# WHISKEY
# CREEK  A PORTER CASSEL MYSTERY

## DAVE HUGELSCHAFFER

*Cormorant Books*

Canada Council
for the Arts
Conseil des Arts
du Canada
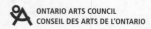

The publisher gratefully acknowledges the support of the Canada Council for the
Arts and the Ontario Arts Council for its publishing program. We acknowledge the
financial support of the Government of Canada through the Canada Book Fund (CBF)
for our publishing activities, and the Government of Ontario through the Ontario
Media Development Corporation, an agency of the Ontario Ministry of Culture, and
the Ontario Book Publishing Tax Credit Program.

This is a work of fiction. The locations are real, as are the names of the
First Nations bands, but all characters and events are fictional.
Any resemblance to specific individuals or events is purely coincidental.

LIBRARY AND ARCHIVES CANADA CATALOGUING IN PUBLICATION

Hugelschaffer, Dave, 1967–
Whiskey Creek : a Porter Cassel mystery / Dave Hugelschaffer.

Issued also in electronic formats.
ISBN 978-1-77086-095-7

I. Title.

PS8615.U315W55 2012     C813'.6     C2012-900269-0

Cover design: Angel Guerra/Archetype
Front cover photo: Rick Arthur
Interior text design: Tannice Goddard, Soul Oasis Networking
Printer: Trigraphik LBF
Printed and bound in Canada.

The inside pages of this book are printed on 100% post-consumer waste recycled paper.

CORMORANT BOOKS INC.
390 Steelcase Road East, Markham, Ontario, L3R 1G2
www.cormorantbooks.com

*For Peter Denney,*
*who would have enjoyed it.*

1

I'VE GOT BOTTLES on my mind lately — whiskey and rum. *Captain Morgan. Canadian Club.* My drinking problem is in the past, but I've got another problem, more abstract. These bottles keep showing up at wildfires, blackened and broken into shards. I've spent a lot of time these last two weeks gluing shards of glass together like an archaeologist reconstructing Bronze Age pottery. My latest project sits on the pressboard dresser at my bedside, several pieces missing, jagged like someone shot off the top.

This bottle wasn't shot, but thrown. It shattered against a tree.

I sit on the edge of my bed, in a tiny room in a trailer complex at the edge of the Fort Chipewyan airport, and ponder the reconstructed bottle. Thin trails of glue have exuded from between the cracks, like grass growing through the gaps in a cobblestone drive. It's not quite five o'clock in the morning and I've been awake for an hour, unable once again to get a good night's sleep. Over the past few months I've grown increasingly tired. Perhaps it's age — I'm forty now. Perhaps aging is just accumulated sleep deprivation. Eventually you become so tired, you just lie down and sleep forever. Catch up. Not a very lucid theory but it's five in the morning. I turn over the bottle, run my fingertips over the ridges.

The bottle was most likely filled with a mixture of gasoline and diesel, a rag stuffed into the open throat, then lit and tossed into the forest. A simple Molotov cocktail; classic of rioters and revolutionaries.

Puzzling, as there's nothing to protest in the forest and it leaves behind plenty of evidence. In my experience as a fire investigator, most wild-fires are started in a manner that leaves little or no evidence. A match. A wad of burning paper tossed into dry grass. Usually, the ignition source is simple and nearly impossible to find. If the arsonist leaves evidence, he's either careless or wants to leave a calling card — which appears to be exactly what's happening with the bottles. They all have three letters etched about an inch above their base.

*F.T.C.*

I hold the bottle up in the light, examine the etching. It was likely done with a small rotary drill; the type used by hobbyists and available everywhere. What the letters mean, I have no idea. Obviously, it could be someone's initials — the simplest of calling cards — and I've compiled a list from the local phone book of names that contain matching initials. It's a fairly short list; Fort Chip isn't much more than a sneeze on the map. Nine hundred people. Two stores. Two restaurants. Plenty of bored kids, which so far is my only theory. But why the letters?

The bang of a door. Heavy steps in the hallway. A heavier knock.

"Cassel — you up?"

"Yeah, come in."

"No time," says the voice. "We got another one."

The steps recede down the hall as I set the bottle back on the night-stand. Number five, more than likely. I pull on yellow Nomex coveralls, grab my hardhat, belt and pack — which seems inordinately heavy this morning. The belt clicks shut and sags against my hip, loaded with water bottle, radio, first aid kit and other assorted indispensable goodies. When I turn on the radio, voices blast like the staccato burst from a machine gun and I wince, turn down the volume. Dispatch is giving directions — the fire is northeast along the lake, in the vicinity of Whiskey Creek. The crew leader responds; tells dispatch they're on their way. Overlaying the voices, the steady thump and whine of rotors and turbo engine — they're leaving without me — and I scramble to pull on steel-toed boots, rush out the door.

I make it outside just in time to see a large white-and-blue helicopter rise off the ground, tilt forward and thump upward into the sky, leaving me to shield my eyes against a blast of sand. When the dust settles I watch the departing helicopter grow smaller. Four other firefighters join me, geared up and ready. They're Native — the local Initial Attack Crew — and normally they would be in a helicopter, headed for the fire. Lately, though, they've had to take second seat to a seven-man HAC crew — specialized firefighters trained in rappelling down a rope from a hovering helicopter. They don't often get a HAC crew staged in Fort Chip, and the local boys aren't thrilled at playing second fiddle to a group of young white university students.

"Scooped again," says Rolly, the crew leader, lifting his hat and rubbing his forehead.

"Yeah," says another. "That's a humbug."

They wander away, sit on drums of turbo fuel by their own smaller helicopter.

I'm not surprised the HAC left me behind; the last fire when I flew with them they had to rappel and were delayed — they aren't allowed to rappel if there is anyone not rappel-certified on board. They had to divert and land me in a meadow a few miles away. I understand their reluctance at taking an uncertified passenger, but I prefer to see the fire upon first discovery, to note the colour of the smoke, initial fire behaviour and — if it might be an arson — any indication of a suspect fleeing the scene. I hate working with less than the optimum amount of information, but this morning I have no choice. I head to the smaller helicopter.

"Let's roll. I need to get out there."

The local boys perk up. Rolly grins, displaying broken teeth and a scarred lip. The pilot, disconcertingly young, is already in the helicopter. He flips switches as we climb in and click together our seat belts, don headsets. I'm in the front; there's only room for three in the back. Sachmo, the youngest of the crew, has to remain behind — another accommodation for the Fire Dick, as I've become known. I signal that one more of the crew should stay behind — with the amount of fire equipment on board, it would be easy to overload the Bell 206. Rolly makes his choice and Sachmo has someone to play ping-pong with while he waits.

The helicopter shudders and the ground drops away.

We bank left over the trees and Lake Athabasca comes into view, deep blue and vast. Despite green leaves on the trees and daytime temperatures that make your skin crawl with sweat, there is still ice far offshore. Spring comes late this far north. The fire season comes earlier — grass is dry and trees are dehydrated, straining to raise moisture from frozen ground. Perfect conditions for the arsonist who's tossing blazing bottles into the bush. I look ahead, over a carpet of undulating Jack pine, and see a distant pall of smoke, miles inland from the lakeshore.

Behind me, Rolly peers over my shoulder. "That bottle guy again, you think?" he says, his voice riding static in my headset.

"Maybe," I say. "We'll see soon enough."

You can tell a lot about a fire from the smoke — behaviour, fuels, moisture — and this smoke looks different from the four previous bottle fires. The previous fires had typical wildfire smoke, white or grey, while this fire is puffing up dark, blackish smoke. Normally, black smoke indicates extreme fire behaviour; ignition proceeding too quickly for complete combustion, but this fire started at night when the humidity was relatively high. In fact, burning conditions are still subdued; the smoke is drifting low and thick. As we approach, I notice the black smoke is originating from a point source on the ground and mixing with lighter wood smoke. Something alien to the forest environment is burning. Ahead and below a thin ribbon opens among the crowns of pine and spruce, vanishing just as quickly as we cross over — a trail, wide enough to be used as a road, and my first thought is we have a vehicle fire. The HAC helicopter swirls smoke through its rotors as it makes a preliminary pass around the fire. I'm about to key my mic and ask them what they see when the voice of the HAC leader breaks in, passing his initial report to dispatch.

"Dispatch, this is vxh. We've got a cabin and vehicle on fire."

"What state is the cabin in?" says dispatch.

"Not much left," says the hac leader.

"Can you see anyone on the ground?"

"Negative."

The hac machine banks, glinting in the sun. We arrive at the fire and take our smaller helicopter to a higher elevation, safely out of the way, begin circling, all eyes focused intently on the ground. Treetops float beneath us, dense green and conical in the drifting smoke. Patches of brown and green earth flash between the trees, intermixed with the bright orange of low flame. I'm hoping to see an upturned face, waving arms. What's left of the cabin rotates into view — a black rectangle sending up tendrils of dark smoke. Sheets of what must be metal roofing form a crumpled black shroud over whatever remains beneath. Whoever remains beneath — no one has broken the ominous radio silence. Finally, dispatch breaks in.

"What are you guys seeing?"

Dispatch doesn't sound calm anymore. I've an anxious clench in my gut.

"This is Cassel in trt. I see no one on the ground."

"What about you, vxh? You see anything, Hendrigan?"

A long pause as the hac machine circles below us. "Nothing, dispatch."

Another pause as the duty officer thinks. Carter Spence is on the desk — a young red-haired Forest Officer on his first posting. I doubt he's ever had a building fire. Or what this could turn into when we get on the ground, search what remains of the cabin. I wait a minute, give him a chance — everyone needs to learn. But I'll only give him a minute before I take charge. As a certified Incident Commander and Fire Investigator, I have as much experience as the Chief Ranger, who I'm hoping is in the duty room by now, looking over Spence's shoulder. As I wait, I concentrate on what I can see on the ground, mentally prepare an assessment.

The fire is about ten acres, although with the drifting smoke, it's difficult to determine an exact perimeter. Terrain is a shallow valley, blocked to the northeast by a rock ridge, which would make a good control point as it is sparsely treed. A narrow creek flows through the fire, close to the cabin, suitable for a pump set-up. Fuel in the valley is dense mature spruce, of considerable height, surrounded as the terrain rises from the valley by dense pine — bad news if the wind picks up and pushes the fire into the crowns of the trees. Vehicle access from the southwest. No visible landing spot close to the fire.

"Dispatch, this is VXH. Commencing rappel."

Dispatch acknowledges, requests the White Message. I pass on my assessment, finish by requesting additional manpower and gear. Hendrigan, the HAC leader, will be the Incident Commander — I've another job to do. The local initial attack crew will return to base, ready should there be another fire. Arrangements made, I tell the pilot to swing wide and look for a landing spot as close to the fire as possible. As we bank away, I catch a glimpse of the big HAC helicopter, hovering above the treetops, and of a firefighter in yellow, rapidly descending a rope into the forest canopy. Then a blur of trees and we're following the trail southwest. It's narrow, meanders through the trees like a game trail. No landing sites possible for miles, which is a shame — I want to walk the road for transfer evidence such as tire tracks, paint scrapes on the trees, anything that might have fallen off or been thrown from a vehicle. This might be another bottle fire, or just an accident, like smoking in bed, but I want to cover all the bases, check the road before a convoy of approaching vehicles obliterates any evidence.

I don't have the time and signal the pilot to look elsewhere.

We try the creek, flying upstream from the fire, and don't go far before the valley flattens out completely into a narrow grassy marsh. It looks soft, but it's covered with patches of low shrub. Most importantly, it has plenty of room for the rotors and I answer the pilot's questioning look with a nod. We drop quickly and the pilot eases the small helicopter into the best spot, close to the stream. The ground is hummocky and we can't touch down so the pilot hovers the machine, one skid on a hummock the other in air, his face intent as he concentrates.

"This'll have to do," he says.

"It's fine," I tell him, and unbuckle, slip off my headset.

The ground is mushy under my feet as I step off the hovering skid, dry yellow grass sinking beneath my boots. A divot forms around my feet, filling with water. As soon as the pilot sees that I'm clear, he pours on the power and the skid rises past me, at the periphery of my vision. Cold air presses me forward, challenging my balance, then I'm alone in the marsh, the only sound the receding thump of the helicopter.

It becomes very quiet and still.

I take a step, find more uncertain ground, which yields alarmingly under my boot as dead stalks of grass tilt in around my ankle. If I'm not careful, this marsh will swallow me whole. Some muskegs are nothing more than a skin of vegetation that has grown like a scab over an ancient lake. You can easily fall through and vanish in the muck. I hadn't expected this marsh to be so soupy so early in the spring. I take a few less-than-graceful steps toward the tree line, my pack flopping over one shoulder, ground sinking. No good — I'm going down, nothing but loon shit beneath me. I have just enough time to heave my pack clear, onto a patch of dry grass, then I'm up to my armpits in icy water, gasping from the shock. I flail at a hummock in front of me, terrified I'll go right under into the brackish water. Fortunately, my boots hit ice, which doesn't help my thermal issues, but is solid. I tug myself out of the muck, on hands and knees, gasping, my chest heaving, spider walk to my pack and drag it to firmer ground.

"Jesus Christ!" Baptized in Whiskey Creek.

When I've collected my wits and my heartbeat has returned from the panic zone, I shoulder my pack, turn on my radio, which thankfully still works despite the soaking, start walking downstream toward the fire. I've got about a mile-and-a-half to go.

My belt radio crackles. It's Hendrigan. "You there, Cassel?"

I fumble the radio out of its holster, my hands rubbery from the cold water.

"Yeah, I'm here."

"I saw you flying up the creek, thought maybe you went fishing."

It's five-thirty in the morning; I'm tired and soaked in black icy water. My sense of ha-ha is at an all-time low. Hendrigan must read my tone, because he turns business, gives a quick update. Rappel complete. Cabin burned to the floor line. Truck burned to a husk. No sign of the driver or owner of the cabin. One dog tied in the bush, scorched but alive. Fire behaviour is moderate, crawling on the ground, the odd tree starting to candle. Pump being set up and should have water flowing shortly. I remind Hendrigan not to touch the cabin or truck and to be on the lookout for anything unusual. He signs off, sounding vaguely offended.

Dispatch barks out of my radio. "You at the fire, Cassel?"

It's Mark Middel, the Chief Ranger. Spence has been benched.

"What's your take?" he asks, before I have a chance to respond.

"I'm on the ground, but not at the fire yet," I tell him, explain about the diverted landing. Middel doesn't sound impressed at having to wait for my detailed assessment. He's had four previous confirmed arsons in the past two weeks and is feeling a bit of pressure, which he generously passes on. He tells me to double-time it to the fire, which works well with my plan to avoid hypothermia. Coveralls cling, cold and heavy, slow me. Water squishes in my boots. A dog howls in the distance, forlorn, and I hope it's not badly burned. A pump starts at the fire, its distant whine steady and familiar.

I move out of the willows and buck brush, away from the creek to where the timber is tall, the understory sparse, pick up the pace. I'm chilled, but fortunately it's been unseasonably warm lately and this morning is no exception. Sunlight dapples the forest floor, spackles Labrador tea and moss with brighter splashes of colour. As I walk I think about the previous arsons. The four bottle arsons were close to established gravel roads, the arsonist likely tossing the bottles from a vehicle. It's tempting to consider this fire might be related but it's never good to assume early in an investigation. You start looking for evidence that fits your theory; ignore what doesn't. I focus instead on my surroundings. An odour of smoke and damp moss. And something else.

I walk a bit further, sniffing the air.

No doubt now — rotting meat.

In the forest, rotting meat usually means a bear in the vicinity. A bear can smell decaying flesh for miles and will aggressively protect its dinner, remaining close to the carcass until it is completely devoured. Alone and unarmed, you don't want to place yourself between a bear and his food. I look for the source of the odour. To my left is a border of willow along the creek; perfect cover for a snoozing bear. A twig snaps loudly under my boot and to my right several large black birds squawk in the trees — another subtle warning sign. Ravens are scavengers and will sit in the trees around a kill, waiting for their turn at the prize.

I'm between the ravens and the willow hedge. Not a great place to be.

I waste no time putting myself on the other side of the ravens. They warble and rasp, picking new roosts. As I walk I look for the kill, wanting to know when I'm clear; stop when I see a black mound of hair. It's hard to see clearly from here but it looks like a bear. Any second it will raise its head and see me but for now it's oblivious and I remain still, waiting to assess its behaviour, my heart beating a bit harder — the second burst of adrenaline this morning.

It remains oddly motionless.

A raven dives out of a tree, lands on the black fur, begins to pick at something.

A bear is not normally this patient. I approach cautiously. The raven flaps away, squawking indignantly. The bear is dead; a hole in its side where smaller scavengers have been enjoying this bonanza. More than likely, the owner of the cabin shot the bear, which made it this far before dropping. There may be another bear close by though, drawn by the odour. I put some distance between myself and the smell.

Twenty minutes later, I'm at the fire perimeter.

The fire burned to the creek and I step across the narrow channel a dozen yards upstream from a whining pump, take a moment to survey the scene. Tall trees, trunks blackened. Smoke thick enough it burns the eyes — it smells of earth, plastic and burning debris, like a smouldering dump. A hose snakes across the ground to where yellow-clad fire-fighters work. A cluster of traps hang in a nearby tree. The gutted truck is about thirty yards away, sitting low on its rims, tires burned away. Beyond the truck is a screened view of what remains of the cabin. One corner rises like a crumbling spire, dovetailed log ends still discernable. I step over low flame which nibbles into damp grass along the creek, head for the cabin. Hendrigan meets me on the way.

"You stopped for a swim?" he says.

"Mud bath," I tell him. "Good for the complexion."

Hendrigan is taller than me and sparse. His stubble is streaked with soot.

"You find any sign of the owner?" I ask him.

He shakes his head. "Just the dog."

"Anything suspicious?"

"Not that I can see. But that's your job."

It's his job too — all initial action crews are trained to protect a suspected origin area and look for anything unusual. That's the theory, anyway. Typically, in the heat of first response, flames get most of the attention and determination of origin or cause is a lower priority. This, however, isn't a typical fire. All indications point to a possible casualty.

"You're certain no one noticed anything unusual?"

Hendrigan notes my tone, frowns. "We looked around a bit, didn't see anything."

"How close did you get to the cabin?"

"No closer than about five yards."

I'd have preferred they'd remained farther back and not contami-nate the area with boot prints, but it's a tough call, preserving evidence while looking for some sign of the occupant. They should have marked a path though — a single line of contamination.

"I want everyone to stay away from the cabin until I clear the area."

Hendrigan nods, looks around to check the position of his men.

"What about the truck? Did you approach that as well?"

"I took a peek," he says. "Nothing in there."

I squat, pull a camera from my pack. Until recently all I ever used were the cheap, disposable cameras. They took reasonably good pictures and you could send the whole camera in for developing, or turn it over to someone else, like the RCMP. It was becoming difficult to find somewhere to develop film so I bought a digital, although I don't really trust the thing — too easy to accidentally lose data. I take a few pictures from where I stand, cover the viewscape within the fire, then walk slowly toward the truck, studying the ground and surrounding tree trunks.

"What are you looking for?" says Hendrigan, walking beside me.

"Walk behind, please."

Hendrigan falls in behind me.

"A few things," I tell him. "I'm looking for anything unusual that an arsonist might have dropped, or anything cast off from the fire, which might give me an indication of fire behaviour. And I'm checking fire travel patterns on the ground and trees."

"To see if the fire came from the cabin?"

"Or if it started outside the cabin. You see that tree over there?"

Hendrigan looks in the direction I'm pointing.

"Notice the char pattern is higher on one side."

"Yeah — on the side facing the creek."

"What direction do you think the fire was travelling?"

Hendrigan frowns. "Looks like it came from the creek and burned toward the cabin, but that doesn't make sense. The fire is clearly burning outward, getting larger."

"Fire burning around a tree creates a slight vacuum on the lee side."

"Pulling the flames higher," says Hendrigan. "The fire came from the cabin."

"According to one indicator. We'll need more, to be certain."

Hendrigan's second-in-command calls over the radio. The helipad is brushed out. Hendrigan discusses next steps while I walk toward the burned truck, noting as I pass more tree trunks charred lower near the cabin. The truck is an older Chevrolet half-ton with a fibreglass canopy. Neither have retained their collectors value. The windows of the truck are open and I peer inside the cab. Wisps of smoke rise from what remains of the seat — an acrid, nauseating smell. Chainsaw files and a screwdriver lie on the blackened dash. Keys are in the ignition — not a good sign. Reaching in through the window, I twist a metal clasp on the glovebox, coax open hinges seized by heat. They make an unpleasant sound. The registration and insurance are charred to ash foil; one touch and they'll disintegrate. But there's something else in there.

A whiskey bottle.

I slip on a work glove, carefully extract the bottle. Canadian Club. Empty. Perhaps the driver was the one who named the creek. Turning the bottle carefully over in my hand, I look for the etched letters I've come to expect, but there's nothing. I set the bottle back in the glovebox, walk around the vehicle, look for anything obvious. Nothing. Pine needle ash. No boot prints. The helicopter thumps overhead, large orange Bambi bucket bulging with water as it swings in for a dump, dribbling water which patters across my hardhat. Behind the truck I jot down the licence plate number. The stickers are just barely legible — it was insured until the coming September. I unclip my belt radio from its holster.

"Dispatch, this is Cassel."

"Talk to me, Cassel"

"Burned-out Chevy half-ton. Cabin is gone."

"Any sign of the occupant?"

I glance at the smoking rubble of the cabin. "Nothing yet."

"Well, keep looking. We're looking here, too."

"I've got a licence plate. Are you ready to copy?"

"Go ahead."

I pass on the number: GFL 434.

Dispatch tells me he'll run the plate through the local RCMP who he's put on notice. Middel sounds edgy. I promise to keep him informed, turn my attention to the cabin. In the Green Area of the Province — the predominantly forested area — residential structures are not permitted, except commercial tourism operations and trapline cabins. Based on the traps hanging in the trees, it's obvious which category this cabin falls into, although at a thousand square feet, it's large by trapline standards. A thousand square feet of rubble. The four corners of the rectangular log structure burned the slowest and stand like the charred fingers of an immense hand, holding a palm full of twisted black metal roofing. The tin sheets didn't simply fall to the floor — a fire is far too dynamic. They heated unevenly and twisted; bent as they collapsed with the roof. Many are curled like dead leaves, forming a jagged shroud over what lies beneath, which still crackles and sizzles. Smoke rises unevenly between the spaces. I try not to think about what might be sizzling beneath.

"You think there was someone in there?" says Hendrigan, startling me.

"We'll find out soon enough. Right now, let's take care of that dog."

Hendrigan nods, leads me past an outhouse, untouched by the fire.

"House and truck go," Hendrigan says. "But the crapper is fine."

The dog is tied by a long chain to a tree about thirty yards behind the outhouse. It's a hound of some sort and as soon as he sees us he sets up a terrible racket, whining and crouching. The poor thing is black with soot from nose to tail and smells of burned hair. Both ears are singed. A gooey discharge has oozed from its nose. There's an old hub-cap filled with water nearby. "Calder brought him that," Hendrigan says, following my gaze. "We didn't know what to do with him."

I kneel in front of the dog, who is ecstatic at the attention, straining against its leash as it licks at my face. Its breathing is raspy — smoke inhalation or superheated air. It's not usually the flames that kill. Lungs sear shut and fill with fluid; he may be dying.

"That's a good boy," I murmur reassuringly.

He places a paw on my forearm, cocks his head. I pull out my belt radio.

"Dispatch, this is Cassel. We need TRT back at the fire."

"What for, Cassel?"

"Medevac."

"You found the owner?"

"Not yet. But his dog is in bad shape."

There's a pause. "You want me to send TRT for a dog?"

"He needs immediate medical care."

I think Middel is about to refuse — he's already lost marks in my book, when I hear him call TRT, send him to the fire. The dog lays its head on my thigh, drools onto my coveralls. I wonder why he's tied so far from the cabin. If I owned a dog, he'd be in my favourite chair in the house. But I'm allergic. Already, my eyes are itching. Soon I'll be drooling worse than the dog. But I wait a few more minutes before moving — the dog is glued to my thigh. He whimpers as we disengage.

"Should we let him loose?" says Hendrigan.

"Better not. Given what he's been through, he may run away."

Hendrigan smiles. "I think he'll just follow you."

I picture a dog running amok through what might be a crime scene.

"He'll be fine here until the helicopter arrives."

Hendrigan returns to his men, working the perimeter. I return to the cabin, circle slowly, take photos, make notes, check fire travel indicators on trees, logs and underbrush. All evidence of fire travel points to the cabin as the origin. Once my preliminary documentation is complete, I find where the door of the cabin once stood, facing the truck.

Kneeling carefully, I begin a more detailed inspection.

This fire was very hot, consuming the heavy log exterior wall and the periphery of the floor, where joists stick out from beneath blackened debris. Little briquettes of charcoal and discoloured nails lie amid white ash. It would have taken a few hours for this much mass to be reduced and the heat to dissipate. Not that the site isn't still hot — heat pulses from the debris, advising caution. I examine a bent strip of metal among the ash. It's a door hinge, seized in position by heat. The door was left open, presenting several scenarios.

The occupant fled the burning cabin; the fire likely an accident.

The fire was set intentionally; the door left open to aid combustion.

If the occupant fled, why would the vehicle remain? Perhaps heat from the burning cabin prevented the owner from reaching it. I picture a man, covered in soot and half-crazed, running from the burning cabin into the darkness. He may be lost and injured. I unholster my belt radio, call dispatch, ask that the incoming helicopter make a few wider sweeps of the area to look for the missing occupant. Dispatch acknowledges.

I holster the radio, return to the task ahead of me.

A building fire is far more complex than a wildfire. There are additional factors in a building that affect fire behaviour and spread. Walls and internal barriers. Synthetic materials, both combustible and non-combustible. Sources of ignition you would never find in a forest. Deciphering these clues requires specialized training, which I do not have. But I do have a good understanding of fire behaviour, and I'm the only investigator available. Given the remote location of the cabin, there may not be another investigator on this fire, unless grounds can be established to bring in more resources. Grounds such as evidence of foul play. I scrutinize the smouldering pile of tin and charcoal, searching for anything obvious.

Any clues are buried beneath the shroud of the collapsed roof.

Given the heat of the debris, should I let it burn out and cool before excavating?

It will be hours until the heat diminishes to a safe level, insulated as it is by the collapsed roof and debris that has caved in from the walls. Days even. I remember blackened keys dangling from the truck's ignition. We can't wait. Chances are nil that anyone in the remains of the cabin might still be alive, but we have a responsibility to lay the question to rest. From a practical perspective, we need to know if a search is required.

I ponder how it might be safe to commence work.

Water in a firehose is over two hundred pounds per square inch pressure. Even if we throttle down the pump, the jet of water will wreak havoc among the debris, mixing and damaging. Fire travel clues and other evidence are often subtle or delicate. We'll have to go in hot but controlled. I peer through the trees, to where Hendrigan and his men are working. I'd hate to pull them off fire suppression duties, but I'll need assistance. The smaller helicopter swings overhead and I look up at the block letters of its call sign, stencilled on its belly. I'll bring in the local crew to assist. Until then, I'll do what I can.

First things first. More photos and notes. Site sketch.

By the time I'm finished, another half hour has passed. TRT is still flying. The dog is still whining. The cabin is still smouldering. I call TRT, confirm they haven't found any sign of the missing occupant and have them land at the new helipad, farther down the creek and outside the fire. I unclip the chain from the dog's collar, pick him. He's not a small dog and makes an awkward bundle, legs struggling, whining, licking my face. He stinks of wet dog, burned hair and shit. I don't have a leash for him and don't want him loose around the helicopter. So I carry him, walk quickly, my eyes and nose running. Through the trees, the helicopter is visible, waiting, rotors buzzing. Someone is walking in my direction, coveralls and hardhat glaringly clean, and I groan.

"Howdy, Porter."

It's Luke Middel, the Chief Ranger's teenage son. Luke is tall and lanky, with a mess of blond hair and a look of unbridled enthusiasm on his smooth face. Ever since my arrival to investigate the bottle fires, he's been begging me to follow along. It's like having a big, ungainly puppy stalking you. Luke must have been waiting at the base for his chance to hop a flight here, but the last thing I need, with a possible casualty, a possible crime scene, and a hot evidence search, is an uncoordinated and overly eager sixteen-year-old without any training. I thrust the dog at him, which he takes awkwardly.

"Here, Luke, I've got an important mission for you."

"Yeah, but —"

"This dog is injured and he needs immediate medical care. You take him to the nursing station and make sure they treat him right."

Luke fumbles with the dog, which squirms in his arms, looking back at me reproachfully for putting him in the arms of an amateur. Luke's hesitation is obvious — he's looking past me at the fire. I fix him with a stern look and send him back to the helicopter. He slouches away, struggling with the dog. I watch until both dog and teenager are safely in the helicopter, then give the pilot the thumbs up. As the machine lifts off I breathe a sigh of relief and return to the ruins of the cabin, where I examine the tangle of debris, look for the best point of entry to start my excavation. I decide the front of the cabin will be best as the debris here is less cluttered. This is also the cabin's path of entry and exit and there may be evidence along this route disturbed by moving and shifting elsewhere.

I pull my leather work gloves snug and get started.

The area just inside the door has no floor and I spend about twenty minutes on hands and knees systematically probing the ash. I find numerous nails, three metal coat hooks and a doorknob. The sun clears the treetops. In no time I'm sweating. The ends of the carbonized floor joists crumble as I brush them with my glove. Farther into the cabin, portions of the floor have survived but are buried beneath the heap of debris. Jagged edges of tin halt further exploration. I stand and stretch, half-damp coveralls chaffing as I move. There isn't much more I can do until my helpers arrive, but I'm not much for standing around, so I start to work at the easily accessible sheets of tin, the metal warm through my gloves. The sheets of twisted metal move reluctantly, scraping with a sound like fingernails on a blackboard, but soon I've cleared enough roof tin and debris that I can progress my search several feet further into the building, where I see the black metal side of what I think is a small woodstove. I take pictures, then step across the ashy threshold into what was the front room of the cabin, my heart beating a bit faster — the woodstove may be the origin.

Floorboards are deeply charred and still smoking. Something sizzles beneath the debris. Just in front of me the side of the stove is fully exposed, tilted on an angle. It's a simple wood heater — a cube of heavy sheet metal with a door in the front. Warped roofing tin, round metal stove pipe, chunks of charcoaled log beam and other debris prevent a complete view of the stove, but from the aspect of the stove's door hinges, it looks as though the door may be open, which could be the cause of the fire — coals having spilled onto the wooden floor. Or the stove door may have been knocked open as the cabin collapsed on top of it. Either way, I'm anxious to have a better look and begin tugging at more sheets of tin.

The tin is tangled with other debris and I succeed in shifting portions of the pile, but little more. Something buried begins to sizzle more aggressively. A length of stovepipe rolls out at my feet and I pick it up, give it a cursory examination, set it aside. Something far more interesting has been exposed — the end of a whiskey bottle, laying on the black pillowed surface of the floor. I squat, pick away bits of charred wood and gently blow away ash. The bottle is broken, but the base is intact. Gingerly, I pick it up, my scalp tingling, expecting to see the familiar letters inscribed at its base, but there is nothing on the crazed, cobblestone texture of the tortured glass. This appears to be an unrelated fire and a picture begins to form in my mind. Lone occupant drinking whiskey, leaves the cabin door open, perhaps as the stove has made the cabin too hot. Or he goes for a piss and forgets to close the door, as he does with the stove when he feeds in wood. The occupant is asleep or passed out when an ember falls from the stove, igniting the floor. My scalp tingles again — the smoking debris has a pungent undertone similar to meat burned on a barbecue. I grasp a sheet of tin and pull hard, hoping to uncover the stove and surrounding area. It moves about two inches. Another try yields another inch — the tin is either tangled solidly in the pile or still connected to something heavy. I pick a sheet of tin further down in the pile and, putting my legs into it, heave upward.

The weight is considerable — it feels as though I'm lifting the entire roof — but the pile shifts, scraping and groaning. A blast of hot air hits me in the face, rancid and filled with smoke and swirling ash. I wince, close my eyes and let it pass, then heave once more. An opening forms beneath the pile of debris. What I see puzzles me. A charred log with blackened branches lying on the floor — a vivid pink stripe where the bark has pulled away. Then a strong odour hits me, of burned cloth and flesh, and I realize, horrified, that the log is a body and the missing bark is skin and clothing, burned to the tin and pulled away from the corpse as a result of my lifting. I see teeth and vacant eye sockets and for a few seconds all I can do is stare, no longer aware of the weight of the debris, the muted hiss of fire or the sounds of the helicopter. Then it all rushes back and I drop the weight and stagger away, gagging, my arm blazing with pain. Blood roars in my ears. Burned trees ahead of me seem to bend and swirl.

# 2
•

A FACE HOVERS above me. Swaying treetops create an odd sensation of vertigo. I'm disoriented, can't remember where I am or what is going on, then I recognize the face — Hendrigan — and it all rushes back. The fire. The cabin. The body. I'm flat on my back on the ground, lift myself onto my elbows. More faces peer down, curious and worried.

"Can you hear me, Porter?"

"Hell yes," I say, more abruptly than I intended. This is embarrassing.

"Maybe you should lie still," says Hendrigan, as I stand up, ignoring proffered hands, brush myself off. Most of the crew stand around me. I'm not crazy about being the centre of attention. "Thanks, but you guys get back to work."

Crew members look uncertainly at Hendrigan, who hesitates before sending them back to their assigned tasks. They walk slowly, glancing back at me, in murmured discussion. "What happened?" asks Hendrigan. "I was heading over to talk to you, and you sort of stumbled backwards and fell over."

I look at the rubble of the cabin.

"I think I got a whiff of something noxious and passed out."

Hendrigan looks concerned. "You sure you're okay?"

"Fine."

"What about your arm?"

The sleeve of my coverall is ripped and dots of blood have created a nifty pattern. When I pull up the sleeve there is a long furrow in the flesh of my forearm. It's barely bleeding, cauterized by the hot edge of a piece of tin.

"Crap," says Hendrigan. "That looks nasty."

He pulls out his belt first-aid kit, spends a few minutes fussing with my arm. It's beginning to hurt now and I wince, grit my teeth. I focus on the cabin, think about the body beneath the rubble. About next steps.

"That'll hold you for now," says Hendrigan, inspecting his work.

"Thanks."

"We ought to get you back to town, so a doctor can look at that."

"I'm fine. Listen." I nod toward the cabin. "There's a body under there."

Hendrigan's eyes widen. "You sure?"

"I didn't want to mention it with everyone around — it'll just distract the guys."

"Yeah. What do we do?"

"You guys keep doing what you do best — control the fire. Keep everyone away from the cabin. This area is now a fatality scene and off limits." Hendrigan is nodding in a distracted sort of way — I've seen it before; a sort of mental shock. A death hits everyone differently and I worry for a moment. He is the Incident Commander. "Are you going to be okay?"

"What?" He shakes his head, frowns. "Oh, yeah. Sure."

"Good. Take a few minutes to make notes on everything you saw from the moment you lifted off base. Pretty soon, this place will be crawling with Mounties and they'll be asking a lot of questions."

Hendrigan squares his jaw, slaps me on the back reassuringly and returns to his men. I unholster my belt radio and hesitate, my eyes fixed on the pile of blackened rubble. The radio frequency is open to all the firefighters, towers and anyone with a scanner. Cause of death and number of casualties have not been determined. Next of kin have not been notified. How to relay the nature of the situation without revealing too much?

"Dispatch, this is Cassel — at the Whiskey Creek fire."

"Copy that, Cassel. How are things going out there?"

"Have you found the owner of the cabin?"

"Negative."

"Well — you can stop looking."

"You've found the owner?"

"Yes."

"What's his condition?"

"Not good. We'll need the RCMP out here."

There's a pause. "Do you need a medevac?"

"No. Just the Mounties."

Another pause. I picture Mark Middel frowning behind a microphone.

"On their way."

I return to the cabin, stand in front of the small patch cleared of debris, take a good look. Despite the obvious danger, and the need to preserve the scene, I want to keep digging, uncover the body — or bodies. Best to wait until the RCMP arrive, let the boys in blue do their thing. I'm responsible for locating the origin, determining cause, and collecting evidence for man-caused wildfires. Usually, my investigation concludes with charging someone, or some company, with the fire-fighting cost.

Today is a bit more complicated.

While I wait for the RCMP, I take a few more pictures, review and expand my notes. I'm not sure how much farther I'll be expected to take my investigation; probably just confirmation of origin. With this in mind, I start a systematic search, documenting fire travel patterns and indicators. The ground is a web of foot trails and low shrub. The shrub carried the fire outward, like a lamp wick, to deeper bush. As I sketch, TRT passes overhead, circling slowly. I catch a glimpse of a face, ruddy and frowning, looking down as the helicopter banks, and of a uniform crest on a shoulder. A few minutes later, TRT lands and a tall Mountie approaches amid the blackened trees. He's scowling, looks tense.

"What have we got today, Cassel?"

His name is Waldren and he has a commanding air about him — brow furrowed and jaw clenched. Then there's the bullet-proof vest, side arm, baton, extensive tool belt and TASER in a thigh holster. It makes him look like an oversized action figure. We've met several times over the past two weeks, to discuss the bottle fires I'm investigating. The RCMP want to be in the loop on any investigation occurring in the area, but don't become directly involved in wildfire arson if there is no crime against persons or property. In their world, trees don't count. This time, there'll be more than trees to worry about.

"Cabin fire," I report. "One confirmed fatality."

He gazes past me. "How badly messed up is the scene?"

"Not too bad. The HAC boys steered clear."

"Good. Give me the tour."

We head toward the cabin. Waldren does a visual sweep of the area as he walks. Firefighters track our progress, momentarily distracted by the uniform. They'd better get over it quick — there'll be plenty more. I motion Hendrigan to join us and he gives Waldren a brief report of what he's done. Waldren smiles, tells Hendrigan he's done a good job. When Hendrigan returns to his men, Waldren's smile vanishes.

"Show me where the fire started."

I go through basic origin determination, following the path of fire back to its source at the cabin. I explain what little scene processing I've completed, point out where I found the body, buried under the smoking rubble. Waldren makes a few notes in his flip pad, walks to the truck.

"When do think the truck went up?" he says, peering into the blackened cab.

"Not long after the cabin. Lots of grease and oil. Doesn't take much."

He carefully opens the glovebox. "Another whiskey bottle."

"I had a look. No markings."

"You disturbed it already?"

"I disturbed a lot of things before I realized there was a fatality."

"Fair enough."

"What else do you need me to do?"

"Stand guard. I'm going for a walk. Forensics will be here soon."

Waldren strides away, down the narrow road among the trees, peering from side to side, looking for transfer evidence. This could be tire tracks, pop cans, cigarette butts — almost anything that might have been dropped or transferred on the path from the fire scene. I'd have preferred he remain to guard the cabin while I search the road. Standing around, damp and tired, isn't a winning combination. I flex my hand, feel a ribbon of pain stretch along my injured forearm. It's going to be a long day.

The next hour is spent fortifying my notes. I try not to think about the corpse roasting beneath the remains of the cabin.

Waldren returns, face beaded with perspiration.

"You find anything?"

"Nothing." He doesn't look pleased. "No tire tracks. Too dry."

It's been a dry spring, following a winter with little snowfall. The fire season started early. Most years, a spring fire like this wouldn't have amounted to much, particularly burning through the night. Waldren amuses himself by taking photos, kneeling like a *National Geographic* photographer on a lion shoot. It's not really necessary, as I've clicked off about a hundred photos and the forensics boys will blanket the site with more photos and video.

"Looks like he got pissed up and left his stove open," says Waldren.

"Hard to tell at this point."

Waldren gives me a look I can't quite decipher. I think he wants to toss theories back and forth, but it's too early. We don't know the identity of the victim, the cause of death, or the cause of the fire. Most of the evidence is buried under smoking debris.

"Do you know who owns the cabin?"

"Guy by the name of Rufus Hallendry," says Waldren.

"You know much about him?"

"Everyone knows him — it's a small town. Liked to drink. Punched out a few Natives now and then and got his share back. Just drunken stuff really, nothing you wouldn't see anywhere else on a Friday night. Mostly he kept to himself though. Lived alone."

"Hallendry wasn't Native?"

Waldren snorts. "Not on the outside."

"And this was his trapline?"

"Yeah," says Waldren, giving me a curious look. "Why?"

This far north, most traplines are held by Aboriginals. For a white guy to get a trapline, it likely was purchased from a Native. Or seized from a Native for some reason and sold off. Either way, it's a bit unusual and I make a note to talk to the local Fish and Wildlife officer.

"Did Hallendry have a junior partner?"

Waldren shrugs. "Good question. I'll have to check with Leroy."

We both look up as TRT passes overhead. A minute later it lands at the new helipad and two men disembark, begin to unload bags and metal cases. It's the Forensic Identification Unit from Fort McMurray. Waldren and I lend a hand, lugging the gear to the cabin. More introductions. Albert Dugan is the senior. He's short and slight. Despite his frail stature, he's got an impressionable handshake. Collin Verdon is the junior specialist, much taller and younger.

"You were first on the scene?" Dugan asks.

"No, the HAC beat me here."

Dugan frowns. "The what?"

"The heli-attack crew." I point at the firefighters. "They rappelled in."

"Has anyone driven the road yet?"

"Not yet," says Waldren. "I walked it, though. Didn't find anything."

"Good," says Dugan. "Can you have it blocked off until we clear it?"

Waldren nods. "I'll get a unit out there right away."

"What about you, Cassel? What have you done so far?"

I go through my routine, summarize my conclusions regarding fire travel and origin, note the bottle I found at the truck, the bottle at the cabin, the open hinges and stove door. I detail my entry into the cabin along a single line of contamination, close out by telling them about the body under the debris. Dugan has his notebook out, is scribbling like mad. I tell him I have notes on all of this.

"Now so do I," he says, without looking up.

I dig my notes and camera from my pack, hand over the memory card to Verdon. He slips it into a plastic evidence bag, which he seals and labels.

"You guys need me for anything more?"

"Maybe." Dugan looks around, at the remains of the cabin and truck, at the firefighters labouring on the perimeter, and thinks for a moment. "Okay," he says, "here's how it's going to work. The area around the structure and vehicle, out for about thirty yards, is my primary scene. We'll flag this off and no one other than myself and Mr. Verdon goes in without my express permission. Sergeant, I'll need you or one of your staff to serve as a guard until I clear the scene. Our secondary scene encompasses everything within a radius of about three hundred yards, as well as the trail leading back to the main road. We'll need personnel to assist in a ground search of that area. Do you have any available manpower?"

It's an open question. Waldren scratches his head.

"We've got a few members," he says. "And there's Parks staff."

We brainstorm, manage a list of about a dozen volunteers, including locals with search and rescue training, staff from Wood Buffalo National Park, and the local Fish and Wildlife officer. Dispatch declines my suggestion of including the local initial attack crew — Rolly and crew are left to play ping-pong again, waiting for the next fire. Another humbug. I offer to serve as the search master, something I've done before, but Waldren pulls rank. Once again, he doesn't want to stand around guarding a pile of smoking rubble — he'll have a junior constable fill that illustrious post. Dugan offers me a consolation prize.

"You can assist with the detailed search."

Calls are made and work progresses quickly. Helicopter TRT will ferry in the additional searchers. Verdon flags off the primary scene with yellow crime scene tape. I contribute by having a granola bar —

my blood sugar is so low I've got a headache. It isn't likely to go away soon — a white forest service truck is rattling toward us at a good clip along the trail, raising dust. The driver is young and grinning like an idiot. Dugan looks up from where he's kneeling, opening instrument cases.

"Who the hell —"

It's Luke Middel, aspiring fire investigator, budding pain in the ass.

The truck slows and lurches to a halt a dozen yards from the yellow barrier. Luke's smile falters when he reads our expressions. Undaunted, he steps out of the truck, clad in bright clean yellow coveralls and white hardhat.

"I thought you blocked off the trail," Dugan says to Waldren.

Waldren looks ready to draw his gun. "He must have beat my man out here."

Luke waves. "Hi guys. How can I help?"

Waldren grinds his teeth. "You've done enough already."

"But I just got here."

"And you're just about to leave," says Waldren.

Luke looks stricken. "But why? There must be something I can do."

Dugan stands. "You likely have destroyed any track evidence on the road."

For a moment, no one says anything. Luke looks back at the road, his shoulders drooping. He sighs deeply and reaches for the truck door. "Where are you going?" Dugan asks quietly. This has more effect than if he'd shouted. Luke freezes, hand in mid-air. "You weren't going to drive back out again were you?" asks Dugan. "That would only double the contamination on the road."

For a few seconds I think Luke Middel might cry.

"You wanted to learn about fire investigation," I tell him. "That would be lesson number one. Avoid scene contamination whenever humanly possible. That doesn't just mean firefighters and bulldozers — it means you."

Hope flickers in Luke's eyes. Dugan picks it up immediately.

"You might as well stay — you're here now. But you stay out of the flagged area. You can help with the secondary search."

Luke is in heaven. He'd be happy searching the outhouse if he thought there might be a clue. Not necessarily a bad thing, but to be taken in small doses. I catch his arm as he walks past, ask him if he took care of the dog.

"Oh sure," he says, beaming. "I dropped him at the nursing station."

Processing a fire scene as complex as a cabin is demanding meticulous work. First, the site is measured and recorded in detail. The position of all notable features are mapped, including the cabin, truck and trail, as well as assorted attractions, such as a small shed that burned, and a blackened tree hung with metal traps. Even the outhouse doesn't escape attention. The entire scene is video recorded, supplemented with still photos. Initial documentation complete, we can start the actual processing.

"You and Collin go left around the cabin," says Dugan. "I'll go right."

The two forensics specialists are dressed in frumpy hair nets and puffy white disposable coveralls they affectionately call bunny suits. They look silly, but the suit keeps both the scene and their clothes from contamination. I'm in grungy coveralls, which Dugan is prepared to tolerate, so long as I remain behind the specialists and follow instructions to the letter. Within the realm encompassed by yellow ribbon, Dugan is king. I'm just concentrating on making it through the day and not messing anything up. It is mid-afternoon and I feel faint, my head buzzing. I could beg off and head to the nursing station, get my arm properly treated, but they're short-handed. I drop to my knees beside Collin Verdon.

"Look for anything unusual," he says.

"And plant a flag," I finish for him.

"You've done this before?"

"Plenty of fires and the odd bombing."

"Bombings are nasty. Fragments everywhere."

We chat as we move slowly and methodically, on hands and knees, around the outside of the cabin. There's a fair bit of glass from a broken window, blackened on both sides, which Verdon explains indicates the window shattered after the fire started. At this point it doesn't mean much, except that a Molotov cocktail wasn't tossed through the window. Given the recent spate of other arsons, that's a relief. We meet Dugan a third of the way around the cabin, processing from the other direction. He might be old, but he's fast.

"You guys find much?" he asks, sitting back on his haunches.

"Not much," Verdon admits. "Glass, broken after the fact."

We move to the front of the cabin, assess how we might start the heavy work of mining down through the debris. It's a daunting task as we can't just heave the debris out of the way. Disturbance to the underlying strata must be minimized. And it's still hot, evidenced by my seared arm, which is throbbing. We spend a few minutes discussing how best to proceed.

"We could set up a sprinkler," Verdon suggests. "Cool it with a steady drizzle."

Dugan shakes his head, frowning. "Wouldn't do much good, and contamination could trickle down. Normally, I'd just wait until it cooled on its own, but that could take days, and we need to see who's under there. I think we just need to get in there and start working, carefully of course." He looks at me. "Can I get a firefighter with a controlled water source to carefully hose down where I tell him?"

I look over to where Hendrigan's men are working. "Sure."

I tug free my radio and am about to call Hendrigan when Luke Middel appears from the periphery of my vision, peering over the yellow ribbon strung between the trees. He's got a piss pack — a water-filled black rubber bag with a hand pump — hanging from his bony shoulders. I swear he can read my mind.

"Anything I can do to help?"

"Well …" I picture further scene contamination. Jets of uncontrolled water.

Dugan looks at Luke. "You ever seen a dead body, son?"

"At funerals," says Luke.

"This'll be a lot worse. Can you handle that?"

Luke frowns thoughtfully. "I think so."

"Okay," says Dugan. "But you tell me if it gets to be too much."

Luke nods, ducks under the yellow ribbon, tendons in his neck straining from the sixty pounds of water on his back. Dugan explains the process. The two specialists will clear a path into the cabin, handing me sheets of tin and other debris, which I will stack out of the way. Luke will apply controlled spurts of water where instructed.

"Are we clear on that?" Dugan says.

Luke nods enthusiastically.

We get to work. The tin is difficult. During the heated collapse of the building, the metal buckled, twisted and bent. Overlapping sheets are held together by metal roofing screws. A ratchet is procured. I get the dubious honour of climbing onto sections of alarmingly warm metal. Slowly, a pile of twisted metal grows aside from the cabin. The smoking, blackened wasteland of the cabin floor develops. Luke stands in the cleared area of the cabin with Verdon, spritzing as directed. Once the roof tin and other large debris is cleared, a grid is established — a network of strings and pins stretched across the ground. More photos and measurements. I stand back, wait and watch.

It's a gruesome sight. There's a lot of smaller debris obscuring what lies beneath, but the outline of the body is obvious, sprawled on the charred black floor. The corpse looks a bit like those statuesque body casts from Pompeii. What's different is this corpse is fresh and not nearly as complete. All that remains of the hands and feet are shards of dark grey burned bone. The skull is black, eye sockets vacant, jaw gaping. The smell is meaty and acrid.

Luke Middel looks at the corpse for the hundredth time.

"You good, son?" says Dugan.

Luke nods, looking pale but determined.

"*I drink alone*," sings Verdon, in a rough, George Thorogood voice.

Gallows humour — without it a fellow could lose his mind.

"You think it's that simple?" I ask Dugan.

"Maybe," he says, stretching out a kink as he stands up. His puffy white cap is flattened and he looks tired. "Although you never can tell for sure until all the data comes in from the scene and the medical examiner, but preliminary findings indicate a simple case of careless drinking. Looks like the stove was left open, and the body is positioned in a manner that is consistent with a person overcome with unconsciousness."

"Basically," says Verdon, "he got drunk and fell over."

"Very drunk," says Dugan.

My radio blares — dispatch calling Hendrigan that reinforcements are on the way. It's late afternoon and the HAC boys will soon be replaced by a crew of local Native firefighters, who will camp at the fire until it is extinguished. Dugan asks if they are driving or flying. Driving, says Middel, who doesn't sound impressed that the trail into the fire is blocked by the RCMP, pending clearance from ident.

"You better go for a walk," Dugan tells me. "Double check the trail."

"You want me to tag along?" Verdon asks.

"I need you here," says Dugan. "Cassel will be fine."

I've been wanting to check the trail. I walk briskly away from the fire, relieved to get away from the cabin. The smell of charred human flesh is nauseating. On the trail, I walk slower, peering from side to side. I'm not expecting to find much — Waldren already scouted the trail, and Luke Middel contaminated it — but you never know. If someone started the fire which killed the occupant of the cabin, chances are they drove in along this trail. I peer intently at the ground in front of me as I walk, scan the forest on both sides. The ground is dry, which is not good for tire impressions. There's no grade to the trail, just twin ruts scuffed into the sand and over tree roots. A few old beer and soda cans litter the side of the trail, which I pick up and sniff. They're old and dry. After a few kilometres, I give up, call Hendrigan, who tells Dugan, who calls the RCMP guard at the gate. A few minutes later, a convoy of trucks rolls past. I hitch a ride, crammed next to a large Native, chewing tobacco.

"I hear there's a dead guy at the fire," he says.

"Where'd you here that?"

"Moccasin telegraph," he says, leaning across me to spit his chew out the window. He's only partly successful. I acquire a new stain.

"Really? We might have to subpoena the moccasin telegraph."

"Yeah." He finds this amusing. I'm less amused.

"What's your name?" I ask, struggling to free my notebook from a pocket.

"Don't sweat it, man. I heard it over the radio. We got a scanner."

"Whose cabin is it?"

"Rufus Hallendry," says the driver.

"What kind of guy was he?"

"Just a regular guy. Good hunter."

"Ah, he was a dink," says a voice from behind me. I try to turn and look back at the source, but I'm in too tight, jammed between the door and a beefy shoulder. I content myself with studying the side mirror. A brown face gazes back at me. Young. Cocky.

"Why do you say that?"

"Ah, he was just a dink. Typical fuckin' white man."

The face jerks, like someone gave him an elbow.

"Present company excluded," he says, with a trace of sarcasm.

"Bobo here is a dink, too," says another, older voice from behind.

In the mirror, Bobo grins. I let it slide. Soon, the green branches and grey tree trunks give way to black poles and ashy ground. The truck pulls to a stop near the yellow crime scene ribbon, which blocks the path. For a moment, no one moves to leave the truck. The forensic specialists, in their white suits, contrast starkly with their blackened surroundings, lending the scene an air of clinical finality. The body is an angular black form and I wonder if the others have noticed. Behind me, Bobo opens the truck door.

"Come on boys," he proclaims. "Let the white men play. We gotta get to work."

He moves to the back of the truck, opens the canopy, pulls out a chainsaw. His companions seem to have ignored him and wait another minute, then they too exit the truck, quietly begin to unload their gear. I head to the ruins of the cabin, where Luke waves at me. I nod, vaguely annoyed by Luke's childishness. Hendrigan makes his way through the black branchless trees, accompanied by Carter Spence, the junior local Forest Officer. Spence must have flown in while I was walking the trail. No doubt he's been put in charge of the fire. He'll supervise the local Native crew until he's confident the fire has been extinguished. He shakes my hand as if we're strangers.

"How you holding up, Porter?"

"Fine. You the new Incident Commander?"

"Yeah." He frowns, looking at my arm. "What happened?"

"Scratched myself, searching the cabin."

He has me pull back my sleeve, inspects Hendrigan's work.

"That's more than a scratch."

"I'm fine. I'll clean it up later."

"No," he says, thinking it over. "You'd better head back."

At the cabin, the two ident specialists are shovelling debris into a pail for screening. There really isn't much more I can do here. I nod to Spence, who tells me that TRT is headed back to base to refuel and that I should thumb a ride. At the helipad, I climb into the helicopter, exhausted, watch the ground recede below, where I see yellow-clad men working hoses among black skeletal trees, white trucks parked like toys.

And the black sprawled form of a burned body.

# 3
●

THE BROAD EXPANSE of Lake Athabasca spreads out before us as the helicopter ascends. Bright blue, mirroring the sky. The far side of the lake, twenty miles away, is a thin line. The helicopter banks right, following the shoreline, and we skim above green trees speckled over the pink and grey granite of Canadian Shield. Thin strips of beach pass below, so white you would think you're in the Caribbean, except for the horseflies, which attack in hordes as soon as you are wet, and water so cold it hurts. Everywhere I look is colour and life — an immense relief from the black mortal remains of the fire. The pilot's voice crackles in my headset.

"Any more casualties?"

"No. Just the one."

Normally on a flight you chat with the pilot. Lulls in conversation are spent in companionable silence. Today the silence is tense and uncomfortable. Firefighting is a dangerous business and we all know of lost friends and co-workers. The presence of a body at the fire has everyone on edge. I focus on the forest below, peering through the bushy crowns of pine, the conical tops of spruce trees, looking for deer or moose. With the population of nearby Fort Chipewyan mostly Aboriginal, and entitled to hunt year-round, chances of sighting an animal this close to town are slim. I shift my gaze inland, toward the area of the previous bottle fires. They've occurred in a relatively concentrated zone within the boundary of the Cree Band's land claim — an undeveloped area of pine. It didn't take long for the Cree Band council to notice and they're looking for a direction to point their fingers. It's caused some tension, particularly for Mark Middel, the Chief Ranger. Pressure he's more than willing to pass on to me.

A few minutes later the airport and fire base come into view.

"Where do you want me to drop you?" asks the pilot.

"The IA base is fine."

The IA base — or Initial Attack base — is a collection of industrial trailers set among a stand of pine trees. The base is located adjacent the small airport, seven or eight miles out of town, to keep the noise of air traffic away from residents and provide a quiet place for firefighters waiting to be dispatched. This has been my home for the past two weeks. In addition to the bunk trailers, there's a cook shack, warehouse and pumphouse. The compound is fenced with heavy wire mesh, topped with barbed wire. The helicopter touches down on a gravel pad, next to a collection of fuel drums. The pilot hot fuels — keeps the engine running — and I help him roll a barrel, flip it upright, then head to my truck, gingerly opening and closing my hand. The injured arm does not appreciate the work and is throbbing.

The drive into town is short and quiet. A black bear in the ditch watches me pass.

Fort Chipewyan is the oldest community in Alberta and has a unique personality. Houses are small and faded, set among trees and humps of granite. Yards are filled with vehicles on blocks or sinking into weeds. A fence made of old tires half buried in the ground is many colours. Another yard has a moose hide in a frame, drying in the sun. Snowmobiles in various stages of dissection are scattered like lawn ornaments. Dogs roam at will. No permanent roads lead to this small community. In winter an ice road is pushed through the snow for a few months. The rest of the year, you either fly in, or take a boat. It makes me wonder what young people here do to let off steam. There are no movie theatres, arcades, or bowling alleys. No shopping malls. I sense boredom lurking in the shadows as I cruise slowly into town, wind from the open truck window ruffling my hair. Perhaps this boredom is what lies behind the bottle fires.

I ease the truck to a stop at an intersection, look both ways.

The town is strung along the curving shore of a small bay in Lake Athabasca. To my left is the squat brown building of the ranger station and several older houses that attest to the lack of a building code. Across and slightly down the street is the government dock where the boats of the Forest Service, RCMP, Fish and Wildlife, and Wood Buffalo National Park are berthed. To my right is Main Street. Beyond the houses and metal-clad buildings, the lake shimmers, fringed with white scud from the wind, carrying a scent of damp rock. Small humped islands covered in trees decorate the outer edge of the bay. Gulls roost on power lines. If you didn't know you were in land-locked Alberta, you would swear you're in Newfoundland.

Mark Middel is at the ranger station, awaiting my report of the day's activities. I'll stop in later, after my visit to the clinic.

I turn right onto Main Street, which roughly parallels the lakeshore. Native children play in the street, kicking a ball back and forth, laughing. They make way slowly. An old dishevelled Native pauses and watches me pass. He's a familiar sight — always pushing a bike, which I've never seen him ride. Two roughly built plywood boxes have been mounted on either side of the rear tire, giving the bike an awkward width. I see him several times a day, often far from town, wearing a faded florescent vest over his torn jacket, picking bottles. He's always stooped as though under a great weight. He watches me with rheumy eyes, cheeks wild with stubble. I wave. He doesn't wave back. I pull into the parking lot of the clinic — one of the few modern structures in town. Sided in corrugated metal, it looks more like an industrial facility than a place of healing.

As I open my truck door, I hear a familiar howling.

The dog from the fire is tied to a rail at the corner of the building. The parking lot is hot, sun baking off the brown metal wall. The dog has no water and obviously has not been attended to. He barks hoarsely, slobbering at my hand as I kneel in front of him.

"Hey buddy, looks like they abandoned you."

The poor animal is wheezing. A gelatinous mass has formed over one burned ear. I untie the leash, lead the dog up the stairs into the clinic. The small waiting room is crowded. The Native receptionist behind the counter looks me over.

"You can't bring that dog in here. This is a hospital."

"He needs medical care."

"The doctor doesn't see animals."

"Is there a vet in town?"

She shakes her head.

"Then where do I bring him?"

"Anywhere but here."

We glare at each other. An older nurse appears behind the counter.

"Is there a problem?"

"This guy brought a dog in here."

The nurse peers over the counter, looks at the dog, who sits obediently at my feet, tongue lolling, eyebrows bunched hopefully. "Oh my," says the nurse. "So he did."

"This dog has been through hell. He requires medical attention."

"So do you, by the looks of it."

In my anger at the dog's neglect, I'd forgotten about my arm.

"We'll take care of both of you but I'm afraid it may take a little while. The doctor only comes once a week."

"What if there's an emergency when he's not here?"

"Our nurses have extra training."

With the nearest fully equipped hospital two hundred miles away I'm not sure it's a great compromise. I ask for a dish of water for the dog and settle into one of the hard plastic chairs, prepared for a long wait. I'm not disappointed. Finally, I get my turn, lead the dog into a small room to await the doctor. Ten more minutes, and the doctor enters.

"Ah — you are the one with the dog."

The doctor is short and stocky, wears glasses. He's Korean and looks weary.

"I am Doctor Cho," he says. "What is trouble today?"

"I've injured my arm, but could you look at the dog first? He's been through a lot."

The doctor looks down at the dog, sitting at my feet. The small room is filled with doggy odours and the sound of panting. The doctor taps on the padded examination bench. "You put dog on table." His accent is harsh. I pick up the dog, who whimpers as I touch his scorched skin, lay him on his side. His tail thumps half-heartedly against the bench's paper covering. Animals seem to know when you're trying to help them and the dog watches us, trust written in his brown eyes.

"What happened?" says the doctor.

I sniff, my nose itching. "He's been through a forest fire."

The doctor looks the dog over. "Your dog?"

"No, we found him at the fire this morning. His owner is deceased."

The doctor probes with his stethoscope, checks the dog's eyes, peers with another scope into his ears. "We clean him up. Give him some cream for burns. He'll be okay."

"What about his breathing? How are his lungs?"

"He'll be okay," repeats the doctor. "Lots of smoke. But healthy dog."

He spends a few minutes cleaning the worst of the burns, applies antibiotic cream. When he's done, he rummages in a drawer, hands me a fist full of small sample tubes.

"Twice every day," he says.

I lift the dog off the examination table, set him in the corner on the floor, where he promptly lays down and closes his eyes. The doctor waits. I start to pull up my sleeve.

"Take off clothes."

I hesitate — it's just a gash on my arm — then shrug off my coveralls. I've been soaked in muskeg, seasoned in smoke and marinated in sweat. My scent makes the dog smell like a deodorant, but the doctor doesn't let on that he notices. He unwraps Hendrigan's handiwork.

"How you injure yourself?" he asks, studying the wound.

"I'm not exactly sure," I admit, not wanting to elaborate.

"You are firefighter?"

"Yes. A fire investigator."

"There is abrasion and burn. You are light sleeper?"

I'm confused at the change in direction. "Yes, but what —"

"Hands and feet usually cold?"

I nod. Again correct, but how this relates to my burn remains a mystery.

"You are tense? Tire easily?"

"Well, I don't know about that —"

"Have you been urinating less than usual?"

By now I'm totally confused. "I thought you were treating my arm."

"Arm is easy to treat," he says. "Rest of you is the problem."

I'm getting defensive. "What's wrong with me?"

The doctor gives me a stern look. With his narrow eyes, square jaw and flat face, he looks imposing. He must sense my unease, because suddenly he gives me a patient smile, as though I'm a child that requires mentoring. "Have a seat Mr. ..."

He opens my newly prepared medical folder and scans.

"Cassel," I tell him. "Porter Cassel."

"Yes, Mr. Cassel." The doctor pauses, no doubt searching for some way to best phrase what he needs to tell me. The pause makes me nervous. I'm not a hypochondriac, but after the doctor's sudden inquisition, it seems any number of possible diseases or conditions might plague me. I haven't been feeling that well these past few months. The doctor purses his lips, touches his fingertips together. "You have an imbalance in your life. Your Yin and Yang."

"Okay," I say, relieved. Mumbo-jumbo. "Could you just —"

The doctor gives me a stony look. "You are sick, Mr. Cassel."

This rattles me enough that I sit on the edge of the examination bench.

"Body is like fish in bowl," says the doctor. "Survival depends on temperature of water, sunlight, food. You are fish. Something between you and water is not right."

Suddenly, I want to get out of here. Perhaps it's just a reaction to an approach that seems nothing short of sorcery. Perhaps it's some secret knowledge that the doctor is looking right into me and seeing what I dread most — that it's not just age creeping up on me. His dark eyes stare back at me. I try to make light of what he's told me — that I'm a sick fish. Seen in the abstract, it's ludicrous, but I'm not reassured.

"Thanks, Doc. I'll keep that in mind. Can you fix my arm? I gotta get back to work."

The doctor watches me a few seconds longer, then shrugs, as though he should have expected as much. He takes my arm, cleans the wound, none too gently. I wince, focus on the dog, asleep on the floor. It occurs to me that I'll have to figure out what to do with him. There must be a relative in town. Until then, he can stay in the yard at the ranger station.

"I give you antibiotics," says the doctor, bandaging the wound.

"Thanks." Good old western medicine. "Could I get a few antihistamines?"

The doctor nods, doesn't say anything. He seems to have decided that further conversation would be wasted on me. He finishes up, indicates I can pull up my coveralls, rummages in a drawer and hands me two vials of pills — antibiotics and antihistamines.

"Three times a day," he says, indicating the antibiotics.

I collect the dog and am about to leave, when he stops me.

"You here next week?"

I think about the bottle fires. "Probably."

"You come see me again. We talk more."

It's well past supper and getting dark when I emerge from the clinic, dog in tow. I lower the tailgate on my truck, thinking I'll have to lift in the dog, but he jumps up on his own, curls up in the box behind the cab. I ease the truck onto the street, head through town toward the junction with the airport road. Children in a yard play on a derelict snowmobile. An old Native woman watches me pass, her expression unreadable. At the intersection, I hesitate, looking at the ranger station. It's been a long day and I want to shower, eat and collapse, but Mark Middel is in the duty room, expecting to be briefed on the day's events. I try to convince myself he would appreciate me in a change of clothes, but that means a trip out of town to the IA base, and I might not return. Reluctantly, I turn into the small gravel parking lot, trudge up the steps. The secretary, Louise Holmes, is behind a desk, doing paperwork. She's the wife of the local Fish and Wildlife officer, which works out well, as she lives across the street. She gives me an understanding smile as I enter.

"How are you doing, Porter?"

"Not one of my better fires."

She tilts her head toward the duty room. "Mark's been expecting you."

Mark Middel sits in a small room filled with buzzing radios, boots propped on a desk. Despite his posture, he does not look relaxed. There's a sheaf of papers in his hand and he's frowning. When he sees me, he tosses the paperwork onto the desk, drops his feet and rubs his face with his hands.

"How does it look out there, Cassel?"

"Bad. Between the body, the cops, and forensics, everyone is edgy."

"That figures." He sighs wearily. "What are the Mounties saying?"

All impressions are preliminary, so I choose my words carefully. "There's evidence of alcohol consumption. The body appears to have been on the floor at the time of the fire. Both the door on the cabin and the woodstove appear to have been open."

"Hallendry got drunk and burned down his cabin."

"That's one explanation."

"You can think of others?" says Middel. He's about fifty, with sandy, receding hair and a small face. His nose looks like he's been in fight in his youth and his skin is coarse with eczema. He's a bit bandy-legged and has a pot belly. Physically, he's not impressive, but he carries an aura of impatience and exactitude about him that is intimidating. He waits, scowling, for a response. I've managed to cope with him these last two weeks by not engaging.

"It's early. We need to finish processing."

"Since you're here, I take it your part is done."

"Essentially. I've confirmed the cabin is the origin."

"Good," he says. "That's good. If it's not wildfire arson, the investigation isn't our problem. We'll mop up and extinguish — the rest will be up to the cops." He leans forward, watching me. "Unless you think this has anything to do with the other fires."

"I don't think so. There doesn't seem to be any similarity."

"You're certain?"

"It's a little early to be certain," I say, glancing out the window which overlooks the parking lot. The dog is standing in the truck box, watching the door of the ranger station. Perhaps I should have tied him. I consider turning him over to Middel for safe-keeping until a relative can be found, then recall Middel's reluctance to send the helicopter for the injured dog. Middel clears his throat impatiently. I force myself to focus.

"This fire doesn't fit the pattern. The other fires were on vacant land."

"Not entirely vacant," says Middel. "It's Cree land claim."

"Sure, but the fires didn't involve buildings."

"Thank God for that. They're pissed enough at losing trees."

I'm thinking it's not the trees they're upset about — it's a feeling they're being picked on, singled out. They're being territorial. It hadn't occurred to me until now but the cabin wasn't on Cree land, which I point out.

"Close though," says Middel. "The trail runs through Cree territory."

"Was there ever an issue with Hallendry driving through there?"

Middel shrugs. "Maybe. What about the bottles?"

"We didn't find a bottle with an inscription."

"But you found bottles. You said he was drinking."

"I said there was evidence suggesting alcohol consumption."

"What's the difference?"

"We don't know who consumed the alcohol."

"You think he had company?"

"Impossible to determine at this point."

Middel scowls. "Where were the bottles?"

"One in the truck and several in the cabin."

"He was drunk before he got there."

"Also impossible to determine."

A cold stare, which I ignore. Middel seems to take most of what I say as a challenge. "In fact," I continue, "it is impossible to determine if the bottle recently held any liquid, as residue would have been vaporized by the fire. The medical examiner will conduct an autopsy and determine a blood alcohol level. Until then, we have no direct evidence that the victim was inebriated."

"But it looks that way."

"That's the obvious conclusion."

The radio demands attention — vxh returning to the ia base with the hac. Spence has camp set up and operations are winding down for the night. I wait while Middel takes care of business. I'm so exhausted it hurts. If I close my eyes I'll fall asleep.

"How's your arm?"

"Fine. Nothing serious."

"Did you log it into the first aid record at the fire?"

"Of course. Mark, did you know Rufus Hallendry?"

"Not real well. I've only been here two years. We went hunting once, after I first arrived, up by Andrew Lake. He bagged one hell of a big moose."

"I didn't realize the two of you were friends."

Middel looks thoughtful. "Shame he did that to himself."

Once again, Middel is jumping to the conclusion that the death of Rufus Hallendry was accidental. There doesn't seem any point in further discussion so I wait while Middel stares at his boot, lost in memory. "I better get going," I say finally, snapping him out of his reverie.

"I'm done here too," he says with a yawn. We head outside together.

It's dark, a streetlight casting a pool of light over my truck, where the dog paces.

"This is the mutt?" says Middel. The dog sniffs at him cautiously.

I nod and Middel asks what I plan to do with him.

"I don't know," I admit, scruffing the dog under the chin. He's watching Middel, clearly nervous. Dogs don't trust anyone that won't return their interest and Middel just stands there, with his hands in his pocket. "Does Hallendry have relatives in town?"

"Not that I know of," says Middel. "I think he has grown kids somewhere."

"I'll track them down. See if they'll take the dog."

"I wouldn't bother. Look at him — he's a mess."

We watch the dog sniff my hand. He does look pretty rough.

"Just put him down," says Middel. "One bullet and his troubles are over."

I suppress a flash of anger, don't look at Middel while it passes. The dog is licking my hand. Silently, I vow to do what I can to help the injured animal find a safe home.

"Was Luke any use at the fire?" says Middel.

I decide not to mention the trail contamination. "He helped a bit."

"Good. He needs some exposure to the real world."

I'm tempted to mention that with a burned corpse at the fire, I'm certain Luke had more than enough exposure to the real world, but bite my tongue. Middel and his son seem to have a few issues, not unlike all fathers and teenagers I suspect. I'm not about to wade into the fray. Middel heads home and I head out of town, windows on the truck cranked down to help me stay awake. At the base, I tether the dog to a tree, get him some food and a bowl of water and collapse on my spongy mattress. I'm certain I'll quickly be dead to the world but my brain has other plans. Just as I begin to drift off, I jolt awake and lie staring at the grainy ceiling, wondering why I can't sleep. This has become a nightly ritual. Tonight, I was hoping the exhaustion and antihistamines would allow me a reprieve. No such luck. My thoughts drift to the Korean doctor and his Asian medical mumbo-jumbo. I'm a fish. My Ying and Yang are out of balance. I'm sick. Perhaps that's why I can't sleep. A mild panic ebbs and flows. I count sheep. I shear them, wash them, skin them. Barbecue them. Still, I lie awake, worrying and frustrated. Outside, the dog howls morosely, the sound resonating with the tension in my chest. I grit my teeth, wait for sleep. Images parade through my mind.

A corpse, burned and eyeless.

A bird on a pile of black fur.

Hendrigan, bandaging my arm.

Just before dawn, finally, mercifully, I drift into sleep.


I'm woken by a pounding on my door. I struggle out of bed, bleary-eyed, thumping my knee in the process, and yank open the door. Mark Middel stands in the narrow hall, wearing his uniform and a frown.

"Jesus, Cassel, you look like shit."

"What can I do for you, Mark?"

"The Cree Band has requested a meeting. I brought you a uniform."

He offers me a bundle of folded clothes, which I do not take. "When is the meeting?"

"In about an hour." He thrusts the clothes at me. "You need to get changed."

"Not into those," I tell him.

"You wore the uniform for years. What's the problem?"

There's no way I'm ever wearing the uniform again, but don't want to argue, so I take the damn thing, reassure him that I will be at the meeting on time, and close door. I set the bundle on my bed, stare at the tan and green cloth as Middel's footsteps recede down the hall. When the outer door slams shut I wince, furious. Years ago, I dressed my girlfriend in a uniform so we could spend a day together in the woods. She didn't work for the Forest Service and it seemed harmless fun, but it got her killed. The last thing I need this morning is a reminder from Mark Middel, trying to bolster the uniformed presence at some meeting. My work now as a contractor doesn't require me to wear a uniform. I toss the bundle of cloth into a corner, head for the showers.

The water feels good and I return to my room in a slightly better mood.

I put on blue jeans and a cotton shirt, take the uniform with me.

The office of the Cree Band is in a low building in the centre of town. The building is long and angled to form a sort of bay around a dusty gravel parking lot. I park next to Mark Middel's truck, set the uniform on the seat and hurry into the building. A slim Native woman with long black hair points me to a boardroom where several Natives sit around a polished wooden table opposite Mark Middel, who looks very official. His expression darkens when he sees I'm not similarly attired.

"You're late, Cassel."

"Sorry," I say. "Traffic."

Middel introduces me to the group as the investigator in charge of the arson fires. Sammy Cardinal introduces himself as the Chief. He looks to be in his late fifties, slim build, grey hair neatly trimmed. The band councillors go next. Buddy Cardinal is the External Affairs Coordinator. Albert Cardinal is Economic Development. Simon Cardinal is the Native Justice Liaison. Rodney Cardinal is Community and Social Outreach.

It's the Cardinal mafia. Nepotism at its finest.

"Mr. Cassel and I are here at your request," says Middel.

"Where's the RCMP?" says the Chief.

"I notified them," says Middel. "They're too busy to attend."

"Why aren't they involved?" says Simon. He looks to be in his mid-thirties, with clear brown skin. His black hair is braided and parted in the middle, pulled tight against his scalp. Two ponytails draped over his shoulder hang halfway down his chest. He wears a fringed buckskin coat with a lot of beading, sits with his arms crossed.

"This is a Forest Service matter," says Middel.

"The fires are on Cree land. That makes it Federal."

"We have an agreement with the Feds," says Middel, his neck colouring.

"That doesn't mean you have enough resources to do the job. There have been four fires so far on Cree land, and you guys have how many people working on this?" Simon Cardinal looks at me, dark eyes hostile. "One guy. You've got one guy."

"Porter is a qualified fire investigator."

"One guy. No wonder you can't make any progress."

There's a tense moment as Simon Cardinal and Mark Middel glower at each other.

The Chief says, "Let's hear what the Forest Service has to say."

Middel tilts his head in my direction. "Go ahead, Porter."

I consider how to start. Simon Cardinal has done a nice job of setting me up to look ineffective, which will be difficult to overcome as there really isn't much to offer. I clear my throat, address the Chief, focusing on a button on his shirt. In Native culture, it is considered disrespectful to look an older man in the eye while speaking. "We've had four fires in the past two weeks. All four fires used the same incendiary device — a bottle of gasoline and diesel with a rag stuffed into the throat. Timing has been consistently three or four days apart. All the fires were started very early in the morning a short distance from the road."

"So they tossed the bottles from a car," says Simon.

"That appears the most likely scenario, although the origin of the first fire was substantially farther from the road, over a hundred yards."

"What do you think that means?" says the Chief.

"The perpetrator might be getting nervous and is exiting the scene more rapidly."

"Not nervous enough to stop," says Simon Cardinal.

"We've started early morning aerial patrols," says Middel.

"Have you found tire tracks?" says the Chief.

"The road surface has been too dry and hard for impressions."

Simon Cardinal rolls his eyes as if he expected to be disappointed. He looks about to say something and I hasten to sum up the investigation. "In fact, we've found no physical evidence, at origin or in transfer, other than the bottles."

The Chief frowns. "So you have no idea who started these fires?"

"At this point," I admit, "we haven't developed any leads."

Middel gives me an unsettled look, as though he expected I'd have more.

"What about the bottles?" says the Chief. "Any thoughts on that?"

"Nothing really. They're just common liquor bottles."

"I've heard they have some sort of code on them."

I hesitate. We purposefully hadn't released this information. In any investigation, there are clues or evidence that are not released by the investigators — called hold back — that only the investigator or the perpetrator would know. Hold back is used to screen genuine suspects from the inevitable crazies that want to claim responsibility, and to trip up the perpetrator. It disturbs me that the Chief knows about the inscription on the bottles. I keep my voice carefully neutral.

"Can I ask how you came into possession of this information?"

The Chief looks over at Simon Cardinal.

"Everyone knows," says Simon. "Firefighters talk."

Although I was careful not to show anyone the bottle fragments with the inscription, and to keep my room locked where I have the reconstructed bottles, there were firefighters roaming the fires when we were looking for the origin. In fact, on two of the fires, it was one of the local IA members who first spotted the fragments. I hadn't stressed to them the need to keep this quiet because the inscriptions were hard enough to spot that I didn't think a casual observer would have noticed. Apparently, I underestimated their powers of observation and now the only hold back I have, on a fire with very little to go on, is common knowledge.

"What do you think it means?" asks the Chief.

"At this point, I'm not prepared to speculate."

"Could the letters be someone's initials?" asks Buddy Cardinal, the External Affairs Coordinator. Buddy is thin, hollow-cheeked, with a large nose. His hair is short and he's wearing a bright red plaid shirt which commands attention.

"It's possible, but not likely."

"Why not?"

"Too obvious — unless the firebug wants to get caught."

There's a thoughtful silence around the table. The Chief is frowning.

"Could the inscription on the bottles be related to the fires being on our land?"

"We have no evidence to support such a connection."

"You don't have any evidence — period," says Simon Cardinal.

"What about motive?" asks the Chief. "Do you have any theories?"

"Nothing so far."

The Chief furrows his brow. I wish I had more to offer him.

"So," says Simon Cardinal, "after four fires, you've got no clues, no motive, and no suspect." His tone is challenging, bordering on insolence. Perhaps he's trying to impress the Chief. Or he's a cop wannabe. Either way, he's testing my patience. I take a deep breath, determined to remain professional. "Yes, that about sums it up."

"Some nutcase is attacking us and you don't know anything."

"Trees are the only thing being attacked."

Simon Cardinal glares at me. He's younger than I am, so I glare back.

The Chief raises a placating hand. "Gentlemen, please, we're all on the same side. It does seem to me, though, that whoever is starting these fires is specifically targeting the Cree Band." Beside him, the lesser Cardinal snorts, which the Chief ignores. "So far, they have done little except burn a few trees but I am concerned these targeted attacks could take another path. The Band has many assets, other than the trees on our land. There's the store in town. The bulk fuel company. The barge and the airline. What if this fire starter becomes more aggressive? Can you imagine what might happen? What assurances do we have that all that can be done is being done and that our interests are protected?"

Middel sits up, alarmed. "There has been no specific threat."

The Chief looks at me. "What do you think, Mr. Cassel?"

"Other than the location of the fires, there's no evidence to indicate the Cree Band is being targeted. The area affected is undeveloped and basically identical to any other area around here, so it's possible the arsonist doesn't know he's active on your land. Given there are very few rural roads here, the location of the fires could simply be a matter of convenience."

"But there is the possibility that we are being targeted."

"Yes," I admit, "it is possible. If so, you probably have a better idea than anyone what might motivate the arsonist. Is there anyone that might benefit financially by threatening the Cree Band? Anyone with a grudge?"

The men at the other side of the table exchange looks. Anything that passes between them is far too subtle for my interpretation, but I get an impression of discomfort. "Nothing comes to mind," says the Chief. "If we think of anything, we'll certainly let you know."

Buddy Cardinal clears his throat. "Any connection with the Hallendry fire?"

"Not that we're aware of," Middel says quickly.

"What caused that fire?"

"Looks like an accident," says Middel.

"At this point," I say. "We don't know. The investigation is still preliminary."

Beside me, Middel shifts in his chair. "The fires are unrelated."

It disturbs me that Middel is broadcasting his theories in such a pre-emptive manner. Perhaps there's some local politic of which I'm unaware. Or he's feeling enough heat over the bottle fires that he doesn't want to add to the pressure. Either way, it's misleading and, quite frankly, unprofessional. "Well, technically, at this point, we don't really know."

Simon Cardinal's eyes narrow suspiciously. "Well, are they connected, or not?"

Middel turns, gives me a stern look, then faces the Chief. "We're still working on it."

The Chief thinks about this. "Who is in charge of the Hallendry fire?"

"The RCMP" I tell him. "Anytime there's a fatality, it's the Mounties."

"Good," says Simon Cardinal.

There's an uncomfortable silence.

"Do you have anything further to add?" asks the Chief.

Middel gives me a wary glance. I shake my head. The Chief rises, thanks us for our time. Simon Cardinal lingers as the others rise. "Just one more thing," he says, looking at me. "Based on the frequency of these fires, when do you anticipate another one?"

"We're overdue."

# 4

WE DRIVE OUT to the fire together. Middel is rigid, gripping the steering wheel. "Don't ever do that again," he says. "Do not contradict me in front of the locals."

"You were jumping to conclusions, Mark."

"Dammit, Porter, there's politics involved. The Cree Band thinks it's a conspiracy."

"All the more reason to stick to what we know."

"Easy for you to say."

I revert to my proven strategy of not engaging and remain silent. Middel doesn't like the silence, grumbles a bit more about my not wearing the uniform to the meeting, and about fighting with the regional dispatcher for more resources, but mostly he grumbles about the lack of progress on the bottle fire investigation, which I could take personally, but don't — I'm just too tired. Last night was rough. Middel's grumbling recedes to a distant drone as I gaze blankly at passing Jack pine.

The trees look odd, with wild erratic clumps of branches. They are heavily infested with dwarf mistletoe. They need a fire to clean out the parasite so a healthy new forest can start over.

Ironic because we're busy putting out all the fires.

My eyes flutter shut and I'm transported.

Fire crackles. Firefighters around me have oddly green faces.

"Porter?"

I blink, lift my head. It takes a second to realize where I am. Middel gives me a worried look as he drives. I had dozed off. I push myself up in my seat.

"You okay? You don't look so good."

"Yeah." I rub sleep out of my eyes. "Just a little tired."

We turn off the gravel road onto the narrow trail that meanders to the Whiskey Creek fire. Trees at the trailhead are festooned with multi-coloured plastic ribbon — orange and blue from the Forest Service; yellow crime scene ribbon from the Mounties. Very festive. A cardboard sign stapled to a tree warns those with no business at the fire to stay away. We bump over roots, which jolt and thump the truck. No chance of falling asleep here.

"You find anything along the trail?" says Middel.

"Nothing."

He nods, as if expecting as much. Twenty minutes later we're driving among blackened trees. Firefighters are splashes of colour in bright orange and yellow coveralls. A pump whines at the creek. We park next to the sacred yellow ribbon marking Dugan's primary scene. Dugan and Verdon squat together inside the rectangular frame of what was the cabin. I stop at the yellow ribbon, wait for permission to enter their domain. Middel ducks under the ribbon, strides over to the cabin, glancing at the burned truck as he passes. Dugan stands, holding out a hand like a cop at an intersection.

"I'll need you to stop right there, sir."

Middel stops, glares back at me, irritated I didn't point out the obvious.

"I'm Mark Middel, the Chief Ranger."

"Dugan and Verdon. Stay right there. We'll come to you."

I join Middel a few steps back from the remains of the cabin. The ident specialists have made tremendous progress since I was last here. The pile of debris over the site has been completely removed, stacked neatly out of the way, exposing the irregular remains of the deeply charred cabin floor. The body, thankfully, is gone and the floor has been swept bare. White string staked above the ground divides the area into a grid. Among the grid, significant features have been replaced, presumably in the location they were found while excavating the site. The stove dominates the scene. Several bottles lie in a scattered group. The bottles are warped and broken, the glass crazed by the heat. Metal chair frames and table legs are laid out, black and skeletal. Several feet away a drinking glass, a crystal tumbler of sorts, lies on its side. The scene reminds me of reconstructions done after a plane crash. The two specialists step carefully over the grid strings, extend gloved hands as introductions ensue. Dugan and Verdon's bunny suits aren't white anymore.

"What do you figure?" says Middel.

Dugan smiles politely. "I figure we're getting close."

"To figuring out what happened?" Middel says hopefully.

"To completion of scene processing. We should have it concluded by nightfall."

Middel thinks about this as Verdon and I gaze at the remnants of the cabin.

"What do you think happened here?" Middel says, trying again.

"It is not something I'm at liberty to discuss," says Dugan.

Middel frowns. "Even with the Forest Service?"

"I'm afraid not."

Any slack Dugan and Verdon have given me as a fellow investigator seems to have vanished, perhaps because Middel is with me. A possible homicide is the exclusive domain of the RCMP. Once the case is resolved, we'll find out what happened, but first an autopsy will be performed and cause of death determined. If there are no suspicious indicators, it will likely be written off as accidental. I can't help wondering if Dugan and Verdon have already written it off. I've been around enough dead bodies to know that any suspicious death brings in plenty of manpower but haven't seen anyone from their Major Crimes unit, or even the General Investigation Section. A medical examiner needs to clear the body for removal and would do this in person if the death was suspicious, but the only manpower are the two ident specialists. Maybe it was just an accident, but I have an uneasy feeling and nothing to support it.

Dugan asks Middel if he knew Hallendry.

"We've been hunting," says Middel.

"Was your hunting buddy a regular drinker?"

"Pretty much everyone up here is."

"When was the last time you saw him?"

"Not for a while." Middel points to the cabin floor. "Is that where the body was?"

Dugan nods. Hallendry's body partially shielded the floor, leaving a reverse shadow. I wonder if anything was found under the body. Evidence in a fire is often preserved under a body — blood, traces of accelerant, footprints — but if anything suspicious in nature was found the cops will be tight-lipped. Dugan touches my elbow to catch my attention. "What do you think about that stove, Cassel? I've looked at the door and the locking mechanism appears quite reliable. Are you familiar with this type of woodstove?"

I step cautiously closer for a better view.

"Enter the scene, if you'd like," says Dugan. "Stay in the first two grid squares."

I step into the grid as directed. One of the squares overlays the void from the body and a tingle runs up the base of my neck. I crouch by the stove, peer inside the firebox, note there are no holes rusted or burned through. The ash contents have been removed, no doubt for screening by Dugan and Verdon, and I wonder if they found anything. I focus on the stove door, which creaks as I swing it shut, drop the locking mechanism into its slot. It seems solid.

"It looks to me like the stove was open before the fire."

Dugan nods. I stand, knees popping, and am hit by a wave of nausea, need to lean on the stove for a moment, pretend I'm examining something until the nausea passes, then step over the grid strings and exit the scene. Dugan watches me, eyes registering concern.

"Do you mind if I take a few pictures?" I ask quickly.

Dugan nods and I head to Middel's truck for my pack, take out my camera. When I return to the cabin, Dugan and Verdon are squatted by their extensive collection of cases and equipment. I walk around the remnants of the cabin, click a few pictures, feeling conspicuously out-gunned in the photo department. My cheap camera is better than nothing as I doubt I'll ever see Dugan's images. As I'm finishing up, Carter Spence, the Forest Officer assigned command of the fire, wanders over.

"If you guys want a break," he says, "lunch is ready."

Halfway back to camp, we run into a delegation heading the other direction. It's the cook, Margaret, a stout middle-aged Native lady with a bosom that would impress a battleship, her helper, young, slender and attractive, and Leonard, the Crew Boss of the Native firefighters. Leonard, small, grey-haired and wiry, is carrying a cast iron frying pan held in front of him in which a lump of something smoulders. We stop as he walks past, mumbling something in Cree, waving a free hand over the smoke.

"Someone burn lunch?" says Verdon.

"I think he's doing a ceremony of some sort."

Firefighters heading toward camp turn and follow the delegation, who stop at the yellow crime scene ribbon. Margaret whispers something to Dugan who nods, escorts Leonard past the ribbon where they do a circuit around the cabin, Leonard wafting the smoke from the frying pan and muttering. The rest of us, local firefighters and HAC, stand along the yellow ribbon, watching. Having completed his circuit, Leonard lifts the frying pan, first east, then west, north and south, calling out in Cree at each direction. Beside me, the young cook's helper sighs heavily and stares at the ground.

"What is he doing?" I whisper to her.

"Offering to the grandmothers," she says quietly.

"What's in the frying pan?"

"Sage. He's asking that no more bad happen at this place."

Leonard finishes with a song that tapers to a series of soft chants and for a few minutes we stand with our heads bowed. When the sage has burned out, Leonard picks up the pan and walks slowly back to camp, followed by the congregation.

"Unusual," says Hendrigan, beside me.

"Why's that, Aldous?"

"Cross-cultural. He was white guy, wasn't he?"

"I don't think that matters. Dead is dead."

Lunch involves SPAM, KLIK and other equally inedible lunch meats, served with soup on a crude table, built the day before out of logs, ripped lengthwise with a chainsaw. Firefighters spoon soup and make sandwiches from platters of sliced meat. They eat quietly. Even Bobo, the crew clown and attention junkie, is reserved. When the cook's helper arrives with more SPAM, I pick up a slice, hold it up.

"Did you hear the one about the priest and the hunter?"

She shakes her head. The firefighters wait, expressions suspended.

"A hunter stops by the church one day while the priest is having lunch. The priest invites the hunter to have a bite with him and offers him some sausage.

"'What's this?' says the hunter.

"'It's meat,' says the priest.

"The hunter sits with the priest and eats the sausage. He has a funny look on his face, but he doesn't say anything. The next week, as the hunter is passing the church, the priest asks the hunter if he would mind bringing him some firewood.

"'No problem,' says the hunter, and returns with a pail of sawdust.

"'What's this?' says the priest."

"If sausage is meat," says Bobo, "then sawdust is firewood."

General snickering — he's stolen my punchline. But they're smiling.

Dessert comes, cherry pie that tastes like cough syrup, but it's sweet and I gobble down a slice, craving the energy. Just as we're finishing lunch, the rumble of an approaching vehicle drifts through the burned trees. The firefighters all turn to watch.

It's another RCMP Suburban.

Sergeant Waldren steps out of the Suburban, escorting one of the largest men I have ever seen. He looks to be in his mid-forties, curly dark receding hair. Huge belly. No neck. He walks with an awkward gait, arms pushed outward by his immense back. Waldren points to the remains of the cabin. Dugan and Verdon leave the table.

I tag along, curious. We meet by the sacred yellow ribbon. Introductions ensue.

The big guy is Charles Hallendry, Rufus Hallendry's brother.

Condolences are offered, hands shaken. I can only get my hand halfway around the big guy's mitt, leaving me with the disturbing knowledge that he could easily crush my knuckles to powder. Fortunately, he isn't in an aggressive mood, seems dazed and bewildered.

"This must be difficult for you," I offer.

"Yeah," he says absently, eyes fixed on the black cabin floor. "What happened?"

"There's not much more that I can tell you," says Waldren.

Hallendry fingers the yellow ribbon. "Can I go in there?"

"Sure," says Dugan. "I'll just give you an escort."

The two men duck under the ribbon, walk around the remains of the cabin. Dugan looks like a child beside the larger man. Hallendry doesn't say much, just stares. The rest of us watch respectfully from outside the primary scene. Dugan points out a few things, such as the stove door being open. When they've circled around, Hallendry stops in front of what was the cabin door. He stares at the body shadow where his brother was found.

"Whiskey bottles," he says, shaking his head. "Damn fool."

Hallendry stares a moment longer then leaves the scene, ducking under the ribbon.

"I've seen enough," he says to Waldren, who nods. They head for the Suburban.

I remember something. "Excuse me, Charles, but there's a dog."

Hallendry stops, looks at me, puzzled.

"Your brother had a dog. We're not sure what to do with him."

He shakes his head. "You keep him."

"Is there anyone else? Another relative?"

"Damn fool," he says again. "I can't believe I flew all the way up here for this."

Hallendry turns away, climbs into the Suburban, which settles noticeably. I'm left wondering, among other things, what to do with the dog. Middel, who was talking with Carter Spence by the camp, walks over, picking his teeth with a sliver of wood, watches the Suburban vanish down the trail.

"Who was that?"

"Hallendry's brother, Charles. You ever meet him before?"

"I think I'd remember. You ready to go, Cassel?"

"In a minute. There's something I need to check."

I ask Dugan if I can take a look at the bottles at the cabin, explain what I'm looking for. Dugan has me glove up, hands me the bottle fragments. I handle them gingerly.

There's no inscription.

Having been unable to acquire satisfactory conclusions from Dugan and Verdon, Middel grills me about the cabin fire during the drive back to town. Unlike the ident specialists, I am within Middel's jurisdiction. And I'm a captive source. We're barely down the trail from the fire when Middel asks the inevitable. "What do you figure, Porter?"

"SPAM should be outlawed."

"About the fire," he says impatiently.

"I don't have the benefit of everything the RCMP have uncovered."

"But you're a fire investigator. You must have some opinion."

I'm a wildfire investigator, I'm tempted to remind him. Structure fires are far more complex and are investigated by a different sort of professional. The fire dynamics of a building are different than those of a forest, as are the fuels — there are thousands of materials in a building fire you'd never find in a wildfire. "Well, let's review what we know," I say. "Both the stove door and cabin door were open before the fire. There were whiskey bottles and one drinking glass found within the vicinity of the body, which was on the floor, indicating Hallendry was likely unconscious or incapacitated."

"I know all that. I want to know what you think happened."

"I think it's too early to think we know what happened."

We hit a root along the trail and the truck thumps. Middel shifts in his seat, looking irritated. "Why do you make things so complicated?" he says. "What more do we need to know to draw the obvious conclusion that he was drinking and passed out?"

I hold up a hand, tick off the points.

"First, we don't know the cause of death. Second, we can't say with certainty that an accelerant wasn't used. Third, we don't know if he was alone. Fourth — hell, what does it matter, this isn't a Forest Service investigation, anyway."

I slump back in my seat, annoyed and restless. Middel is wearing me out. My head feels as though it's filled with cotton. I'm nauseous. Everything hurts. I'm not a hypochondriac, but what the doctor told me is eating at me. I can't remember the last time I really felt well. I lean back my head, close my eyes. Mercifully, Middel lapses into a grumpy silence. A half hour later, we arrive in town. Middel drops me at my truck. I climb in, start it up, lean on the steering wheel, thinking, then drive three blocks to the nursing station.

Maybe the doctor hasn't left town yet.

## 5

THE WAITING ROOM at the clinic is empty today. The receptionist behind the counter gives me a questioning smile. "No dog today?"

I shake my head. "Is the doctor still here?"

"I believe he was just on his way out. Let me check."

She vanishes into the bowels of the small building, returns a moment later.

"You're in luck. Come with me."

The receptionist shows me into an examination room. I expect another long wait but Doctor Cho arrives almost immediately. "Ah — the fireman," he says. "No dog?"

"I left him at home today."

"Good. How is your arm?"

"Sore, but that's not why I came. I've been thinking about what you said before."

"Okay. First we look. Take off clothes."

I strip down to socks and boxers, expecting the doctor will listen to my heart and lungs with his stethoscope, test my reflexes, perhaps draw a little blood for tests. Instead, he silently examines me, touching my neck, checking my palms and the alignment of my hips. I feel more like a horse at auction, being examined by a prospective buyer, than a patient. He frowns, steps back. "Well developed shoulders and chest."

"Yeah, thanks, but —"

"Lower part of body thin. Hands and feet cold."

Now I really feel like a horse. "Listen, I don't mean to be rude, but I came here expecting a medical examination. If that's not going to happen, let's not waste each other's time."

The doctor looks offended. "Mr. Cassel, you do not understand. Medicine is not only treating sick part of body. Medicine is about all of body. How parts work together. Disease not caused by abnormal body part, but by disharmony of whole body. Very important also is situation and condition in which body is placed. Harmony is foundation of good health."

"Sure, I'll buy that, but —"

"We start by determining your constitution and physical type. The nape of your neck is developed, and you have slender waist. You are determined and talk easily. You have a lot of acid in your stomach and when it is empty your stomach hurts. You tire more easily than most of those around you. You are usually healthy, but when you get sick, you become ill quickly."

This analysis is delivered in rapid impatient sentences as though the doctor were instructing a medical class. The tone is unsettling, but what I find more unsettling is that everything he has told me fits. Episodes of illness, fatigue, hunger, even social situations where I found myself talking suddenly until I was almost dizzy.

"How do you know this?"

"You are *Taiyang*," he says, as if this should mean something to me.

"Is that serious?"

Dr. Cho finds this response amusing.

"Just who you are. Very rare."

"What does that mean?"

"You must be cautious of becoming angry or sorrowful."

I focus on a poster on the wall — the lymphatic system — searching for reassurance that I am in fact in a doctor's office. The last time I really became angry and sorrowful I ended up in detox and I find the doctor's penetrating diagnosis intensely discomforting.

"You are usually tense? Light sleeper? Frequent diarrhea?"

"Yes," I say slowly. A shiver runs up my spine.

"Fire type," says the doctor.

I chuckle, a bit nervously. "That's for sure."

"Not firefighter," he says. "Fire *type*."

"Hard to tell them apart, sometimes."

"Fire type very driven. Easy to lose balance. Tell me about your job."

"Well …" I sigh, take a deep breath and sit on the examination bench. What I thought would be a routine medical exam has warped into something sublimely bizarre but fascinating in its accuracy. "I'm a wildfire investigator. When there's a forest fire, I try to figure out who started it, and why."

"Your arm," says the doctor. "You are working on a fire here."

"Several. One very nasty."

"This nasty fire bothers you?"

I think of the burned corpse. "Yes, I guess it does."

The doctor looks thoughtful. "This job very hard for you. Fire type will not stop."

There's a moment of silence as I ponder his prognosis. I've always been good at taking things to extremes. Until now, I hadn't appreciated that this tendency might actually make me sick. The doctor pulls a stethoscope from his black bag and proceeds with a routine examination. The stethoscope is cold on my skin. The blood pressure sleeve causes my fingers to tingle — my pressure is a bit elevated. While I'm putting on my shirt, the doctor rummages in his black bag, pulls out a small package wrapped in brown paper, which he hands to me.

"You make tea. One teaspoon with cup of water. Four times every day."

I look at the package in my hand. "What's it supposed to do?"

"Taste very bad but make you feel much better."

I leave the clinic feeling unsettled and restless, drive out of town to the IA base. The big white-and-blue HAC helicopter gleams in the evening sun. I wander past the warehouse where the HAC boys lounge around a picnic table, ready for action, playing cards.

"It's the fire dick," says Hendrigan.

"Solved the big case yet?" asks one of the men.

I shake my head, continue on to the kitchen, make myself a sandwich from a platter of cold cuts, grab steak bones for the dog. I apply cream to his burns and we share a meal behind the cook shack. The dog, tethered by a long chain to a pine tree, squats and chews the bones. He looks rough, but seems to be doing fine.

"What am I going to do with you? You don't even have a name."

The dog looks up briefly, continues with its supper.

"Hey, Scorch."

The dog looks up again. Given his burn patterns, the name seems appropriate. When the dog is done his supper, I unsnap the chain from his collar. He runs around, chasing squirrels and barking. Hendrigan and a few of the HAC boys wander over to check out the excitement. It's a lazy evening without much to do.

"You guys want to start a fire in the pit?"

The question comes from Rudy, one of the HAC boys. Rudy has a guitar and we've spent a few nights around the fire, roasting hot dogs and listening to his three chords.

"I don't know," says Hendrigan. "It's too warm out for a fire."

There are general grunts of agreement and we drift back to the picnic table, where a few of the men resume their card game. Rudy, disenchanted, brings out his guitar and sits away from the group, picking a melancholy tune. I'm challenged to a game of ping-pong, which I quickly lose, vaguely distracted, but not sure why. It hits me when I walk out of the trailer, into the warm evening air. What Hendrigan said is bothering me.

*It's too warm out for a fire.*

It's been unseasonably warm the past few nights — warm enough that I've thrown off blankets and opened windows in the stuffy bunk trailer. Why then would someone start a fire in their woodstove? The only explanation would have been to cook, and I don't recall seeing any pots within the vicinity of the stove at the remains of Hallendry's cabin. I use the base radio at the cook shack to call the fire lookout tower closest to the Whiskey Creek fire.

"Cambridge tower, this is the IA base."

"This is Cambridge. Go ahead base."

"What was your minimum temp two nights ago?"

"Standby one."

All towers have a set of minimum and maximum thermometers. These thermometers are the usual mercury-filled glass type, with the addition of small plugs which remain at the highest or lowest reading until reset daily by giving the thermometer a good shake.

"Base, this is Cambridge. I had a minimum temp that night of 16c."

At only four degrees below room temperature, it makes no sense to start a fire for warmth. If there's no evidence that Hallendry was cooking, then perhaps the stove wasn't the cause of the fire. The stove door could have been opened to make the fire look as though it were accidental. What if Hallendry was drunk and passed out and someone deliberately burned down his cabin? If I knew there was some evidence that he'd been cooking, I'd feel a lot better.

None of this is my responsibility. My work ended with confirming the cabin as origin.

What if no one else thinks to check?

I debate a moment longer, head to my truck.

The sun is low on the horizon, glinting in my rear-view mirror as I drive the dusty gravel road to the Whiskey Creek fire. On the trail, trees cast long shadows that strobe across my windshield. When I arrive, Dugan and Verdon are gone and the crime scene tape has been removed. I stand in front of the black rectangle of what was once a cabin. It's eerily silent, chainsaws and fire pumps rested for the night. In the distance, seen between black tree trunks, is the fire camp, placed just at the edge of the burn. Tents are sun-bleached yellow among green branches.

Orange-clad firefighters, smeared with soot, cluster around the over-size picnic table. A figure in yellow, with a white hard hat, moves in my direction. Carter Spence, the young Forest Officer, appointed Incident Commander.

"Hello, Porter. You're a bit late for supper."

"I'm not here for supper," I say, staring at the remains of the cabin. There's nothing left but the deeply charred remnant of floor, the stove, and the bottom of the log wall, framing the scene like a picture. Miscellaneous debris, such as table legs and chair frames, are neatly stacked off to the side. The bottles are gone, on their way to the RCMP crime lab. I wonder if any pots or pans are making the same journey, gaze at the pile of metal debris, searching for the shape of cookware, but the pile is too dense and tangled.

"When did the crime scene guys finish up?"

Spence adjusts his hard hat. "About an hour ago."

"Did they say if they were heading right out?"

"No, but I just saw the RCMP plane fly over."

Damn. I should have come earlier.

"Why?" says Spence. "What's up?"

"Nothing, maybe."

I take a closer look at the pile of metal household debris. It's a big pile — you'd be surprised how much metal is in the average cabin. I'm going to have to dig and I pull on leather work gloves, start to pull apart the pile. Spence watches, curious.

"What are you looking for?"

"Pots. Pans. Any sort of cookware."

"What would that prove?"

"I'm wondering if he was cooking."

Spence looks tired, his freckled face streaked with ash and sweat, but he pulls on his own pair of gloves and begins tugging debris from the pile, setting it aside. We work together for a while, find three cast iron fry pans, several metal pots with handles burned away, a muffin tin, four enamelled metal cups, an enamelled teapot, and plenty of cutlery.

We stand back, inspect the result of our labours. We've taken a small mess and made it bigger.

"Now what?" says Spence, rubbing his forehead with the back of a gloved hand.

"I don't know. None of this stuff proves whether or not he was cooking."

"Do we put it back?"

"Later, maybe," I say absently, wandering around the scatter of debris. If there was some way to determine if the fire was deliberately set, Dugan and Verdon would have looked for it. Perhaps they already found what they needed. I wish they would have told me more. I wish I knew more about structure fires. The doctor was right — I just can't help myself. I wander around for a few minutes, scrutinizing the cabin floor, the stove, and the debris, and am just about to give up when something catches my eye. In the pile of roof tin, there's a section of metal which is bulged and has what I think is a faint temper line. Temper lines look like subtle rainbows and occur when metal is heated unevenly — something I learned in knife-making. With my gloved hand, I rub away the fogging of ash that covers the metal and take a closer look. Sure enough, there's a meandering temper line. I'm not sure of the significance of this, wonder how widespread this might be across the roof. I turn to Spence, who has been watching.

"Could I borrow a few men?"

"Sure. What do you want to do?"

I explain I want to lay the scorched metal roofing on the ground as it would have been on the cabin and Spence nods, returns with a half-dozen men. It's a big job, pulling the tin from the pile, flattening out the badly bent and warped sections, fitting them together like a huge ugly puzzle. By the time we're done, the entire crew is working, fitting the pieces together. Even the cook and her helper have turned out to watch the show. Finally the last few pieces fall into place and we all step back to admire our handiwork. Once again, we've taken a small mess and made it bigger.

Bobo, the clown of the group, says, "Looks like someone steam-rolled a cabin."

Muted chuckling, which I ignore, focusing in the fading evening light on the metal collage on the ground. The sheets of tin are long and narrow, curled and twisted as a result of heat and the structural collapse of the roof. Bands of faint rippling and distemper, which appeared isolated on any particular strip of metal, form a more complete picture when matched together. An area, approximately a quarter of the roof, is slightly more bulged, with faint lines like a fading aurora along the edge of the bulge. I point this out to Spence.

He frowns. "Are you sure?"

The tin was mounted to roof planks so the distortion isn't continuous. You have to look for the pattern. It's a bit like those 3D puzzles that look like wallpaper.

"Look harder."

He squints, looks harder. "It's faint, but I think I see it."

The firefighters watch, curious about the result of their efforts. I walk around the tin mat we've created, firefighters backing out of my way, try to align how the roof sat on the cabin. It's not difficult, as the chimney flashing serves as a tie point, clearly matching where the stove was located beneath. From there, I easily deduce the location of the cabin door. The faintly distorted area of roof tin surrounds the stove, includes a wide area over where the body would have lain, and leads like a teardrop to the door, where the distortion is most pronounced. Clearly, there was a rush of heat below this area and I get an excited tingle as it occurs to me that Dugan and Verdon couldn't possibly have known this without replicating what we've done.

"What does it mean?" asks Spence.

I shake my head, unsure and not wanting to be distracted. A coal falling from the open stove and igniting the floor would have created a fire growth pattern similar to this, but something about the pattern still bothers me. A burning area of wood should create a fairly even heat, in my experience. This pattern indicates a more sudden rush of heat from one area, followed by a sustained burn. The answer comes to me suddenly, with a jolt.

Accelerant.

If an accelerant were used, such as gasoline, it would create a sudden billowing rush of heat. The heat would be intense, but would dissipate rapidly as the accelerant was consumed, to be replaced by the steady heat of the burning cabin. I walk around the charred cabin floor, frowning, wondering if Dugan checked for hydrocarbons; worrying he might not have and that key evidence will have been missed. Memories of the burned corpse cause an anxious clench in my gut. I walk onto the charred floor, which crunches under my boots, squat and examine the black, deeply pillowed surface of the heavy planks. After the fire, it would be impossible to determine if an accelerant had been sloshed on the floor — it would have been consumed, along with the top surface of the wood. As I turn on my heel and stand, a narrow slit forms where my boot heel has pressed — a thin section in the weakened floor where the planks join.

I stare at this narrow slit.

"We need a Pulaski and chainsaw," I tell Spence.

He looks perplexed. "What?"

"Now — dammit. And a flashlight."

"Okay," he says, looking offended, and calls the Crew Leader. A firefighter trots off and returns with a chainsaw and regulation safety gear, such as earmuffs and Kevlar chaps, which he proceeds to put on in what seems slow motion. It's getting dark and I want to grab the chainsaw and do the work myself. Finally, he's ready, along with another firefighter, holding a Pulaski — an axe with an opposing heavy hoe blade.

"You see those lines of nail heads?" I tell the firefighter with the saw. "That's where the floor joists are." I indicate an area by the stove, sweep my arm toward what was the back of the cabin. "I want you to cut out the floor boards between these two joists, from here to here."

The man nods, starts his saw and begins to cut. Chips fly as he rips one long cut along a line of nails. He walks back to where he started, lines up the tip of the whining saw and presses it into the floor, cutting another parallel line through the planks. We watch as the sections of plank drop about eight inches to the ground below, leaving a stark white line of virgin, unburned wood where the planks of the floor have been severed. When he's done, there are about twenty sections of floor-board loose in the trough between the two joists.

"Shine the flashlight over there."

I take the Pulaski from the waiting firefighter and, using the hoe end of the tool, flip the sections of board over, starting near the stove and working my way to the rear of the cabin. Spence follows my progress with the flashlight. As the sections turn over, they reveal their clear, unburned surface. I make it about halfway along the trough before finding what I'm looking for. One of the sections of floorboard is burned along the edge of the underside, as is its companion.

I lift the piece and show it to Spence.

"See that? How it's burned underneath?"

Spence takes the section of board, turns it over, inspecting both sides. Several firefighters lean in, curious. Spence frowns, hands the board back to me.

"Why is it burned on the underside?"

"I think an accelerant was poured on the floor and leaked through the cracks between the boards. When it was ignited, it burned through, along the edges, under the floor."

"Why didn't it burn the whole floor underneath?"

"Not enough oxygen. The main fire above used all the air."

There's a significant pause. Spence looks concerned. "Now what?"

"Now I tell the RCMP."

Fortunately, my camera has a flash; it's dark by the time I take a few pictures of the under-burned floorboards and turn my truck away from the fire. The narrow trail seems endless as I thump slowly over roots and ruts. When I emerge onto the gravel road I press hard on the accelerator, anxious to tell Waldren what I've found. The compound enclosing the RCMP station and staff housing is deserted, a lone streetlight illuminating the front of the blue detachment building.

I park in front of the doors, mount the concrete steps.

The door is locked, windows dark. A sign indicates I should press the buzzer in case of emergency. I'm not sure this qualifies but press anyway. Nothing happens for what seems a long time. Finally, a door slams behind me. A form trudges across the gloomy yard, from the direction of the RCMP staff houses. Sergeant Waldren looks tired, slows as he approaches.

"Cassel," he says. "You buzzed?"

"I found something you might find interesting."

He raises an eyebrow, waits.

"Did you know an accelerant was used at the cabin fire?"

"No." The other eyebrow goes up. "That is interesting. Dugan made a point of mentioning that he'd found no evidence of an accelerant. How did this revelation come about?"

I briefly explain the process I used at the cabin.

"Good work. We'll check it out at first light."

"Okay." I'd hoped he would return to the fire with me immediately.

He reads my tone, smiles wearily. "It's not going anywhere."

I consider pressing him but notice several vehicles parked in front of his house. People are visible through his living room window. He has company. Reluctantly, I leave him to return to his visitors. On the way out of town I shift uncomfortably in my seat, wishing I could have followed through immediately with Waldren. It's both exciting to have found something that was missed, and disconcerting. I wonder how many RCMP forensic specialists are fully trained in arson investigation and try to put the matter out of my mind for now — morning will come soon enough. At the kitchen in the IA base I heat water, follow the doctor's instructions and make the mystery tea. It comes out black and if bad taste is the measure of medicinal effectiveness this stuff could cure cancer. I gag and cough, gulp water to chase away the bitterness.

Minutes later the aftertaste fades and I feel calm, peaceful, wander back to my room in the bunkhouse.

For the first time in months, I'll have a good sleep.


The next morning I'm awake early. I lounge in bed a few minutes, luxuriating in the sensation of feeling rested, then have breakfast and make another cup of the wonder tea, which fills me with a sense of detached well-being. Apparently, I have underestimated traditional eastern medicine. I brew enough tea for my prescribed dosage during the day, fill a Thermos, and call Waldren. He'll meet me at the fire in a half hour. Outside, the dog whimpers for attention. I decide to take him with me and, after treating his burns and giving him a bite to eat, I load the dog into the back of the truck. Even my dog allergy seems better this morning. Whistling, I wheel out of the IA base, gravel crunching under my truck tires, and head for the fire.

My sense of well-being is short-lived.

Waldren has beaten me to the fire and stands with Carter Spence in front of the remains of the cabin, which isn't much. The remnants of the floor are gone, nothing left but the spines of a half-dozen floor joists, still smouldering. Several firefighters with Wajax water bags slung on their backs are half-heartedly spritzing the hot spots. Waldren and Spence turn in my direction as I approach. "What happened?" I ask.

"It appears your evidence has consumed itself," says Waldren.

I look at Spence. "It was fine when I left last night."

"I don't know what happened," Spence says defensively. "I was sleeping when someone started hollering. I came out of my tent and the damn cabin floor was on fire."

"When was this?"

"About three o'clock in the morning."

"Did anyone see anything?"

"Like what?"

"Someone running away. Anything like that."

Spence looks puzzled. "You think someone did this on purpose?"

Waldren frowns, looks at me.

"Who knew about what you had found?"

"Just the people here," I say quietly enough my voice won't carry far.

We glance at the firefighters with the water bags on their backs, and at the camp farther away. Everyone here last night would have understood the significance of the under-burned floorboards, thanks to my enthusiastically recruiting their assistance. I hadn't considered there was any risk from the crew. The only risk would be if the arsonist that started the cabin fire was actually on the crew, which seems unlikely as they would have been mustered quickly in town, not knowing where they were being sent until they arrived. I suddenly recall what the firefighter said who had been sitting beside me when I hitched a ride back to the fire.

*I hear there's a dead guy at the fire.*

The crew knew of the fatality by scanning the radio traffic. Perhaps someone joined the crew with the intention of monitoring the situation and cleaning up any remaining evidence. To destroy the floor, the perpetrator would have had to wait until everyone was asleep, sneak out of his tent, start the fire, then sneak back into his bed or raise the alarm.

"Who first noticed the fire?" I ask Spence.

"I'm not sure. I'll find out."

While Spence makes inquiries I ask Waldren if there's cellphone coverage.

"Not yet," he says. "Would be nice, though."

Spence returns with the cook and the crew leader, introducing them as Mary and Reggie.

"Who raised the alarm about the fire?" I ask them.

The two exchange looks which I interpret as worry, not guilt. The cook, Mary, is a short heavyset Native woman with grey braided hair. Reggie, the crew leader, is tall and thin, with a pockmarked face and nasty scar over the bridge of his nose.

"I got up to take a pee," says Mary.

"What did you see?"

"Soon as I get up from my bed, I see bright, you know, like somebody got a big campfire going. I figured maybe some of the boys couldn't sleep. When I get out there, there is big flames, whole thing on fire, and nobody is around."

"You're sure you didn't see anyone?"

"Oh yeah," she nods emphatically. "Just me. I go get Reggie."

"She kicked me," says Reggie.

Mary shrugs. "He wouldn't wake up."

"Everyone else was asleep?" I ask.

"Yeah," says Mary. "So I wake up the boss."

I look over at Waldren and Spence, wondering what else I should ask. They shrug. I thank Mary and Reggie and they return to camp. Spence dismisses the few firefighters that have been wandering around with Wajax bags on their backs, tells them to go for breakfast.

"What do you figure?" Waldren asks me, when it's just the three of us.

"I'm not sure. This secondary fire seems too coincidental."

"It does seem odd," Waldren admits. "But there are only two possibilities. Either this secondary fire started on its own, or someone started it. If someone started it, they would have to have a vested interest in destroying the evidence. This could have been the arsonist or someone related to, or friendly with, the arsonist. The kicker is they would have had to know there was evidence here, which limits the suspects to the individuals at the fire."

"Unless someone got a message out of camp."

"What about your fire radios? Can we check on those?"

Radios are not like phones. There's no record of calls. But there is one thing.

"Carter, can you have everyone here turn off their radios for a few minutes?"

He nods. When he's gone, I explain to Waldren.

"I want the radios off so there isn't any listening-in while I make a call."

When Spence gives me the thumbs up from the camp, I key my own radio — the only radio at the fire that is still active — and call the local fire lookout tower. "Cambridge tower, this is Cassel at the Whiskey Creek fire."

"This is Cambridge. Go ahead, Cassel."

"Did you have your radio on last night?"

"Roger that, Cassel."

"Would you have heard any traffic during the night?"

"Yeah. I always keep it going, and I'm a light sleeper."

"Anything last night about a cabin floor?"

There's a perplexed hesitation. "Nothing like that."

I thank Cambridge, holster my radio. "Seems to rule that out."

"Was the cabin debris thoroughly extinguished?"

"When I was working the debris I went in hot, which is how I injured my arm." I picture Luke Middel with his Wajax bag, helping Dugan and Verdon. "Ident worked the scene with a minimum of water. Come to think of it, no one really hosed down the floor."

"So there could have been an ember or two under there?"

I nod reluctantly. Despite my certainty last night, doubt circles like a vulture.

"That seems the most likely explanation," says Waldren. "Someone here might have started the floor fire but it seems a stretch. Looks to me like the fire was still smouldering under the floor, then it took off after you disturbed it."

"Regardless, I know what I saw."

"You don't normally investigate structure fires do you, Cassel?"

"No, but I know fire."

"Maybe the guy spilled a drink and it seeped through the floor."

"It wouldn't explain the pattern of temper lines on the roof. He'd have had to spill a lot of booze and it would have had to be a lot stronger than what they sell in the stores to burn like that. I think we're looking at an aggressive accelerant here. If we could have ripped up the rest of the floor, we could have traced the whole accelerant use area."

Waldren frowns, pacing for a moment. He squats, rubs some ash between his fingers.

"It sure would be nice if you had some evidence, Cassel."

"I do," I say, suddenly remembering the pictures I had taken. I head to my truck, pull out my backpack, rummage inside, thankful that I took the time last night to snap a few images. I fiddle with the camera as I walk over to Waldren, who waits patiently as I fumble with the buttons. There seems to be something wrong — I can't find the pictures.

"What's the matter?" says Waldren, watching.

"I'm not sure. There must be something wrong with my camera."

"Do you mind if I have a look?"

Reluctantly, I hand him the camera, watch as Waldren gives it a quick once over.

"Nothing wrong with the camera," he says. "It's just empty."

Waldren doesn't hang around much longer. He seems to have lost interest in the Whiskey Creek fire, which I find frustrating. The discovery of physical evidence of accelerant use, quickly followed by destruction of the evidence and loss of the pictures in my camera, seems an obvious indication that something deeper is going on here. Waldren doesn't come right out and say it, but his tone suggests I didn't know how to use my camera and simply bungled the job — if there was anything to take a picture of, which I suspect he doubts. It leaves me feeling unjustifiably incompetent. I do manage to extract a promise from Waldren to pass on my theories to Dugan and Verdon, and to invite them back to inspect the roofing tin. Then he's gone, his RCMP Suburban kicking up dust along the trail out of the fire.

I spend a few more minutes examining the ashy remnants of the floor as the work day starts at the Whiskey Creek fire. Firefighters pick up shovels and Pulaskis, don Wajax bags, head to the fire perimeter to seek out hot spots. Carter stops by to see what I'm up to, then joins his men on the fire line. I kneel in the ash among the few remaining bits of floor joist, prospect for something, anything, that might remain to indicate what occurred, but there's really nothing left to examine as fire is a wonderful cleanser. It is, in fact, one of the leading methods of destroying evidence at a crime scene. Any serious crime is exponentially more difficult to solve when the scene has been incinerated, then hit with water and the boots of firemen. Criminals know if they drop a match the chance of getting caught is reduced. From a practical perspective, this means you can never initially assume that a fire is just a fire. Clues of any primary crime are much harder to find, if any remain at all. Indications that a fire might be arson may be the only clue that something deeper is amiss — which is why I'm so frustrated that all evidence of the under-burned floorboards are gone. I return to my truck, go through my pack again. Last night I checked the pictures I had taken — a nifty feature you can't do with the old film cameras — and confirmed I had good images of the under-burned floorboards. There's a slim chance I accidentally deleted the pictures, or they were erased when I shoved the camera back into my pack, but I doubt it as the camera is designed to require a series of manual steps to delete pictures. Either my digital camera paranoia is justified or someone tinkered with my camera, and I search in my pack for anything amiss. Other than the missing pictures, nothing seems to have been disturbed.

Except for me, that is — I'm definitely feeling a bit disturbed.

I left the pack in my truck. Whoever tampered with the camera had to have done so last night at the IA base, which means there were two separate incidents to eliminate the evidence presented by the floorboards. If someone at the fire was responsible for burning the floorboards, they would have had to travel unnoticed from the fire to tamper with the camera, then returned unnoticed. Not impossible, as Mr. Spock would say, but highly improbable. It could be that someone at the fire had a partner who sabotaged my camera, but this would have required communication that is not available. This leaves only the possibility that an outsider is responsible for both acts, although I have no idea how anyone outside of the fire camp could have known about the significance of the floorboards.

Cursing, I stuff gear back into my pack and let the dog out of the truck.

I need to walk. And to search.

An outsider would have had to travel to the fire in the middle of the night. Given the distance from town, this would mean some mode of transportation, likely a vehicle, possibly a horse, that was parked a distance back from the fire so as not to arouse attention. Most likely access was along the trail and I head in that direction, calling to the dog.

"Come on, Scorch. Over here, boy."

The dog runs toward camp, then hesitates, looking back at me. I probably should have snapped a leash on him to keep him away from the camp and firefighters, but it just didn't seem right, considering this was his home. I'm having second thoughts about the dog when he trots back in my direction, stopping to sniff at the ashy remains of the cabin. I give him a minute, then start walking down the trail. The dog runs past me, bunting my hand with its head.

"That a boy."

I walk quickly, both to cover ground and to burn off pent up energy from my anger and disappointment. The dog stays about forty yards ahead, meandering, sniffing the ground occasionally. I'm not sure what I might find but keep going. Perhaps the arsonist was careless and I'll get lucky. After about a mile, Scorch doubles back, circling, and stops to pee on a tree. I stride past, expecting the dog to move ahead of me after it's done its territorial business. Instead, he wanders into the bush.

I stop. "Come on, Scorch. Over here."

Thirty yards into the forest, the dog looks back at me.

"Come on you mutt. Don't run off and get lost."

Scorch seems to consider, then sniffs the ground again and continues to trot further into the forest. I watch, wondering if I should just let him do his own thing. Eventually he'll return to the fire camp, where there's food. As I'm watching it occurs to me that he isn't wandering randomly but is sniffing the ground, following a scent. He's onto a deer or something.

Or could he be following a human scent?

I hang a ribbon on a tree branch for later reference and start to follow the dog.

He's definitely onto something, sniffing, circling back here and there. We move together deeper into the forest, farther from the trail. In the distance a fire pump starts up, providing a vague directional reference. Other than this, I have no idea where I am. Too late, I realize that I'm basically lost and will have to rely on the dog to get me out of here. Scorch seems oblivious to my concern, leading me amongst trees and around brambles. An hour drags by, then another. I'm hot, sweaty, thirsty and convinced that I've foolishly followed a dog after a deer or coyote when Scorch stops and circles back, sniffing the ground.

"What's up, you mutt? Lost your furry prey?"

The dog continues to circle, looking for a lost scent. As I follow his progress I see a small clearing among the pines. There's an old campfire ring, a few bottles and cans. Tent poles are propped against a tree. The camp appears not to have been used recently but there are tire tracks in the bent grass and a broken shrub where a vehicle recently turned around, tight among the trees.

Most interestingly, there's a burgundy paint scrape on the trunk of a large pine.

# 6

I DOUBT WALDREN will be impressed with a paint scrape on a tree, miles from the crime scene and discovered by a mongrel dog, so I decide to look into a few things, see what turns up. I start by tracking down Charles Hallendry. Fort Chipewyan is not a big place and if Hallendry is still in town he shouldn't be hard to find. Ten minutes of cruising around in my Forest Service truck yields Hallendry coming out of the local store with a bag of groceries. I wheel into the parking lot, pull close to Hallendry, who looks at me warily as I lean an elbow out the open truck window.

"Have you got a minute?"

"Maybe later. I gotta head to the cops to sign some papers."

He'll need to go over to his brother's place in town, try to figure out what to do with all the damn stuff. I can meet him there in an hour. I jot down the address, spend the hour returning the dog to the 1A base, where I give him a treat for a job well done. I give myself a treat as well — more of Doctor Cho's Bitter Happy Tea. I cruise into town feeling tired from the long walk but remarkably relaxed. Perhaps I can work out a deal with Doctor Cho to distribute this stuff — I know plenty of people who need to lighten up. I might be a little too relaxed because I miss my turn and have to double back. When I get there Charles Hallendry is struggling out of a cab.

"Thanks for seeing me," I say, extending a hand.

"Yeah, okay," he says. His hand is like grabbing a warm pot roast.

Hallendry invites me inside. I follow him through a gate in a sagging page-wire fence, past a collection of derelict snowmobiles nestled amongst the weeds, and into an old wood-sided bungalow. Inside it is immediately apparent that Rufus Hallendry lived alone. The debris of a poorly kept life is scattered everywhere. Kitchen counter is crowded with dirty dishes crawling with flies. It smells like a landfill. A toaster has a pair of small vice-grips attached to the prong where there used to be a lever. The living room contains a couch with bald spots, a coffee table covered with empty whiskey bottles and sticky glasses, and an overflowing ashtray. A small wood stove occupies one wall. Stray bark chips and ash are scattered across a rug of indeterminate colour. Propped against another wall are several long narrow stretchers with animal hides pulled taught. This was definitely the home of a single, hard-drinking trapper.

"Look at all this crap," says Hallendry. "What am I supposed to do with it?"

"You could have a garage sale."

Hallendry doesn't find this amusing.

"Are there other relatives who would be interested?"

"Interested in what?" says Hallendry, standing in the living room and staring at the coffee table covered in whiskey bottles. "We've got a sister who lives in Holland. Dad's gone. Mom's in a home. His ex-wife hates his guts."

"Where does she live?"

"Calgary."

An old wood-cased television squats in a corner, supporting a collection of framed pictures. One is a faded family group shot. Another is obviously the two brothers, younger, with Charles much slimmer. I pick up a photo of two children, a boy and girl, smiling in a photographer's studio. The girl is missing her front teeth.

"These his kids?"

Hallendry sighs, shaking his head, wandering around the living room, opening a drawer to peer inside, squinting at a Native ceremonial drum hanging on the wall. I'm not sure he'll answer but it seems he's just collecting his thoughts. "Yeah, those are his kids," he says heavily. "Damn shame for them, having a father like that. They came up here a few times to visit — twice, I think it was. Didn't work out."

"Do you think the kids would like the dog?"

"They live in an apartment. She's allergic."

Hallendry wanders into the kitchen and I hear the slap of cupboards opening and closing. "You want some coffee or something?" he calls.

"No. Thanks. Did your brother have any enemies?"

"Sobriety."

There's an awkward silence, followed by more rummaging sounds from the kitchen.

"Do you mind if I look around?"

"Help yourself."

I look at a few things of little interest in the living room and move to the bedroom. Messy bed. Dirty clothes everywhere. Old pressboard and laminate dresser filled with the usual things you find in a dresser, and few partial bottles of Jack Daniels. The bathroom is frightening, but I take the time to examine the medicine cabinet — always good to know what prescriptions a person is using, particularly if they have a mental condition. There's nothing unusual in Rufus Hallendry's medicine cabinet — pain killers, anti-fungal cream, a collection of used toothbrushes. There's a tiny laundry room that needed to be used more frequently. No basement. I venture outside to the backyard, where there's a dingy single garage.

Stench of grease and mouse turds. Old Honda quad up on blocks. Workbench scattered with tools. A shelf with trapping gear and boxes. I spend a few minutes going through the boxes. Rags. Old truck parts. Nothing of interest. My eyes track back to something hanging over the workbench. A string of what appears to be shrivelled, blackish sacks about the size of golf balls — animal parts of some sort. I step onto an overturned pail for a closer look.

"Pig galls," Hallendry says, standing in the door.

"Why would he have pig galls?"

Hallendry shrugs. "Bait, I guess. I run a hog farm down by Stettler. In winter I send up pails of frozen guts and crap like that for my brother. He's uses them to make some sort of concoction for his trapping."

Hallendry comes in, looks around. He's so large the garage seems smaller.

"This quad might still be good," he says, lifting the end as though it were a toy.

I step down from the pail, go the shelf, where there are large jars filled with a strange blackish sludge. No label. I set one on the workbench, where I can get a better grip on the jar.

"I wouldn't do that," says Hallendry.

Too late. The lid comes off, instantly filling the garage with a stench so intensely putrid that I reel back, gagging, my eyes watering. Hallendry jolts as though hit by the shockwave from an explosion.

"Close it!" he hollers.

I stumble to the workbench, dizzy, holding my breath, screw the lid back on the jar, stagger for the open door. Charles Hallendry is already outside, leaned against the garage wall, retching and dry heaving.

"What the hell was that?" I gasp.

"I think," he says between breaths, "you found my brother's long-range trapping lure."

A long-range trapping lure, it turns out, is a concoction of animal parts and scent glands that are mixed together in a slurry, placed in a jar and left in the sun to putrefy. The more it stinks, the better, as it is used to attract predators from miles away. Every trapper has their own preferred blend. Rufus Hallendry has created a mix that should be classified as a biological weapon. When we finally catch our breath, Charles Hallendry slaps me on the back, laughing.

"You should have seen your face."

My spine may be broken, but it's good to see Hallendry smiling.

We return to the house which no longer seems to smell so bad.

There's a truck parked at the curb and someone knocking at the door. Hallendry answers, blocking my view of the visitor.

A man's voice: "Is Mr. Hallendry in?"

"I am Mr. Hallendry."

"Uh — the other Mr. Hallendry."

A moment's hesitation. "You'd better come in."

Charles Hallendry backs into the kitchen, allowing the visitor to enter. He's young, well groomed, dark hair slicked back, and is carrying a briefcase. He introduces himself as Clive Owenson. Mr. Hallendry was expecting him.

"I'm sorry," Hallendry mumbles, "but Rufus is dead."

It takes Owenson a few seconds to process this. "What?"

"He died two days ago."

"Oh, umm, I'm terribly sorry. My condolences."

There's an awkward silence. I'm waiting for Hallendry to ask the man what business he had with his brother, but a moment drags by, so I intercede.

"Is there something we can help you with?"

"Well, umm, maybe, I guess."

"Can I get you some coffee?" says Hallendry.

"Well, okay. I'm with Aggregated Land Services and we represent Phultam Uranium. We've been negotiating compensation for a core-hole program on Mr. Hallendry's trapline. I was stopping by to finalize the agreement, although now I'm not sure what can be done." He looks hopefully at Charles. "Perhaps if you're a relative you could sign on behalf of Mr. Hallendry."

Hallendry shrugs. "Maybe." He looks at me. "What do you think?"

"That's up to you. Sounds like family business."

Hallendry considers. "Okay, I'll have a look."

We move to the kitchen table, clear away a clutter of dirty cups. Owenson opens his briefcase and extracts a neat package of paper, which he lays in front of Hallendry.

"You'll need to sign the last page."

Hallendry frowns, reading, refusing to be rushed. I'm sitting across from him and read upside down. It's a standard project notification, required by legislation. I've seen hundreds of these back when I was a forest ranger and don't recall anything about a compensation clause. Hallendry reaches the last page, which isn't part of the standard package.

Owenson hands him a pen, waits expectantly.

"Excuse me," I interject, "but when did it become a requirement to directly compensate a trapper? I thought compensation was taken care of through the Trapper's Compensation Program, to which all the companies contribute."

Hallendry pauses, pen in hand, expression suspended. Owenson looks like a guilty kid with his hand in the cookie jar, which is odd because he's giving, not receiving. "Well," he says slowly, "technically, you're correct. Who did you say you are?"

"I'm with the Forest Service," I say, intentionally vague.

Owenson seems to relax. "This is a company-to-company transaction," he says as though he's given this pitch more than once. "We recognize that our operations affect the operations of the trapper, so we're prepared to offer additional compensation to offset the cost to the trapper of moving his traps, inconvenience, that sort of thing."

"And this is completely voluntary?"

Owenson glances at Hallendry, who's listening with obvious interest.

"Let me put it another way. What happens if you don't pay?"

Owenson leans back, lets out a big puff. "Honestly, what usually happens is the trapper complains to the ERCB that he wasn't adequately consulted and then we have to file a non-routine application, which takes months instead of weeks. There can be hearings and all sorts of delays. It's a major pain in the ass."

"But the trapper doesn't have a case."

"Like that matters," says Owenson.

I can't help smiling at the simple brilliance of the scheme — using the weight of the system for additional concessions. Hallendry has a trace of a smile tugging at the corner of his mouth. "What sort of compensation are we talking about?"

"Two hundred dollars per core hole."

"How many core holes?"

"In this program, I think there are thirty-eight."

I blink. "This program is worth almost eight thousand dollars to the trapper?"

Owenson nods. "That's about right."

Hallendry smiles. "I think I can sign this."

I'm stunned. This is only one program. If a trapper has a trapline with a lot of industrial activity, he could be making an incredible amount of money — far more than trapping would ever yield. "Is this normal?"

Owenson shrugs. "It's just the cost of doing business."

It's late in the afternoon when I depart the Hallendry estate, the long-range lure lingering in my olfactory passages. Something else lingers as well — my surprise at the lucrative cottage industry that has developed among trappers. Traplines have become money machines in a way that has nothing to do with their original intent. Seems like a good motive for jealousy, greed or murder. Not a compelling motive for the uranium company, as they simply pay off anyone who threatens to slow them down, but certainly motive for anyone who covets his neighbour's trapline. I head to the local Fish and Wildlife office, conveniently located across the street from the ranger station, hoping to arrive before quitting time. With minutes to spare I pull my forest service truck to a stop in front of the small building.

"Cassel, hold up."

It's Middel, calling from across the road. Damn — I don't really want to talk to him.

"I've been waiting for your report on the cabin fire all afternoon."

"I'll do it tonight," I say quickly, and duck into the Fish and Wildlife office, nearly colliding with Larry Holmes, the lone local Fish and

Wildlife officer, as he heads for the door. He backs up, smiling sheepishly. "Sorry, just about ran you over."

Larry Holmes is never likely to run anyone over. He's nearly a foot shorter than me and slight in build. His easy smile and polite manner seem at odds with the sidearm, pepper spray and baton on his belt. He smoothes back his hair, as though it might have become ruffled in our near collision.

"What can I help you with, Porter?"

"I've got a few questions about traplines."

Holmes nods agreeably, ushers me into his tiny office where he settles into his chair behind an old wooden desk. The walls around us are crowded with stuffed animals. Grouse, ducks and weasels all seemed poised to explode into action.

"What can you tell me about the trapline held by Rufus Hallendry?"

"I'd have to check the file — I've only been here a year."

Holmes excuses himself, returns a few minutes later. He settles back in his chair, lays a thick manila file folder on the desk, rifles through the contents. "Hallendry bought the line about twelve years ago." He hesitates, raises an eyebrow. "This is interesting — he acquired the trapline for the transfer fee of forty-seven dollars and fifty cents."

"How'd he manage that? I thought traplines were hot properties."

"Not twelve years ago. And not up here. Ever since the greenies started protesting fur back in the eighties, the trapping industry has been in the toilet. In fact, for a while, you could hardly give away a trapline. Says here the line was previously owned by a Native fellow who passed on — Oliver Mercredi. Relatives weren't interested in taking it over so we advertised it."

Holmes shows me a faded newspaper ad for the vacant trapline.

"Policy was that if a Native owned the line, then first choice is transfer to another Native, but it looks like to no one applied." He flips pages. "They even offered a trapping course to try to interest some of the younger folks. Still no takers, so they transferred the line to the first guy that came along and asked."

"Rufus Hallendry."

Holmes nods. "For less than fifty bucks."

I shake my head, think of the hefty payout by Phultam Uranium. I wonder where all the money went; whiskey, no doubt. "What else can you tell me about the line?"

Holmes flips more pages. "No junior partner."

"Who gets the trapline?"

Holmes shrugs. "I have no idea. Whoever Hallendry left it to in his will."

The will, if he had one, wouldn't be in the file — probably in some safe-deposit box somewhere, or in a lawyer's office. I try to think of what else of interest might be in the file, ask if there is any way of determining how actively Hallendry was trapping the line. Holmes flips back and forth in the file for a few minutes. "According to his fur catch records he didn't trap much, which isn't unusual. We used to take traplines away from people when they didn't trap them, to transfer to bona-fide trappers, but we gave that up when the industry tanked."

I thank Holmes and he follows me out, locking up. I wander across the road, thinking about how traplines have become money machines, and wonder what the Mercredi family thinks of missing out on such a golden opportunity. I'll mention this to Waldren the next time I see him. This turns out to be a lot sooner than I think.

I'm working late at the ranger station, pecking away at a keyboard, using my distinctive one-finger style, when Middel barks at me from the duty room. My first thought is that he's hollering at me to learn how to type — my woodpecker technique has sent more than one co-worker off the deep end — but it's something else.

"Cassel — you got your bag handy?"

"In the truck."

"We got another fire."

I abandon the report I'm painstakingly compiling, join Middel in the duty room.

"Plane reported it, coming into the airport. Hop in your truck and go for a look."

I nod, head across the road to where my truck still sits under a single yard light in front of the Fish and Wildlife office. I race out of town, toward the airport. It's a dark moonless night and any fire should be easy to spot. I don't go far before I see a faint distant flickering glow and my pulse quickens. All of the bottle fires have started at night, as did the Whiskey Creek fire. Night is the time for foul play. There's only one road to the airport and I watch for approaching headlights that might be an arsonist fleeing the scene.

No one passes me. The radio in the truck blares. It's Middel.

"We've got a better location. It's by the old gravel pit."

I'd been there a week ago, target shooting with Reggie from the local IA crew, and I let Middel know that I'm familiar with the location. As I turn onto the narrow road leading to the pit, I see an eerie orange glow above treetops a mile away and immediately sense there is something different about this fire. I had assumed the fire .was in the pine trees around the old gravel pit, as there is nothing in the pit itself — just a big hole in the ground — but from the way the flickering glow seems to bounce off the treetops it looks like the fire is right in the pit. More than likely it's just kids with a big party bonfire, having a good time, but when I clear the edge of the trees by the pit I see something else.

A pickup truck at the bottom of the pit is engulfed in flames.

"Damn." I ease my truck to a stop on the earthen ramp leading into the pit, assess the scene. Flames gush upward from vacant windows. The gravel pit indicates a need for privacy and I wonder if it could be a suicide. These thoughts race through my mind as I step out of my truck and scan the tree line at the top of the pit, looking for any hidden observers. Flames from the truck illuminate the walls of the pit but the forest beyond is a black void. I focus my attention on the truck, note that it's an extended cab four-wheel-drive with a lift kit and oversize tires. It looks new and fairly expensive. Curls of black smoke rise and vanish into the night. I hope there is no one inside because it would already be too late.

Middel's voice blasts from the radio in my truck. "Cassel, what's your position?"

I reach in through the open door, grab the radio mike.

"Vehicle on fire in the gravel pit. No sign of persons responsible."

"The IA are right behind you. Do you need anything else?"

"A water truck, and some light."

I barely hang up the radio when the IA crew arrive. Reggie walks up beside me, shaking his head as his men pull out equipment. There's not much they can do until the water truck arrives. Even then, a burning vehicle is a hazard best approached cautiously. Fumes from burning rubber and plastic are highly toxic. Then there's the gas tank.

A loud *whump* lifts the back of the truck a few feet off the ground.

"There she goes," Reggie says, standing beside me.

"Yup. You pass anyone on your drive out here?"

Reggie shakes his head. "What do you want us to do?"

"Wait for the pumper. Do you know that truck down there?"

"That's Sammy's truck," Reggie says quietly. "He just bought it."

"Sammy who?"

"Sammy Cardinal. The Chief."

While we wait for the arrival of the water truck, I go for a walk in the trees along the edge of the pit, thinking about Sammy Cardinal and his smoking hot ride in the pit below. Unless Sammy started his own truck on fire this is not going to make the situation easier with the Cree Band. My first hope, once we douse the flames, is there won't be a body in the truck. My second hope is there won't be a bottle with a familiar inscription. I walk among pine trees close to the edge of the pit, aim a flashlight into the dark pine forest, looking for a hint of someone watching. Arsonists are often spectators — part of the allure of starting a fire; releasing a force more powerful than one's self and watching it grow. It's a compensation of sorts. Today, if anyone is compensating, they're not visible, and I'm not sure the motive is psychological. Like the Cree Band council, I'm beginning to wonder if they are being targeted.

I return in time to greet the volunteer fire department with their vintage 1958 red pumper truck. I get Reggie's crew and the VFD working together, setting up a foam injection kit. They'll fill the inside of the burning truck with soapy foam and suffocate the fire. Until they're done, there isn't much for me to do but watch and wait. I call Middel, give him a brief update, inquire as to what else he knows about how the fire was reported. Arsonists sometimes report their own fires, to make sure firefighters arrive in time for a good show. No such luck today; the regular flight from Fort McMurray spotted the fire and called air control, who called us. Nobody was seen leaving the area. Above the drone of the water truck, the whine of an approaching engine becomes audible. It sounds like a chainsaw being revved. Soon a single light plays wildly across the top of the pit. Gravel crunches.

Luke Middel peers down at me over the handlebars of a dirt bike.

"I got here as soon as I heard, Porter."

"Wonderful. You stay right there."

Luke looks crestfallen but a burning vehicle is a dangerous situation. He waits at the top of the pit while I direct operations from below. Soon the fire is out and the burned truck is a dark husk. White foam drools from vacant windows. The firefighters stay back as I approach, flashlight in hand. The surrounding ground has been transformed into a gravelly, soapy muck that slides under my boots. I aim the beam of my flashlight into the front of the cab, revealing a blackened cavern with metal seat springs in a soapy slurry, a skeletal steering wheel, but no corpse. Heart squeezing a little harder than normal, I shift the beam of light to the back interior of the cab — the most likely place for a body, tucked out of view.

There's no back seat left — or body — and I let out a relieved sigh but walk around the truck, peer in from the other side, just to make sure. No obvious signs of criminal activity, but anything could be under the thick layer of foam inside the truck.

"What's in there?" Luke calls from above.

I ignore the question, have Reggie and crew turn off the foam, throttle the pump on the water truck down so a weak stream of clean water comes from the nozzle, then open the truck's doors to allow the foam to dribble out while I use the hose to gently wash bare the debris. More seat springs emerge, along with two screwdrivers, a crescent wrench and the clips and wire of a set of booster cables. Luke has his own flashlight and manages to blind me from above.

"Would you turn that thing off," I holler at him.

"I was just trying to help."

"If you're going to use that thing, come down and point it where it will do some good."

Luke wastes no time in scrambling down the gravelly slope.

"This is so cool," he says. "I love this CSI stuff."

"Just pay attention and do what I say. Don't touch anything."

Luke peers in from the far side of the truck.

"What does all that stuff mean?"

"Well," I say slowly as I examine the debris, "it looks like a clear case of reverse hot-wiring. See the cables with the clamps? They must have used that with the screwdrivers to reverse hot-wire through the floorboards."

Luke frowns. "Are you serious?"

"Probably what started the fire," I tell him.

Luke reads my expression, realizes I'm leading him on.

"You shouldn't do that," he says. "I'm young and impressionable."

I can't help smiling. Despite his fumbling over-eager manner, Luke is a good kid. I straighten my back, which comes into alignment with an audible crack, and get to work, carefully examining the debris on the floor. Luke assists with his flashlight.

"Is that a broken bottle?" he says.

He points the beam of light at the gas pedal and I wash the area clean of foam. Jagged shards of bottle glass appear. With gloved hands I pick out the pieces, examine them in the beam of the flashlight. The bottom of the bottle is a single round piece with a jagged fin protruding. Plainly visible are three letters, etched in the glass.

*F.T.C.*

"Isn't that the same thing from the other fires?" says Luke.

"Yes," I say quietly, tell him to stay put while I head up the steep earthen ramp to my truck to retrieve my crime scene kit. An RCMP Suburban rolls to a stop, strobing red and blue lights across the walls of the pit. Waldren gets out, his gaze traveling from the truck in the pit, where Luke waves enthusiastically, to the firefighters clustered in a group near the fire engine, and finally over to me. "What's going on, Porter?"

"Someone dumped a truck here and set it on fire."

"I can see that. I thought your jurisdiction was limited to forest fires."

"Technically, but I got the call. I was the first responder."

"I don't see any trees down there. This is an RCMP crime scene."

I'm not sure what the big deal is. The Forest Service frequently respond to burning vehicles, as would any fire department. We're less concerned with what is burning than in making sure the fire is contained and extinguished. I may have overstepped my bounds by processing the truck for evidence, but the lines of authority are not always clearly drawn. Until today, at any rate. I take a moment to keep my emotions in check, determined as always to remain professional. "Apparently that's Sammy Cardinal's truck," I offer.

"Damn," says Waldren. "This will not go over well."

Luke, tired of waiting down in the pit, is making his way up the ramp. Waldren pulls out his radio, calls in using a series of codes I don't understand, requests ident. He's holstering his radio when Luke joins us.

"Pretty weird it's the same guy from the other fires," he says.

Waldren frowns. "You found another bottle?"

Luke nods. "Yeah. It had the same inscription."

Waldren massages his forehead as though he's getting a migraine.

"Now what?" says Luke.

"Life gets complicated," says Waldren.

Now that the same calling card has been found at both an RCMP crime scene and the bottle wildfires, they're all officially RCMP business. Hence the complication. The burned truck represents a significant escalation from the wildfires, in which the RCMP have had little involvement. I've kept Waldren in the loop on the wildfires as a courtesy. That's all about to change, he informs me. Ident will process this scene and will be interested in visiting the wildfire arson scenes as well. My role in this production has yet to be ironed out. Regardless of any good intentions I've had, my compromising their crime scene won't make relations any easier. Waldren stands with his arms crossed, watching, as I dismiss the IA crew and local volunteer firefighters. Luke is also sent home. Then it's just Waldren and me at the edge of the pit, headlights of our trucks casting craggy shadows. Waldren is ominously silent as we wait for ident. We're both stuck here until they arrive: Waldren is on guard duty and I'm required to brief the forensic specialists. We've got an hour or two to kill. I use the time to run a few things past Waldren.

"Did you know Hallendry was collecting payments from a uranium company?"

Waldren looks at me, face half in shadow. "What?"

"Phultam Uranium was paying him for a core hole program on his trapline."

"I've heard that happens. Cost of doing business up north."

"That could be a motive."

"Could be," says Waldren, turning his attention back to the pit. I wait, expecting he'll say more, but he remains silent. I have the uneasy feeling our relationship has been damaged, which concerns me. To be effective we have to work together. "It would be interesting to know who gets the trapline now," I venture.

"That would be in Hallendry's will, which we're searching for."

"So you're still open to the possibility that it's murder?"

"Personally, I think he got drunk and burned down his cabin. But yes, Porter, we look at everything. We do have some experience with investigations."

I grit my teeth, let my annoyance subside at Waldren's belittling tone. His subtext is clear — back off and let us do our job. Only the RCMP seem to have missed a big piece of the puzzle when they missed the burn pattern under the floorboards. Unfortunately it's a part of the puzzle that is now gone forever.

"What did the ident guys say about the roof tin?"

"They said that accelerant can cause evidence of uneven heating in roof tin, but they hadn't noticed anything close to a clear indicator. They were surprised you claimed to have found evidence under the floor."

"What was their explanation?"

"Burn-through from above."

I shake my head. "I don't think so."

"Well, you can take it up with them when they get here."

There's a long, uncomfortable silence. Waldren checks his watch. I try a different tack.

"What do you know about Hallendry's activities before the fire?"

Waldren considers for a moment. "Look, Porter, this is an ongoing investigation and I can't tell you anything that isn't directly related to your fire investigation or is not public knowledge. You know that. But since it is public knowledge, I can tell you that Hallendry was seen drinking in the bar the night before the fire, and that he left about eleven o'clock that night, apparently on his own. Now you don't have to go around asking people questions or otherwise giving the impression the RCMP aren't doing their job, and that you have to do it for us."

He's watching me, eyebrow raised. I nod, feeling distinctly browbeaten.

We spend the next forty-five minutes in professionally neutral silence until headlights approach. Dugan steps out of another RCMP Suburban, accompanied by Constable John Markham. Dugan looks rumpled and tired, explains that he just got off a murder scene. His manner is brisk and curt as he fires questions at me; has me show him exactly what I've done; what I've moved. He doesn't chide me for contaminating the scene. He just does his job, filming, photographing and collecting. The bottle fragments go into an evidence bag. He has me run over the IA base and bring back my reconstructed bottles from the previous fires, which also go into evidence bags. He's not interested in discussing the under-burned floorboards. Ditto with the tin. He doesn't want to revisit the cabin scene. Basically, he just wants my information on the truck fire, and he wants me to stay out of the way.

After I'm dismissed from the truck fire, I head to the IA base where I feed and salve the dog, eat leftovers, then make a big cup of bitter tea and collapse on my bunk. I'm expecting to quickly fall asleep and am looking forward to another restful night, but soon I'm wide awake, my mind tumbling thoughts. The change in pattern of the bottle arsonist worries me. It could be a copycat, but the lettering seems etched by the same hand. He's moved from relatively harmless remote fires to auto theft and destruction of property. Now that I'm sure the cabin fire was set deliberately, the possibility that the bottle fires are related can't be ignored. If they are related, the absence of a calling card at the cabin is understandable. It would be logical not to want an obvious connection to a fire that could be considered a homicide. Or it could just be two different arsonists, as the bottle fires seem planned and the cabin fire suggests a crime of opportunity. To complicate matters, my relationship with the RCMP seems to be deteriorating. Frustrated, I get up and head into town, radio blaring. Driving with music usually settles my mind, but there isn't enough road. Ten miles later I'm at the edge of town. Instead of continuing into the settlement, I take a fork in the road, head to the Lodge.

The Fort Chipewyan Lodge sits on a rocky promontory overlooking Lake Athabasca. From what I've learned in the past two weeks, the Lodge was a venture between the Native bands, several companies from the massive tar sands development upstream, and local government to promote tourism. I'm not sure how the tourism industry is doing but tonight the parking lot is full. I bypass the lobby, climb narrow stairs and emerge into the crowded confines of the Trapline.

The Trapline is the only legal bar in a town that, until a few years ago, was a dry community. The sale of alcohol had been strictly prohibited for two hundred years until, according to Reggie, the Lodge was facing bankruptcy. It seems to be doing fine tonight — tables crowded, jukebox thumping, air thick with smoke. I pause at the threshold, look for a seat. It's going to be a challenge. The bar was inserted into an attic that was clearly never intended as a place of business. The room is a long narrow wedge, tables and benches crammed tightly together. There are no empty seats. Fortunately I'm here to mingle, not drink. In my experience, bars are an excellent place to pick up information. Lips loosen. Defences drop.

This bar is also the last place that Rufus Hallendry was seen alive.

"Heya bud." A tall slender Native with a heavily pockmarked face crowds in close as I edge my way to the bar. His nickname is Tuber; why, I have no idea. He's a constant presence around town, usually with a bottle of Five-Star whiskey crammed into his pants.

"You wanna drink?" he says.

I doubt he's offering and I nod politely, move past him to the bar, where a harried Native lady is busily mixing drinks. When she asks me what I want, I hesitate — drink has done me few favours in the past — but decide I'd better have a real drink. Pop is served in a different sort of glass, which would advertise that I'm not drinking. Anywhere else this might not be a big deal, but here it would be conspicuous, so I order a rum and Coke.

"That looks good," says Tuber, flecks of spit landing on my face.

I order him one of the same. He drapes an arm over my shoulder.

"Yooz a good shit, you know that, bud?"

"Hey, Tuber, you knew that trapper — Hallendry?"

"Oh yeah," he says expansively. "He was a prick."

"Were you here two nights ago when he was in?"

Tuber gives this some thought. "Yeah, he was here. Prick."

"Who was he drinking with?"

"He never buys nobody no drinks."

"So, he was drinking alone?"

Tuber frowns thoughtfully, looking around. He grins, spotting someone familiar. "Hey, Cork," he says, waving his free arm, motioning over a big Native. "This here is my bud. He's all right."

Cork is a few inches taller than my six feet but where I'm gangly he's solid, shoulders wide as a doorway. He looks like he could run through the forest and knock over trees. He lumbers toward me, frowning in a way that I hope is good-natured.

"You're that fire guy," he hollers over the country music.

I nod. It's hard to keep a low profile in a small town, particularly when ninety-five percent of the population is Native and you're a white stranger working for the Forest Service. Cork offers an enormous dirty hand to shake. I manage to hold my own, barely.

"Why do they call you Cork?" I holler back. Here, everyone has a nickname.

"I pull out the cork," he says, grinning, "and it's all done."

I suspect it has something to do with his drinking prowess. I nod, slip out from under Tuber's arm, try to make a casual getaway. I'd like to talk to the bartender, see what she can tell me about Hallendry's activities that night, but Cork has other plans. He drapes a heavier arm over my shoulder.

"You should meet my niece," he says.

It doesn't seem like a request so I let him guide me over to a corner table where several large women and two Native men in ball caps sit hunched, nursing drinks. He introduces me as the Fire Guy, which elicits friendly nods all around. Working for the Forest Service in such a remote location — two hundred miles from the next town and with no road access — I have status. The Forest Service is one of the primary employers and a Forest Service employee usually means a paycheque. I'm quickly offered drinks, which I decline but are ordered anyway.

Cork looks around. "Where the hell is Collette?"

The men shrug. The women giggle. Collette has apparently come up behind us.

"Damn," he says, turning to her. "I'm going to put a bell on you."

She grins, punches him in the shoulder.

"Meet my bud," says Cork, gesturing in my direction. "He's the Fire Guy."

Collette smiles briefly and looks away. She's young, nineteen or twenty, slender and seems shy, perhaps because I'm a stranger. She's easily the most attractive lady in the bar. The most attractive, in fact, since I arrived in Fort Chipewyan. Her black glossy hair hangs nearly to her slender waist. Dark eyes, warm brown skin and high cheekbones give her an alluring exotic look. I find myself glancing away, to avoid staring.

"She's a hell of a looker," says Cork, grinning. With one thick finger he lifts her chin, as though showing her off. Collette slaps his hand away, gives Cork an impatient look which he laughs off. The women chuckle, clearly enjoying an opportunity to embarrass both the forestry guy and Cork's niece. Space is created at a bench against the wall and, despite my protests, I'm absorbed into the group and handed another drink. If hospitality is the measure of successful tourism, this place is a gold mine. Cork sits beside me, effectively barricading me in the corner. From the far side of the table Collette gives me an understanding smile. I smile back sheepishly, take a slug of my drink.

The rum goes down smooth, fiery and familiar.

"You're checking out those bottle fires?" says one of the middle-aged Native ladies.

"That's right."

"You figure out who done it?"

"No. Do you have any idea?"

She looks thoughtful. "Me — I think it's that damn Chip band."

"Really? Why is that?"

She digs a can of chewing tobacco from a pocket, works a wad of it under her lip.

"They always been jealous of the Cree Band. Goes way back."

"Interesting. Anyone in particular come to mind?"

She shrugs. "Could be any one of them."

"So you're obviously from the Cree Band."

"Yeah." She high-fives the lady next to her. "Cree Band forever."

"Cool," I say. "Did you guys know Rufus Hallendry?"

Cork laughs. "Everyone knew Smokestack."

I picture the smoking remains of Hallendry's cabin — the charred body beneath — and the irony of his nickname gives me an eerie chill. One of the men talks about a fight involving Hallendry, in which he got his nose broken, and there's more laughter. Other stories emerge about Hallendry — his drinking, hunting and grouchy hermit lifestyle. It's entertaining and gives me a better picture of the man but doesn't really provide any usable information about the night of the fire or a motive for his murder. The conversation meanders from stories about Smokestack to the commercial fishery, which one man argues has been affected by the huge tar sand developments upstream along the Athabasca River.

"I pull up my fish," he says, "they got red spots all over them."

I look over at Collette. She's been covertly watching me since I sat down.

"It's not just the fish that are getting sick," says Cork. "That shit in the water must be doing something to us, too. How many people got the cancer last year?"

Heads nod around the table. Cork draws deeply on his cigarette.

"Damn cancer," he says. "It's in the water."

There's a commotion by the stairwell. Sammy and the other Cardinals come into the bar, animated by the burning of Sammy's truck. The news spreads through the bar like a ripple. Several men join the group by the door. A tense conversation ensues, inaudible against the pulsing music. Cork and the other men at our table turn to watch. The group by the door move to the bar, order drinks. Cork says something in Cree to the other two men, who nod. One of them looks at me. "You checked out Sammy's truck tonight?"

"I was at the fire."

"What do those bottles mean?"

News sure gets around fast in this town.

"I wish I knew," I say. "What do you think?"

He frowns, tugs at the brim of his ball cap. He's younger than me, perhaps in his late twenties, has a scraggly black goatee. "I don't know," he says, "but someone is after the band."

"What makes you think so?"

"The fires are on our land. Now they hit Sammy's truck."

If the arsonist is trying to make a statement against the Cree Band, he's succeeding, and I wonder what else might be going on in the community. It will be difficult for an outsider to get under the skin of such a tight-knit Aboriginal community, particularly if there is friction between the various groups. I excuse myself, nudge Cork to open a path, and head for the washroom. I go about two steps before I'm hit by a wave of dizziness, have to steady myself on the back of a nearby chair. I've downed only two drinks but feel disproportionately inebriated. The dizziness passes and in the bathroom I splash water on my face, look at myself in the mirror. My eyes are glassy. Better slow down. Leaving the tiny washroom I head for the group at the bar, catch Sammy Cardinal's attention.

"Cassel," he says, handing me a drink. "You did a good job on my truck."

"Glad someone thinks so. When did you notice your truck was missing?"

He frowns. "It was gone when I come home. I thought the wife had it."

"When was that?"

"Oh, maybe six-thirty, seven o'clock."

"Where was your wife?"

"Down the road, visiting her sister."

"When you realized she didn't have the truck, did you report it stolen?"

He looks amused. "It's not like that. In our culture, we share. Goes way back."

"But you weren't sharing tonight, were you?"

His expression darkens. "You let me know when you learn something."

The other men are watching me, listening to the exchange. They look ready to shoot someone and I have the uncomfortable feeling they're waiting for me to point the gun. Tensions are high and I'll have to be careful what I tell anyone in the community. Sammy and his group filter into the crowd and I take the opportunity to quiz the bartender about Hallendry. She's short, pudgy, has a serpent tattoo on her neck.

"Yeah, he was here that night," she says, reaching for a bottle.

"Did you see if he was drinking with anyone?"

"You kidding?" She arches an eyebrow. "In here, everyone drinks with everyone."

"What time did he leave?"

"Look, I'm not a clock," she says handing a drink across the bar to a customer.

"Did he leave with anyone?"

She sighs, tucks a strand of loose hair behind her ear. "I don't know. I think he left on his own. He lives by himself, you know." An impatient group has formed behind me at the bar. "Anyway," she says, "I gotta work. I told all this to the cops."

"Shooters!" someone bellows behind me.

It's Cork, Tuber, Collette, and the two men from the table. They're all grinning.

"Line 'em up," Cork says to the bartender. "Come on, Fire Guy."

The drink in my hand is half gone already. I don't remember drinking it. "No thanks," I say to Cork. "I have to work in the morning."

"We all have to work in the morning," he says.

"Just one," says Collette, giving me a challenging look.

Our eyes connect. Somehow, I don't want to disappoint her. "Just one."

I'm passed a test tube filled with an orange liquid. It goes down like a bolt of lightning. I've barely set the empty tube into a jug on the bar when another tube, this one filled with blue liquid, is thrust at me. I hold up my hand. Enough is enough.

"Oh, *come on*," says Collette. "You gotta try this one."

There's a moment of indecision. Elbows and backs bump against me from all sides. I'm pressed so close to Collette that I can smell her and she smells good. A voice inside me whispers that I'm not supposed to be drinking, and that I'm not looking for anything, but the voice seems distant and detached. I listen a few seconds longer for the voice, but all I hear is the blare of country music. I'll have just this one more and then I'll get in my truck and back to base to sleep.

No, I'll call a cab —

Beside me, Cork bellows something incoherent, pumping a fist in the air. The shooter in my hand is empty. I feel numb and confused but, rather than alarming me, it feels pleasant. I smile, nod at Cork and Tuber and Collette. I have the distant realization that I'm getting drunk, that I am drunk, but I no longer care. I've been working hard. One night of fun won't kill me. I'll slow down, pace myself. Around me, people are moving.

"Come on, Fire Guy," says Cork. "Party at my place."

So much for slowing down.

Cork's house is at the far end of town locally referred to as Dog Patch. I'm crammed in the back seat of a car, with Tuber one side of me and Collette on the other. Houses and trees flash past in the headlights. Everyone is laughing. The car smells sweetly of alcohol and the garlic sausage Tuber is eating beside me, which he generously offers to share. I decline, which Collette finds very funny. We lurch to a stop at the curb, spill out of the car into the warm night. Memories of past parties and binges mingle with the present and I feel a primitive and familiar anticipation.

I need to slow down. Focus on why I'm here. Find out about Hallendry.

We move inside. The house is small and quickly feels crowded. There is an immense TV turned to a music channel. All the hard furniture is old pressboard. The soft furniture consists of a sagging brown couch and love seat. There's a stuffed fish on the wall. The clock is one of those fake brass star things from the seventies. I'm on the couch beside Collette, holding a drink in an immense mug. It's one of those German steins with a pointy lid that keeps biting my nose.

"You knew that trapper — Hallendry, right?" I say to her.

"Sure. Everyone did," she says, tipping the lid on my drink back up for me.

"What am I drinking?" I say, sipping from the mug.

She leans close, takes a sip. "Everything, I think."

"That's what I was afraid of."

She smiles. "I like you, Porter. You're a good guy."

"Yeah — thanks. What's a nice girl like you doing at a place like this?"

"I live here."

I give this some thought, wonder who the other people are around me.

"About that trapper," I say, but she's talking to someone else. I must have missed something. Time has become elastic. I look up at someone who's sitting on the arm rest. A brown face and scraggly goatee look down at me. I think his name is Philbert.

"Do you know who Smokehouse was drinking with a coupla nights ago?"

"You wanna smoke?" says Philbert.

"No." The music is loud. I take a drink, get my nose tweaked by the lid, wave away an offered cigarette. "Smokestack — who was he drinking with at the bar."

"Yeah, the bar," says Philbert. "Same as you."

I frown, consider how to get my question across to Philbert when someone stumbles across my outstretched legs and my mug tips into my lap, soaking my crotch. I stare at it for a second, then look up. Cork sways uncertainly in front of me.

"Crap, bud. Sorry about that."

"Come on," says Collette, pulling me to my feet. "Let's get you cleaned up."

She grabs my hand, leads me through the crowd. It's all I can do to stay vertical and avoid the knees and legs around me. The big screen TV captures my attention for a second — a blonde looking up at the camera, suggestively displaying her cleavage — then I'm tugged away and into a room. A door closes. Something bumps the back of my legs and I fall onto a bed.

Suddenly, Collette wavers above me and there's a tugging at my jeans.

"No," I slur. "I gotta get going. I can clean myself up."

She grins. "Who said anything about cleaning you up?"

Her face is right in front of me, framed by black hair. I can see down her shirt, where her cleavage sways suggestively. I realize with mild shock what is happening, alarmed that I let it get this far. I need to tell her that I'm engaged. That I have to get out of here.

"Listen." I push myself up on my elbows.

She shoves me down, breathes in my ear. "You just lay back and enjoy, sweetie."

I feel my jeans being tugged down. "No — I gotta ..."

There's a buzzing in my ears. She's smiling.

I focus on her face as it fades away.

# 7

CONSCIOUSNESS COMES SLOWLY, accompanied by bright light, nausea, and a throbbing headache. The first thing I see is the side of a cardboard box. My hip is aching and I quickly realize why; I'm lying on my side in a scatter of flattened cardboard boxes behind some building. Slowly, I push myself to a sitting position. There's a battered dumpster in front of me. Farther back are the crooked wooden crosses of an old grave-yard. Further still is the broad expanse of Lake Athabasca, shimmering painfully in the sun. I squint, puzzled.

How did I get here?

Rum. Shooters. Alcoholic swamp juice.

Defeated, I lay down again on the cardboard boxes. They smell like rotten lettuce. Above me, small scuds of white cloud move slowly across a blue canvas. Why did I start drinking again? Sheer unadulterated stupidity. I have a pattern of drinking when things go badly and I try to remember what triggered this episode. We found a body at the cabin fire. Rufus Hallendry. I was at the bar to ask questions about Hallendry's activities the night he died. Technically, I was working last night, but somewhere I crossed a line. My nausea deepens to disgust and self-loathing as I recall Collette leading me to her bedroom. I remember tripping backwards and falling on her bed, then her above me, tugging at my pants.

And then — nothing.

What happened after, and for the rest of the night, is a mystery.

I push myself up and sit staring at the sparkling expanse of the lake, trying desperately to remember, to fill in the void between then and now. I've never blacked out like this before. I've always remembered the events of a night of drinking, even though I might have preferred to have forgotten. In the past, my recall seemed a curse but this chasm in my memory is more disturbing and I strain to mine the dark shaft of last night's amnesia, searching for any clue that I did the honourable thing — that I pushed myself off Collette's bed and staggered away from the house in Dog Patch. I want to believe this so badly I can almost see myself doing it, as though by sheer will I could manufacture the memory. I want to believe because now, after years of healing, my life is on track and I have a new fiancée.

Christina Telson — unique, contrary, and everything I want.

I shudder to think that I might have destroyed the trust between us and cringe at the thought of facing her. Sickened in heart and body, I force myself to push these thoughts to the back of my mind and get moving. I'm a mess, my pants blotched and stiff from spilled drinks, my shirt smeared with unfamiliar stains. I'm behind the Northern store — the local grocery — and I head through town, walking along an alley paralleling Main Street. I need to make it to the parking lot of the Lodge to retrieve my truck, preferably without being seen. The tricky part will be bypassing the ranger station. The Lodge sits on a rocky promontory overlooking the lake and the shortest route is past the ranger station, through the fenced compound and Mark Middel's house, then past the RCMP office and a few hundred yards uphill along a rocky path. The alternative is a lengthy detour and the way I feel I'm willing to chance the shortest route.

I stop as the ranger station comes into view.

"Damn."

My truck is parked in front of the ranger station, directly in front of the window of the duty room, where Mark Middel spends much of his time. I have no doubt that someone reported a Forest Service truck in front of the Lodge late at night and that Middel moved it to the office, with the intention of ambushing me when I came to collect it. I have a brief flash of hope that it's still early enough in the morning that no one is at the office and I can sneak over and take the truck to the base. Clean and composed I would have at least a chance of facing him with dignity.

I check my watch only to find that I have no watch — sometime last night I lost it.

The base is ten miles out of town and I have no choice but to retrieve my truck. I slink across the road. No signs of life from the office as I cross the small gravel parking lot. Sensing possible victory, I reach the truck, which fortunately is not locked. I slide onto the seat, feeling like a kid stealing the family car, gently close the door and reach for the keys.

No keys. I'm going to have to go into the office for the spare key.

I peer through the window into the duty room. No sign of life. Quietly, I step out of the truck, tiptoe up the wooden steps, which creak obligingly. The office door is unlocked, which makes me nervous, but there is no one at the front counter, beneath which is a box containing spare keys. I barely have to enter the office, really. Maybe, if I'm lucky …

"Cassel," Middel says from somewhere behind me.

I jump, caught red-handed in the act of reaching for the key box under the counter. I turn, prepared to be apologetic. Middel stands by the door of the duty room, his uniform looking very crisp and official this morning in contrast to my dishevelled appearance.

"I can explain." The most abused line in history.

Middel looks disgusted. "My God, Cassel, look at you."

His remark draws the rest of the staff into view. The receptionist, Louise, comes out of the stationary room. The seasonal radio operator, a young local gal, peers past Middel's shoulder. Even Carter Spence, who must be in from the fire for a quick update, peers at me from his office. My humiliation is complete.

"What the hell happened to you?" says Middel.

"Well —"

Middel points. "In my office."

Reluctantly, I step into his small office, acutely aware of my incriminating odour. Middel comes in, scowling, closes the door and stands behind his desk, glaring at me. In theory, what I do after hours is entirely my business. In reality, in a town this small and with the profile of the Forest Service, what I do after hours is a bit more sensitive — something I should have taken into account when I stepped into the Trapline last night.

"You left a Forest Service truck in front of the bar last night."

"It's also a hotel," I remind him.

"Are you staying there?"

"No, obviously not —"

"Obvious?" he says. "You want me to explain 'obvious' to you?"

I decide it's a rhetorical question, remain silent.

"You're working for the Forest Service. People here look up to the Forest Service. Maybe it's not such a big deal leaving your truck up there normally. Maybe it's not such a big deal having a beer or two after work. But this town is a powder keg right now — and look at you. You stink like a brewery, you look like shit, and you're late for work."

I want to remind him that I'm a contract fire investigator and that I set my own hours, but reminding him that I'm an expendable contractor doesn't seem a wise approach at the moment, so I just stand there and grit my teeth. Besides, I'm not exactly on solid moral ground this morning. He fumes and goes on a few minutes longer, a vein throbbing in his forehead. When he seems about out of steam, I politely inquire if I can go take a shower.

"Do that," he says, tossing me the truck keys. "And then get to work."

I step quickly out of the office, gun my truck out of the parking lot and head for the base. My head feels like a gang of amateur autobody mechanics are pummelling it with rubber mallets. I grip the steering wheel, try to focus on the road while a mixture of panic and fury blossoms in my chest. How could I have been so stupid? Now what am I going to do?

Work the case, damn it, that's what I'm going to do.

At the base, I feed the dog, who looks to be in better shape than me this morning, then take a long hot shower that leaves me limp and tired. I manage to eat a few pieces of toast while I make a large cup of bitter medicinal tea, gagging as I force myself to gulp it down. After I'm done I feel almost human. What I need now is a long drive with plenty of loud music — blues and hard rock — but I'm trapped in a community without road access, so I sit on the edge of my bed in my tiny room that smells like moulding pressboard and stare at the nightstand that until recently held my collection of reconstructed bottles. Like my dignity, they too are gone. I lay back, close my eyes, hoping for a few minutes of oblivion. No such luck — I hear the staccato rattle of a dirt bike. Luke Middel is the last person I need to see this morning.

Clump of boots in the hallway. The unlatched door opens as he knocks.

"Hiya Porter," he says, standing in the doorway.

"What is it, Luke?"

"There's something in town you need to see."

I drop my head back onto the pillow. "Can't it wait?"

"I think you'll want to look at this right away."

"Why's that?"

"I think it explains what the letters on the bottles mean."

I take Luke and the dog with me into town. Scorch paces in the box of the truck, wind ruffling his fur. Luke is animated, talking fast, leaning forward like he can't wait to get there. He was cruising around town on his bike, after having stopped by the post office, when he saw it, although he won't tell me exactly what he's found. Suspense I can do without today. There were a couple of guys hanging around, too, he says. We pull past the Northern store.

He points. "There they are."

A half-dozen young Native men crowd in the alley next to the

Northern store. They stand with their arms crossed, ball caps turned back. One of them is hefting a baseball bat. They frown at us as I wheel the truck around in the street for a better view. On the brown corrugated metal side of the store someone has spray-painted large orange words.

*Fuck*
*The*
*Cree*

The words are stacked on top of each other, so the first letter of each word lines up. For extra emphasis, the vandal sprayed a long straggling loop around the first letters of each word.

FTC.

"What do you think?" says Luke.

My first thought is that I woke up on the back side of that building this morning and only missed seeing the graffiti because I walked past the other side of the store. My next thought is that I was lucky I stumbled away from there before the crowd with the baseball bat showed up and there was a misunderstanding. These boys look upset. Their expressions turn from suspicion to anger when they see the Forest Service emblem on the side of the truck.

I roll down the window. Scorch growls softly as they approach.

"Look at this shit," says the man with the bat, pointing it at the offending words.

"Yeah," says another. "On our goddamn store, too."

"You guys have any idea who did this?"

"Hell no," says the guy with the bat. "But someone's gonna pay."

I nod, commiserate for a minute. No point trying to calm them down; it might only inflame the situation. I get what little information seems to be available. Someone discovered the graffiti about an hour and a half ago — shortly after I regained consciousness — and told the store manager, who called the RCMP who have come and gone. The men here are waiting around, hoping the artist will return to admire his work. They know all about the Chief's truck and the fires on their reserve land out of town. They figure someone is out to get the Cree Band and have plenty of theories. It might be the Chipewyan Band or the Metis. Maybe even some white skinhead. Anyone not in the Cree Band seems to be a suspect and these lads want blood. From their expressions, any blood might do and I retreat from the alley, watch the crowd recede in the rear-view mirror.

"Now what?" says Luke.

"Now I take you back to your bike and you go home."

"Aw, come on, Porter. Let me help out."

"Doing what, exactly?"

Luke thinks, his young face intent. "There must be something we can do."

I'm about to tell him that investigations are nothing like what you see on TV, where they condense everything to an hour, less commercials. We hardly ever find those conveniently unique clues. Investigations are long, tedious and often unrewarding work. Arson is the most difficult crime to solve; wildfire arson doubly so. On top of that, I feel like a giant used me for chewing gum and I just want to curl up somewhere and die for a few hours. But he keeps looking at me, all fresh-faced and enthusiastic. It's annoying, but maybe if I throw him a bone he'll leave me alone. "What were you thinking, kid?"

"Well," he says thoughtfully, "we could return to the scene of the other crimes, look for more clues, stuff like that. Maybe we'll get lucky."

"Okay," I say, resigned. "We'll swing over to the Dore Lake road on the way back."

The Dore Lake road, where the bottle fires originated, is along our way. I figure we drive a few miles down the gravel road, get out, wander around the black patches in the forest for a few minutes. I'll look appropriately thoughtful, then drop Luke at his bike and crash on my bunk for a few hours. Later in the day, when my brain starts functioning again, I'll give this business of the graffiti some thought.

"Over there," says Luke, pointing to a highly visible burned area.

"Thanks kid, I almost missed it."

We park on the side of the road and Luke and Scorch are out of the truck before I manage to unbuckle my seatbelt. I follow somewhat less enthusiastically. Luke walks around for a few minutes, checking behind trees. Scorch follows him, peeing on the trees. They make a great team. "Where'd the fire start?" says Luke.

I go through basic origin location, pointing out the fire travel patterns on the trunks of the trees, point out where I found the bottle. Luke squats, examines the origin area in great detail. I yawn, look down the road as a vehicle slows and passes. Farther down the road is the familiar solitary figure of the local bottle picker, taking his bike for a walk. Luke stands up finally, follows my gaze. "I wonder if that guy knows anything," he says.

I'm about to dismiss his remark when it dawns on me that he might have a point. The old bottle picker is out along this road all the time. We wait as he approaches, shoulders hunched, resolutely pushing his ancient bike. It's been a good day for him — his plywood boxes are crammed full. A white plastic shopping bag bulges from one side. As the old man approaches, Scorch trots out to greet him, nuzzling his hand and jumping up on him. Luke and I follow.

"Good morning," I manage to lie.

The old guy nods at me and returns his attention to the dog.

"He seems to like you," I add, trying to elicit a response. Nothing. His face is weather-beaten, cheeks covered in white stubble. A grey ball cap is pulled low, shielding his watery eyes. I wonder if he speaks English — many of the elders in these remote communities still speak only their native tongue. Scorch licks his hand and the old man looks up at me, his face creasing into a smile.

"Good dog," he says stiffly.

"You know this dog?"

"I see him sometimes. He comes on road with me."

We introduce ourselves. The old bottle picker is Frank Cardinal.

"You've got quite a haul today," I say, gesturing to his cargo. He looks back at his bulging bag of bottles as though noticing them for the first time. A shape pressed from inside the bag against the plastic catches my attention. It's short with angular ridges and it takes my sluggish mind a moment to realize it's a drinking glass. A tumbler. The pattern and shape are the same as the drinking glass at the cabin fire.

"Can I have a look at what you found there?"

The old fellow looks at me as though he doesn't understand. I step over to the rear of his bike, peer into the plastic bag of bottles. He watches me but doesn't say anything. I reach into the bag, feel down through the bottles and cans until I grasp the open shape of the tumbler and pull it out. It looks like the brother of the tumbler at the cabin.

"Do you mind showing me where you found this?"

He hesitates, then points farther down the road.

"Could you show me exactly where?"

He's worried about leaving his bike. It takes some doing, but I convince him to join me in the truck, while I have Luke remain with Scorch, guarding the old man's bike and treasury of bottles, and we head down the road. I'm wondering how good the old man's memory might be for something as transient as the location of a piece of refuse in the ditch but he points without hesitation to a spot along the road and we stop, get out for a closer look. There's not much to see, just a spot at the base of a small bush. The bush likely caught the tumbler as it was thrown out a window, preventing it from shattering on the ground.

"Can I keep the tumbler?"

Frank Cardinal frowns, shakes his head.

"Can I buy it from you? I'll give you five bucks."

He considers, shakes his head again. A few more offers and finally he agrees — for twenty dollars I've purchased the most expensive glass I own. I carefully zip it into a plastic evidence bag from my pack, which the old man seems to find amusing.

"More," he says.

"Are you kidding? You already got twenty bucks out of me."

He smiles, points farther down the road. There's another tumbler. We drive a half mile further, where he leads me into the ditch and points to a scatter of broken glass. The fragments clearly have the same ridges and my foul disposition this morning brightens. This tumbler hasn't been handled since it left the hand that tossed it into the ditch — an evidentiary bonus. I thank Frank and turn toward the truck when he grabs my sleeve, sticks out a hand.

"This one is broken," I tell him.

He thrusts the hand at me again and I give him ten dollars, show him my wallet is now empty. Satisfied, he climbs into the truck and waits for me. I pull some bright fluorescent ribbon from my pack and hang it on a nearby sapling to mark the spot, then return Frank to his bike. Seemingly pleased with the morning's labours, he heaves his bike upright and continues to trudge sedately along the shoulder of the road, peering into the ditch for more treasure. Luke loads Scorch into the back of the truck, then hops in beside me and asks me what I found. I hold up a hand for silence, use the radio in the truck to call the ranger station and request the RCMP. The young radio operator tells me to stand by and a moment later Middel comes on.

"What's going on, Cassel?"

"Please have Sergeant Waldren meet me on the Dore Lake Road."

There's a pause. "Okay. Come see me as soon as you get in."

We drive down the road, park beside the dangle of bright ribbon. Luke peers at the marker, looks ready to burst at the seams. While we wait for the RCMP, I tell Luke what little there is to know, caution him that he must keep this to himself. He nods, eyes wide and serious.

"So I helped, huh?"

"Yes, Luke, you did help. Thanks."

A few minutes later, an RCMP Suburban pulls up beside us, enveloping us in a cloud of road dust. Waldren waits for the dust to clear, then joins Luke and me at the side of the road. He looks tired and irritable, gives Luke a brief nod.

"What have you got, Cassel?"

I show Waldren the fragments of tumbler, and the intact one, propose that the tumblers found in the ditch are the same type as the one found at the cabin. He frowns thoughtfully as I present my theory that two or more people were drinking with Hallendry the night he died and took their glasses with them, to make it look as though Hallendry were drinking alone.

"Why would they do that?" says Waldren, squatting and looking at the shards of glass.

"Someone wanted Hallendry out of the picture and they wanted it to look like an accident. Hallendry was receiving payoffs from the uranium company and that trapline was worth a lot of money. With Hallendry gone, the trapline would become available."

"Maybe," says Waldren. "But Hallendry didn't have a will. We looked."

"What about the family that lost the trapline to Hallendry?"

"The family that didn't want it?" says Waldren.

"That was before they started exploring for uranium."

"True, but the trapline was transferred. They have no way of reclaiming it."

"Maybe that's not their motive. Maybe it's payback for losing the line."

Waldren stands up, shrugging as through he's stiff and sore. "That's a lot of 'maybe,' Cassel. Keep in mind that anyone could have tossed those glasses in the ditch. They sell the things at the Northern, in packages of a half dozen. I'll bet every house in town has a set of them. And if you've been drinking with Hallendry, why not just leave the glasses at his place? Put them back in the cupboard, where they belong? Fire is going to wipe out any fingerprints."

All true, but killers don't necessarily know that.

"It is still possible they came from the cabin," I insist.

Waldren looks down the road. "Anything is possible. Too bad you didn't find these an hour ago. Ident just left this morning, headed for another scene."

"I have my kit in the truck."

"Okay. We'll bag these, send them in for printing."

After bagging the fragments and handing them over to Waldren for processing, I return Luke to his bike, tie up the dog and head into town to meet Mark Middel at the ranger station. Middel ushers me into his office and closes the door. I take a seat in front of his desk, acutely aware of our exchange the last time we were here, only hours ago. Now, Middel's focus has changed.

"Why did you need the cops?"

I relate my discovery of the drinking glasses, make sure to mention Luke's involvement, which pleases Middel. I mention my theory about a possible link to payments for uranium exploration, conclude with Waldren's remarks and his plan to send the tumblers in for fingerprinting. Middel leans back in his chair, looks thoughtful.

"You really think those whiskey glasses are from the Hallendry fire?"

"That's my theory so far."

"What about the graffiti on the Northern store?"

"It looks like the same lettering from the bottle fires."

Middel sighs heavily. "This is not good."

"Have you spoken to the Mounties about it?"

"Yeah. They're fairly tight-lipped. What have they told you?"

"Nothing I haven't passed on."

Middel is silent for a minute, thinking again. I shift, uncomfortable. The nausea of earlier this morning has returned, bringing with it an achy weakness. My mouth is dry and I'm having difficulty concentrating. I'm no stranger to hangovers but this feels different. It occurs to me suddenly that Middel has been talking to me.

"I'm sorry, what was that?"

Middel frowns. "Are you okay? You're pale and your hands are shaking."

I look down at my hands, clasp them together. I had an aunt with Parkinson's. Her hands used to shake. A jolt of fear passes through me. "I'm fine, just a little tired."

"Tired?" He snorts. "Hungover is more like it. Anyway, Sammy

Cardinal was in this morning and he's furious. That graffiti was the last straw for him, particularly after his truck was torched. He's positive the Cree Band is being targeted and he wants answers. Do you have anything to report? Any progress at all?"

"Well," I say slowly, squeezing my hands to keep them still, "I think he may be right. Whoever is lighting those fires has been leaving their calling card for a reason. The graffiti might be someone else, piggy-backing on what's happened, but I think it's the same guy. I think he waited until he had everyone's attention, then dropped his bombshell."

"He's certainly got everyone's attention," Middel says bitterly. "But why?"

"I have no idea, but we have the RCMP involved now, working on the truck."

Middel waits, expecting more. When I don't elaborate, he leans forward, staring at me. "That's it, Porter? The town is going to hell and all you can offer is that the RCMP are involved now? Is that supposed to make me feel better?"

I have a sudden surge of anger, want to tell Middel that he can go to hell along with the town, but manage to suppress any outburst. He dismisses me, telling me to keep working on it and to let him know as soon as I have anything. I nod, rush from his office, just wanting to get out of there. This sudden emotional volatility is unusual and has me a little freaked-out. I nearly collide with a Native lady at the counter who blocks my retreat. She's having an argument with Louise, the receptionist, who turns to me for help.

"You tell her, Porter."

"What?"

Louise introduces the woman. "This is Helen Mercredi — Bernice Mercredi's mother. She wants her daughter's cheque, but I've told her she'll have to wait until the rest of the crew is released. That's our policy when someone leaves early."

Helen Mercredi, although short, is a large woman and when she crosses her arms indignantly over her ample bosom I see no way past her. I force myself to focus.

"What is the problem, Mrs. Mercredi?"

"I just come to pick up Bernie's cheque and she says I gotta wait."

"Where was your daughter working?"

"At the fire," she says, scowling at Louise. "She got sick, had to come home."

People want to leave fires for lots of reasons. Sometimes they're sick. Sometimes they just say they are. To discourage people from leaving whenever they feel like it, which causes chaos at a fire operation, the Forest Service has long had a policy that anyone who leaves prematurely doesn't receive their paycheque until their crew has completed their rotation. If you arrive together, you get paid together. I raise my hands in helplessness and inform the irate Mrs. Mercredi that her daughter will have to wait like everyone else. She gives me the evil eye and storms out. I use the opportunity to follow her and point my truck toward the IA base, where I rush to the first toilet I can find and vomit. Weak and dizzy, I make myself a cup of bitter tea, lie on my bunk. The tea seeps into my blood and the nausea and edginess melt away. I fall asleep, thinking that I'll need to see the doctor again, thank him for the tea, and get some more.

When I open my eyes again, the light in my room has changed. I feel dehydrated but much better. Nothing like a quick nap. Then I see my clock and curse. It's nearly suppertime — I've slept away the afternoon. I roll onto my back and stare at the ceiling. The past few days seem to have taken a lifetime. The Whiskey Creek fire and Hallendry's burned body. The burned truck. A long night of drinking and disgrace. The graffiti. Middel, hollering at me. Luke. The bottle picker. Then that angry woman, blocking my escape from the ranger station.

What was it she wanted?

Something suddenly clicks and I push myself up, sit on the edge of my bunk, rubbing my forehead, trying to sort out exactly what it means. The woman wanted her daughter's cheque because she'd left a fire early, sick. There's only one active fire and the only women are the cook and her helper.

The cook's helper left the fire early.

Damn — how had I missed that? I shove on my boots and head into town. The public door on the ranger station is locked, but the rear entrance is open. With an active fire, there's someone in the duty room until dark. Today, it's Tabra, the young local radio operator. I nod to her as I pass the duty room, head for Louise's desk. The timesheets and reports for the Whiskey Creek fire are neatly tucked in a file holder on a credenza next to her desk.

I lay out the file, quickly find what I'm looking for.

Bernice Mercredi left the fire late in the evening on the second day, about an hour after I left on the night I ripped up the floorboards. I try to remember any impression of Bernice Mercredi that night — if she looked ill — but I was too involved in what I was doing to notice. On the other hand, she would have noticed everything I was doing and, like everyone else at the fire, would have known the significance of the under-burned floorboards. She might have been sick and had to leave, or she might have left for another reason. Either way, she is the most likely conduit of information from the fire that night and I need to talk to her. I replace the file, ask Tabra if she knows where Helen and Bernice Mercredi live.

"Oh sure," she says, flashing me a smile. "They're up on Sesame Street."

It's not just people here that have nicknames. I clarify exactly where that might be and, following Tabra's description of the house, pull to the curb at six o'clock. Helen Mercredi frowns at me though a dusty screen door.

"You come to bring the cheque?"

When I shake my head her frown deepens.

"Is Bernice home?"

"No, of course not," she snaps. "Why do you think I come to get her cheque?"

"Do you know where she is?"

"McMurray."

"I thought she was sick."

"She is sick. She stays at friends. No doctor here today."

I'd forgotten the doctor services several remote communities and is not always in town.

"What was wrong with her?"

"She's got an irritable bowel. Bad stomach ache."

"Did she have an appointment with a specific doctor in McMurray?"

Helen Mercredi snorts. "Yeah, right. Like it's that easy on short notice. She goes to emergency at the hospital."

"Did you ask her to call as soon as she got there?"

"Yeah, but she doesn't always call, you know. Teenagers."

"Even if she's sick?"

Helen Mercredi sighs. "She's head strong, that one. Does what she wants."

"Have you spoken with your daughter since she left?"

"I call twice, but no answer."

"Does your daughter have a cellphone?"

"They cost money, you know. Can't use them here anyway."

"Who did you call, then?"

"My friend," she says, crossing her arms. "Why?"

"Just routine follow-up."

"You don't sound routine. She in some kinda trouble?"

"I doubt it. I just need to speak with her. When did she leave?"

"Day before yesterday. Afternoon flight."

"Do you have the phone number where she's staying?"

She considers, then opens the screen door. "You come inside. I get the number."

I step inside while she vanishes down a hallway. The house, although shabby outside, is clean and modern inside, full of newer furniture and a large screen television. Three small Native children sit on a rug and stare transfixed at the screen, oblivious to my presence. Helen Mercredi returns with a scrap of paper and a cordless phone. I don't want to question her daughter in detail in front of her, but I'd like to know where she is, to set up a longer conversation, and dial the numbers on the scrap of paper. I let it ring a dozen times.

There's no answer.

I leave the Mercredi residence frustrated. Bernice Mercredi is the closest thing to a lead I've had yet. She's the most likely link to whoever snuck into the fire and burned up the floorboards. I shove a borrowed school picture of her into my pocket as I leave the house and scan the street for any burgundy vehicles with scrapes. No luck. More than likely she mentioned the floorboards to someone after leaving the fire and the information got around. I have to find out who she talked to and this is something best done in person, where I can watch her reaction, read her body language. I need to go to Fort McMurray and I return to the ranger station, drive into the compound, park in front of Mark Middel's house. He comes to the door, wiping his mouth with a napkin. I've disturbed his supper. "Come in, Cassel."

"No thanks, this will just take a minute. I need a flight to McMurray."

He raises an eyebrow. "You making some progress?"

"I'm not sure. As soon as I have something, I'll let you know."

Middel nods, thinking, no doubt wondering if he should press me for details. Fortunately, he lets it slide, as I don't want to mention anything until I have something substantial. He mentions the HAC helicopter will be going into McMurray tomorrow morning, before the daily fire hazard builds, for a mechanical inspection, and I can bum a ride.

"Could Luke look after the dog while I'm away?"

"Yeah, I guess so."

"Thanks. He's tied up at the IA base."

I head out, hesitate at the end of the driveway by the ranger station. Across the road is a large, white, two-storey log building. It's the local museum. I have a history question to ask that might have relevance to arson or murder.

The museum is open for another hour, which I find surprising.

"Tourist hours," says the curator. "Just started this week."

The curator is a summer student named Kim, working on her master's in anthropology. She's short and slim, red-haired with freckles and a ponytail. Just looking at her makes me feel old. Her master's thesis is on intergroup behaviour and EuroCanadian relations among the tribes of the lower Athabasca region. The museum is a perfect gig for integrating her school work with her employment situation. She tells me all of this in a nonstop tirade as she leads me into the museum. There's no one else in the place. I ask her if she gets many tourists.

"Not many," she says, smiling, leading me through displays of furs, wooden washing machines and assorted historical debris. I wait until she's given me the full tour, which takes about ten minutes, steer the conversation to matters of more recent history.

"Do the bands here get along well?"

She smiles again. "They seem to be doing okay now, but there used to be a lot of friction. The Cree historically positioned themselves to be the middlemen between the European fur traders and other tribes. They provided labour. They served as guides and translators. Basically, they made themselves indispensible to the fur traders, even going so far as intermarriage. This is where the Metis evolved from originally — French fur traders and the Cree."

"How do the Cree get along with the Metis?"

"Okay, I guess," she says, standing in front of an upstairs window overlooking the lake. "The Metis don't have official status under the Indian Act, so they're not entitled to a land claim settlement and associated benefits. Some of them have been vocally bitter."

"But there are three groups here, right?"

"Yes. There's also the Chipewyan, or Dene, which means 'the people.' Historically, they were nomadic hunters that operated farther north and were less directly involved with the fur trade. In fact, the Cree made sure of this, jealously protecting their position as middlemen, so there's been a historic sense of distrust between the Chips and the Cree."

"Do you think that still exists today?"

Kim frowns, looks uncertain. "I'm not sure — it's hard to tell as an outsider. That's one of the reasons I came here to do research." She brightens, puts a warm hand on my arm. "Fort Chipewyan is a fascinating area. Sort of a microcosm, isolated like it is, without a road."

"How is your research going?" I ask, moving my arm.

"Oh, sort of slow," she says wistfully. "What do you do?"

"I work for the Forest Service."

"Ooh." She flashes her lashes at me. "A forest ranger."

I nod, thank Kim and quickly excuse myself. Why is it now that I'm engaged women find me attractive? Some higher power has a wicked sense of humour. Hot with the shame of my previous night's activities, I head for the IA base where I feed the dog, rub salve on his burns, and make myself an extra-strong cup of Dr. Cho's Happy Tea. It hits me like anesthetic and in minutes I fade into a merciful sleep.

The next morning my alarm clock wakes me for the first time since I arrived. Normally I'm awake long before and have no need for an alarm, to the point where I've stopped setting it. Last night though, I suspected I might need it, with the magnum charge of tea, and I yawn, feeling rested and ready for the day. It's a marvellous sensation. I stuff a fresh change of clothes into my pack, have a bite of breakfast, feed the dog and meet the pilot of the HAC helicopter at his machine. A few minutes later the rippling grey expanse of Lake Athabasca is below us as we head south. Soon we are over the Peace-Athabasca river delta — a marshy expanse formed by the confluence of these rivers at the south end of the lake. The delta, I've learned from locals in the past two weeks, is an integral part of the Native lifestyle, used for trapping muskrats, fishing for walleye, hunting migratory birds and buffalo. Much of it falls within Wood Buffalo National Park. It also contains the Chipewyan land claim area, which is great for trapping and fishing but useless for building — an issue of perpetual jealousy with the Cree Band, who have a land claim area underlain by rock. The Cree Band land claim is also where the bottle fires have been occurring. I ponder possible motivations as we pass over the delta. The pilot distracts me by pointing out a herd of bison.

"Amazing," I say, peering down through the Plexiglas bubble.

"As soon as they step out of the Park, the Natives shoot them."

We make small talk as we follow the Athabasca River south. An hour later the smoke stacks and excavations of the oil sands come into view. Looking down is like passing over another planet. Vast stretches of forest have been peeled away to reveal a black ominous landscape, pocked with pits and huge glistening wastewater ponds, some of them alarmingly close to the river. Massive refineries squat in the centre of each wasteland. Trucks as large as apartment buildings and cranes as high as skyscrapers — they all look like toys from this height.

"I've flown over it a hundred times," says the pilot. "Still impresses me."

It's hard not to be impressed with the sheer scale of the operation. Then there's the money — a hundred billion dollars of investment. Energy royalties that fund projects all across the country. Not that there haven't been issues. Open any newspaper lately and there'll be articles on carbon release and global warming, habitat destruction, river contamination, dead ducks, and the heavy energy cost to separate the oil. My concern today is on a smaller scale and as we touch down at the base in Fort MacKay I look forward to finding Bernice Mercredi.

Fort MacKay is a tiny settlement at the end of the road, about a forty-five-minute drive north of the city of Fort McMurray. I check in with the base commander, pick up keys to a borrowed truck and head south again. Soon I'm in the bustle of a genuine boom town. Fort McMurray has grown from a logging town of fifteen thousand to a petroleum city of nearly one hundred thousand in a decade. Everything is being built at once and there isn't enough of anything. Traffic clogs streets not designed to handle high volumes and it takes an hour to cross halfway through the city. I check the address given to me by Helen Mercredi against a map I found in the borrowed truck. The map is a few years old and the neighbourhood I'm looking for isn't shown. I take a few wrong turns, which burns up another hour, before finding the correct house in a cul-de-sac at the edge of a raw clearing.

The house, like the neighbourhood, can't be more than a year old. Spindly birch trees are anchored by ropes and stakes in a front lawn that still shows the checkerboard of new sod. As I reach for the door handle in my truck, I notice my hands are shaking again, take a moment to compose myself. I had a big cup of tea this morning, but neglected to take any with me, and I could really use some right now. The air smells of turned soil and diesel fumes as I walk up the newly minted sidewalk. The door is answered by a tall Native woman.

"Hello, I'm Porter Cassel, with the Forest Service."

"Carol," she says. "What does the Forestry want with me?"

"Do you know Helen and Bernice Mercredi?"

She frowns. "What's this about?"

"I'm looking for Bernice. I was told she's staying here."

"Her mother said she would be coming down for a few days but she never got here. I thought maybe Helen changed her mind. Is there something the matter?"

"I just need to talk to her. Routine fire stuff."

Carol digests this. "Well, she's not here."

"Have you spoken recently with Helen Mercredi?"

Carol frowns. "I called her. Bernie was supposed to take a cab here, then I was going to take her to the doctor, depending how her stomach was. Sometimes it gets better by itself. Anyway, when I called her, one of the kids answered. I told him to tell his mom to call me back. When she didn't, I just figured Bernie was feeling better, and they changed their minds."

I think of the kids playing video games at the Mercredi house, picture them answering the phone, rushing back to their game, forgetting to pass on the message. A sliver of apprehension works its way into my chest. No one knew that Bernice Mercredi was missing.

"I've been out a lot and haven't given it much thought," says Carol.

"So you haven't heard anything from Bernice Mercredi?"

"Is something the matter? Did something happen with Bernie?"

"We're just trying to locate her."

Carol's expression clouds.

"Could I speak with your daughter?"

"Why?" she asks suspiciously.

"I understand Bernice and your daughter are friends."

She turns and hollers in Cree into the house. A younger voice answers. I can't understand the language, but the tone is surprised. A moment later a younger version of Carol appears, long black hair hiding one eye. The girl looks to be about sixteen or seventeen. She stares at my boots. I introduce myself again, which elicits the slightest of nods.

"I was wondering if you'd heard from Bernice lately."

Her gaze flickers across my face and she shakes her head. This is awkward, her mother looming beside her, scrutinizing the conversation. I want to ask personal questions she may not want to answer in front of her mother.

"Is there somewhere else Bernice might have gone?"

She shrugs, staring at my boots again. The mother says something sharply in Cree.

"Maybe to the mall," says the daughter.

"Which one?"

"Peter Pond."

It seems an odd response, given that Bernice was supposed to have arrived yesterday.

"Is there anyone else she might be staying with?"

The girl looks at me, searching my face, and I wonder if there's something going on here of which none of the parents is aware — something a friend wouldn't reveal to a parent, much less a stranger. A party. A secret boyfriend. Perhaps she was running away. Whatever it might be, she won't tell me, answering instead with a typical teenage shrug.

"Where does she like to go to party?"

The mother prods her daughter — as interested in the response as I am.

"Answer the man."

She shrugs again. It occurs to me she's probably underage.

"Listen," I say, dropping my voice, "this is really important. We need to find Bernice and make sure she's okay. I need to know if there's someplace you've gone with her to party; someplace she might get into trouble. Someone's house, maybe. Or a bar. I'm not here to cause you any trouble — I just need to know about Bernice."

She looks at me again, evaluating. "We go to the Oil Can sometimes."

A subtle intake of breath from her mother.

"How often do you go there?" I say.

"Sometimes on Fridays."

"I thought you were going to study group," the mother says.

"We didn't go every Friday. Just sometimes."

"Oh — that makes it better, does it?" says the mother, crossing her arms.

I raise my hands. "Let's just focus for a moment, please."

They both glare at me.

"When you were at the bar, was there ever anyone that caused you concern?"

She shrugs somewhat flippantly. "Not really. We can take care of ourselves."

The mother snorts. I don't want to wade into a mother-daughter argument, so I thank them for their time, leave my contact information and head to my truck where I use my cell phone, which until I arrived in Fort McMurray had been useless, to call Helen Mercredi and see if Bernice has called or come home. She hasn't. Her mother's voice is strained.

"Where is my daughter? Where could Bernie have gone?"

"She could have snuck off to see someone. Do you know if she had a boyfriend out of town? Or if she had any reason to take off?"

The line is silent for a moment, then a small voice: "No."

"I'm here now, Mrs. Mercredi, and I'll keep looking. It might be a good idea to call the RCMP, file a missing persons report. They have more resources than I do."

The line is silent again.

"Are you there, Mrs. Mercredi?"

"Yes," she says distantly. "Thank you for helping."

I assure her that I'll let her know as soon as I find anything.

I sit in my truck, watch the house where Bernice Mercredi was supposed to be, ponder my next move. Leaving the fire to see a doctor may have been a ruse to spend time with a boyfriend. Or maybe she learned something at the fire and felt the knowledge put her at risk, so she bolted. Either way, it'll be difficult to find her if she doesn't want to be found. I'll need to work this like any missing persons case — on a timeline. A day-and-a-half ago, her mother dropped her at the airport for the regular afternoon flight to Fort McMurray. She would have arrived about five o'clock that afternoon. She was supposed to take a cab to her friend's house but didn't arrive. The airport is some distance outside the city, so she would have needed to take a cab from there to wherever she was going. I could canvas the cab drivers, but that'll take quite a while in a city of one hundred thousand. The other possibility is that someone was waiting for her at the airport. Either way, she may no longer be in Fort McMurray. She could be anywhere by now, either by road or on another flight. Or, just maybe, she went from the airport directly to the hospital.

The Northern Lights Regional Health Centre is a large building in the old downtown core of Fort McMurray, located not surprisingly on Hospital Street. I park in the public area and contemplate how best to approach my inquiry. The medical profession are, rightfully, quite conservative about releasing information. Today that will not be working in my favour, as I need to know if Bernice Mercredi has been treated here. I decide the emergency department, where she would have gone, makes the most sense.

Emergency rooms are all pretty much the same. This one is no exception. A room full of weary patrons droop in rows of hard plastic chairs. Another line of patrons wait at a counter. I join the line, wait for my turn to speak with the admitting nurse. When my turn comes, she evaluates me through a Plexiglas safety partition, asks what she can do for me today.

"I was wondering if you could tell me if Bernice Mercredi was seen here."

The nurse frowns. "I can't help you with that. Medical records are confidential."

"Is there any way to determine if she was here?"

She eyes the line behind me. "She might have been admitted. You can call the switchboard. They'll check for you. There's a phone by the entrance. Anything else, sir?"

I'm about to thank her and head to the phone when it occurs to me that I feel really awful, itchy, twitchy, achy, and as though my muscles are filled with sand, and I'm in a hospital anyway, so I ask to see a doctor, show her my shaking hands. She raises an eyebrow, scribbles something on a clipboard and sends me to another counter where my personal details are taken. I'm told to take a seat — my name will be called. While I'm waiting, I use the public phone to call the switchboard. A polite feminine voice answers.

"Northern Lights Regional Health Centre."

"I was wondering if you could tell me if Bernice Mercredi has been admitted."

"One moment, sir."

A minute goes by, during which I hear humming.

"There's no one listed by that name, sir."

I thank her, the sliver of apprehension in my chest burrowing deeper. If Bernice Mercredi didn't come here at all, she either never made it this far or never intended to come. Both scenarios suggest something amiss. I take seat on an uncomfortable plastic chair and wait. And wait. The experience is a bit monastic and I could use the time to connect with my inner self except I'm not really sure I want to meet the guy right now. I'd have some tough questions. So I read outdated copies of *Reader's Digest*. Finally, my turn comes and I'm ushered behind a cloth partition, where I wait again, sitting on a paper-covered exam bench.

The doctor arrives. He's old, white-haired, looks exhausted.

"What can I help you with today?" he says.

"I don't feel well. I'm nauseous and my hands are shaking."

He looks at my hands. "How long has this been going on?"

"I haven't been feeling well for months now. Difficulty sleeping. No energy. The shaking started more recently. And I'm itchy."

"Itchy?" he says giving me a critical look.

I nod, scratching my ribs.

"Any recent changes? Drug or alcohol problems? Family medical history?"

"Nothing new. All in the past. Aunt that has Parkinson's."

I'm impressed by the brevity of our conversation. I don't think anything will impress the doctor, though. He prescribes a thorough checkup. His stethoscope is predictably icy on my chest and back. Reflexes are tested, urine sampled. And a blood test, which I manage to pass without fainting. Barely. Dizzy, I struggle to retain my dignity, stumble out of the hospital, sit in my truck, breathing deeply. I might be a macho firefighter, but needles undo me. I'm just starting to feel better when my cellphone rings and I scramble to free it from the holster on my belt, hoping it's Bernice Mercredi or news of her.

It's Christina Telson. My fiancée.

"Howdy, Porter. How's my cute little fireman?"

My recuperation is short lived; I don't feel so good again.

"I'm fine," I mumble. "How about you?"

Telson proceeds to tell me about her latest freelance job. She's a journalist, a champion of the truth. I only half listen as she talks. My own truthfulness remains in question. I know I have to tell her, but not like this, not over the phone. I need to face her, be with her, let her know with all of me how much the episode with Collette was a mistake. So I stall, contribute minimally to the conversation, my heart hammering, my palms sweaty, until she notices.

"You okay, Porter?"

"Yeah, fine. I'm just really busy right now. Can't talk long."

"You don't seem to be able to talk at all. What's up?"

There's an awkward silence. I don't want to lie to her.

"Look," I say, "I gotta go. I'll call you later."

"Okay," she says, sounding distinctly put-off. Then she's gone and I feel alone and dirty. I've never cheated on anyone. Now I literally have a hard time looking at myself in the mirror. I swallow a lump in my throat, brace my arms against the steering wheel and tense my whole body for as long as I can hold it. When I let go I'm faint and limp but the blunt pain in my chest is a bit better.

I need to drive.

I wheel the truck into traffic, fight my way up the hill leading out of town, passing recklessly until I'm on the highway where I open the windows and crank up the tunes. Wind whips hair into my eyes as they blur with tears. I thought I could hold it together until I had a chance to face Telson but her voice, disembodied, pieced my chest like a knife, leaving an invisible wound. I'm not sure how long I drive before I notice it's getting dark. I want to keep going but I'd only be running from myself so I turn back.

It's full dark by the time I see the lights of Fort McMurray. I'm calmer now, the adrenaline and emotion spent. I turn off the radio, absorb the sounds of night traffic as I roll downtown, searching for Bernice Mercredi. It's a long shot. In the dim artificial light of the streets everyone looks the same. I pass the Oil Can several times as I loop back on Franklin Avenue. I'm not crazy about spending the evening in another bar, but the Oil Can is the closest thing I have to a lead, so I park in the only available spot near a dumpster. I'm shoved aside at the door by a large Native who curses as he makes his way past me.

"Watch it, asshole," he throws over his shoulder.

For a few seconds I'm tempted to go after him, but then I shake my head, amazed, as the anger subsides. Not like me. Too much stress lately. I take a deep breathe, move to the bar, order a beer, look around. It's a typical older drinking establishment. Dim light. Low ceiling. Small crowded tables. The clientele are mostly Natives and mine workers. Several middle-age women in high heels and tight cocktail dresses lounge along the bar, watching. Cougars, stalking younger men. Or hookers — sometimes it's hard to tell the difference. I make a circuit, glancing at faces, trying not to look conspicuous as I search for Bernice Mercredi. No luck, but it's early. Around the corner from the bar I see a crowd leaning in, edge my way closer.

A long Plexiglas structure sits on a low table. They're racing hamsters. For five bucks you can pick your thoroughbred. I buy a ticket for number three in the next race. Halfway through the race my hamster stops to lick itself, then turns around. A fool and his money are quickly parted. I make another circuit through the room, looking for Bernice Mercredi. No luck but I recognize several faces from Fort Chipewyan. There's an older Native that works for Wood Buffalo National Park, and the weatherman from the airport. A beaded buckskin jacket is familiar and I nod at Simon Cardinal, the Native Justice Liaison from the Cree Band. He returns my nod, wanders over to where I'm standing along the bar.

"It's the Fire Guy," he says. "You making any progress?"

"Some, but I'd like to be making more."

"Can I get you a drink?"

My beer, which I had planned to drink slowly, is nearly gone. Given recent events, I know I shouldn't be drinking anything, but I'm shaky and there's a dull pain in my chest from my conversation with Telson. I tell myself I'm in control, and intend to remain that way, but I need a bit — just enough to calm my nerves. I generously allow Cardinal to buy me a whiskey.

"Thanks." I take a sip. Damn that tastes good tonight.

"No problem. I heard that Sammy's truck was firebombed with one of those bottles."

I nod. "I'm sure everyone's heard that by now."

"You got the cops helping you?"

"I think it's more the other way around."

Cardinal claps a hand on my shoulder, gives me an earnest look. "You need anything, you let me know. Anything the Cree Band can help you with, you just gotta ask. We want to find the prick that's after us." He looks around, lowers his voice. "You find him, you let me know first, okay? We'll take care of it."

"I'm not sure I can do that."

"Just let us know," he says, giving me another hard look. Then he nods and walks away, telling me to take care of myself. I watch him go, think of Middel's concern that the town is a powder keg. Telling anything to the Cree Band at this point would be lighting the fuse.

I lounge, try to look casual as I wait to see if Mercredi will show up.

The whiskey goes down too smooth. Careful Porter.

I switch back to beer, watch the hamster races, place a few more bets. A slender feminine hand with long purple fingernails is warm on my arm. I've roused the interest of one of the cougars and she's moved in for the kill. Then it occurs to me I'm as old as she is.

"Hello darling. You look lost. You looking for something?"

"Someone," I say, and immediately regret the response.

"Well," she smiles, batting fake eyelashes at me. "You just found someone."

"I'm actually looking for a girl of about nineteen."

"You and everyone else."

She frowns when I pull out the photo of Bernice Mercredi.

"You a cop?"

I assure her that I'm harmless — that I'm just looking for a girl that didn't come home when she was expected. She barely looks at the picture.

"You sure you haven't seen her?" I say, holding it up.

Someone shoulders me aside — a big guy with a bandana over his head. He looks like a biker and I assume he's the bouncer, or maybe the woman's pimp.

"This guy bothering you?" he says to the lady.

"Mind your own damn business," I snap at him.

Normally I'm not that brave or confrontational, but tonight I'm edgy, frustrated and anxious. And, apparently, a bit intoxicated. The big guy gives me a deliberate poke in the chest, hard enough to bruise. "You just watch your mouth, shit for brains."

Anger boils up like fire climbing a tree. Where it came from I have no idea but it's overwhelming. He's in front of me, getting in my face, all eyeballs and stubble. The frustrations of the past week fill my senses and my heart races. Everything around us vanishes and his face becomes startling clear. I can see every pore.

He pokes me again. "Listen, shithead —"

I hit him.

# 8
•

**THE DRONE OF** the plane throbs in my head as we pass over Lake Athabasca. I'm on the regular commercial flight, crammed in with locals returning from Fort McMurray. A hyperactive boy of about seven is in the seat next to me, bouncing up and down while I try to sleep. I have a headache, black eye and several other bruises. I didn't get much sleep last night. The holding cell at the RCMP detachment wasn't very comfortable. In the heat of battle we managed to destroy several chairs, a large speaker by the dance floor, and the hamster racing equipment. Fortunately, the hamsters escaped injury, which is the only bright light of the evening. Apparently I went berserk, which is completely out of character — a fact I tried to impress upon the two RCMP troopers who hauled me away. They weren't keen on conversation. The local sergeant called Waldren in Fort Chipewyan, and after lengthy discussion they decided I could be released, so long as no one wanted to press charges. Mr. Bandana wanted nothing further to do with me. The bar owner just wanted payment for the damage.

So now I'm broke, humiliated and still have to face Waldren and Middel.

I'm relieved there's no one at the airport to meet me. Hands shaking, eyes darting nervously, I walk the half mile to the IA base. A quick shower, leftovers in the cook shack and a big cup of bitter tea and I feel marginally better. Scorch provides some quality dog therapy, licking my face and hands. It occurs to me that I'm not nearly as allergic as I was before I visited Dr. Cho — another benefit of his wonder tea. I spend a few minutes with the dog, then reluctantly set off for town. I have an appointment with the RCMP at 3:00 p.m. — a briefing with the team that will be investigating the bottle fire that destroyed Sammy Cardinal's truck. The briefing was no doubt one of the mitigating factors in my being released this morning. I park in the fenced RCMP-compound, check in at the reception counter in the detachment office. A clerk talks to me through a sheet of bulletproof glass, hands me a sign-in form through a narrow slot above the counter, then vanishes. Waldren appears, scowling when he sees me from the other side of the glass. He unlocks the door.

"Jesus, Cassel. You look like a truck hit you."

"I think his name might have been Mack."

"Don't pull that shit again. I've used up my favours."

I nod, in no mood for confrontation. Waldren leads me to a small conference room where Constable Markham and ident specialist Dugan sit at a table. Their expressions register surprise at my bruised appearance. There's a new face here as well, a big guy in plain clothes. I take a seat facing a blank flip chart, grab a notepad from a pile on the table. I feel more professional with something in front of me. Waldren and Dugan sit on my left. The new guy stands at the head of the table, opens the ceremonies.

"Good afternoon, I'm Corporal Roland MacFarlane, from the General Investigative Section in Fort McMurray. You must be Porter Cassel," he says, looking at me. I nod. MacFarlane is wearing faded jeans and an AC/DC T-shirt. His unkempt black hair is receding heavily at the temples in the classic V-shape. He has a dragon tattoo on his right forearm and badly needs a shave. He looks more like an aging rugby player than a cop. Perhaps that's the idea. "Good to have you on our team," he says generously. "Due to the multi-jurisdictional nature of this investigation we've thrown together an ad-hoc joint forces operation, code named 'Kitten.'"

"Kitten?" says Waldren. "Couldn't we have something with a bit more bite?"

"Yeah," says Markham, "like killer whale?"

"All the good names were gone. Don't worry — I don't think any less of you."

"Meow," says Waldren.

"What would the Forest Service role be in this?" I ask.

"We'll get to that," says MacFarlane, "but basically we would like to parallel your arson investigation relative to the Molotov cocktails. The only way we are going to catch the perp, who we believe may be escalating or posturing toward more acts of arson, is to keep on the same page, share information."

"Sounds good to me."

"There is one important thing I'd like to stress," he says, pausing as though searching for the right words. "To make this work, you'll need to follow our rules."

Everyone is looking at me. I nod, feeling distinctly cowed.

"We'll begin with a briefing on facts to date. You can start, Mr. Cassel."

I clear my throat, mentally try to organize the past few weeks. "I'm a fire investigator contracted to the Forest Service, based out of Edmonton, and I travel where ever I'm needed. I arrived here on the third of May, in response to a wildfire arson reported by the local office. The local initial attack crew responded to an early morning fire along a road about fifteen kilometres from town, reported by a fire tower. Upon actioning the fire they discovered the remnants of a bottle. My investigation revealed that the bottle was the origin. There were charred remnants of cloth with the bottle, consistent with a Molotov cocktail. Since the initial arson, there have been three more bottle fires, all along the same stretch of road, and then the truck fire in the gravel pit. All of the bottles had the letters FTC etched at their base."

"Five fires with the same signature," says MacFarlane, jotting this on the flip chart.

Waldren goes next, detailing his participation in the bottle fires which, until the truck fire, has been minimal. He came out to the first bottle fire for a quick look but when it was apparent there were no human values threatened, he was content to receive periodic updates. Dugan adds his summary from processing the scene at the truck fire, starting with a pointed statement that the scene was heavily compromised when he arrived. There were no apparent sources of ignition from the vehicle itself. Other than the bottle, no suspicious items. No fingerprints due to cleansing by the fire. Bottle segments were collected and are awaiting further analysis at the lab, although little additional is expected.

"Let's talk about those bottles," says MacFarlane. "What do we know about them?"

"They're all booze bottles," I say. "Captain Morgan. Canadian Club. And a rectangular bottle that I believe was the Five Star brand."

"So they're a mix," says MacFarlane. "Whatever was at hand."

"They could come from anywhere," says Waldren. "Everyone up here drinks."

"Or they could have been found in the ditch," I say, thinking about the bottle picker.

"What about this signature?" asks MacFarlane. "What does it mean?

"Fuck the Cree," I say, and everyone looks at me. "It was on the store."

"And you think that tagging is the same?" says MacFarlane.

"Looks that way," says Dugan. "I sent photos of the bottle inscriptions and the tagging to our handwriting expert. Although it's not as easy to draw conclusions from writing done with an etching tool and a spray can it looks like the same author."

"What about location or context?"

"The bottle fires were on Cree land," I say. "And the truck belonged to their chief."

"They also own the store where the tagging occurred," says Waldren.

MacFarlane makes more notes on the flip chart, then looks at us, chewing thoughtfully on the end of the marker. "So we've got someone who either has a grudge against the Cree Band or is trying to focus attention on them. Any theories?"

"These bands have been at each other's throats for hundreds of years," says Waldren.

"I've done some research at the museum," I offer. "Same conclusion."

"That may well be," says MacFarlane, "but in my experience an escalation in any long-standing feud is triggered by some event. Has anything significant occurred recently?"

Waldren shrugs. "Who knows — they rarely tell us anything. Native communities are virtually impenetrable to an outsider. If they have an issue, they settle it themselves."

"We'll need a Native liaison," says MacFarlane.

I think about Simon Cardinal's offer of help from the Cree Band, but decide it had too many strings attached. Waldren volunteers Constable Markham, who will put out feelers with the bands and the Metis. MacFarlane scans the flip chart. "Okay," he says, "that seems to cover the bottle fires. Now, what about that cabin with the fatality? What do we know so far?"

I go through my arrival at the Whiskey Creek fire and my preliminary processing of the cabin scene, end with my discovery of the body. Waldren offers his chronology. Dugan takes over from there, covering information I already know, until he mentions a belt buckle found some distance from the body.

"Does that mean the vic wasn't wearing his pants?"

MacFarlane hesitates. "Yes, that was our conclusion, but we're keeping that as holdback evidence. Please ensure you don't mention this to anyone outside of this room."

"What about the autopsy?" says Waldren.

Dugan pulls a sheaf of papers from a folder in front of him, puts on reading glasses. "Identity confirmed through dental as one Rufus Earnest Hallendry. Third degree burns over ninety-five percent of the body with heavy charring throughout. The five percent of the body not burned was on the back, where some skin remained in contact with the floor. Nearly complete tissue damage and carbonization of bones in the extremities." He looks up at us. "This was a very hot fire, gentlemen." He adjusts his glasses, flips a page. "Airways display black soot, and soot was found on the base of the tongue and in the trachea. Blood sampled from within the chest cavity indicates a carboxy-hemoglobin level of thirty-two percent."

"Excuse me," I interrupt. "What does that mean?"

Dugan looks at me over his glasses. "Carboxy-hemoglobin is a measure of how much carbon monoxide is in the blood. His level matches with the soot in the airways to indicate he was alive during the fire."

I shudder — being burned alive is every firefighter's nightmare.

"Continuing on," says Dugan, "we have tox results that indicate a blood alcohol level of 4.5 grams/litre." He looks around. "Does anyone know if the victim was a regular drinker?"

"Oh yeah," says Waldren. "Definitely."

"Good to know," says Dugan, "because this much would kill an inexperienced drinker."

"So the drinking didn't kill him?" says Markham.

"Determining how drunk someone is can be difficult as bodyweight, health and drinking habits all influence the level of impairment. But if this guy was a regular heavy drinker, I would have to say the drinking was not likely the cause of death, although the victim would have been severely impaired and likely unconscious. Smoke inhalation and searing of the lungs would have done the trick."

"That impairment explains why he couldn't get out of the cabin," says Waldren.

There's a thoughtful silence as we all try not to think about what it was like in the cabin.

MacFarlane asks: "Anything else noted that might explain why he couldn't get out?"

Dugan flips pages for a moment, scrutinizing the report. "Injury analysis can be difficult with burn victims. Heat will contract the muscles and break bones post-mortem. But Sandow did this autopsy, and he's good with burns. No discernable pre-mortem injuries were noted."

"So let me summarize," says MacFarlane. "The victim had been drinking to the point of incapacitation. He left open the cabin door as well as the door on the woodstove. He was found lying on his back near a table, with whiskey bottles and a drinking glass in near proximity."

"And he wasn't wearing any pants," Waldren adds.

MacFarlane looks at us. "Is there anything suspicious about this death?"

"Not really," says Waldren. "Looks pretty clear-cut to me."

"Excuse me," I say, looking at Waldren.

"Oh, yeah," he says. "Cassel thinks he's found something."

All eyes turn to me. Everyone here but MacFarlane knows I have concerns.

"I was curious why Hallendry would have had his stove going when the overnight temperature was 16c and there was no evidence of cooking."

"He could have been making tea," says Markham.

"Or looking for a reason to take off his pants," says Waldren.

"A teapot was not found within the vicinity of the stove," I say, ignoring Waldren's sarcasm. "I'm sure ident can confirm this."

Dugan nods. "Carry on," says MacFarlane.

"I found evidence of distemper in the metal roofing tin which, when I laid out the sections, seemed to indicate a rush of heat in the area over the body."

"Really," says MacFarlane. "You laid out the whole roof?"

I nod. Dugan looks a bit defensive, but I plough on.

"I cut out a segment of the floor and discovered a pattern of under-burning which I think was caused by a flammable fluid dripping through the cracks in the floor planking. I believe this indicates an accelerant was used."

MacFarlane's eyes narrow. "You think this was arson?"

"Frankly," I say, "I think this was murder."

There's a silence — which I should have expected, contradicting the RCMP.

"What's your interpretation?" says MacFarlane, turning to Dugan.

Dugan looks uncomfortable. "We observed minor distemper on the roof tin but that's to be expected. A structure fire does not create an even heat. In my experience, the degree of distemper noted by Mr. Cassel is not unusual in a normal fire."

"But you didn't lay out the roof tin?" says MacFarlane.

"It wasn't necessary," says Dugan.

MacFarlane frowns. "What about the under-burned floorboards?"

"We didn't observe this," says Dugan.

"That's because you didn't pull up the floor," I say quietly.

Dugan doesn't look at me. "There didn't seem to be the need."

"What do you make of these floorboards?" MacFarlane says to Dugan.

"I would have liked to see them. They may have been significant."

"Can you still do an assessment of the floor?" says MacFarlane.

"I'd love to," says Dugan, "but apparently it was destroyed."

MacFarlane frowns. "Destroyed?"

"Burned," I say. "During the night following my discovery, what remained of the floor was burned. I don't think this was accidental. I took pictures, which someone accessed in my truck during the night and deleted from my camera. I also found a purplish paint scrape on a tree a few miles from the fire, where a vehicle turned around. I think someone discovered that I was on to the fire being intentionally set, and cleaned up what evidence remained. I think the cook's helper, a girl named Bernice Mercredi, who left early from the fire, the same night as the remaining cabin floor was burned up, mentioned what I'd found to someone, and the word got out. And I found two drinking glasses, which match the glass at Hallendry's cabin, in the ditch along the main road that leads to the site."

"Interesting," says MacFarlane. "Have you spoken with the Mercredi girl?"

"No, she's missing. I went to McMurray to find her."

"Ah," he says. "I see."

There's an awkward silence. No one says my theory is half-baked and circumstantial, but no one is saying anything, which is not a good sign. MacFarlane isn't taking notes. "When was she reported missing?"

"Her mother reported her missing last night," says Waldren.

"How long has she been gone?"

"About two days."

"How old is she?"

"Nineteen, I think."

MacFarlane ponders, tapping the felt marker against his chin. "Normally, someone of age has to be missing for seventy-two hours before we even consider them missing, or there has to be a strong suspicion of foul play. In my experience, in remote communities like this, people vanish and reappear constantly. They go on a drunk. They go fishing. They just go into the bush to get away. Do you really think this girl may have information of value?"

"She's my only lead so far."

"Okay." MacFarlane nods, making a decision. "We'll keep an eye out for her as a person of interest. The next thing I want to pursue is any possible connection between the fires started with the Molotov cocktails and the Hallendry fire. Any theories?"

"Nothing obvious so far," says Waldren.

"What do you think, Cassel? You've worked both fires."

"Both fires involved alcohol bottles, but beyond that I've found nothing to suggest a link. The bottle fires seem to be targeted at the Cree Band, but there doesn't seem to be any obvious connection between the Cree Band and the Hallendry fire. The Hallendry trapline was generating a revenue stream from payments from a uranium exploration company. Previous to Hallendry acquiring the trapline it was held by a Native, who likely belonged to one of the bands. There could be an expectation of gain by removing Hallendry, or it could be some sort of a punishment."

MacFarlane takes notes. "Any more theories?"

No one seems to have anything to add.

"Okay," says MacFarlane, "let's talk structure. I'll be the lead as the primary investigator. Cassel will be the fire behaviour specialist and liaison with the Forest Service. Markham will be Native liaison. Waldren will be logistics and team commander." He flips back a few pages on his chart. "Tasks to be accomplish in the near term are a review of all information relating to the bottle fires with ident and myself — that obviously will be you, Cassel — and establishing the Native liaison function. Markham, you need to set up lines of communication with the bands and let it be known that we are interested in any information regarding intertribal friction. Oh, and we'll put the word out on that girl of yours, Cassel."

The meeting is over. I stand up, move to the door when MacFarlane intercepts me, pulls me aside. He waits until the room clears then closes the door, fixes me with a hard eye.

"I hear you have a reputation of being a wildcard."

"Mere flattery," I assure him. He's not amused.

"We're not going to have problems are we?"

"Not if I can help it."

I spend another hour with the Mounties, bringing Dugan and MacFarlane up to speed on the minutia of the bottle fires — frequency, time of day, discovery — and other details that catalogue what happened. None of this has yet to lead me in any direction. Dugan wants to see the arson scenes so we go for a field trip, stand amongst the blackened patches of forest along the gravel road. I point out fire travel indicators, show him the point of origin at each fire. He takes pictures, makes notes. I have all of this documented but he wants his own data to add to the collection. Then we part ways and I ponder my next move. I know Middel is itching for an update on project Kitten, but I'm not keen on facing him after the incident in McMurray. Besides, I haven't learned anything new, other than the belt buckle — and that's hold

back evidence that can't be mentioned. I decide instead to check with
Helen Mercredi, see if she's heard from her daughter.

She looks anxious as she opens her screen door.

"Holy. What happened to your face?"

"Nothing. Bit of an accident."

"You find out anything about Bernie?"

I shake my head and she invites me in, insists I leave my boots
on and sit in the kitchen. I remove my boots anyway, take a seat at a
gleaming oak dinner table. The bleep and ping of video games comes
from the next room, mixed with the giggling voices of children. She
makes coffee. When we both have our steaming mugs she sits across
from me, looking worried.

"Where did you look in McMurray?" she says.

"I checked the hospital, but she hasn't been admitted. She might
have been treated, although they wouldn't tell me. That's something
you could follow-up, as her mother."

"Yes — thanks. I will. Anywhere else?"

"I checked a couple of places where she might go with a friend."

"Nothing?" she asks again, as if there might miraculously be a
different answer.

"Mrs. Mercredi, are you sure your daughter even went to McMurray?"

"Of course. I bought her ticket, dropped her at the airport."

"Did you actually see her board the plane?"

"I have no time." She points her chin at the next room, from where
children can be heard fighting over a turn on some game. "I have the
kids to take care of."

"So you can't confirm she ever left Fort Chip?"

She shakes her head. "I should have stayed longer."

"Can you think of any reason your daughter might not want to call
home?"

She looks offended. "Like what?"

"A party she wasn't supposed to go to. Some argument you might
have had."

Doubt casts a shadow over her expression but quickly passes. "She's a good girl."

"Could she have been faking being sick?"

"I guess, but why?"

"I'm not sure. Has she made any new friends lately?"

"I don't know. She's not a little kid anymore. She doesn't tell me everything."

Helen Mercredi sips her coffee, thinking. There's an awkward silence. I recall Bernice Mercredi at the fire, serving up lunch, and how the firefighters kept eyeing her. She certainly isn't a kid anymore, which makes me wonder again if she left the fire simply to meet up with a man somewhere. If so, it's unlikely she would have told her mother.

"Mrs. Mercredi, does she have any close friends in town I could speak with?"

"Yeah, lots of friends. There's Annie and Nancy and Darlene —"

"Which would be her closest? A friend she might share secrets with?"

"Oh, that would be Collette Whiteknife. They're pretty tight."

"I'll look into it," I say, standing. She follows me to the door, watches me lace up my boots. As I'm opening the screen door, she grabs my arm.

"Thanks for doing this," she says. "For looking for my Bernie."

I leave her there, a pleading look in her eye.


The Fort Chipewyan airport is a small facility located at the end of the only paved road. The runway is sandwiched between a lake and a rock quarry, which doesn't leave a pilot much room for error. The terminal building is an aged single-storey, with a faded sign welcoming arrivals to the oldest community in Alberta. This is where the fur traders first set up shop in the province. My concern is far more immediate — I want to confirm if Bernice Mercredi boarded a plane. A bored-looking older Native lady sits reading behind a small counter emblazoned with the logo of the local airline, which I recall is owned by the Cree Band. Her plastic name tag reads "Marge." She peers over her paperback as I approach.

"I was hoping you might be able to help me."

"Sold out," she says. "Funeral tomorrow."

"I'm not looking to buy a ticket."

"Well, I'm not selling anything else."

I drum my fingers on the countertop. "Did Bernice Mercredi board a flight lately?"

Marge sets her book aside. "What you want with Bernie?"

"I just need to determine if she was on the flight."

She frowns, gives me the once over.

"Can't tell you that. Against policy."

"Can you make an exception? I'm just trying to get hold of Bernie. Her mother asked me to look around in case Bernie is in some trouble."

Marge's eyes narrow. "You with the cops?"

"I'm just helping out her mom."

"Can I see some identification?"

I pull out my wallet, show her my driver's licence. She examines it closely before handing it back. "What day would this have been?" she says.

"Her mother dropped her here on Tuesday."

Marge taps an index finger on her chin, thinking. "I remember Helen buying the ticket, then she left. Then I think Bernie went to the bathroom. Later, I saw her outside, having a smoke. But that's it."

"Was she smoking with anyone in particular?"

"I don't know. The other passengers, probably."

"Can you confirm if she boarded the plane?"

"I don't watch them all board. I got other stuff to do."

"Is there some record on the other end?"

"Not officially, but we do a head count. Let me check."

Marge picks up the phone, talks for a moment in rapid-fire Cree.

"We were one short that flight," she says. "Maybe that was her."

I thank Marge for her time, head back to my truck. I wonder if Bernice Mercredi is playing games, sneaking around. Perhaps she's seeing an older married man. If this were the case, why would she leave the fire after only one day of work? I drive back to town, distracted by hunger and fatigue. It's suppertime and I debate calling it a night, but decide to stop by and chat with Collette Whiteknife, see if she can shed some light on Bernie's private life. I follow the directions given by Helen Mercredi, have a strange feeling as I turn down the street to Collette's house. The feeling deepens to consternation as I pull to the curb. It couldn't be.

I knock on the door. It's opened by an attractive young Native lady.

"Collette Whiteknife?" I ask.

"Hello Porter Cassel," she says. "I knew you'd be back for more."

It takes a few seconds to recover from the shock. Ever since my fall from grace at the party I've been dreading running into Collette again. I suppose I knew there was a possibility that the Collette Whiteknife mentioned by Helen Mercredi might the same Collette I had sex with but I had put the possibility out of mind, reasoning that there had to be plenty of women with that first name, even in a small community like Chip. Now she's right in front of me, grinning like a fox that's cleaned out the chicken coop. Worst of all, she thinks I'm back for more of the same.

This is going to make it difficult to talk to her.

"Yeah … um … hello. I'm not here to see you. I mean — for that."

"Really?" She bats eyelashes at me. Damn, she is good looking. A perfect disaster.

"Please don't do that."

"What?" she says innocently. "So why are you here?"

"I need to talk to you."

"Hmm. I thought you weren't here to see me. Maybe you're here to see my uncle."

She hollers something over her shoulder in what could be Cree, or Chipewyan, or ancient Greek for all I know. A moment later a shadow falls over her as Cork comes to the door. He sees me and breaks into a big toothy grin.

"Fire Guy," he says. "Your head feeling better?"

"Yeah, fine. Actually, I was just here to see Collette."

"I'll bet you were," he says, his smile widening.

"No, it's … never mind. Collette, have you heard from Bernice Mercredi lately?"

Collette frowns. "No. I heard she went to McMurray, to see the doctor."

"I heard that too. Can I speak with you? Privately."

Collette hesitates, seeing that Cork is still grinning, apparently enjoying the awkward situation. "I gotta go uptown," she says. "Drop some movies. You can give me a ride."

I nod and she vanishes inside to get the movies. I sit in my truck, practise my Zen breathing. It's supposed to calm you down when you're stressed; something Telson taught me. Thinking about Telson creates more tension and I have to breathe harder. By the time Collette appears I'm practically hyperventilating. I need to regain my cool before I get dizzy, crash the truck on the way to the video store. She climbs in, sweeps hair from her face.

"What's the matter with you?" she says. "You look all red."

"Nothing," I squeak.

We drive, not directly to the video store, just randomly around town. I need time to talk to her. She waits, sitting loosely beside me, no seat belt.

"Put on your seat belt."

"Why? If I did, I couldn't do this."

She slides right next to me on the bench seat, lays a warm hand on my inner thigh. I slam on the brakes, nearly putting her into the window. She flops back onto the seat, elbowing me in the solar plexus.

"Holy shit, Porter. You got a full load of powder, or what?"

I glare straight ahead for a moment, grip the steering wheel with both hands, not trusting myself to speak. We're on main street, not far from the store. Customers watch us as they load groceries into their trucks. I take a deep breath, start driving again, staring ahead.

"Move back to the passenger side and put on your seat belt."

She chuckles playfully. "Don't be like that."

"Now."

My tone is glacial. She sniffs, slides over, slowly buckles up.

"So it's like that," she says. "Good for a night, but not good enough for later."

I look sidelong at her as I drive. She's upset, lips pursed, a tear in her eye.

"No," I say, "it's not like that at all. You're a very attractive girl, but I never intended anything to happen. Now I just want us to remain professional."

"Professional?" she says, mouthing the word distastefully.

"I'm here to do a job. Nothing more."

"Well, you sure did a job on me."

I'm thinking it was the other way around. Even so, I know I'm being harsh, but I can't see there being any other way. I need to draw the lines clearly here.

"Bernice Mercredi is missing," I tell her.

"What? What do you mean — missing?"

"Gone. Missing. Her mother brought her to the airport but she never got on the plane. No one knows where she is. That's why I need to talk to you. I know the two of you are close. I'm hoping you know something you're not telling anyone. I'm also hoping you're smart enough not to keep it hidden from me, because I'm investigating a suspicious death and there's a chance your friend Bernice might know something about it. And if she does, her missing is a big deal."

"Suspicious death?" she says. "What are you talking about?"

"That trapper, Hallendry. His death is suspicious."

"Everyone is saying he just got drunk and burned down his cabin."

"Do you know where Bernice Mercredi is, or not?"

There's a long silence. Collette is frowning, thinking hard.

"Okay," she says slowly. "I might know something, but you never heard it from me."

"I think I can manage that."

"You have to promise."

"I can't make that kind of promise. But I'll do my best."

"Well, she's been talking about this guy. Older. Married. I told her she's nuts."

"I need a name."

"I can't do that," she says. "Besides, I don't know. She was so paranoid she never even told me. She was so excited. He was going to set her up with an apartment in McMurray, pay for her to go to school at Keyano College. For now she was just sneaking around with him. I told her it was kinda gross, an older married guy like that."

"I'm an older guy. You went for me."

"Yeah," she smiles. "But you're different. Trust me."

I let that slide, sorry I brought it up. "Where do they meet?"

Collette groans. "She'll kill me if you go there."

"Where, Collette?"

A long sigh. "A cabin up the river. A few miles before the weir on the Roche, to the east on a little tributary. It's an old trapper cabin that no one uses anymore. We used to go there to party, just me and her and a few other girls. Not many people know about it anymore. I'm pretty sure that's where they go."

I have her give me detailed directions, then drive to the video store.

Collette looks back at me through the open truck window.

"Go easy on her," she says. "I think she really loves him."

My next stop is the government boat wharf, just down from the ranger station. I'm supposed to check in at the office if I'm going to borrow the boat but I want to keep this under the radar. I'm not out to expose Collette Whiteknife's affair or cause trouble for anyone — I just want to talk to the girl. The Forest Service boat is a small white aluminum craft with a windshield and console and a seventy-five horsepower Mercury. I check the gas and decide there should be enough — the cabin isn't far from town and I only have a few hours of daylight left. Just enough time to roar out there and ask a few questions, then back for a big cup of tea and a badly needed night of sleep.

I putter out of the tiny bay by the dock, round Monument Point and gun the engine, bringing the boat up on step. Waves slap at the bow as I motor away from town along the lakeshore, pass the red buildings and church of the Catholic mission. There used to be a residential school here which housed Native children, taken from their parents in a forced education and assimilation program. Beyond this is an old conveyor belt and rusted ironworks from some old boat loading facility, long unused. I cruise onto the Roche River where it leaves Lake Athabasca. If you follow this river far enough, it merges with the Peace River to become the Slave, which flows north to the Northwest Territories and eventually the Arctic Ocean.

My voyage will be considerably shorter tonight.

The river flows between massive granite cliffs where peregrine falcons nest. This is my favourite time of day as everything is lit up vividly by slanting evening sunlight. The confluence with a smaller tributary comes into view and I swing right, slow the boat, watching for the markers mentioned by Collette. Another turn down a smaller creek, followed by more meandering bends, and I see a flash of metal.

This must be the place.

Tucked tight under an overhanging hedge of willow is the stern of a small boat. It has a console, no windshield. The way it's tucked under the branches suggests an attempt at concealment and I manoeuvre closer. Nothing in the boat but a bit of fishing tackle scattered on the bottom. The engine cover of the small outboard is still warm. I pull up under a large spruce tree, tie up my boat and scramble onto shore.

There's a grassy clearing and an old grey cabin with a low sod roof. The cabin is built of logs and is tiny, perhaps a dozen feet square. The door, made of grey hewn planks, is closed. A small window has been shuttered with plywood. Despite the boat hidden under the willows, it looks as though no one is here. Perhaps Bernice Mercredi and her lover are inside, hiding, hoping I'll leave. No doubt they would have

heard my boat motor. It makes sense they would come to this location, as it is well hidden but not far from town. They could be peeking
through some crack in the logs, watching me, hoping their secret
won't be revealed. This fits with everything Collette told me — the
location, the need for privacy — but still it seems odd. No smoke
coming from the rusted stovepipe jutting from the roof. No sign of
recent activity in the clearing in front of the cabin.

It could be they're just being careful.

I knock on the door.

The door is heavy, muting my knocks. I knock harder. No answer.
I try the door, half expecting it's locked from the inside. It's not and
swings open to a dark room.

"Hello?"

No response. I peer into the gloom, wait for my eyes to adjust.

An old stove, legs rusted away on one side, sits tilted in the shaft of
light from the door.

There's no one here. I sense as much as hear movement behind me.

As I turn there's a blur coming at my head. I don't raise my arm
quickly enough.

Pain explodes in my temple. A splash of colour and dots.

Blackness.

Pain pulses through my head as my eyes flicker open. Darkness.
Confusion. Nausea. Something coarse against my face. I move my head,
which causes another ripple of pain. Blobs of light and dark resolve
slowly into the dusky outlines of tree trunks and branches. A terrible
stench fills my nostrils; meaty and decaying.

Where the hell am I? Any why?

I squint against the throbbing pain in my head, find my hands
beneath my chest and push up against something rough that shifts
uncertainly. I try to stand, stagger and fall, pick myself up again,
dizzy and reeling. I'm in the forest. It's evening, the light fading. Soon
it will be dark and I have no idea where I am. My mind struggles

unsuccessfully to connect my last memory with my surroundings. Panic threatens and I force myself to breathe slowly and deeply. It helps but the smell causes me to gag. I look down to find the source of the putrid vapours and it occurs to me that the large black shape on which I've been lying is a dead animal.

A rotting carcass. My clothes are smeared with the corpulent juices.

In the coarse grainy light of late evening, the black hide of the dead animal blends with the moulding leaf litter on the forest floor. Judging by the shape of the carcass and the coarseness of the hair, it must be a moose. The chest cavity has been opened and plundered — I can stick my boot inside — and there are chunks of pink showing on the hindquarters. Something has been feeding here. Weak and woozy I lean over, brace one hand on the side of the carcass, force myself to have a closer look.

Claw marks torn into the flesh, wide and deep.

I stand, stumble back, my scalp tingling. I've been lying over a bear kill and I look around, eyes wide, breathing suddenly ragged. When it comes to bears there are four encounters that can be fatal. The first is a surprise encounter in which the bear is startled and attacks defensively. The second is coming between a mother bear and her cubs, in which her maternal instincts trigger an attack. The third is coming between a bear and its food, in which it sees you as a competitor. The fourth is a predatory attack, in which the bear intends to eat you. I'm in more than one category here — I'm standing over the kill, and I smell like food.

But I'm lucky so far — there's no bear in sight.

Heart pounding, I edge away from the dead moose, stumble as my boots encounter the splayed legs. Regaining my balance I hesitate, wonder where to go. The bear could be anywhere. A sliver of moon fills the forest around me with a silvery light. Although tree tops are silhouetted against the night sky, there's barely enough light to see the dead moose at my feet. I could be headed directly for the bear. There's a sudden and distinct snorting sound from the dark not far away. My heart goes into overdrive and I tense, waiting to hear the sound again, to see something darker shift and move in the underbrush.

More snorting and sniffing — the bear catching my scent. I still can't see him but I think he's off to my left. Cautiously, trying to step quietly, to breathe silently, I move right, to put some distance between the bear and I, so I'm less of a threat. Right now I'm standing right over its dinner. I make it two steps when I hear the unmistakable sound of something large moving rapidly through the underbrush, heading in my direction. Willows and rose bushes slap and crack and then I see the bear, huge and dark, catch a glimmer of moonlight in its eye. It's moving fast, headed toward me. I have only seconds to make my decision.

Run or stand my ground?

In bear awareness and defence courses, mandatory for most forest workers, one is instructed that a charging bear is often bluffing and it is best to stand one's ground as running will trigger a predatory response in which the bear will come to believe, since you are running away, that you are something yummy to eat. If you stand your ground, your bowels may loosen embarrassingly, and you may risk cardiac arrest, but the bear will often break off its charge and not attack. If it does attack, one is best served by dropping to the ground and curling into the fetal position with your hands protectively over the back of your neck. Most likely, the bear will take a few bites, but if you remain still, will lose interest and go away. However if a bear is actually charging you because he is hunting and you are food, then you must, by all means, run away. Standing one's ground in this situation will only make it easier for the bear to eat you, as will lying conveniently on the ground, much like the dead moose beside me. So, to sum up, in the first two or so seconds of the charge, you need to determine if the bear looks like it wants to eat you or simply chase you away — a difficult feat in broad daylight with several hundred pounds of muscle and teeth charging straight at you. A bit more difficult in the dark.

I decide that since I'm by his food, and that I smell like his food, that there's a pretty good chance he'll want to eat me or, at the very least, lay a serious beating on me for taking an interest in his supper. So I run. In the dark. This is a risky proposition to start with as it is very likely an unseen branch will jab your eye, causing agonizing pain and blinding you; it's even riskier with a bear chasing you. I try to compensate for the stick-in-the-eye thing by frantically waving a hand in front of me as I run, to sweep aside any potential daggers. This is only partially effective as branches slap my face and arms, scratch my neck. My hope is the bear will only chase me until it reaches the moose carcass, where it will remain to establish ownership.

I'm disappointed — the bear keeps coming, gaining on me.

I crash through a tangle of brush, nearly fall, reach blindly for a handhold, catch a slender aspen and yank myself in another direction. I'm zigzagging through the forest, avoiding trees and nasty brambles that threaten to trip or stop me outright. The bear, judging by the crashing and snapping rapidly approaching on my backside, is taking a more direct route. My shoulder glances off a tree trunk, nearly knocking me over, in the process of which I half-turn and see the bear is nearly upon me, white teeth gleaming in the moonlight. I veer toward a large spruce tree and lunge upward, grab hold of a stout branch, and climb like a terrified squirrel, face slapping and scratching against branches. A dozen yards up I stop, chest heaving, clinging to the tree as though it were a source of nourishment.

A dark shape in the tree below me lunges upward, clawing and scraping the tree trunk. Smaller branches snap. The bear pauses and looks up at me. Clearly it's trying to decide if I'm worth further effort. I holler and curse a bit, knowing it likely won't make any difference but needing to do it anyway. The bear hangs onto the tree a moment longer, a few yards below me, then scrapes down, circles the tree a few times making intimidating whuffing and growling noises, then ambles over the dead moose, where it flops down by the belly cavity.

Wonderful. I'm stuck in a tree in the dark in unknown territory. My Forest Service radio, which had been on my belt, is gone. I yell some more at the bear.

It snorts and trots over, so I shut up.

The bear settles down again at its buffet. It's too dangerous to attempt a get away in the dark so I settle into my tree. I use my belt to strap myself securely to a thick branch in case I fall asleep — no pun intended. Now that I'm secure I have time to think — to wonder why I'm here in the first place. Panic and a throbbing headache have jumbled my thoughts but gradually they clear. I was in the Forest Service boat and found the cabin where Bernice Mercredi and her secret lover were supposed to be hiding. There didn't seem to be anyone in the cabin but there was definitely someone in the vicinity, as they had stashed their boat under the willows along the edge of the river. Most likely they heard my approach and when I didn't pass by they became concerned. I picture some older man taking the lovely Bernice by the hand and leading her out of the cabin, to hide in the forest. Then he circled around, likely hiding just behind the cabin. When I opened the door he clubbed me over the head and dragged me to the moose carcass.

I shift on my perch in the tree. As uncomfortable as the branch on which I'm sitting has become the actions of my unknown assailant make me more uncomfortable. Why not simply fade back into the bush until after I've left? They would have had plenty of time to make their getaway. Instead their actions suggest a level of premeditation. Clearly, by placing my unconscious body across a bear kill, they intended to kill me and have it appear to be an accident. This seems excessive to protect a simple affair. The older man must have a lot to lose. Perhaps there was something incriminating in the cabin. But what would be worth such drastic action to prevent discovery? An affair might include frilly underwear, flowers, perhaps a bottle of wine. Not exactly evidence worth fighting to the death over. I shift again, back aching, and snuggle closer to the tree. What if there was a body in the cabin? Perhaps the older man murdered Bernice Mercredi and I was about to stumble onto the scene of the crime. She might have been pregnant and threatened to expose him. Pregnancy would fit with her leaving the fire because she felt unwell. Gazing down at the vague black shape of the bear I begin to form a plan. Wait for my chance to make a break from the tree, then find the cabin and have a look inside. Then back to town and notify the RCMP.

I shift again to relieve the pressure on my legs. It's going to be a long night.

Dawn begins to creep through the trees when I jolt awake. I've been drifting off a few minutes at a time, dreaming I'm trapped under a pile of logs or in a crashed car, hard edges digging into my body. It's a good thing I've strapped myself to the tree because I wake up doubled over, head drooped onto the crotch of a branch, cheek pressed against the coarse bark. My view downward through branches produces an instant vertigo and instinctively I flail and grab for support, wrapping my arms around the tree trunk. When my breathing returns to normal I look around, discover the moose carcass is unoccupied. The bear is gone.

I release the belt from around the branch and begin painstakingly to descend from my aerial prison. A night spent draped over hard narrow branches has not improved my dexterity. Dizzy with hunger and thirst, I fumble, slide painfully against rough bark. The last branch seems higher off the ground than I remember and I drop hard, pain shooting up my stiff legs.

"Ouch."

Something rustles in the brush and I freeze, heart thumping. Turns out it's just a mouse. No sign of my furry companion. I'm tempted to investigate the moose carcass to see if my human assailant left any clues, but I don't want to risk encountering the bear again. In my present condition I doubt I could make it back up a tree. Instead I work my way through the forest away from the carcass, hear the telltale gurgles of moving water, see a glimmer through the trees. A river. I doubt my assailant would have moved my heavy unconscious body far from the cabin.

I'll follow the river, find the cabin. With any luck, my boat is still there.

Two hours later I'm hot, sweaty and exhausted, struggling through dense willow and alder along the river. I've gone in both directions and have seen no sign of the cabin or my boat. In fact, nothing here looks familiar. I've encountered low boggy areas and swampy creeks that required detour and, although I was lost to begin with, now I'm more lost. My assailant could easily have dumped me into his boat and taken me a great distance from the cabin in a fairly short period of time. I could be anywhere and struggle to suppress a natural urge to panic.

Think logically, Cassel.

I find a comfortable spot along the river and sit down, lean against a tree. The key in survival situations is to keep your wits and not to expend valuable energy reserves. I have fresh water to drink and can last weeks if I really have to. I close my eyes for a minute and begin to drift into the warm fog of sleep. Instantly I'm dreaming. A boat is coming to my rescue.

My eyes snap open — it's not a dream. The roar of an outboard motor approaches.

It occurs to me that it could be my attacker, returning to ensure the bear finished the job, and I step back among the dense sheltering foliage of willow and alder. Downstream the boat comes into view and I focus to discern features on the two hunched passengers. I have no idea what my attacker looks like. Then I notice the boat is different — no console. I step out from the bushes and wave at the passing boat. The driver peers in my direction, then waves back and turns to shore. It's a grey-haired couple, out for an afternoon putter. I ask if they'd mind my hitching a ride to town. They nod, smiling. Despite the oddness of the situation and the reek of my clothing, they don't ask questions. I have them drop me at the government wharf, where my truck sits, head straight to the IA base, where I feed the dog, who's frantic for food and attention, poor thing, shower, and toss my disgusting clothes into the wash machine. I put on clean clothes, head to the kitchen trailer, where I have a large cup of Dr. Cho's nerve tea. It hits me hard.

I fall asleep at the table.

The cook wakes me, coming in to start supper. I've slept nearly three hours, my head on the hard wooden table. Seeing the time — just past three in the afternoon — I rush to the washroom, splash cold water on my face. There's a flat red spot on my forehead where I can see the grain of the table imprinted in negative. The black eye from the fight in McMurray is curing up nicely. My face and neck are scratched from my run through the dark woods. I look like a zombie from *Night of the Living Dead*.

To compensate, I comb my hair. Now I look like a tidy zombie.

I pop a few Advil and head to the RCMP station, meet Corporal MacFarlane as he's leaving the detachment office. He stops, watches, as I ease the truck over to where he's standing. He's wearing a worn leather jacket, green cargo pants and black combat boots. He gives me an inquisitive frown as I roll down the window.

"Cassel — what have you been up to? You look like crap."

"That would be an upgrade. Someone tried to kill me last night."

MacFarlane's eyes narrow. "What happened?"

I tell him about checking the airport for Bernice Mercredi, and my subsequent discussion with Collette Whiteknife. Finding the cabin and regaining consciousness draped over a dead moose, followed by a night spent in a tree. My theory about why I was assaulted and left as bear bait. MacFarlane digests it all without interrupting. When I'm done he smoothes down the prow of his hair, looks thoughtful.

"You can find this cabin again?"

"No problem. I'd like to use one of our helicopters, fly out there."

MacFarlane considers. "Stay right here."

He vanishes into the detachment building for a few minutes, emerges with Waldren. Both Mounties squeeze into the truck with me and we head for the IA base. On the way I call Middel on the truck radio, ask him if I can use one of the machines for a quick flight along the river north of town. His response is terse.

"What for, Cassel?"

"I need to look for something."

"Can you take the boat?"

"That's one of the things I need to look for."

"Maybe you should come see me first."

"I have the RCMP with me and we need to get going."

"Okay. Take TRT. But come see me right after."

I acknowledge and moments later we're at the IA base, then lifting off and heading north. I'm in the front seat; the two Mounties in back. I tell the pilot to follow the river and all four of us watch for the cabin. It doesn't take long to find it from the air. We do a wide circle, looking down. No boats are visible. There's enough of a clearing in front of the cabin for the small helicopter to land and at our request the pilot takes it down. As we land, MacFarlane's voice comes through my headset.

"You stay here, Cassel. Keep the meter running. Waldren and I will check it out."

I wait as the Mounties disembark, run in a crouch below the whirring rotor and approach the cabin. Waldren pulls his gun and flashlight and they position themselves on either side of the cabin door. At a nod from MacFarlane, Waldren goes in, gun ready. A few seconds later MacFarlane follows. A moment later they come back out. Waldren's gun is holstered. They confer, then walk back to the helicopter. I was expecting they would signal the all clear so I could take a look, but they climb in behind me, don their headsets.

"What?" I ask, as soon as I know they're online.

"Nothing," says MacFarlane. "Rat shit and cobwebs."

"There was nothing there at all?"

"Zip," says Waldren. "No one's used that place for years."

I frown, thinking. MacFarlane asks if there's anything else I'd like to look at.

"The moose kill," I tell them. "And I'd like to find my boat."

The helicopter rises from the clearing, follows the small river. We cruise at about a thousand feet. I'm certain I can find the moose kill but after a few passes along the river I have to concede defeat. The kill was under the forest canopy, and by the time I was picked up by the old couple in the boat I had no idea where I was relative to the kill. Nothing below us looks familiar.

"What now?" says MacFarlane.

"Let's swing north along the Roche, see if we can find my boat."

If my assailant cut loose my boat, it would float north with the current. We fly for another ten minutes, following the lazy meanders of the river. A moose standing on a sandbar seems oblivious as we pass overhead. In the distance it appears the river is blocked by an over-sized beaver dam. As we draw closer, it becomes apparent the dam is manmade.

"What's that thing across the river?"

"That's the weir," says Waldren. "The river can flow both ways."

"How can it do that?"

"Depends on the water level in the delta."

Today the river flows visibly north. Something white bobs next to the weir.

MacFarlane peers over my shoulder. "Is that your boat?"

As we approach I recognize the Forest Service boat. Good thing there was a weir or the boat would have floated all the way to Fort Fitzgerald, where it would have been ground up by the twenty-five miles of rapids between there and Fort Smith. The helicopter touches down on the narrow weir, where the Mounties and I get out, then departs for a superior landing site where it can shut down and await our signal. It gets very quiet as we walk along the narrow weir.

"An itsy-bitsy spider went down the water spout," sings Waldren.

On one end of the dam is a winch with a boat cradle and short stretch of rail to allow boats to pass over. It's against this cradle that the Forest Service boat has drifted, scratching up the side. Middel will not be pleased. I stand on my toes on the edge of the track, manage to reach the boat and pull it close enough to climb aboard.

"Anything unusual?" says MacFarlane.

I do a quick inventory. "Looks fine."

Waldren uses a stick to fish the bow rope from the water, holds up the end.

"Wasn't cut," he says.

"Whoever jumped me could have just untied it."

"Or it wasn't properly tied to start with," he says.

"No — I tied it securely. I didn't want to get stranded."

Waldren looks at MacFarlane. Something subtle passes between them.

"What?" I say.

"Nothing," says Waldren. "Can you take the boat back?"

I check for gas, start the motor.

It runs as though nothing unusual happened.

Waldren and MacFarlane take the helicopter back, leaving me with the boat and my thoughts. I get the impression that the Mounties have become skeptical of my story. I can work alone, but it's far better to have the RCMP on my side. I brood as I ride the boat back up river, motor roaring, wind ruffling my hair. It bothers me that there was no sign the cabin had been used. Why would someone be out here, waiting for me, unless it was a trap? This would mean I'm making someone nervous enough to try to take me out. It would also mean that Collette Whiteknife is part of whatever is going on.

Ahead on the left bank of the river, a large spruce tree juts horizontally over the flowing water, it's tip curved upward, still growing as it surrenders to gravity and the collapsing river bank. Branches along the length of the trunk reach like a green wall into the water, creating what canoeists call a sweeper — a dangerous obstacle that can entangle a boater and hold them in the water against the current. As I pass I notice something floating, caught against the branches. A rag or some bit of debris. Something about the way the rag is floating, the sway and tremble of the branches that have caught it, suggests there may be more density to the debris than mere cloth and I slow the boat, allow the current to tack me closer.

A mass of dark fur — a dead animal.

Not fur. Hair.

The wake coming from my boat rocks the floating debris and I see the curve of a head, the whiteness of scalp beneath the black hair, the edge of an ear. Dear God — this is a person. My first reaction is to panic that the person is drowning and I have only a moment to turn them over, but this quickly fades, replaced by horror and revulsion. It's far too late for a rescue. This will be a body retrieval. I reach for my radio, to call dispatch and the RCMP, remember I lost my radio the night before, or my assailant stole it. I hold the boat under low power in the current next to the end of the sweeper, wonder what to do. It would be tricky and dangerous to get in front of the sweeper as I can't control the boat and retrieve the body at the same time. I could leave the body where it is and return for help but the body might slip loose, sink into the river and be lost. I owe it to whoever that is to at least try to bring them in.

I manoeuvre the boat to the downstream side of the sweeper, opposite the body, and use a hatchet to chop away troublesome branches so I can tie the bow rope to the trunk of the tree. Chopped branches float away in the brown water. Once the boat is secure, I lay belly-down on the narrow covered bow and reach more rope through the screen of branches, feeling in the cold water for the body. Branches press against my face, needles prickling against my cheek. I grab what I think is an upper arm, cold and firm, and shudder. With my other hand, careful not to fall forward into the river, I tie the rope around the dead arm, then scramble back, breathing hard, as the boat rocks. I take a moment to allow the boat to settle, as well as my nerves, then whack off more branches so the body can pass through the sweeper and under the tree. With the body loose, I pull it alongside the boat and turn it over.

Bernice Mercredi's pale dead face stares vacantly at me from the cold water.

"Damn," I swear softly, thinking of her mother's pleading look.

*Thanks for doing this. For looking for my Bernie.*

I push the thought aside, focus on the business at hand. The body is stiff and awkward, the weight causing the boat to lean and rock dangerously. I give up trying to pull her in over the side, float the body to the back of the boat, tug her up over the stern, past the outboard motor. The cuff of her jeans catches on the propeller and it takes an awkward moment of leaning over the warm shroud of the motor, intimate with the musty organic stench of her river-soaked clothes, to free her. She tumbles into the boat, arms flopping, head thumping on the bottom of the boat. "Sorry," I mumble.

Her position, so unnatural, drives home the situation.

I prop her against the side of the boat, brush long black hair away from her face. It's hard to accept this is the same girl who was at the fire, serving up platters of sandwich meat, smiling shyly at my recycled joke. She was so young and full of life. Now her eyes are cloudy, skin pale, lips parted and slightly blue. I suppress a boil of emotion and focus on a closer examination, looking for any indication of how she came to be in the river. The coroner will conduct an autopsy, but I'm here now and I want to ensure I note anything unusual. I do a basic first-aid body examination to feel for injuries, run my hands over her head and neck, then down her arms, legs and torso, check for physical injuries such as broken bones or the bulges and swellings of pre-mortem trauma. I find nothing unusual. A quick look at her hands and fingernails for evidence of a defensive struggle reveals skin that is pale, wrinkled and slightly bloated, as though she were washing dishes for a long time, but nothing more.

I look up river, lined on both sides with dense forest. What would a young, fully clothed woman be doing floating in the river? Did she really have a secret lover? Was he simply tired of her and tossed her into the icy water? Or would he have to hold her under while she struggled for air, wondering how her lover could have suddenly turned so cruelly against her? Or is this about something altogether different? I look again at Bernice Mercredi, lifeless in the bottom of my boat, and sigh. I have no answers for her.

The trip to town seems inordinately long. The corpse behind me in the boat causes a prickling on the back of my neck as I steer upriver. I look over my shoulder sporadically, to remind myself this really is happening and isn't a morbid product of my imagination. Close to the lake I kill the engine and allow the boat to be taken slowly and silently by the river as I rummage under the covered bow. I don't want to tie up at the dock with an exposed body in my boat, or to leave her like that while I dash to the ranger station to call the RCMP. Fortunately, there's a small blue plastic tarp and some rope, which I use to wrap Bernice Mercredi in a makeshift body bag. When I'm done, it's hard to tell that it's a body in my boat and I putter toward the government wharf, not looking forward to breaking the news to the community. Luke Middel stands at the end of the dock, fishing rod in hand.

"Hiya, Porter," he says, casting in my direction.

"Put that thing away," I tell him as the lure splashes close to the boat.

He frowns, reeling in, then helps tie the boat up at the dock, gazing curiously at the blue package in the bottom. "You get a monster lake trout?"

"Go get your dad, Luke. And tell him to bring the RCMP."

Luke stands uncertainly on the dock, gazing into the boat.

"Now, dammit."

He looks at me, startled, then turns and runs down the dock, boots clomping. I stand on the dock, gaze across the lake. In the past few days life seems to have become tenuous and unpredictable. I shift my gaze to a hump of rock, focus on the stone pillar of the historical monument that marks the original location of the trading post. I want to look anywhere but back into the boat; want to think about anything but what lies ahead. My thoughts are broken by the gun of an engine, the crunch of gravel under tires, and the patter of more boots on the dock.

"What's going on?" says Middel, striding toward me.

Luke runs to catch up with him, joining Waldren and MacFarlane.

"What's the big emergency?" says Waldren.

"I found something," I say, pointing into the boat.

MacFarlane frowns. "Is that what I think it is?"

"You may not want to open it here."

"Good call," says MacFarlane, looking around. On the high rock next to the harbour several kids watch the action on the dock. "We'll take it to the station, in the garage, call ident." He looks at Waldren. "Pull the Suburban as close as you can. Porter, give me a hand when the truck is ready."

"What's going on?" asks Luke.

"Go home," says Middel.

Luke wanders reluctantly down the wharf, glancing over his shoulder. Waldren pulls the RCMP Suburban tight against the edge of the road while MacFarlane and I step into the boat. Even soaking wet, the bundle seems light between the two of us and I wonder fleetingly why it seemed so hard to lift her into the boat. MacFarlane crouches in the open back of the Suburban and we set her down, the blue tarp crinkling. He steps out, closes the back doors.

"You're with us, Porter."

I sit in the back seat of the Suburban, where prisoners are transported, watch the two Mounties in front of me through the black steel mesh as we turn away from the harbour, pass the ranger station. Mark Middel and his son stand by the side of the road, their expressions questioning, and watch us pass. The Mounties have their own questions as we drive.

"Who is it?" says MacFarlane.

"Bernice Mercredi."

"Jesus," says Waldren. "Where did you find her?"

"A few miles upstream of the weir, caught in a sweeper."

MacFarlane shifts to look back at me. "Why'd you move her?"

"I thought we might lose her."

We pull into the RCMP compound, past the faded blue staff houses, to the back where MacFarlane opens the bay door of a metal-clad garage. Waldren backs the Suburban in, closes the door. The garage is windowless and it's suddenly dim as our eyes adjust to the weaker artificial light. The two Mounties open the back doors of the Suburban.

"Where do you want to put her?" asks Waldren.

MacFarlane looks around, points to some folding wooden tables tucked next to a shelf. We set them up and the Mounties lift the package from the back of the Suburban, lay it across the tables. MacFarlane carefully unwraps the bundle until Bernice Mercredi lays exposed, face up, the tarp trailing to the floor around her.

"Christ almighty," says Waldren. He's sweating profusely.

"You go call HQ," says MacFarlane. "Fill them in. Request ident."

Waldren hesitates, staring at the dead woman, then leaves. MacFarlane takes off his leather jacket, walks around the body on the table, looking but not touching. "So, Cassel," he says, not taking his eyes from the body, "tell me this theory of yours again."

"Like I told you at the briefing yesterday, this girl was the cook's helper at the fire where Hallendry died. She left the same night I discovered the under-burned floorboards, complaining that she felt ill. My first thought was that she had casually mentioned to someone that I'd found the floorboards, and what that meant, and word travelled to Hallendry's killer, who returned during the night and disposed of the evidence by lighting up what remained of the floorboards. He also must have gone to the IA base and accessed my camera, in my kit in the truck, and deleted my photos of the floorboards. Now I have to wonder if maybe she had a more direct role. Maybe she left the fire specifically to tell someone that I had found evidence that the fire was deliberately set."

"Why would she do that?" says MacFarlane, peering in the dead girl's open mouth.

"I don't know," I say, rubbing the back of my head, still sore from being clobbered the night before. "Maybe she knew whoever started the fire. Maybe she was at the cabin the night Hallendry died, drinking with him. You should check her prints against any you find on those drinking glasses. In fact, you should also check them against Collette Whiteknife."

"You think she's involved?" MacFarlane says, looking at me sharply.

"She told me where to look for Mercredi. Then I was attacked."

MacFarlane stands up from his bent position over the body, thinking. Water seeps off the dead girl's clothes, running across the blue tarp and dribbling onto the floor. In the enclosed space the faint odour coming from the body is stronger. Musky and aquatic. "You think both girls were at Hallendry's cabin?" says MacFarlane.

"It's the only connection I can think of."

"Interesting," he says, scratching his chin.

"How long do you think she's been in the water?"

"It's hard to tell in rivers this far north, especially at this time of year. Water is so cold. Based on the degree of wrinkling on the extremities and the odour, I'd guess two or three days. Coroner will have a better estimate."

"She was dead before I started looking for her."

"About that," says MacFarlane. "You could have come to us first."

"It was just a hunch."

MacFarlane sighs. "Communication is a wonderful thing, Cassel."

There's an awkward silence. We're faced off across Bernice Mercredi's dead body. Fortunately, Waldren comes in, breaks the silence. "HQ are briefed in McMurray. Ident is on the way, ETA about an hour," he says a little breathlessly. "They also wanted to know if you need more resources."

MacFarlane nods, eyes resting on me a moment longer. I get the impression he's sizing me up, assessing how he might handle me. It makes me nervous. He shifts his attention to Waldren, asks him a few questions involving people in the RCMP I do not know. Then he looks at me again, his expression guarded.

"What are you going to do now, Cassel?"

"I'm not sure. I'd like to talk to Collette Whiteknife."

"We'll take care of that. I've got a few questions for her."

"Can I sit in on that interview?"

Waldren and MacFarlane exchange glances.

"We'll let you know," says MacFarlane.

It seems they're done with me, so I excuse myself. MacFarlane stops me at the door of the garage, calling out from where he stands by the body. "Just one more thing, Cassel, so there's no misunderstanding. You stay in town or you tell us before you go anywhere. And you discuss any potential lines of investigation that may affect what the rest of the team is doing before you take action. Are we clear on that?"

I nod, glancing one last time at the dead girl I barely knew.

# 9

AFTER I LEAVE the RCMP compound I'm not sure what to do and drive to the government dock, sit in my truck for a few minutes and watch the lake. Small humped islands covered with trees look like something from a postcard. The undulating water looks serene and indifferent. I could use a bit of calm — Bernice Mercredi is dead and I don't know why. I'd like to talk with her mother and find out if Bernice had been acting strange lately — if she'd made any comments to her mother before heading to the Whiskey Creek fire. What she told her mother when she arrived home the next night. I'd have to clear it with MacFarlane, who still has to break the news to her of her daughter's death. I'd also like to corner Collette Whiteknife and ask her a few pointed questions about why she sent me to the tiny cabin along the river, but that too is out of bounds.

The truck radio barks, startling me. "Cassel, do you read?"

It's Middel. He must have seen me drive past the ranger station.

Reluctantly, I key the mic: "Cassel here, go ahead."

"Can you come to the station? We need to talk."

I confirm, spend another minute gazing at the lake, composing myself, then drive to the ranger station. Middel ushers me into his office, closes the door, waits for me to take a seat. When he's behind his desk he tents his fingers together, gives me a penetrating look.

"What's going on, Cassel? You haven't exactly been keeping me up-to-date."

"I realize that, Mark, but I'm not sure that I can."

Middel frowns. "What do you mean?"

"The RCMP are involved now. I'm on a joint forces operation with them."

"Does that mean you can't keep me updated?"

I shift uncomfortably in my seat. "Well, yes and no. It's sort of complicated. The Mounties are involved in both the Whiskey Creek fire and the bottle fires, now that there's been property damage. There seems to be some evidence that Rufus Hallendry was murdered, and now Bernice Mercredi is dead. That was her in the boat."

Middel stiffens. "You're kidding."

"Unfortunately, no."

He looks around his office as though the faded posters and printed emails on the walls might provide some guidance before his eyes settle on me again. "Jesus Christ, the Cree Band are going to go crazy."

"The Cree Band?"

"They're going to think this is all about them," he says, leaning over his desk. I'm not sure why he's so worried about what the Cree Band might think, considering we have two potential homicides. Perhaps he's been so focused on responding to the Band's pressure that he hasn't quite made the jump yet. "Can you tell me anything?" he says.

"I'm not sure. I'm not really sure what I can do anymore."

Middel reaches for the phone. "I'll call the RCMP. You work for me, after all."

"True, but they're a little busy just now."

Middel's hand falters. He slumps back in his chair, nodding.

"I have to get going, Mark."

He waves me vaguely out of his office and I leave him sitting at his desk, dazed and confused. I feel a bit sorry for him. Louise, the receptionist, asks me if everything is okay, her expression concerned. I'm not sure what to say, just nod to her and rush out. Back in my truck, I drive uptown, craving the freedom of the open road to salve my troubled thoughts. I drive as far as I can through town, then turn and double back, stop at the Northern Store. The side of the building where the offending graffiti had been tagged is shiny with fresh brown paint. I go inside, needing some quick energy, grab a handful of chocolate bars and a bottle of milk. The girl at the checkout is young and Native, looks bored.

"Hey," she says. "What happened to your face?"

"Haven't you heard? Bruises are the new chic."

"Yeah, right." She gives me an appraising look. "You're that cute fire guy."

"No, I'm the crotchety fire guy old enough to be your dad."

"That's not what Collette told me," she giggles.

Damn — everyone in town must know. I take my bag of goodies, ready to flee from the store, when a poster on a bulletin board by the door catches my eye. The poster advertises a candidate forum for the Cree Band elections. Four names are listed to run against the incumbent Chief. Three of the names I don't recognize, but one I do — Simon Cardinal — and I hold my bag of groceries while my stomach rumbles, wondering why that particular name bothers me on the poster. Simon Cardinal has been aggressive and annoying, but there's something more. Then it comes to me — Simon Cardinal was the first person outside the Forest Service or the RCMP to mention the FTC inscriptions on the bottles and I'd like to know where he heard about it.

"Hey, Blondie," calls the clerk. "What you doing tonight?"

"Politics," I call over my shoulder as I go through the door.

The forum starts in an hour and a half, and I intend to be there.

I head to the IA base for a real supper, take Scorch for a walk and arrive late for the candidates' forum, slip into the school gym unnoticed. At the far end of the gym, several folding tables have been set up at which sit the candidates for Chief of the Cree Band. Sammy Cardinal, the current Chief, sits in the centre, flanked on either side by two challengers. He looks regal tonight in a beaded and fringed buckskin jacket. One challenger on his left is a much younger man with a leather jacket of a more recent era, his hair brush-cut short. Beside him is a thick middle-aged Native wearing a denim jacket. On Sammy's right is a man in a bright red plaid shirt. Next to him sits Simon Cardinal, familiar with his long double braids and his own distinctive buckskin coat. The gym is a sea of Natives, crammed together on plastic folding chairs and standing several rows deep along the walls. Up here, the band election is a big deal.

I squeeze in next to a big Native who seems to have created a bit of an eddy in the crowd. He turns to look at me, seems surprised to see a white face. I smile and nod, hope there wasn't a membership requirement to attend. I picture the big guy picking me up like luggage and tossing me through the double doors. Fortunately, he turns his attention back to the speakers.

They're talking about their lack of a band constitution.

"I agree we need this constitution to lay out the powers of chief and council," says the speaker in the denim jacket. "This would be the first thing I would work on."

"Another first thing?" says Simon Cardinal. "That's three so far."

There's a ripple of laughter from the crowd. Simon is a bit of a showman.

A woman seated in the crowd calls out: "What about that tribal council?"

There's murmur of discussion. Chief Sammy Cardinal holds up a hand for silence and the murmurs fade away. Sammy has presence. "As you all know," he says clearly, "this is something I have been working on for some time now — a coalition of bands to tackle the bigger issues. This is why I decided to run again. I want to see this through."

"How can we trust the other bands?" hollers a young Native not far from where I'm standing along the wall. I lean forward to get a better look at him. He's from the group that I encountered by the graffiti on the Northern Store — the fellow with the baseball bat. He doesn't have the bat with him tonight, but his expression is the same. "Someone out there is after the Band," he says. "And I'm sure as shit not joining up with them."

There's a thunder of discussion and shouting. Chief Cardinal looks dismayed, but lets it go for a few minutes before he raises his hand. It takes longer this time for the ruckus to die down. "Please," he says, "let's not let the actions of one diminish what we are trying to do here."

"How do we know it's only one?" says Simon Cardinal.

The Chief smiles patiently. "We have no idea who has been doing these things," he says. "It could be one person, or several, but we must not let it distract us."

"Bullshit," someone yells. "This isn't just a distraction. It's an attack."

"It *is* a distraction," says Chief Cardinal. "I should know — I lost my new truck. But still, it is a distraction. We have issues much larger than a few burned trees, a bit of graffiti, or a burned truck. We have social issues. Alcoholism. Domestic violence. Unemployment. Our young people leave because they can't find jobs. Or they stay and get into trouble. We have health care issues. We need our own hospital. We need to understand what those big mines upstream are putting in our water. We need to develop our tourism industry. We need to market our crafts so the elders can sell what they make and get a decent price."

"We can do all that ourselves," says Simon Cardinal. "The Cree Band for the Cree Band."

There's a burst of applause from some of the crowd. The Chief lets it pass.

"No, we can't," he says firmly to the crowd. "These are bigger issues."

"We've done fine so far," counters Simon. "We own the fuel company. The airline. The barge. The store. Part of a hotel in Fort Mac. The Cree Band is doing just fine. If we join up with the other bands, they will just pull us down. They don't have the resources like we do. What will they bring to the table?"

"Their voice," says the Chief. "So we can all be heard together."

Simon waves this thought off as though it were a pesky fly. A grey-haired lady has been hovering near the table and when the Chief pauses she darts behind him, tapping him on the shoulder and whispering something into his ear. He straightens in his chair, his expression hardening. He thanks the woman, takes her hand for a second, then turns to the crowd and holds up a hand to quiet the buzz of conversation that has sprung up.

"Friends, neighbours, Band members, I have just received terrible news. Bernice Mercredi has died. We're not sure of the details, but I am greatly saddened at the death of one of our young people. Out of respect for Bernice and her family, let us halt the night's proceedings immediately and reschedule. Let's go to the Mercredi family and give them our support."

For a moment there's a stunned silence, then chairs scrape as everyone stands. I'm swept outside, decide against questioning Simon Cardinal tonight. I work my way through the crowd to my truck. Daylight has faded. The lake is dark and slick.

I roll quietly out of town, window open, lost in thoughts of mortality.

I'm pulling through the open gate of the IA base when my truck radio bursts to life. It's MacFarlane, on a Forest Service frequency — he must have acquired one of our radios as part of our interagency co-operation. Come to the detachment immediately. Someone will meet me at the door. I make a U-turn, headlights sweeping over the sleeping helicopters, and head back to town, wondering if they already have a lead on what happened to Bernice Mercredi. Several vehicles are parked in front of the faded blue detachment building. Waldren is waiting, directs me to park next to the line of vehicles.

"What's going on?" I ask as I close the door of my truck.

"Inside," says Waldren, gesturing to the building.

He leads me past the counter with the bullet-proof glass. This late, the receptionist isn't working, but there are plenty of people in the small building. Several older men with severely short hair lean over a table, stop talking as I'm led past. Waldren takes me to a vacant cubicle near a hallway, points at a chair, tells me to sit. I feel a bit like a dog, but I obey. He vanishes down the hall, returns a moment later with MacFarlane, who's wearing faded jeans, a plaid shirt, and sneakers. Despite his amiable appearance he wastes no time getting down to business.

"We've got Collette Whiteknife under surveillance. We're going to bring her in."

"Are you charging her?"

"What for?" says MacFarlane. "We're just going to talk to her."

"Good. I have a few questions of my own."

"Negative, Cassel. We can't let you participate."

"Why not?"

"Against procedure."

"Then why'd you call me?"

"I want you to sit right here, look like you're waiting. I'm going to bring Whiteknife in here, right past you. I'm not sure why she sent you to that cabin, but I want her to see you so I can observe her reaction, see if she's surprised you're still around."

I nod — I'm looking forward to her reaction as well.

"Once we've got her in," says MacFarlane, "we'll allow you to observe. We've got video and there's a monitor in the next room. Waldren will set you up. For now, just sit here and wait. Don't say anything to Whiteknife when she comes past."

I nod again and MacFarlane pulls a radio off his belt. "Bring her in."

Then he's gone and I'm left to wait in the cubicle. It's clear from the empty desk and bare walls that the cubicle was cleaned out, no doubt so there wouldn't be anything confidential laying around for my reading pleasure. I twiddle my thumbs, tense, wondering about Collette and how she fits with what's been going on here. It occurs to me that she may tell them about our encounter at the party and I get an unpleasant feeling in my gut.

A door opens in the direction of the reception counter. Voices.

"Right this way."

Suddenly she's there, walking beside Constable Markham, who's gently guiding her by an elbow. She's wearing a loose shirt which hangs to one side to reveal a shoulder. Her long black hair is pulled back except for a few strands, which frame the strong pleasant features of her face. She smiles at me, apparently pleased to see someone she knows.

"Hi Porter."

She gives me a little wave and a wink, then she's gone and I'm left sweating and conflicted. She didn't seem at all surprised to see me, which suggests that she had no idea what was going to happen at the cabin, or she's a good actress. I have difficulty believing she had a conscious hand in my attempted murder, but something still doesn't seem right. I hear a door close down the hall, and then Waldren comes to get me, leads me into a small room.

"Take a seat," he says. "Enjoy the show."

The room looks like it used to be a closet. There's nothing here but a small metal desk and two chairs. On the wall is mounted a flat-screen monitor, with a wire running to the ceiling. On the monitor Collette Whiteknife sits at the end of a table. All I can see of MacFarlane is a worn sneaker, a sock, and the hem of his jeans. I turn up the audio, take a seat.

MacFarlane's voice is a bit muffled.

"Can I get you something to drink? Coffee or a pop?"

Collette smiles shyly. "No, I'm fine, thanks."

"Do you know why you're here?"

"Not really." She brushes a strand of hair aside, tucks it behind an ear.

"I'm sure you've heard by now that Bernice Mercredi has passed away."

Collette's expression hardens subtly. Cheek muscles clench and lips purse.

"We're just doing some background research," MacFarlane says mildly. "Talking to young people in the community. Just routine. Did you know Bernice?"

"Yeah. Of course. We went to school together."

"Grew up together, I'd imagine," MacFarlane says casually.

"You could say so. It's a small community."

"Sure is," MacFarlane says with a chuckle. "When I flew in I thought 'what a picturesque little place,' the houses sitting on the pink and grey granite. Can you tell me a little about the community? What it's like growing up here?"

Collette twists in her seat like a child who has been asked a question they don't know how to answer. Although she's certainly no child, it drives home just how young Collette really is, and how naive, growing up in such an isolated community. I wince, thinking again about the party.

"It might look pretty from the air," she tells MacFarlane, "but it's kind of a boring place to grow up. Not much to do here. Mostly, we watch a lot of TV. Hang out. Bug our parents to take us to McMurray for shopping and stuff."

"What do you do for excitement?"

"Not much excitement here. Race skidoos and boats. Water ski sometimes."

"And a little partying too, I'll bet," says MacFarlane, dropping his tone conspiratorially.

Collette shrugs. "I guess."

I tense, hold my breath, certain she'll mention the party where she took me. From there, it'll only get worse.

"Hey, I used to be a kid too, you know. Not a crime to have a good time."

Collette nods slightly. "Yeah, we let loose every once in a while."

MacFarlane is doing a great job of putting Collette Whiteknife at ease, getting her to loosen up and talk. The subtle art of interrogation. I've been on the other end a few times and I can appreciate a master when I see one.

"You and Bernice party together much?"

"Yeah, sometimes. Why?"

"No reason," MacFarlane says easily. "I just thought she might have talked to you, you know, about how things are going. I have three daughters myself, a few years younger than you, and I know how girls talk. Boy problems. Gossip. Stuff like that. Did Bernice ever talk about that stuff?"

Collette hesitates, as though pondering what she can tell him.

"We're just doing background," MacFarlane assures her.

"Background?"

"Just trying to determine her state of mind these past few days."

Collette frowns. "You think Bernie killed herself?"

"It's a possibility," says MacFarlane. "What do you think?"

"I don't know. She did get depressed sometimes."

"What about?"

Another shrug. "Just stuff."

"Did she become depressed often?"

"Every once in a while," says Collette, smoothing her hands on her jeans.

"What about lately? Like the last week or so? Anything set her off?"

Collette looks thoughtful. "Now that you mention it, she did seem a bit down."

"Just a bit? When would this have been?"

Collette twists in her chair again. "I don't know."

"What about after she got off the fire? How was she then?"

Collette's eyes flick sideways, which I've noticed happens when people are getting creative. She shakes her head. "I didn't see her after the fire."

There's a silence, during which I presume MacFarlane is taking notes, or pretending to. Silence can be an effective tactic — a void which creates discomfort in nervous people. I watch Collette watch MacFarlane. She's sitting perfectly still, like a hunted mouse waiting for the shadow of a hawk to pass. MacFarlane clears his throat. "So the last time you saw her was the night before the fire, at the party."

"What?"

"The party at the cabin," MacFarlane says, as though they had already discussed this.

"I don't know what party you're talking about."

"Oh, you know," he says, like she's playing an amusing game.

Collette tilts her head. "I'd think if I was at a party I'd remember it."

"Yeah, you'd think so," MacFarlane says softly. "But sometimes people don't. I know that's happened to me on occasion. Pretty embarrassing." He leans forward and I get a good view of his receding hairline. When he sits back there's something on the table beside Collette's elbow. It's the glass tumbler I found in the ditch, in a clear plastic evidence bag. "But you were there, Collette," he says. "At Rufus Hallendry's cabin. Your fingerprints are on this glass."

Collette's expression freezes as she looks down at the tumbler.

MacFarlane says: "You know who else's fingerprints are on this glass?"

Collette swallows, shakes her head.

"Bernice Mercredi's fingerprints. Isn't that interesting?"

There's a long silence. Emotions struggle subtly in the muscles of her face as Collette tries to keep her expression neutral. I wonder where MacFarlane got her prints for comparison, or if he's just testing her. Her chin begins to quiver and she reaches up, covers her face with her hands, lets out a single stifled sob.

"Just tell me what happened," MacFarlane says gently.

"No," she says through her hands, voice choked. "It's too embarrassing."

"What's so embarrassing? Getting drunk and not remembering?"

"No." Collette shakes her head, hands still covering her face.

MacFarlane waits. After a few moments, Collette drops her hands.

"I didn't know he would do that," she says, voice trembling.

The back of MacFarlane's head shows as he leans forward. "Who did what?"

Collette stares at the floor, teary and vacant.

"Who did what?" MacFarlane says, harsher.

"Raped us," she shouts suddenly. "He raped us, okay."

I recoil at the intensity of her response. Collette's hands are over her face again and she's sobbing uncontrollably. I think MacFarlane will go to her, comfort her — I want to go to her — but he sits back and waits until the storm subsides. When she's done and drops her hands, he offers her a tissue.

"You okay?"

She takes the tissue. "How can I be okay?"

"Tell me what happened, Collette."

It takes her a moment to collect herself, then she sniffs, stares at the floor, talking quietly.

"We were drinking at the Trapline, Bernie and me, and he was there."

"Rufus Hallendry?"

"Yeah. We were all having a pretty good time, then Bernie starts to get stupid sad, like she does sometimes when she's had a lot to drink, and we decide to call it a night. We're walking home when he pulls up beside us, offers us a ride. We know the guy, right, so we say sure. Then Bernie says she's feeling better and we should go back to the bar. He says why not go make a fire, have a bush party, watch the stars. He's got off-sales. Sounds like a cool idea. When we get to his cabin there's no one else there. They're coming, he says. We go inside and he starts his stove and we do a few hot knives."

"You were smoking hash?"

"Just a few knives, on the stove, you know. Heat the tip, suck it up through a toilet paper tube. We started to get high and he poured us drinks. Then —"

Collette stops, her expression working, eyebrows bunching.

"Hey, it's all right," says MacFarlane. "Just get it out."

"No one else came," she says quietly.

"He raped both of you?"

"Bernie first, then me. Said he'd kill us if we said no."

MacFarlane gives her a minute. "What did you do after?"

"You kidding? When he was drunk enough, we ran out of there."

"Was the stove open when you left?"

Collette tilts her head, gives MacFarlane a puzzled look. "You shitting me? Guy raped us and you're asking if I took the time to notice if the stove door was open when I ran outside? Get real. Next you're gonna ask if we took the time to burn down the cabin."

"Did you?"

"As if. Not a bad idea, really, but all we had in mind was to get the hell out there."

"Right," MacFarlane says absently.

Collette watches him, intent.

"So, after you left the cabin, what happened next?"

"Like I said, we got the hell out of there. Went home."

"Walked? Drove? Took the train?"

"Walked, obviously."

"That's a long way from town. You walk the whole way?"

Collette slumps back in her chair. "Mostly. We hitched at the highway."

"Who picked you up?"

"My uncle."

"And his name would be?"

"Rodney Whiteknife. Everyone calls him Cork."

There's a lull as MacFarlane gives Collette time to calm down. My mind is racing. Collette Whiteknife and Bernice Mercredi were raped at Hallendry's cabin. It fits the evidence. The belt buckle indicating Hallendry was naked from the waist down. The stove going and open to heat up the knives. The drinking glasses. The door left open as the two girls fled.

"Was Mr. Hallendry conscious when you left?"

Collette looks up at the question, eyes hard. "He was stumbling around."

"And you didn't see anyone else on your way out?"

She shakes her head.

"What did you two do after your uncle picked you up?"

"Nothing. We went home."

"Did you tell him what happened?"

She frowns, stares at the floor. MacFarlane leans forward.

"This is very important. Did you tell anyone what happened at the cabin?"

She sighs heavily, sits up straighter, seems to collect herself. "You wouldn't understand. You're not a girl. You're not Native. You don't live up here. We don't talk about stuff like that. We just try to forget it. There's nothing that can be done."

MacFarlane's voice drops, gentle but firm. "There are things that can be done, Collette — things that need to be done — but we'll talk about that later. Do you know Porter Cassel?"

"Yeah," she says. "He's a nice guy. We were consensual."

I grimace as though someone kicked me in the gut.

"What?" says MacFarlane.

Collette looks a bit shy. "When we did it, we were consensual."

"I'm sorry, but I'm not sure I heard you correctly. Did you have sex with Mr. Cassel?"

Collette nods. I feel faint. MacFarlane's face suddenly fills the monitor, glaring at me. Seconds later, he's in the room, glaring at me. "You slept with her?" he says, voice controlled but unmistakably furious. "Our key witness — our only witness — and you slept with her?"

I nod, mute, unable to offer a defence. MacFarlane turns away from me, rubs his thinning hair furiously for a moment. When he turns to face me his hair is wild. He points to the door.

"Get out of my sight, Cassel."

"I didn't know —"

"Get out of my sight. And out of my investigation."

# 10
•

THE NEXT MORNING I'm not terribly motivated to get out of bed. Despite a late-night cup of Dr. Cho's happy tea I did not sleep well, disturbed by thoughts of Collette Whiteknife and of burned and drowned bodies. Of young women lured to a remote cabin and raped. And of my guilt at having strayed. When I tried to block out these thoughts, images surfaced like long-submerged driftwood in the river of my imagination, only to be caught in an eddy and circle endlessly. MacFarlane pointing to the door, a vein bulging in his temple. Luke Middel with a burned dog in his arms. Simon Cardinal grinning at me in the bar in Fort McMurray. By the time the first weak rays of light seep into the room, the bed sheets are a tangled sweaty mess. Irritated and angry, I toss the sheets aside and struggle free, sit on the edge of my bed, nauseous and shaking.

Dr. Cho's guttural voice haunts me: *You are sick, Mr. Cassel.*

I shake off the thought, stumble into the shower. When I emerge it's still too early for anyone to be up. In the empty cook shack, I brew a strong cup of Dr. Cho's tea. It tastes how a mixture of battery acid, urine, and tree bark might taste, causing my throat to pucker, but calm soon settles over me and my eyelids begin to droop. I'm in danger of falling asleep when I hear boots on the wooden landing outside and the door bangs open. It's young Constable Markham, his uniform exceptionally crisp this morning.

"Cassel — they want you in town."

I picture MacFarlane pointing at the door. "What for?"

"Ident wants you to show them where you found the body."

I groan, not looking forward to what could only be a tense and awkward day, tell Markham I'll be right there. I quickly feed the dog, check his burns, which seem to be healing well with no sign of infection. He licks my hands. Although he causes my allergies to flare up I'm loathe to leave him this morning — he seems to be the only companion that isn't judging me. I scruff him behind the ears, tell him I'll be back later, and follow Markham to the government dock, where Dugan, MacFarlane and Waldren are waiting. Only Dugan gives me a nod. We step aboard the RCMP boat, a newer deep V-hull model, cram together among Dugan's cases of crime scene gear. Waldren takes the helm, guides us out of the harbour and brings the boat up to speed.

It's too noisy for conversation, a blessing this morning, and I watch the shoreline bob past as we cut through the waves. We travel downriver for a half hour before I spot the sweeper. The gap I've cut through the branches looks like a missing tooth. Dugan signals Waldren to slow while he takes a series of pictures. Then he runs video as we approach the sweeper, records my narrative as I describe how I freed the snagged body and pulled it into my boat. Dugan takes a sample of river water for diatom comparison with water found in Bernice Mercredi's lungs. This will determine if she drowned in the river or somewhere else. We do a slow cruise to the weir, then return to the sweeper. Dugan and MacFarlane go ashore on opposite sides of the river, where they struggle through the brush for a few hundred yards. When we retrieve them upstream they're both sweating and scratched. Dugan has twigs caught in his wispy white hair.

"Nothing," he says, wiping his brow. "You find anything?"

MacFarlane shakes his head. "She could have gone in anywhere."

"What about that cabin you mentioned?"

I direct them along a narrower tributary channel to the cabin. We cruise slowly past the spot on the bank where I found the other boat, look for any visible evidence. Nothing. After securing our boat, Dugan examines the river bank, looking for boot prints, but the vegetation is too dense. We work our way in a pattern across the clearing in front of the cabin. I find an old tobacco can, overgrown with moss. MacFarlane finds a rusted muskrat trap. Despite my hopes to the contrary, the cabin yields even less. I was certain there would be some evidence of recent occupation, but as I stand inside I'm puzzled. A rusted and collapsing stove is clearly not safe for use. A pole bunk has no mattress. A shelf is lined with dusty soup and tobacco cans, filled with nails and bits of debris. The smell is funky and organic, like mushrooms and wood rot. Nothing here is even remotely recent. This is definitely not a hidden love nest. I join MacFarlane, Waldren and Dugan in the grassy clearing.

"I don't know, Cassel," says Waldren.

"Tell me the story again," says MacFarlane.

"Like I said before, I talked to Collette Whiteknife about Bernice Mercredi. The two of them were supposed to be pretty tight. She told me Bernice was secretly seeing some older guy, married by the sound of it but she didn't know who, and she thought they might go to this cabin to do their thing. I grabbed the forestry boat and came out to talk to Bernice about why she left the fire. There was a boat here when I arrived, but I didn't see anyone. I went to the cabin and was standing just inside the door when I was hit."

"And you woke up draped over a moose carcass."

"Yes."

"In a place you can't find."

"Yes."

"Do you have any idea who hit you?"

"No."

There's an uncomfortable silence. MacFarlane scuffs bare a spot on the ground with his boot, frowning, then looks at me. "Doesn't that seem a bit improbable?"

"I'm getting the impression you guys don't believe me."

"You're not the most reliable source, Cassel."

"Why would she send you out here?" says Waldren. "What's in it for her?"

"I don't know, but she must have had a reason. What did she tell you?"

"She claims she never told you to come out here."

"What?"

"Said you asked her about Mercredi, but she hadn't heard from her in a few days."

"That's it? She never mentioned the affair Mercredi was supposed to be having?"

MacFarlane shakes his head.

I look at the Mounties. "There is something really wrong here."

"No shit," says Waldren. "Hey, let me tell you a story. Forest Ranger decides he's going to investigate a series of apparently unrelated deaths and follows a lead out to an old cabin by the river. But this Forest Ranger is a bit careless and he forgets to tie up his boat properly, so it floats away. He's so embarrassed he makes up some cock and bull story to cover his ass."

"I'm not a Forest Ranger."

Waldren raises his hands expressively. "I'm just being hypothetical here."

"This is bullshit," I say, fuming, heat prickling across my back.

"Settle down," says MacFarlane. "We're all flying blind here. So far we've got a dead guy burned in his cabin, with no presentable evidence of foul play. A girl who claims she was raped, which cannot be substantiated, and a drowned girl who was prone to depression."

"They must have something in common," I say.

"Yeah," says MacFarlane. "You."

"What are you getting at?"

"Look Cassel." MacFarlane places a hand on my shoulder, perhaps in an effort to calm me. It isn't working. "The only common element so far is that you seem to somehow be in the middle of everything. You claim to find evidence we missed. You arrive first at the scene. You find the body."

Waldren chimes in: "You shack up with our only lead."

"About that," says MacFarlane. "What is your relationship to the Whiteknife girl?"

"There is no relationship. I met her at the bar. We went to a party together. I had too much too drink. It was a complete surprise to me that she might be involved."

"Is that a problem of yours? The drinking?"

"A long time ago. It's under control."

Waldren snorts. "Doesn't look that way to me."

He's right. I want to explain that I haven't been myself lately, but it's hard to define and would only sound like a lame excuse. The only reason I was at the bar, both here and in Fort McMurray, was to further my investigation, but I doubt that will impress them. And the only evidence of the incident at the moose carcass — my reeking clothes — was lost to the washing machine at the IA base. My credibility is at an all-time low.

"Look," says MacFarlane, using the same ingratiating tone he used on Collette Whiteknife. "I know you're just trying to help us out here, but you have to see it from our side, Porter. We need to run a tight investigation and so far you haven't exactly been an asset in that department. What I need you to do is just take a break, let us do our jobs here."

"Take a break. What does that mean? What am I supposed to do?"

"If we need you, we'll let you know."

It's mid-afternoon by the time the RCMP boat docks in Fort Chipewyan. As we disembark, Dugan handing cases of equipment to Waldren on the dock, it's clear that a line has been drawn between my investigation and the RCMP. In fact, I'm not sure I still have an investigation and I walk away from the dock without further discussion, avoid the ranger station, have a hamburger at the local café. Ponder my future in Fort Chipewyan. The waitress is a young Native woman, with a nasty scar on her cheek, but a nice smile. I think of Collette Whiteknife — she seems to be ground zero for my recent credibility problems.

I need to talk to her.

I pay for my burger, leave a generous tip for the friendly waitress, drive to Cork's house, park along what might be considered the curb. The front yard is overgrown with weeds, amongst which an immense stump squats. Towels are hung in windows in place of drapes. Unattended garbage has collected along with an impressive pile of bottles near the side door. I wonder what life event caused Collette to live with her uncle. When I rap on the door it's Cork who answers.

He grins when he sees me. "Fire Guy. You wanna come in for a beer?"

"I was just looking for Collette."

"She went camping. Williams Point, across the lake."

"When will she be back?"

He shrugs. "Coupla days — maybe a week."

"Maybe I'll have that brew," I say, thinking it's odd that Collette would go camping right after her interview with the RCMP. She's the closest thing they have to a lead and I expected the RCMP would have asked her to stick around as they're bound to have more questions. I have a few questions of my own. I follow Cork inside, where he leads me to the fridge, hands me a can of beer. His kitchen table is covered with mechanical parts from what looks like a boat motor. The pungent smell of gasoline fills the house. He lumbers into the adjacent living room, where he flops down into a broken recliner. I look around, at the immense TV, muted and turned to a fishing show, take a seat on the sagging brown couch — the same place I sat on that fateful night.

"What's new, Fire Guy?"

"Not much," I say, noncommittal. "What about you?"

"Boat motor is shot," he says, gesturing with a nod to the kitchen.

There's an awkward silence. Cork slurps his beer. I hold the cold can in my hand and wonder how to approach this. Much like the guy on the big screen, I'm fishing. He's after sail fish in the Caribbean and having plenty of luck. I'm hoping for a nibble about Collette.

"How's Collette holding up?"

"Fine, I guess," says Cork, grinning, his affable smile filled with crooked teeth. I wonder if he knows anything about the rape of his niece. Collette claims she never told him and I doubt the RCMP would mention it. Collette, however, wasn't entirely truthful with the RCMP in regard to what she told me.

"She was close to Bernice Mercredi, wasn't she?"

Cork's expression clouds. "Yeah. They were buds."

"Must have hit her pretty hard."

He gives me a resigned sort of shrug. "She doesn't let on much, but I know it bugs her. Happens too often up here with the young people. Nothing to do. Nowhere to go. They get depressed." He sighs, rubs the heel of his foot on the carpet. "I think that's why she went camping," he says quietly. "Had to get away."

"You think it was a suicide?"

"Doesn't everyone?"

"Well, we don't know the actual cause of death yet."

Cork's jaw clenches. "If someone did this, I'll kill the bastard."

I believe him. The beer can crumples slowly in his large hand.

"You picked up the girls the night of the fire, right?"

"What?"

"The night Hallendry's cabin burned. You picked up Bernice and Collette."

"Yeah. I heard they were going to some bush party and it was getting late. I was kinda worried, you know, so I took a drive. Found them walking on the highway."

"Why were they on the highway?"

He shrugs. "Don't know. Parties. Things happen."

Tell me about it. "You never asked them?"

"Nope." He drains his beer, crumples the can noisily flat between his palms and tosses the aluminum disc in the direction of the door. "They're big girls and I don't pry into their business. I figured they have something to tell me, they will. They know I got their back."

"Were they upset when you picked them up?"

"A bit, I guess. Tired mostly."

"Were their clothes ripped or stained? Anything like that?"

Cork turns in his recliner, thick shoulder facing me.

"It was a bush party. Why you want to know — Fire Guy?"

Cork seems to sense there is more to what happened than I've told him. I recall Middel's caution that the town is a powder keg.

"No reason. I just wanted to see how Collette is doing."

"You're pretty sweet on her, aren't you?"

"She's certainly had an effect on me."

He gazes at the big screen, where a fish is being gaffed.

"You treat her right," he says quietly.

There's an awkward silence, then he asks if I want another beer. I've barely touched the one I have, but suddenly want to get out of here. I quickly guzzle the beer, set the can on an end table, tell Cork I've got to get going. He doesn't insist, doesn't bother rising from the recliner, just watches me leave. Outside, an RCMP Suburban is pulled up behind my forestry truck. Waldren, uniformed, is walking up the drive. He stops when I emerge from the house, waits as I approach.

"Cassel — what a surprise. What brings you here?"

He sniffs once subtly in my direction, raises an eyebrow. Damn — the beer.

"Just a social visit," I say, slip quickly past him.

I feel his eyes behind me as I drive away.

I'm barely back in my truck when the radio blares at me, jangling my frazzled nerves. It's Middel. He's been trying to get hold of me all day. I'm to come to the office at once. Reluctantly, I wheel the truck around. Louise, the receptionist, gives me a friendly but nervous smile, her eyelids flickering quickly. Through his office door I see Middel rise from behind his desk, wave me in. I close his office door, an anxious clench in my gut. I'm not sure what I can tell him — anything I might say isn't good. Neither of us sit.

"Where's your radio, Porter?" he snaps. "I've been calling you all day."

"Lost," I tell him.

"Lost?" he repeats, scowling. "How'd that happen?"

"Long story."

He thinks about this, shakes his head. "I don't want to know." He fixes me with a stern look. "What I do want to know, though, is how things are going with the RCMP and the Mercredi girl's death. Have they got anything new?"

"Not that I'm aware. Ident processed the body and there'll be an autopsy."

"Anything else? What about the Hallendry fire?"

"Like I said before, I'm not sure what I can tell you right now."

"You'd have to check with the RCMP" he says, finishing my thought.

"That's right."

Middel leans forward, hands on the back of his chair, lips pursed. Something is up.

"What's going on, Mark?"

"Here's the thing, Porter," he says, forehead creased. "MacFarlane called, told me you were no longer active in the investigation."

"Which investigation?"

"Any investigation."

"Okay," I say slowly. "But I'm still working for you, right?"

Middel sighs. "I wish I could say yes, but given the degree of involvement by the Mounties, this has essentially become their investigation." He pushes the chair away, raises his hands helplessly. "If you can't work with the Mounties, you're of no use to us."

"You're firing me, Mark?"

"Call it a layoff," he says, crossing his arms over his chest. The body language is clear. "The bottle fires will be taken over completely by the RCMP. If they require technical assistance with the arson, they'll source their own specialist."

"So that's it? I'm just supposed to leave with my tail between my legs?"

Middel doesn't say anything, just stands with his arms crossed above his pot belly and rocks back on his heels. He avoids my gaze as I wait for a response, which apparently I already have. I rub a rand over my forehead, rake fingers through my hair. "Crap."

"I've had Louise book you a seat on the next regular flight tomorrow afternoon."

I nod, thinking about Bernice and Collette, and Hallendry's burned body. Then I walk out of Middel's office, past Louise, who pretends to be busy, avoiding me. I sit in my truck in front of the ranger station for a few minutes, stare at the ugly brown building. It occurs to me that there's nothing left for me to do here. The anxious pressure in my chest has returned and I grip the steering wheel to stop my hands from shaking. I could use a beer, or a whiskey, or at least a long drive with music cranked up high. Neither is a possibility right now, but I could brew a strong cup of bitter tea, take the dog for a walk. Resigned, I start the truck, drive to the IA base. In my room I pull out the brown paper package that contains the tea and find there's only a trace left. Did someone steal the rest? No — I must have used it up. Damn. I could really use a cup of tea. After a moments hesitation I crease the paper, pour the remnants directly into my mouth, where it bites bitterly into my tongue. I wince and spit into the garbage can, sit on the edge of my bed, tongue burning. What now?

I don't sit for long before I'm forced back into my truck. I need more tea.

The waiting room at the nursing station is crammed, the nurse explaining as I fidget at the counter that the doctor just arrived at noon. When I try to explain that I only need to see him for a minute her demeanour becomes frosty. I'll have to wait my turn, like everyone else. Ashamed that I've broken the unspoken etiquette of the queue, I sit on one of the hard plastic chairs and work on my patience. I'm itchy, my hands are shaking, and there's a dull hollow pressure in my chest. Noises around me seem painfully loud as children squabble. I try unsuccessfully to distract myself with the outdated housekeeping magazines. Finally, mercifully, my name is called. I pace the two available steps in the tiny examination room until the doctor knocks and slips in.

"What is problem today?" he says.

"Nothing major," I say quickly. "I just need more of that tea you gave me."

"Tea is helping?"

"I feel better when I drink it. Calms me down."

Doctor Cho nods, asks me to sit on the exam bench and open my shirt. He proceeds with a quick exam, placing his cold stethoscope on various parts of my torso. I breathe accommodatingly. He checks my eyes, takes my blood pressure. This is all very routine — I had expected more.

"How is job going?" he asks as he pulls off the blood pressure cuff.

"Done for now," I say, not wanting to get into it. "Going home."

The doctor nods again. Something occurs to me.

"What do I do when I run out of tea the next time?"

"No problem," he says, waving the thought away.

"I don't seem to be able to function without it. Does that mean I'm getting worse?"

"No problem," he repeats. "Tea helps body regain natural balance with environment."

"Well, my water seems to be getting dirtier."

Dr. Cho looks puzzled until I explain the reference to his earlier diagnosis. He looks vaguely amused. "Balance takes time," he says. "I give you plenty enough tea. You much better when all tea is gone." He leaves for a moment, returns with another small package wrapped neatly in brown paper. I thank him and return quickly to the IA base, where I heat a kettle of water in the kitchen. The cook, Mary, a squat Native lady, watches as I measure the tea into a small mesh tea egg. The texture and colour of the dry tea is different, which I pass off to it being a different batch, but when I lower the tea egg into the water, the colour of the tea is also different. Lighter. I let it steep longer, waiting for the expected blackness to develop. The tea darkens but not to the same colour as the previous batch. I shrug, give it a try. It tastes different — not acidly bitter like before. In fact, it tastes a lot like a very strong regular tea. I gulp it down, wait impatiently for the warm numbing relief to spread throughout my body.

Nothing. I set the cup on the counter, frown at the soggy tea egg.

"What?" says Mary. "You no like your tea?"

"It's just tea," I say, and scoop up the brown package, drive back to town. It's late in the day, sun low on the horizon, when I park in front of the nursing station. The waiting room is empty. A tired nurse behind the counter tells me the doctor is done for the day. Unless it's an emergency, I'll have to wait until tomorrow. I briefly consider if my concern could be considered an emergency, but discard the thought. I tell the nurse I just need to speak with the doctor. Could I get his phone number? Or where he's staying? The nurse shakes her head — this is against policy. If they allowed the doctor to be disturbed after hours for non-emergencies, he would never get any rest. Frustrated, I leave the clinic, stand in the parking lot and gaze irritably down the empty width of Main Street. My head feels filled with sand, my chest aches with anxiety and my hands restlessly beat a rhythm against my thighs.

If I could just talk to the doctor, we could straighten this out.

Beside the clinic are four flat-roofed boxy white portables that look as though they might be for temporary accommodation. It seems reasonable they would house the doctor close to the clinic in case of an after-hours emergency. The doctor answers when I knock on the door of the second portable, frowning in the doorway.

"Can I help you?"

"I'm sorry for disturbing you after work, but there seems to have been some mistake with the tea you gave me. It isn't doing anything for me." I offer him the brown-wrapped bundle. "Is it possible you give me the wrong tea?"

The doctor doesn't bother with the bundle. "Tea is fine. Patience is lacking."

"But I had expected the tea would make me feel better, like before."

"Are you doctor?"

"No, but —"

The doctor's tone becomes harsh. "You must drink tea and be patient. Do not disturb me after work. Not appropriate. Good night to you."

The door slams and I'm left bewildered by our truncated conversation. I consider knocking again, insisting on his examining the tea he gave me, but there doesn't seem any point. I return to my truck, wonder what to do next. I stare at the clinic building, grip the steering wheel, fight a blossoming panic. I feel as though I'm losing my mind. Guilt over betraying my fiancée, mixes with the shame of having been dismissed from the investigation. This is underlain by a sharp but indefinable impression that I've missed some critical clue and that when I leave Fort Chipewyan I'll have lost my only chance to sort this all out. These emotions mix with physical sensations that indicate I may be seriously ill. It's all too much at the moment and I start the truck, drive directly to one location where I know relief, although temporary, can be found. I park in front of the Lodge and climb the stairs to the Trapline. In quick succession, I down three whiskies, ignoring the other early evening patrons. Warmth radiates from my midsection and my thoughts lose their rough edge.

"You want another one?" says the waitress, a slender young Native gal.

"No thanks." I blink, surprised at myself for being here. "I'm fine."

She scoops up my empty glasses as I stand. The floor seems a bit spongy as I make my way across the room. I pause at the door, then return to the bar and buy a bottle of vodka, for later — just in case. Brown bag in hand, I make my way down the stairs. I haven't drunk seriously for years and hold the railing on the stairs as I make my way to the parking lot. I'm in my truck, driving down the narrow trail to the highway, before it occurs to me that I shouldn't be driving. I'm not really drunk, but I'm not really sober either. I don't want to drive all the way to the IA base on the highway, and I remember

Middel's admonishment not to park a forestry truck in front of the bar. I can't just stop here, so I decide to drive the short distance into town and park the truck by the ranger station, convince myself that this is a good compromise — it's so close, there's minimal risk, and I can avoid embarrassment — the classic mistake of impaired drivers everywhere.

I pull onto the highway. Less than a minute later, I see the grill and lights of an RCMP Suburban in my rear-view mirror. My heart jumps into my throat. The Suburban must have been headed into town, just a few curves away when I pulled onto the highway. Constable Markham looks at me, his face deadpan behind sunglasses. Even though I'm not speeding I slow down a bit. Just another mile and I'll be in town, then a few hundred yards more to the ranger station.

Behind me, red and blue lights flash and the siren goes off for a second — just long enough to let me know he means business. Reluctantly I pull over and with my boot slide the brown bag with the bottle of vodka farther under the seat. I force myself to release my death grip on the steering wheel and crank down my window as Markham walks up.

"Hello, John," I say, surprisingly calm. "What's up?"

"How you doing, Porter?" he says peering into the cab. "You been drinking?"

"What? What makes you say that?"

"Well, you just turned out from the Lodge."

"It's a hotel too," I say, repeating a previous excuse I used with Middel.

"And your breath stinks like whiskey," says Markham, wrinkling his nose.

"Yeah, okay, I had one."

He gives me a hard look. "Just one?"

I'm not a great liar. "Maybe a bit more."

Markham looks down the road, chewing his lip thoughtfully for a minute as I wait, tense, for the hammer to fall. "Tell you what I'm going to do," he says slowly. "You're going to drive nice and slow and I'm going to follow you into town. You're going to park the truck at the ranger station for the night. Then tomorrow you're going to get on that plane and stay the hell away from Fort Chip." He gives me a hard look. "We understand each other?"

"Perfectly," I say through gritted teeth.

He nods, returns to his Suburban. I pull away from the shoulder of the road, flushed, furious at myself. In the past week, I've managed to make nearly every possible mistake, both personal and professional. Markham follows close behind, pulls beside me as I park. Fortunately there's no one in the ranger station to witness my humiliation. Markham reaches a hand though his open side window as I walk around the front of his Suburban.

"Keys," he demands.

Feeling like a kid caught playing hooky, I hand him the keys.

"You need a ride anywhere, Porter?"

"No thanks."

Markham cranks up his window and pulls away. I stand in the parking lot of the ranger station for a minute, feeling low. I could have used a ride from Markham, but I felt bad enough that he pulled me over and didn't want to extend the embarrassment. I walk to the highway, falter when I reach the junction, stare down the long empty road. It leads out of town, toward my exit from Fort Chipewyan. I realize I'm not quite ready to go.


Helen Mercredi doesn't seem surprised to see me, invites me into her home. She's aged in the past few days, eyes moist and sad, surrounding skin bruised and sagging. She moves slowly as though sedated as she leads me into her kitchen. I hesitate at the threshold; there are several people at the table — an older Native couple and a younger man with unruly black hair. I had come with thoughts of apology for not finding Bernice alive, hoping this gesture might provide some small consolation. I wasn't prepared for a group.

"This is my mother and father, and my brother Derrick," says Helen.

The three nod politely.

"This is Porter Cassel," she says. "He found Bernie."

The elder Mercredi rises. He's a thin man, grey hair neatly parted in the middle to hang in two long braids. "Thank you for bringing our granddaughter back to us," he says, shaking my hand. I'm not sure why — perhaps it's the look in Helen Mercredi's eyes, the warmth in the old man's gnarled hand, or the deep sense of loss that permeates the room — but I'm suddenly overcome with grief. The room blurs as I struggle to hold back tears. My throat constricts painfully and my legs are weak. I slide onto a chair, nodding an acknowledgement. There's an awkward silence, broken by Helen Mercredi's offer of coffee.

I nod and finally manage: "I'm sorry for your loss."

She returns the nod, sets a cup of coffee in front of me.

"The cops find anything new?" says Derrick.

"They'll do an autopsy. Other than that, I really can't say."

"But you're working with the cops, right?"

I hesitate. "My part of the investigation is over. I'm leaving tomorrow. I just wanted to stop by and offer my condolences. I only wish I had been able to do more. Perhaps if I had started to look for her earlier —"

My voice cracks and I clear my throat to hide my lapse.

Helen Mercredi reaches across the table, takes my hand in hers, looks me in the eye. "It's okay, Mr. Cassel. We know you did all you could. Like us, you too are suffering from this tragedy. I want you to take a sweat with us tonight. You also need to heal."

"Thanks, but I'm all right."

Her grip on my hand tightens. "It's all set up. We have room for you."

I nod — it seems the least I could do.

The sweat has been set up out of town at a secluded location along the lake. Crammed into the Mercredi family minivan, we bounce and jostle along a dark narrow trail, headlights revealing a rutted path. The minivan thumps and spins as we climb an increasing slope to arrive at a high bluff overlooking Lake Athabasca. Seated in the back, I am the last to exit and, temporarily blinded from the interior door light, stand in the sudden darkness while my eyes adjust. No moon tonight. Below, the lake is nearly invisible but for a dim gun metal sheen of reflected starlight on the water. My eyes are drawn to the nearby orange glow of a simmering campfire and the small illuminated world it reveals. A group of Natives stand by the fire, men dressed only in swim trunks, women in long cotton nightgowns. Towels are draped over their shoulders as though ready for a day at the beach but their expressions are solemn. Next to them is a large waist-height dome which I take to be the sweat lodge. The new arrivals join the group. I tag along, am introduced to Rodger, the medicine man, and his wife Eva. Rodger appears to be in his early sixties, short, with heavy features, a pot belly and bandy legs, his dark skin shimmering with sweat in the firelight.

"Welcome," he says, shaking my hand. "Is this your first sweat?"

I nod and he smiles. "We'll go easy on you, then."

Around me, the men from the minivan strip down. They've worn their swim trunks under their clothes. I've made no such preparations and wonder if I'm expected to simply strip down to my underwear. Noticing my uncertainty, Helen Mercredi hands me a towel, inside which is a pair of swim trunks. I thank her, change in the dark behind the minivan, join the group in the circle of campfire light. We wait respectfully by the sweat lodge as Rodger holds a small cast iron frying pan in which he is lighting something on fire.

I move next to Helen Mercerdi to get a closer look.

"Sage," she whispers. "He's doing the blessing."

Rodger chants a brief prayer in Cree as he offers the sage in the four cardinal directions, then enters the sweat lodge, followed by his wife, disappearing into the darkness. I go next and crawl into the waist-high opening to a position at the back, until Rodger, a dim bulky shape, stops me.

"Clockwise," he says softly. "Always clockwise, like the path of the sun."

Obligingly, I crawl clockwise along the round perimeter of the dark dome. In the light entering from the campfire I see the arched willow branches that form the curve, overlain by heavy brown canvas. My nostrils fill with a coarse familiar scent, evoking memories of childhood campouts. There's a pit in the centre of the floor, in which I see the dull glow of heated rocks. I skirt Rodger and his wife, seated near the pit, take a position against the curved wall. As others enter, crouched single file, I notice a bucket of water beside Rodger, with a bundle of willow twigs and a long hand-carved pipe. When everyone is seated, a dozen of us by my count, Rodger calls for the door to be closed and a heavy flap of canvas drops to cover the opening.

The darkness is sudden and absolute.

"Welcome home," says a deep voice. "Mother Earth is here for you."

Around me the world has ceased to exist. The voice of the medicine man seems to originate somewhere inside my head, like an unexpected but not unwelcome thought. He sprinkles powdered herbs on the hot rocks in the pit, filling the air with a pungent aroma that stings my eyes. In the dark the specks of herb blaze on the rocks — a tiny universe of bright orange stars — before quickly winking out. Invisibly, water is mopped onto the rocks, a soft swoosh like a whale spouting, and there's an immediate rush of heat.

Sweat prickles on my bare skin as the medicine man speaks.

"The sweat lodge is our spiritual womb. It is made from everything the Creator has given us. Rocks and wood and water and earth. The Creator provides everything for us, everything we need to live, and in exchange we give ourselves back to the Creator. I understand one of us has recently returned to the Creator. I encourage you now to think of this person, and of your family and friends, and of yourself, and to pray."

More swooshing as water is mopped onto the rocks. The heat increases dramatically, filling my nose and sinuses. The medicine man begins to sing — a loud, wailing song; sounds not words, but not unpleasant. I think of Bernice Mercredi at the fire camp, smiling at my corny joke. I try not to think of her in the river, or lying cold and pale on the tarp in the RCMP garage. I'm not a religious man, but I hope for her sake that there's something good for her on the other side. Sitting cramped in the dark, holding my bare legs, head drooped, sweat dripping like hot beads down my neck and back, my thoughts begin to drift from Bernice Mercredi to her secret lover. Who might he be? What might he do if told of the rape? He would be furious, perhaps enough so to kill Hallendry. I shift to relieve a cramp in my leg, careful in the dark not to kick anyone. A new thought drifts — an image of two young Native women walking down the highway at night. I can picture this so perfectly in the sensory deprivation of the sweat lodge that it seems almost a memory. Why would Bernice, hungover and having been up virtually all night, walking many miles, even have gone to the fire? After the rape, that location would be the last place she would want to go. But for some reason she was there. Perhaps the arsonist responsible for the under-burned floorboards sent her, to watch the investigators and listen to talk among the firefighters, for any sign that foul play was suspected. This fits with her leaving after I discovered the burn indicators on the floorboards. It also explains the pictures deleted from my camera. I lean forward in the dark, try to focus on this thought. Bernice is dead. Collette, who claims she was at the cabin with Bernice, sent me to an ambush. Now Collette is out of town and can't be questioned. Someone is attempting to control the situation and I picture Cork, introducing me to Collette. Telling me Collette has gone camping. He claimed to have picked up the girls after they left Hallendry's cabin but didn't ask them about where they were or what happened. I recall the look on his face when I questioned him, and the way he crushed the beer can when I mentioned that it had yet to be confirmed that Bernice's death was suicide.

*If someone did this, I'll kill the bastard.*

How would he have reacted if he learned of the rape the night he picked up the two girls?

I shift in the dark to relieve a cramp in my legs. I'm trying to follow this line of thought but am losing focus. The singing has stopped and I wipe sweat away from my forehead. The medicine man calls for the lodge to be opened and from outside someone lifts the flap, revealing the bare and glistening legs of my silent companions. I wait, expecting the sweat is over, but it is only an intermission. I count as eight more large glowing rocks are passed in on the tines of a pitchfork. A few more words from the medicine man, which I barely register, and the flap is closed. Darkness reigns and once again I am alone in the heat with my thoughts and impressions. More glowing sparks when powdered sage is sprinkled on the rocks. As the sparks wink out I see in my mind's eye the cabin by the river, grass blowing in the wind of the helicopter rotor-wash. Whoever attacked me had to be someone bigger and stronger than Collette, who could carry my unconscious body into a boat, then to the rotting moose carcass. I try to picture how this might have happened, as though the image will enter my mind as easily as the voice of the medicine man, who sings in duet with his wife — a steady ululating sound — but I can no longer control my thoughts. They have slipped away like the hot beads of sweat rolling down my back. I'm rocking back and forth to the rhythm of the singing, the swoosh of water mopped onto the rocks and the shake of the rattle. Sounds so ancient they seem to come from the earth itself. In a moment of understanding, startling in its simplicity, I sense a connection to a distant past. To roaming bands of ancestors, hunting, sitting around a campfire. The signing stops and the medicine man calls for the lodge to be opened.

Cooler air wafts in. Another intermission.

Rodger lights up a hand-carved pipe. He's a dim bulky figure in the flickering orange light, primitive, eternal. He hands me the pipe and I draw a breath. The smoke is mild and tastes vaguely like a pine forest fire. I hand the pipe clockwise to the next person in the circle. Next is a plastic tub of blueberries, then a bottle of water, from which I take small samplings. The pipe returns to me and we continue to pass it and the berries and water around until they have all been consumed. A ceremony of sharing and community. The lodge is sealed again. More water; more heat; more singing. A scent like bread dough and hot stones. I slip into a trance, rocking slowly. The sweat lodge is womb-like in

more than a spiritual sense. Hot and dark. The rattle sounds like a
heartbeat. The song tapers off and Rodger confers with his wife in
Cree. A question is asked and answered and, although the words
are unfamiliar, I have the overwhelming impression it is my parents
speaking and I am a child again, secure in a warm bed in the dark. The
ceremony continues and my mind empties. Time becomes meaningless. The heat is ratcheted up to a level that causes mild delirium.

Suddenly, it's over and the flap is open.

Helen Mercredi nudges me. "We go outside now."

I hadn't realized she was so close to me, had in fact forgotten that I
shared the small space with anyone. Bloated with heat, I move lethar-
gically, have difficulty crawling out of the sweat lodge. Outside it is
cooler, a breeze washing gently over my steaming skin. The campfire
has died to a pocket of coals. Stars above are a dazzling panorama,
impossibly vast. It feels like a rebirth and it occurs to me that the dull
aching tension that's been in my chest since shortly after arriving in
Fort Chipewyan is finally gone.

The mood in the minivan on the drive back to town is subdued but
companionable. I have the driver drop me at the ranger station, thank
Helen Mercredi and her relatives for the privilege of sharing a sweat
with them, then use the unlocked back door to enter the ranger station
and retrieve the spare key for my truck. I'm relaxed and a bit drained
from the sweat but no longer impaired. I drive to the IA base, feed
Scorch, spend a few minutes of quality canine time. He's healing well.
Despite the allergy, I'm growing rather attached to the mutt, although
I can't see a way of keeping him. It's therapeutic, scruffing him under
the chin, and I ponder the sweat lodge and my thoughts about Cork.
Questioning him isn't apt to be productive but surveillance seems in
order and I head back to town, park in a dark alley where I can watch
his house.

Light seeps around the towels hung in the windows and an older-
model pickup truck is parked in the driveway. I watch from my own

truck, pondering. When I last visited Collette, just prior to the incident at the cabin along the river, she ducked back into the house to collect rented videos to return to the store. Perhaps this was just a cover. I wonder if she needed to speak with Cork, find out what she should tell me. Then, while I was driving around town with Collette, Cork headed down river in his boat to ambush me. This possibility sheds a different light on my initial encounter with Collette at the Trapline. Perhaps she wasn't smitten by my rugged good looks but came on to me because Cork coached her. After all, he was the one who introduced me to her. The party that night was at his place. And, although my memory is a bit fuzzy, I think it was Cork who spilled the drink on me, giving Collette a perfect reason to get me alone. In retrospect it seems almost comical — the guy twenty years older thinking the woman is attracted to him — but I'm not laughing. The effect of this lapse in judgment on my part has reverberated through my time in Fort Chipewyan, affecting my ability to focus and, more significantly, my relationship with the RCMP. If Collette and Cork are involved in Hallendry's murder, what better way to discredit my status as an investigator than by having Collette sleep with me?

I grip the steering wheel and release a breath I hadn't realized I'd been holding. The calm instilled by the sweat lodge has slipped a bit and I wonder if Collette really is camping. Perhaps Cork didn't want me to talk to her and she's at home, in the house, right now. I peer intently through the windshield of my truck at the house, as though by sheer force of will I can determine if she's inside. No use — my X-ray vision isn't what it used to be. I watch a few minutes longer, but nothing is happening. I can't wait here all night; I'll fall asleep. I leave my truck, walk quietly around the block to a back alley and approach Cork's house from the rear.

The alley is rocky and uneven and in the dark I stub my toe on something hard, thankful for my steel-toe workboots. They're a wonderful piece of footwear; not only do they protect my feet and provide excellent ankle support, they're black and suitable for almost any occasion. I once wore them to a dance, much to the horror of my girlfriend. On the bright side, my feet emerged unscathed from her three-inch stiletto heels. The alley is lined with crooked rotting fences over which I see crude A-frame doghouses, partially illuminated from back windows. The last thing I need is to arouse a pack of angry dogs.

I tiptoe as quietly as my workboots will allow.

A low-roofed ancient two-bay garage squats dimly behind Cork's house. In the dark I nearly neuter myself on a tangle of sharp rusty metal which, when I click on my hand-dandy keychain flashlight, appears to be a failed attempt at modern art, stacked on an old table saw. Shielding the beam of my light so as not to arouse the curiosity of a neighbour across the alley, I peer through a dusty fly-specked window into the garage.

I get a view of a dusty fly-specked window. I need a better flashlight.

Stymied, I stand in the dark, wondering what I expected to find back here and, as a second thought, try the knob on the garage door. It's unlocked. I hesitate for a moment, thinking about what might happen if I'm caught breaking and entering. How impressed the RCMP might be. But it's really just entering, no breaking required, and, furthermore, I won't even enter. I'll just open the door and sweep the beam of my flashlight over the contents.

Shelves, junk, more junk, and a boat are revealed progressively in the sweep of the weak beam. Something about the boat is familiar and I return the light to study it more closely.

It appears to be the boat from the cabin by the river.

I don't need to debate a deeper incursion into the garage. I step carefully inside, use the pale beam to light my footsteps, swing the beam over and into the boat. Same small console. No windshield. Even the fishing tackle scattered on the bottom looks familiar. A mixture of dread and anger washes through me. I want to confront Cork but given his size and motivation to keep whatever has transpired hushed-up, I don't think this would be wise. I click off the light, stand in the dark garage, appreciating the scent of grease and mouse turds, and wonder what to do. I could go to the RCMP, but they don't believe my explanation of what occurred at the cabin. I leave the garage, hesitate in the alley. There's an open route from the garage past the dark side of the house, which is shorter than retracing my footsteps through the alley. And I might be able to see in through a window on my way past, look for any sign of Collette. I tread slowly and quietly along a sidewalk, scuff over ridges of grass and dirt which have welled up between the slabs. The lighted side windows of the house have yellowing drapes covering them, blocking my view into the rooms. As I pass the door a light blazes on, illuminating a wide circle around me, and I dart down the driveway, duck behind the truck, then cross the road to the safety of another dark alley and find my truck. Inside, I watch the house. After a few minutes, the exterior light goes out. It must have been triggered by a motion sensor. Fortunately, no one inside seemed to have noticed. On the other hand, I noticed a few things when the light went on. The truck was the same burgundy colour as the paint scrape on the tree to which Scorch led me from the Hallendry fire. And the truck had a scrape on the front passenger side, where a patch of paint had been rubbed off.

Cork was involved in both the Hallendry fire and my attack.

I imagine a number of scenarios involving the RCMP but arrive at the same conclusion; they no longer believe anything I say. I have completely lost credibility with them. Any attempt to explain my loss of credibility with a story that is based solely on my word, and for which I have no direct evidence, would not be well received. I sit in the truck and stew over this Catch-22. I'm expected on a plane tomorrow afternoon so whatever I'm going to do will have to be done soon. Unfortunately, all I can think of doing is watching Cork's house, to see if Collette shows herself, then getting her alone and challenging her with my theory. If anyone might let something slip, it'll have to be her. So I wait.

And wait.

On television nature shows, you see how master predators stalk their prey, waiting patiently, immobile yet ready to spring into action. That's not me. I've never been very good at stakeouts. In fact, I stink. My mind wanders. I get distracted. I fall asleep. Or I lose my patience and do something risky. Tonight I try to play mind games to keep alert, do a little mental arithmetic, but I've never really enjoyed math so it just irritates me. So do my hands, which have started to shake again. I felt so good when I emerged from the sweat lodge, so cleansed and renewed, I hoped that whatever had been ailing me was done with, but the itching has returned, along with a swell of anxiety in my chest and a dull throb at the back of my head. None of this is conducive to sitting patiently for hours in the dark.

Fortunately, I don't have to wait that long.

The exterior light across the road blazes on and the side door opens. I peer intently through the dusty windshield, hoping to see Collette, but it's Cork, probably dumping more empty bottles on his refuse pile. He holds the door open a few seconds, looking around, then walks quickly to his truck. He's carrying something, a small box of some sort, but I don't get a good look because he seems to be shielding it from view. Perhaps I'm imagining things but he seems nervous, his manner hurried and secretive. I wait while he backs out of the drive and heads down the street. When I see him turn right I start my truck and follow.

I've had some experience tailing vehicles. Usually, just to keep things interesting, I'm driving a fairly conspicuous vehicle in some remote location with little traffic and even less for cover. I'm working on the basis of continuous improvement, slowly honing my skills so that eventually I can sit right next to a suspect and they won't even notice I'm there. I won't get much practice tonight though — it will be easy to follow under cover of darkness. There aren't many roads and I just need to stay far enough back.

Ahead of me, the truck swings past the Northern Store and around an uphill curve. He's on a dead-end road, heading to the old Catholic Mission. Not wanting to arouse his suspicion, I pull over shy of the crest of the hill, park the truck as close to the side of the road as possible, and run uphill to where I can observe his progress. It's fairly easy, given that his bright red tail lights are the only set on the road. Suddenly, his lights go off and I wait, listening. He's about a mile away and I hear the crunch of tires and the creak of the truck's suspension. There's a bright flash of red brake lights, closer to the lake where I didn't think there was a road, then silence. He's stopped and I wait for the gleam of an interior light as he opens a door. Nothing. Either he's not getting out, or his door light isn't working. This leaves me in a bit of a jam because he's a mile away, clearly up to something, and I can't drive closer without his seeing my lights or hearing my truck. I jog downhill, open the hood of my truck so it looks like it just broke down, then jog quickly along the road toward Cork and his truck.

In the starlight the road ahead of me is a ribbon of darkness barely discernible from the surrounding rock and grass. By the time I've covered most of the mile I'm breathing heavily and have to force myself to slow my respiration so I can hear what Cork might be doing. Nothing. Then a shielded flashlight beam several hundred yards away in the direction of the lake. I leave the road, pick my way over nearly invisible ground, feeling in the dark for anything that might trip me. I've seen this area from the lake, on my way to the cabin along the river, and remember old metal conveyor belts and rusty piping — loading works from some abandoned port. Ahead and downhill, a sloping skeletal structure is a faint black silhouette against the dull sheen of water and it is near the base of this that the shielded light flickers and bobs. I'm within a hundred yards when I whack my shin painfully on something hidden in the grass and release a muffled grunt. The flashlight sweeps suddenly in my direction and I drop, press myself into the long dry grass. Light plays over nearby grass tips then vanishes. I raise my head, watch from my concealed position.

There's a metallic clank and scrape, loud in the night, then I hear footsteps rustling through the grass, making their way toward the road. I hear Cork breathing heavily as he passes near where I lie. If he turns on his flashlight, he'll see me. He continues past, labouring uphill. The arthritic creak and thud of a truck door, then an engine starts and headlights switch on. A rusted conveyor appears against yellow grass and shimmering water, then the swath of light swings over the road and I'm alone, listening to the sound of Cork's receding truck.

I head downhill in the direction of the rusted ironworks, the memory of the image revealed by the truck lights my only guide. I must have a spot of light burned on my retina as there seems to be a faint glow floating a few feet above ground. But the glow doesn't move when I do, doesn't waver as I move my eyes. As I draw closer the glow seems to increase. It's a strange greenish sort of luminescence, like a comic book glow of radioactivity, and my imagination constructs a bizarre scenario. This is uranium mining country and Cork has planted a package of the deadly stuff out here, perhaps for pick-up by some terrorist organization. Using the glow as a beacon I arrive at the conveyor belt, use my tiny flashlight to navigate a path around the rusty hazard, nearly breaking my leg in the process.

I'm not well prepared; I need a better flashlight — I'd make a crappy Boy Scout.

The greenish light is coming from a bin in the conveyor. The radio-active nugget is a simple plastic glow stick. A green one. It sits on a small cardboard box. There might be a lot of reasons for a man to wander around in the dark, in a hazardous area, to leave a box in an abandoned conveyor belt, but I can't think of any. He's not just hiding something — he's left it here for someone else to find. I wonder what in the box is so clandestine it requires such an odd sort of courier service and am reaching into the conveyor when a set of headlights emerge over the hill where I left my vehicle. It may be someone from one of the scattered houses farther along the road, returning home, but it may also be the recipient of this box, in which case I have to get to some cover from which I can safely and invisibly identify the person.

But first I need to peak inside the box.

I lift the box from the conveyor bin, fleetingly hope it's not a bomb of some sort, and set it on the ground. Working quickly, I unfold the top interlocked flaps of cardboard and pop them up, shine my tiny flashlight inside. A glass jar with a metal lid. The vehicle slows and comes to a stop almost directly uphill from my position. The headlights remain on, illuminating a swath of grassy hillside above me. I lift the glass jar to see what's inside, frown as I peer at the blob floating in clear liquid. The lights go out, plunging the area into darkness, and a car door slams. Another beam of light appears, swinging widely — a flashlight, much more powerful than mine. I return the jar to the box, close the flaps and set it carefully back on the conveyor, place the glow stick on top, and walk as quickly and quietly as possible in the dark, hoping not to encounter anything rusty and sharp. I make it about twenty yards before the flashlight homes in on the conveyor belt and begins to brush the area with strokes of light. I crouch behind a large concrete block that serves as the foundation of the upper end of the conveyor structure.

The flashlight appears to float over the ground, the powerful beam concealing the identity of the holder, who is clearly more uncertain than Cork. It takes several more sweeps of light over the area to reassure the holder the coast is clear, then the light descends to the conveyor and the box is lifted. I had hoped the change in angle of the beam of light might afford an opportunity to identify who was picking up the box, but the light remains too powerful, too intense and blinding. The beam is darted around randomly a few more times, as though spooked, then moves uphill as the holder returns to their vehicle.

I want to run after the light, grab the person, demand to know who they are and what they're doing. What's in the jar seems worse than uranium. But I don't want to destroy any future line of investigation for the RCMP. Better that I gather what information I can and I follow cautiously up the hill, ready to drop into the tall grass, hoping for a view of the holder as they enter their vehicle, perhaps a glimpse of a licence plate number. I want to know who is holding the box. I want the RCMP to find them in possession of the glass jar and its terrible contents, floating in clear liquid.

A severed pair of human testicles.

In my rush I must have made some sound that rose above the thrash of footsteps from my target because suddenly the light swings around and I drop for cover behind a spindly young pine tree, shorter than me, flatten myself against the cool ground. I'm perhaps forty yards downhill and wait, tense, my heart racing, as light plays wildly around me. Then the sound of a car door opening and closing and an engine coming to life. Damn — I'd hoped to catch a glimpse of a face in the flash of the interior door light, but missed my chance. When the headlights point away from me, I rise and jog swiftly uphill, knowing I'll be invisible to the driver, catch a glimmer of tail lights as the driver brakes at the edge of the road. It's a car; I can tell by the spacing and height of the headlights and the high-pitched whine of the engine, then the unknown car is gone.

Unknown except for one detail: It has a broken tail light.

I'll find it sooner or later. There are no roads out of Fort Chipewyan in summer.

ONCE AGAIN I'M at the RCMP detachment in the middle of the night, pressing the button by the door. This time there's someone inside — the windows are all lighted. A bolt scrapes and the door opens. MacFarlane gives me a questioning look.

"What now, Cassel?"

"Can I come in? I need to talk to you."

He moves back, makes way, and I step in. He waves for me to follow and leads me through the building. Voices drift from an office in the corner. Waldren opens the door, peers out at us. MacFarlane waves him over, leads us into a small interrogation room at the rear. It's the same room where they questioned Collette, what seems an eternity ago. I wonder if they're taking video. MacFarlane pulls a chair away from the small table, motions that I should sit. Waldren ducks out, returns with another chair, and the two Mounties sit against the wall. Waldren looks formidable — dark uniform, black handgun and baton on his belt. MacFarlane is wearing a khaki shirt and jeans. Both look weary and serious.

"Okay, Cassel," says MacFarlane. "You've got our attention."

Suddenly, I'm not sure where to begin. The night seems to have warped into an era of its own, filled with heat, sweat, hallucinations, breaking-and-entering, surveillance, jogging under the stars, uranium, terrorists, and testicles in a jar. I know some of this is only impression and thought, but it seems jumbled in my mind. I'm sweating profusely, my hands are shaking, and it feels like an iron rod is being pressed upwards through the base of my skull. I swallow nervously. It makes a dry clicking sound.

"You okay?" says Waldren. "You look terrible."

MacFarlane frowns at me. "Are you on something?"

"What? No — listen, I have to tell you something."

"That's why we're here," says MacFarlane.

I take a moment, squeeze shut my eyes, try to clear my mind. It would take about a week of sleep. I decide to start my narrative after the entry into the garage. "I was watching Cork's house tonight."

"Cork?" says MacFarlane.

"Rodney Whiteknife," Waldren explains. "Collette's uncle."

"Have you found her yet?" I ask.

MacFarlane shakes his head. "No. I hear she went camping."

"Maybe," I say. "Doesn't it strike you as odd that she can't be located?"

MacFarlane massages his forehead. "Everything about this JFO strikes me as odd, not the least of which is you, Mr. Cassel. Obviously we are concerned and are looking for her."

"Have you tried Williams Point, across the lake?"

"We've flown over it," says Waldren.

"And?"

"Didn't see her camping party, but they may be somewhere else."

"Camping party? Who is with her?"

"Coupla local boys are missing as well, supposedly camping."

MacFarlane shakes his head. "Never mind that, Cassel. Did you say you were running surveillance on Rodney Whiteknife?"

"I have reason to believe he was the one who attacked me at the cabin."

"Really?" says Waldren. "And what reason would that be?"

"I recently learned that it was his boat that was out there."

Both Mounties ponder this for a moment.

Waldren says, "That's what you came to tell us in the middle of the night?"

"There's more, isn't there?" says MacFarlane.

"Yes. At about 10:45 tonight, Cork, Mr. Whiteknife, left his residence, carrying a small box. I followed him to the south end of town, past the Catholic Mission. He blacked out his truck and dropped the box by an old conveyor. A few minutes later, someone picked up the box, although I couldn't get a look at who it was. Their car had a broken tail light, though."

MacFarlane is frowning thoughtfully. "Any idea what was in the box?"

"I had an opportunity to look. It was a set of human testicles."

"What did you say?" says Waldren.

"Testicles," I repeat. "Nuts. *Kahones.*"

The Mounties exchange incredulous looks.

"Let me get this straight," says Waldren, a wicked grin tugging at the corner of his mouth.

MacFarlane holds up a hand. "Are you serious, Cassel?"

"Completely. Perhaps I should have taken them."

"Perhaps," MacFarlane repeats distantly, obviously thinking.

"You didn't need to take them," says Waldren, refusing to be silenced. "You got plenty of your own, coming in here with a story like that."

"Anything is possible," says MacFarlane. "In fact, it fits with our theory."

Waldren looks aghast. "You're not taking this seriously, are you?"

"Revenge castration fits with the rape story," says MacFarlane.

Waldren rolls his eyes. "No disrespect intended," he says to MacFarlane in a tone that suggests otherwise, "but we caught this clown drinking and driving earlier tonight. In fact, look at him, trying to sit still. He's got the DTs so bad he's practically vibrating. And you're disclosing elements of our investigation to him."

Furious, I clamp my shaky hands together, glare at Waldren.

MacFarlane, much to his professional credit, remains cool.

"Porter," he says mildly. "Is it possible you misinterpreted the evidence?"

"I suppose anything is possible," I say, echoing his earlier sentiment. "But that's what it looked like to me. They were suspended in a clear solution — alcohol maybe."

"Okay." MacFarlane gives me a weary smile, his voice carrying only a trace of the strain he must be feeling. I was expecting worse, particularly after his outburst following Collette's mention of having slept with me. His calm demeanour may be a bad sign. "Here's the thing," he says carefully. "What you found is very interesting and may in fact be what it appears to be. I am concerned, though, that, once again, you've done this on your own. That means we have no direct evidence to support your claim."

He pauses, raises his hands as though trying to mould something out of clay.

"Essentially," he says, "you have become an unreliable witness. If we had to drag you into court to testify, the prosecution would chuckle with glee. They would make mincemeat out of you. And not just out of you, but out of our case. If we actually found the evidence, your fingerprints would be all over it. Are you getting what I'm saying here?"

He has an almost pleading look in his eye.

I nod, flushed and irritated. "I'm flying home tomorrow."

As he shows me out I get the impression he doesn't believe me.

The next day there's nothing left to do but finish a bit of paperwork, then tuck my tail between my legs and board the plane, so I'm in no great hurry to get out of bed. I lie on my bunk at the IA base and stare at the ceiling. The tiles have squiggly holes in them that look like worms were having a party. I hear Scorch outside, yowling, and realize I need to figure out what to do with him. Reluctantly I push myself to a sitting position and am overcome by a wave of nausea. When the nausea subsides it leaves behind an anxious pressure in my chest. I lay back on the bed, close my eyes. The whine and of an over-wound two-stroke engine seeps through the wall, growing painfully in volume until it suddenly dies. Boot steps in the hallway. I groan, not wanting to see anyone this morning.

A knock on my door. "Porter — you home?"

I wait until there's another knock, hoping he might go away.

"Yeah, I'm home, Luke."

"Can I come in?"

"All right." I sit up, rub my hands over my face as the door opens.

"Wow," says Luke Middel. "You look terrible."

"Thanks for the feedback. What can I do for you?"

He's wearing a weathered backpack and hesitates in the doorway. Tall, awkward, blond hair in a mess, he looks like a lost surfer and seems impossibly young and innocent this morning. I realize how caustic I sound and relent, invite him into the room. He smiles uncertainly, drops his backpack and sits on the lone chair opposite the bed.

"My dad said you were going this afternoon and I wanted to say goodbye."

"Oh — right. Looks like my time here is at an end. Thanks for your help."

His smile broadens. "You're welcome. I wish there was more I could do."

"Well, there may still be something you could do for me."

"Sure, Porter. Just name it."

"Would you like a dog?"

Luke's smile falters.

"He's been through quite a bit and needs a home."

"You don't want him?"

"I'd love to keep him, but I travel constantly. And I'm allergic."

Luke ponders this. "Maybe. I'm not sure about my dad."

"Well, you think about it Luke, but I need to know by noon."

"Okay. You've got until noon, right? You wanna go fishing?"

I consider, not really wanting to do anything, but Luke looks so hopeful. I need some time to work on him about the dog, or find another alternative, so I agree, ask Luke to give me a few minutes to get ready. When he's out of the room I massage my eyes until I see spots. I'm not sure I'm up to polite conversation this morning, even if it involves fishing. I lift a hand and watch my fingers twitch. There has to be something seriously wrong with me to feel this terrible all the time. There's a way to make it stop and I reach under the bed and pull out the bottle of vodka I bought at the Trapline the previous night, appreciate the heaviness, feel the smoothness of the glass. For a time, vodka was my drink of choice because it was hard to detect on my breath. I just had to act sober. A few hard pulls from the bottle this morning and I'll be okay for a while — long enough to go fishing with Luke. I unscrew the cap, put the mouth of the bottle to my lips, feel the familiar bite on the tip of my tongue, the odour like rubbing alcohol, and hesitate, knowing if I continue it may be a long time before I stop. I think of Bernice Mercredi and Collette Whiteknife, and of Luke Middel, waiting for me to go fishing with him, and lower the bottle, take it to the washroom, dump the clear contents down the sink, disgusted with myself and sick with the knowledge of how close I came. I made the mistake once, years ago, of not dealing with what needed to be dealt with, and I'll never do that again.

The empty bottle thuds as I drop it into the trash can.

I find Luke behind the trailer, playing with Scorch, and we load the dog in the back of my truck, head to the public dock, where Luke assures me it is possible to catch a ten pound walleye. A friend of his did it just last year, he says, grinning, as we walk past rows of boats tied to the long dock, gently bobbing and clunking in the undulating water. It's a beautiful morning, water sparkling in the sun, gulls calling to one another. A light breeze cools the skin, carrying a scent of rock and aquatic things. The dog walks beside us and the sound of our boots on the dock makes a familiar clunking sound. I'm overcome with an almost giddy sense of relief and well-being, as though I'd dodged a bullet and earned back my life. We set up at the end of the dock, which Luke claims is the best spot, and I promptly lose three of his hooks.

"I'll head up to the Northern and buy a few more," I tell him.

He nods, keeps fishing. The Northern store is only a few hundred yards away, up a dirt track, and I whistle a tune as I walk under a sky that seems too blue to be real. Inside I grab a half-dozen lures and several chocolate bars. My good mood evaporates when I see Cork pushing a cart between the aisles. My first impression of him as an affable, easy-going partier has been replaced by anger and a deep sense of unease. This is the man who clubbed me unconscious and draped my body over a rotting moose kill, hoping to have a bear finish me off. I follow him surreptitiously until he spots me, in the meat and dairy aisle.

"Hey, Fire Guy," he says, grinning. "How's it going?"

I ignore the question. "Have you seen Collette?"

"Why? You missing your little girlfriend?"

He grins wickedly, amused with himself. I want to punch him in the face.

"I need to talk to her," I say. "It's important."

He steps closer, getting into my space. "Yeah — I'll bet you do."

"Where is she?"

"Having fun without you," he says, noxious breath wafting over me. I stand my ground, exercising admirable self control. He inspects my basket, sees my fishing lures and chocolate bars. "You should have some eggs," he says, reaching a carton from the display, setting them in my basket. "They're good for you." Then he winks at me, turns his back and returns to his shopping, humming under his breath. I return the eggs to the display, watch him examine a package of pork chops, have to remind myself of MacFarlane's caution last night. It takes some effort, but I force myself to pay for my purchases and leave the store. Back at the dock, I stalk past the boats and several new fisherman that have taken up positions, hand Luke a chocolate bar.

"Had a good one," he says. "Let it go. Didn't know how long you'd be."

I nod, force myself to make small talk, fuming about how unfair it is that Cork is right here and I can't do anything about what he did to me, or what he might have done to Collette. I have to step away from this and let the RCMP, who don't believe most of what I have told them, take over, while I fly back to Edmonton to ponder my damaged reputation and future as a fire investigator with the Forest Service. I catch several fish, which I release with a minimum of comment, look up to a large sleek boat entering the harbour.

"Whose boat is that?" I ask Luke.

He squints against glare coming off the water. "That's Simon Cardinal."

The boat must be thirty feet long, dwarfing in both size and power the other boats moored along the dock. My first impression on seeing the boat was that some big shot from Fort McMurray — an oil company executive or hotel owner — was pulling in. That it's Simon Cardinal I find interesting and set down my rod, tell Luke I'll be right back. I wander along the dock, watch the boat cruise in. Simon Cardinal grins down from a high cabin as he steers the boat to a berth. On final approach, he cuts the engine and drifts the last few yards. Several locals crowd the side of the boat, watching the dock. I offer to help them tie up and they toss me a rope. Once the boat is secure, Simon steps down, smiling, waves a hand over the rail in my direction.

"Hey, thanks buddy."

Two middle-aged Native men and three smiling women disembark, carrying a cooler full of fish. We chat amicably about how their fishing went and I complement them on their catch. They lug the cooler away and I turn my attention to Simon, still on the boat, fiddling with something on deck.

"That's quite a boat you got there," I say.

"Isn't she a beauty?" he says. "Come aboard and I'll show her to you."

Luke, who's joined me to check out the catch, waves me off, telling me he's already seen the boat and wants to keep fishing while the action is good. He returns to the end of the dock, where Scorch is tied, pacing restlessly, and I climb aboard Cardinal's boat.

It's obviously a sport pleasure boat, not a commercial fishing vessel, and still has that new-boat smell. The stern bristles with downriggers and spare rods. Spacious live well to keep the fish fresh. Seats are upholstered in leather. It's got GPS and sonar. There's even a mini-bar. I wonder where he got the money.

"What's a unit like this worth?"

Simon gives me a self-depreciating shrug. "About a quarter mil."

"Wow. Wish I had one of these. How'd you manage it?"

"Won the lottery."

"Really?"

"Scratch-and-win ticket in McMurray."

"You lucky bastard," I say, shaking my head.

"It happens," he says, smiling.

"Hey, I was wondering about something else," I say, casually running a hand along the smooth stainless steel rail. "Back at that band council meeting you mentioned the inscription on those bottles found at the fires on Cree land."

He stares at me.

"The 'FTC,' if you remember."

Simon's expression hardens suspiciously. "Yeah?"

"I was just wondering where you heard about that."

He shrugs, eyes darting to the side. "Just around, you know."

"No, I don't, actually. That was supposed to be confidential."

"Oh." He laughs. It sounds a bit forced. "Someone should have told the IA crew."

"You heard it from the IA crew? I just want to be clear on this."

"I didn't know it was a big deal. I don't want to get them in trouble."

"Don't worry about it. Honest mistake. Where'd you catch all those fish?"

"About a mile from Old Fort Bay," he says. "You should come out some time."

We bullshit a few minutes longer about fishing before I thank him for the tour, leave him standing on the deck. He watches us fish for a few minutes longer, after which I tell Luke I have to get going and pack my bags. Reluctantly, he reels in and we head back to the IA base. On the drive I ask Luke again about the dog.

"Yeah, I guess so," he says.

"What about your dad?"

"We've got room. If dad has a fit, I'll find the dog a good home."

At the IA base I tell Luke he can drop by later and retrieve Scorch from behind the kitchen trailer, thank him again for his help and tell him he'll make a fine fire investigator one day. Then I pack my bags. On my way out, I stop at the helipad, where the local IA crew lounge in the shade of the fuel shack, close to the helicopter. Rolly, the leader, raises his hand in greeting but no one moves. They're deep under the influence of stand-by, willing only to move out of sheer boredom or for a fire call. I squat in the shade with them, tell them I'm on my way out. This doesn't make much of an impact, but they nod and smile.

"Better work on your ping-pong," says Sachmo, the reigning champion. "For next time."

"I will. Hey, did any of you guys ever talk to anyone about those bottles we found?"

"Like what?" says Rolly.

"About that inscription — the letters."

The four Natives look at each other, shake their heads.

"You're positive? No repercussions, I just need to know."

"No, man," says Rolly. "We thought you must have told someone."

I thank them, drive into town pondering Simon Cardinal and his flashy new boat. At the ranger station, I exchange nods with Louise Holmes and Mark Middel, pretend to be working on fire reports while I use the computer in Carter Spence's temporarily vacant office to search the internet for information on lottery wins. I find the page for the Western Canada Lottery Corporation. Winners are listed with names and photographs, their expressions stunned. The locations of the wins and a brief story are listed for each winner, some for amounts far less than what Simon claims to have won, but Simon is not listed, even though I go back two years. I check the clock. I have about an hour before I need to head to the airport.

There is one more thing I need to do.

Simon Cardinal is still on his boat, lounging in one of the leather upholstered captain's chairs, drinking beer. I don't wait for an invitation, just climb aboard. Simon is alone, which is good. He blinks up at me, lazily indicates an open cooler filled with ice and silver cans of beer.

"Porter Cassel," he says, as if we hadn't seen each other for a long time.

I stand silently over him, blocking his sun.

"You want a beer, buddy?" he says. "Or you come to go fishing?"

"Neither," I say, and fall silent. This seems to unnerve him.

"Well, then, what the fuck do you want?"

"I want you to stop fucking everything up."

An eyebrow goes up. "What?"

"You heard me, Cardinal."

"Look," he says, starting to peel himself out of the chair. I place my steel-toed workboot on his chest and shove him roughly back into his cushy seat where he flops, thumping his head.

He gazes up at me in wonder. "Are you out of your fucking mind?"

"It was a simple arrangement. Why couldn't you leave it simple?"

He stares up at me, confused, trying to work it out. I hope he hasn't had too much to drink. I hope I'm barking up the right tree. The way I figure, it doesn't matter if I ruffle a few feathers here, because I'm on my way out. A little theatre is all I have left.

"What the hell are you talking about?"

"You were doing fine with the bush fires."

He squints up at me. "Man, you're fucking crazy."

"Then you got carried away. Burned the Chief's truck."

"I don't know nothing about that."

"You can drop the act, Simon."

He doesn't much like this, studies me with cold, calculating eyes. He also doesn't like that he's sitting while I'm standing and he tries to rise again but he's had a few beers. I shove him back into his chair again, harder this time — another use for my favourite footwear. The chair turns, does a full rotation, Simon's arm flying wildly out. He grabs at a handhold, stops himself, sprawled in the chair, staring at me as though I might have dropped from an alien spacecraft.

"You don't know who you're fucking with," he says, drawing it out.

"You took a perfectly simple plan and messed it up. Now the Mounties are involved."

Simon's eyes are the only things that move as he looks me over, trying to see where this is going. Ever since the election debate it's been in the back of my mind that Simon is getting mileage out of the bottle fires and the tension it's causing among the bands.

He laughs at me suddenly.

"Nice try, asshole. You're the investigator."

"Of course. I'm your backup."

"Yeah — right."

"Did you really think they would just hand over a wad of cash to an amateur?"

"Bullshit, man. You're just some dumbass forestry guy. You got nothing."

Despite his bravado, doubt creeps into Simon's smug expression. I'm flying by the seat of my pants, trying to sound believable while keeping it vague as I have no idea if Simon is guilty of anything, who might have hired him, or why. But too many things don't add up and his increasingly concerned expression only convinces me to push harder.

I look around, lower my voice.

"Why do you think there hasn't been any progress in the investigation? It's not because you're some master criminal, I can tell you that. It's because I'm controlling the investigation."

"You — you're controlling it?"

"The cops only know what I let them know."

"You're full of shit."

"Really, Simon? I'd love nothing more than to cut you loose but I'm a professional, unlike you. First thing you do is go out and buy the biggest boat in Fort Chipewyan. Why not just nail a sign to your ass? Then you make up some crap story about winning the lottery that anyone can disprove with five minutes on the internet. Frankly, the people with the money are getting nervous. And I'm sick of trying to cover your ass."

Simon Cardinal goggles at me. I wait, certain he'll clam up.

"This is total bullshit," he says, standing up quickly, bracing himself in case I try to push him down again. It occurs to me just how risky this is and I wonder if he might come at me with a knife or gun, and if I can dive overboard in time.

"I did my job," he says. "They'll never re-elect Sammy."

"Yeah, but you're sloppy. The RCMP are involved."

He rubs his forehead furiously for a minute.

"I need more money."

"What?" I'm stunned that my ruse was effective.

"You heard me. Another hundred grand. No — two hundred."

"You must be kidding."

"The risk has gone up. So has the price."

This is fantastic. Still, I step back, look at the water.

"You're the reason the risk has gone up, Simon."

"Just fucking listen to me," he says, face contorted, forehead beaded with perspiration. A foot begins to tap. He's on the edge. Seems like good time to break this off.

"Look, the money isn't my end of it. I'll let them know."

I turn, descend on wobbly legs to the dock, feel Simon's eyes on me as I walk to my truck. I have an unbearable premonition he'll shoot me in the back but make it to my truck unscathed. I lock the door, insert the key, hands jittery on the steering wheel as I roll onto Main Street where I stop, realize I have no idea where I'm going or what I'm going to do.

The only thing I know for sure is that leaving Fort Chip isn't it.

I make a few loops through town, wonder what to do next. Simon Cardinal is clearly behind the bottle fires with the intention of sabotaging the Cree Band election, but I have no idea who hired him. I doubt it's one of the other bands as I fail to see how they would benefit by having Simon become chief, rather than Sammy, who has a position that is more sympathetic to the other bands. It could be an outside interest, concerned about the bands forming a coalition. I need to determine who is sponsoring these fires — a responsibility that clearly would fall to me if I were still working for the Forest Service. As it stands, I'm supposed to be on a plane in ten minutes. Should I go directly to the RCMP? Or talk Middel into hiring me on again? Or both? Given my recent history with the RCMP, will they believe what happened? Or simply give me another lecture about interfering in what is now entirely their investigation? My head is reeling, not just from the confrontation with Simon, but because I'm hungry. I head to the Lodge, take a seat with a panoramic view of the lake, order and quickly consume a large burger and fries. I still haven't sorted out what to do and continue to ponder this as I head to the washroom. I'm standing at the urinal when a stranger enters and takes a position at the urinal next to me.

"Good day Mr. Cassel," he says, staring at the wall.

It's generally considered rude to engage in conversation while urinating, particularly with a stranger. At least I'm pretty sure he's a stranger. I'm trying not to look.

"Do I know you?"

"We have some business to discuss."

"Really," I say as casually as possible, feeling particularly vulnerable. I quickly finish, move to the sink to wash my hands, standing sideways to keep the stranger in view. He's middle-aged, slender and wiry, with grey-streaked black hair, pulled back into a short ponytail. At first glance he looks Native, but closer observation suggests a more exotic heritage. He's soft-spoken, with a slight English accent, wears a plaid shirt and jeans. There's a cellphone on his belt, indicating he's from out of town, as cellphones don't work here. I can't help wondering if he's been sent by whomever hired Simon Cardinal and I look discretely for the bulge of a gun under his clothes.

"Yes." He moves to the sink, washes his hands.

"I'm sorry, but I didn't get your name."

"You can call me Joe." He dries his hands, tosses the paper towel into the trash and steps casually to the side, blocking the door. "I'll need you to take a ride with me."

I tense, a prickle running up my neck. "You need to step aside, Joe."

"You're missing your plane. I thought I'd give you a ride."

There's an awkward moment when I wonder if he'll move out of my way, then he turns and walks out of the washroom. I follow him out of the Lodge, more comfortable now that he's in front of me, curious who he is and what he wants. He walks to a black Suburban with tinted windows, turns to face me. "If it makes you more comfortable, you can drive."

"Not until I know who you are."

He looks around the parking lot. No one else is visible.

"It's about operation Kitten," he says quietly.

"You're with the RCMP?"

"I'll explain in the truck."

He opens the driver side door, walks around the front of the truck and climbs into the passenger seat, waits patiently. Glancing around the parking lot, I take a seat behind the steering wheel, close the door, drive away from the Lodge. At the highway, I turn toward the airport, not because I plan on boarding a plane, but because it's the only long stretch of road.

"Start talking, Joe."

"It's a bit ironic. In my business, that's usually my line."

"What exactly is your business?"

"Surveillance. I work for Special 'O.' We've been watching you."

"What?" I look over at him. He's watching me now.

"Here's the thing, Porter," he says, tenting his fingers together. "Ever since you've been involved in operation Kitten you haven't exactly been playing by the rules. This has been made clear to you on several occasions yet you persist in your — how shall I say — unorthodox methods. Even after you've been told to back off, you remain embroiled in the investigation. Frankly, we can't have you running around saying the things you are saying without some corroboration."

"Wouldn't corroboration indicate a working relationship?"

"I'm not talking about sanctioning anything you do. I'm talking about determining how much truth there is to your claims and, if evidence is obtained, protecting admissibility."

"How long have you been watching me?"

"I can't reveal the details of our operation."

"Can you corroborate my discovery of the testicles?"

Joe hesitates. "Unfortunately, no. That was pre-surveillance."

They must have started early today. When I returned from the store with the fishing lures, there were several new fishermen on the dock, although I hadn't paid much attention to them. I ask Joe if they heard my conversation with Simon Cardinal on his boat but he stops answering my questions, directs me to an isolated rental fishing lodge along the lakeshore. The lodge is nothing more than a cluster of faded clapboard cabins. Only one seems to be in use, in front of which are two older-model trucks. Inside I find Waldren and MacFarlane, both in civilian clothes, seated at a table, scrutinizing paperwork and surrounded by coffee cups.

Waldren gives me a wistful half smile as we enter. MacFarlane motions me over.

"Grab some caffeine, Cassel, and take a seat."

I fill a cup, join the Mounties at the table. MacFarlane and Waldren look exhausted, with bags under their eyes and sagging jowls. They must have been up all night. MacFarlane shuffles together the paper on the table, slides it into a folder, out of sight.

"Okay," he says, giving me a hard look, "I'm going to lay this out as simply as I can. As Joe here told you on the drive over, we've had you under surveillance. We probably should have started earlier, but we had no idea you would be so bloody determined."

"That's one word for it," says Waldren, waggling a toothpick between his lips.

"Anyway, we were treated to your performance on Simon Cardinal's boat just recently."

"It was a performance, wasn't it?" says Waldren, raising an eyebrow.

"Of course," I say, a bit defensively.

"Good," says Waldren. "I'd hate to have to take you down."

MacFarlane raises a hand. "Enough," he tells Waldren, then gives me a critical look, eyebrows raised. "I'm not going to get into what I think of your methods Porter, you already know my feelings on that subject, but it appears that you are now in a unique position to provide a certain value to the investigation. That is if you want to be a team player."

He sits back and watches me.

"What did you have in mind?"

"We want you to continue in the role in which you presented yourself to Simon Cardinal. We need you to get him to incriminate himself on record."

"Don't you have that already, since you were watching me?"

"I wish it were that easy," says Joe. "When you were talking to Cardinal, we could only monitor the conversation for your safety, but we couldn't record anything. We can only record if an RCMP member or agent is involved. Now that Cardinal has incriminated himself verbally, we can move to one-party consent under Part Six of the Criminal Code."

"So you need me to be an agent?"

Waldren cringes. MacFarlane nods. "In addition to incriminating himself while being recorded, we need you to work on getting him to reveal who hired him. We're also very interested in any possible involvement in the death of Rufus Hallendry or Bernice Mercredi."

"How would this work?"

"You contact Cardinal, tell him you need a private place for a conversation. We'll watch him the whole time. Special 'I,' our surveillance technical specialists, will set up for the meet. Remote microphones, cameras, telescopes. Then you just play your part."

"What if something goes wrong?"

"Don't worry," says Joe. "We'll have you covered."

We spend the next few hours working out the details. It's best if we pick the location, to maximize the effectiveness of the set-up, but there aren't a lot of options in a small remote community like Fort Chipewyan. Joe would prefer a building or small park, but we settle on Simon Cardinal's new boat. It seems most believable that I tell him we need to go fishing. I'm given use of a satellite phone, which I use to make the call.

"Simon, this is Porter Cassel."

"Don't call me on the phone."

"Listen, dipshit, we need to go fishing. Can you manage that?"

"Yeah, we can do that. When?"

"Tomorrow, early. How about six o'clock?"

"All right. You'd better have good news."

"We're going fishing. Just be ready."

I hand the phone back to Joe, who explains that during the night, while Special "O" watches Cardinal, Special "I" will wire up the boat, placing microphones in several locations. As insurance in case of equipment failure, I'm given a remote microphone, planted in a pair of sunglasses. I try them on. They look exactly like ordinary sunglasses. I feel a bit like James Bond. I'm also given a lovely orange baseball cap, which I'm to put on if I'm in trouble. A team will be waiting nearby, posing as fishermen in a boat. In addition, observers with long range telescopes will be watching every move. For a guy used to operating on his own, it's a bit overwhelming. We do some role playing, cover a few "what if" scenarios. Then they cut me loose. Joe drives me back to the Lodge.

"What about the Forest Service?" I say, looking at the decal on my truck.

"Don't worry. It's all taken care of."

I test this out right away by driving to the IA base and calling Middel on the radio, requesting a fire patrol with the IA crew and their helicopter. Middel's reply is subdued but he acknowledges. The crew aren't surprised to see me — plans change quickly in the fire business.

"Where are we going?" says Rolly.

"South side of the lake."

We can't fly far enough over open water with our single-engine aircraft to legally cross Lake Athabasca, so we follow the lakeshore around to the Williams Point area, where we search for campers among sand dunes that look imported from Saudi Arabia. We find one group and land the helicopter. It's a family and although they're greatly impressed with the helicopter, they haven't seen Collette Whiteknife.

We spend another hour flying, cover a lot of ground.

Collette Whiteknife is nowhere to be found.

# 12

I DRIVE BACK to town, troubled by a gnawing apprehension that Collette Whiteknife is in danger. Cork is clearly a part of what has been happening in this little town, and his snide self-satisfied jab at me in the store only strengthens my suspicion that he is exerting some sort of control over Collette. I wonder if he tried to exercise control over Bernice Mercredi, and it didn't work, so he drowned her. The RCMP seem to believe the rape story, and it's not a stretch to imagine Cork going after Hallendry and mutilating him. If Cork did murder Hallendry, which the circumstantial evidence suggests, any witnesses or confidants are in a vulnerable position. That he had no qualms about attacking an investigator suggests that he's a particularly dangerous individual. It occurs to me that Special "O" is busy watching Simon Cardinal tonight, and therefore not watching me, and I drive past his house.

The lights are off and the driveway is empty.

I circle the block, thinking. I could conduct my own surveillance again on Cork's house, but I doubt Collette will be returning anytime soon, and Cork likely won't be repeating the drama of the previous night. His house is invitingly dark and I toy with the idea of having a look inside, to see if there's anything to suggest where Collette went, or to support my statements to the RCMP. It would be best if anything incriminating inside the house was actually found by the RCMP but, unfortunately, everything they have on Cork is either far too circum-stantial, such as the paint scrape on the tree miles from the fire, or has come from me — and I've been thoroughly discredited. Not the stuff of search warrants. If there is anything critical to the investigation in that house, I'll have to be the one to find it.

I slip on my work gloves, park a few blocks away and take a circuitous route along the alley of sagging fence boards, arrive again at Cork's garage, which is still unlocked, and slip inside. The boat is gone, suggesting Cork is on the lake, hopefully for another hour or two. The filtered light coming through the dusty windows allows a more thorough inspection than last night.

Junk and more junk.

A wooden shelf is filled with cans of rusty washers and bolts. Cobwebbed leg-hold traps. Coils of snare wire. Tangled fishing nets. A wire, strung just below the ceiling and pulled taut, is crusted with bits of dried blackened flesh. In a corner under a pile of boxes is an old snowmobile with no hood and a ripped seat. I open a few boxes but find nothing you wouldn't expect in a garage in a remote bush community. I slip out of the garage and walk confidently up to the house, knock on the door. If you're seen entering a house, it should at least look like you're supposed to be there. No answer. The door is unlocked. I go inside.

"Hello," I holler. "Is anyone home?"

Silence.

I scan the living room to make sure no one is sleeping on the couch, then wipe my boots and walk through the kitchen to the back of the house. In Collette's room, the bed has not been made, blankets in a tangle, and I try to ignore the warm flush of guilt that blossoms in my chest. I will face Christina Telson later, tell her what happened and live with the consequences. Now, I have business to attend to and check under the bed, under the mattress, look for a diary or anything that might offer a clue about Collette's involvement and where she might have gone. There are no mementos of her younger days and I wonder again what happened with her parents that she would be living with her uncle. A quick pass through her dresser and closet reveals nothing of use. I move to Cork's bedroom, which is messier and has an unpleasant smell. Shotgun shells litter his nightstand. Porno magazines are scattered under the bed. A dresser drawer holds a small stash of cash — a few hundred dollars in folded bills. Nothing provides any clue about his involvement or Collette's location. The bathroom medicine cabinet reveals anti-fungal, Advil and birth control pills. At least she took precautions. I wander through the living room, check under end tables by the couch. Kitchen cupboards are full of the usual kitchen things. The fridge smells like rotting onions. I make one more pass through the house, open a small broom closet. A ball of plastic shopping bags and an ancient vacuum cleaner. I'm about to give up when I notice a fold of blue fabric behind the vacuum cleaner, reach in and pull it out.

It's a small duffel bag. It's not covered with dust like everything else in the closet and I tug open the zipper, find a wad of women's clothing, a toothbrush and deodorant. This is someone's overnight bag and my pulse quickens. If it were Collette's it would be in her room, not stuffed into a closet. I'm suddenly nervous, sweat prickling up my back, and peer out a few windows, through the gaps between the towels hung as drapes and the window frames. No one in sight. In the kitchen, I find a local phone book, use Cork's phone. It's clumsy, dialling while wearing work gloves, but I'm determined not to leave fingerprints.

Helen Mercredi answers on the third ring.

"Mrs. Mercredi, it's Porter Cassel. I need to ask you a question."

"Okay," she says, sounding concerned.

"You said you dropped Bernice off at the airport with her bag."

"Yeah, that's right."

"What does that bag look like?"

"The bag? I don't know — I think it was a blue one. Sort of two-tone."

"What was inside?"

"Just the usual stuff — clothes, toothbrush. Why? What's going on?"

"We just need to know what it looks like, in case we find it."

I thank her, hang the phone back in the cradle, look at the blue two-tone bag on the floor beside me. The RCMP need to find this, but they need to find it where it was, so I carefully reposition the bag in the closet, behind the vacuum cleaner, and slip out of the house.

Daylight is failing as I park in front of the cabin the RCMP are using as their remote command post. It takes a moment before anyone answers my knock. When the door opens, MacFarlane gazes woozily at me, hair wild and matted.

"Cassel," he says, yawning. "You're interrupting my one hour of sleep today."

He motions me inside, fills a coffee cup, stares at me blearily.

"I've found a lead on Bernice Mercredi."

"I thought you were laying low until tomorrow morning."

"I had a hunch I had to follow."

"Really," he says, squinting hard. "I'm shocked."

"There's a connection between her and Rodney Whiteknife."

"This the guy you call Cork?"

"He intercepted her at the airport, on her way out of town."

"And you know this how?"

This is the tricky part. I'm not sure we have time to play games.

"Have you found her overnight bag?" I ask.

MacFarlane frowns, waking up. "No — but something tells me you did."

"It's at Rodney Whiteknife's place."

"Dare I ask how you came to know this?"

"It might be better if you didn't."

There's a pause as MacFarlane digests this. I'm hoping he's invested enough in my role with Simon Cardinal not to take exception to the obvious truth about how I came to know about the location of Bernice Mercredri's bag. He sets down his coffee cup, rubs his hands over his face, massaging his eyes, then looks at me.

"Has the bag been compromised?"

"It's in the position I found it."

He thinks about this some more.

"This is a significant development, Cassel."

"That's why I looked for it. That's why I'm here."

"Okay." He nods, seems to come to a decision. "We can't go in based on your find, or it would never hold up in court, but here's what we're going to do. I'm going to review this with the team, work on an angle to develop probable cause and secure a search warrant. That could take a day or two. Until then, we'll bring in some more resources, put eyes on the house. If that bag moves, we'll know. But you gotta stay away from there."

"I can do that. Any news on the whereabouts of Collette Whiteknife?"

"The boys we thought were camping with her have been located."

"Was she with them?"

"No. Collette Whiteknife is officially missing."

I don't get a lot of sleep that night, worrying alternately about Collette Whiteknife and the meet scheduled for the morning with Simon Cardinal. I toss and turn, twist the blanket into knots, give up trying to sleep about four in the morning and make a pot of coffee in the cook shack. At five o'clock I head to the cabin by the lake, as planned, for final confirmation that everything is a go. It is. Joe, my undercover handler, goes through the script once more, confirms I have everything memorized, hands me the special sunglasses and hat.

"Just act natural," he says. "Don't look for the surveillance."

Then I'm sent on my way.

I drive to the public wharf, walk down to the water, feeling conspicuous. The rising sun is still low on the horizon, the air cool and smelling of damp rock. Fog is layered over the water, concealing the humped islands at the edge of the bay. Simon's boat rocks gently, rubbing against the plastic bumpers on the dock. The metal railing is cool and damp in my hand as I climb aboard. Simon emerges from the cabin, in jeans and his trademark buckskin coat.

"Untie those ropes," he says, pointing at the dock.

I untie the mooring lines. Simon cranks up the motor, loud in the early morning stillness, and we putter out of the docking area and into the fog of the bay. The boat surges, bow rising until it reaches cruising speed, and levels. The fog concerns me but begins to break up soon after we pass a shrouded island. We skim rapidly over the water, wind whipping, and in no time are miles from land. The shore, partially shrouded in fog, looks from this distance like narrow skips of scraped paint. Isolated by the vast expanse of surrounding water, I wonder how surveillance is possible, and if anyone will see my distress signal if the need arises.

The engines are cut and the boat settles, rocking gently. Simon leaves the cabin, joins me at the rail. Vivid light plays across the water as the sun clears the fog bank. It would be a great day to be fishing, which I mention to Simon.

"Yeah?" he says, looking around. "But we ain't here to fish."

"That's a shame," I say, slipping on my sunglasses.

"Maybe for you. I can go out anytime."

"I know," I say, using this as a lead-in for the first part of the script. "You've got the big boat. That's part of the problem. Flashing this thing around like a dick in a whorehouse. Didn't it ever occur to you that it might not be a good idea? That people might wonder where you got the money?"

The idea is to get Simon to repeat his story about the lottery win, so it can be recorded and admitted into court, but Simon doesn't bite.

"Fuck that," he says. "It's my money."

"It was payment for a job you haven't completed."

"What?" He frowns, steps toward me, his long dark braids swinging. "I did my part. I started the fires. I got the Cree Band suspicious of everyone else. That was *my* band," he says, poking himself in the chest. "You got no call to tell me I didn't do what I was supposed to."

Bingo. This is easier than I thought it would be.

"You having second thoughts about your band?"

"Screw that. My band will do just fine on its own."

"You can stop campaigning. I'm not voting for you."

Simon Cardinal glares at me. A big hunting knife hangs from his belt and he may have a gun on board. I'm armed with a pair of sunglasses and an orange baseball cap. A glance past him over the light chop of the water isn't reassuring. If there's a boat waiting to back me up, it's nowhere in sight. It occurs to me, with the patches of fog, they might not even know where I am. Things are going well though — he's already admitted to starting the fires. I just have to keep him talking and direct the conversation.

"But you're not done."

"Bullshit," he says. "That's all I had to do."

"I didn't think I had to explain this to you, Simon, but part of any operation is discretion. Making it look natural. Something you're not so good at."

"It's my goddamn money," he says, stepping closer. "Don't tell me how to spend it."

"The election isn't over yet," I say quietly.

This seems to catch him off guard and he frowns for a minute as the boat rocks gently beneath us. I look at the cabin of the boat, wonder where they stashed the microphone, and if they included video. They warned me not to look for surveillance because the suspect can pick up on that, and I look over the water, then back at Simon.

"You guys still need me," he says, smiling to himself.

"Don't count on it. You can be replaced."

"Like hell. I'm in the perfect spot. My Band. My election. I know the people. You've got no one. So what about it?"

"What about what?"

"The other two hundred grand," he says.

"Here's the thing, Simon. The cops are involved. I can't control the entire investigation anymore." I hesitate before dropping the big lure. "And that business with the trapper who was killed has them really spooked."

For a few seconds Simon Cardinal just stares at me, then he moves, far quicker than I had expected, charging straight at me. Standing in front of the rail I don't have a chance. He drives his shoulder into my chest and I go over like a kid tricked in a playground. Head first, the water swallows me, breathtakingly cold, and I see the white hull of the boat. Shafts of sunlight radiate through bluish-green water. The surface appears, silvery and undulating above me and I kick, break through, sputtering and gasping.

"Christ! Are you nuts?"

Simon Cardinal peers down at me from the rail. "Now we talk."

"Bullshit. Throw me a rope."

He grins as I tread water. "How long can you do that?"

I glare at him. I've lost my sunglasses and the orange baseball cap I had tucked in the back pocket of my jeans. It occurs to me that the RCMP may wait to see what develops. They had warned me that often a suspect will feel the need to exert control before resuming with the business at hand, in which case they do not want to interfere prematurely and risk blowing the operation. I hope that's all that's going on here, because I have yet to see the hint of another boat. It occurs to me that I may be on my own.

"Okay," I say breathlessly, "what do you want to talk about?"

"Nothing much," he says casually, running a hand along the rail above me, beyond reach. He disappears from view and for a few minutes I tread water, hoping not to hear the sound of an engine starting. I have no life jacket and am not a great swimmer. It's hard to see a body from any distance at water level. But Cardinal returns, grinning, with a fishing rod.

"I've reconsidered your suggestion," he says, unhooking the line.

"Cut the crap," I holler at him.

"Crap?" he says, shrugging his shoulders. "What crap? I'm just fishing."

The cold is taking my breath away. I'm beginning to go numb.

"Six to ten minutes," he says, casting out leisurely. "They say that's all a person can take, this early in the year. After that, the cold water begins to shut you down."

The lure plops into the water some distance away.

"Heart failure is usually what does it," he says, reeling in.

"Jesus Christ!" I say, teeth chattering. "You want to talk — let's talk."

"Okay," he says, as though the thought just occurred to him. "You first."

"They're really worried … about the dead trapper."

"Wasn't me." Another cast.

"Well, they're worried," I say, looking around, hoping to see an approaching boat. With my eyes right at water level I can't see anything more than a few yards away in the chop. "So they're cutting you loose."

"What?" he says, his reeling paused, braids dangling as he looks down at me.

"You're too risky," I say, following the script. It's meant both to worry him enough he'll contact his employer, which will be recorded, and to tease out any possible involvement he might have with the Hallendry fire. Aggravating him at the moment may not be in my best interest, but my head aches and it's becoming hard to focus, so I stick with what I can remember.

"So they're just dumping me?" he says, angry, gripping the rail.

I nod, bob under, struggle to the surface, spitting water.

"Billions of goddamn oil dollars and they're just cutting me loose?" he shouts.

"Maybe … maybe I can to talk to them."

Simon Cardinal crosses his arms, regards me coldly from the rail.

"Maybe I should just cut *you* loose, Fire Guy."

I bob under again. Cardinal is a dark blurry shape looming above me. I don't have much time left. I struggle for the surface, clothes clinging, binding, trying to pull me down. I gag on icy water, break the surface, cough it out.

"I know the investigation. I could talk to them."

Cardinal thinks about this for an agonizing moment, then shrugs.

"Okay, Fire Guy." He tosses a knotted rope. "But the price has gone up."

I barely hear him as he hauls me up, over the rail. I flop like a dead fish onto the deck.

He nudges me with the tip of his boot. "You still alive?"

I nod. "Motherfucker."

"Half a million," he says, grinning.

It's not a great ride back to town. Even in the cabin of the boat, sheltered mostly from the wind, I shiver uncontrollably. When I grew up on the farm, we'd had a dog fall through the ice. It took a long time to get him out and I remember how small and frail and miserable that poor soaked dog looked as it quivered and shook. Today, I am the dog. Simon Cardinal, on the other hand, looks quite comfortable in his dry jeans and heavy buckskin coat. He ignores me on the ride back to town. At the dock I climb off his boat, boots squishing, without further conversation.

In my truck, I turn the heater to max, rev the engine impatiently to warm it up. The RCMP instructed me to go about what would seem normal business until after lunch, then to meet them at the cabin along the lakeshore. I head to the IA base, where I peel off cold clinging clothes and stand in a hot shower until I'm bloated and groggy with heat. I dress in dry clothes and lie on my bunk, exhausted, eyes closed, let the world drift away.

It doesn't get to drift far. Boots in the hallway. A knock on my door.

Joe, from Special "O," peers in.

"We need to talk, Porter."

"Go away," I mumble. "I'm not so happy to see you right now."

He closes the door, takes a seat across from my bed.

"How you doing?"

"Pissed." I push myself up to sitting. "Where the hell were you guys?"

"We were watching. You seemed to have it handled."

I have a strong urge to reach out and touch him. With my boot.

"If you call nearly drowning handling it. That asshole almost killed me. I'm curious, just speaking hypothetically, but at what point would you have intervened?"

"We were waiting for your signal."

"That would be when I stopped coming up for air."

"Yeah — we were a bit worried there for a minute."

"Just a bit? Was this some sort of payback?"

He ignores the question. "We lost you in the fog. We did have a scope on you when he pushed you into the water, but we decided to hold when he didn't leave immediately. I appreciate you being a bit pissed at the moment but I gotta tell you, on a professional level, I think you did a hell of a job, hanging in there."

"Wonderful. I hope you got what you needed."

"Well." He hesitates. "There was a problem."

"What sort of problem?"

"The mics crapped out. We need you to do it again."

"You can't be serious. What happened?"

"We're not sure yet," he says, rubbing his forehead as though giving it deep thought. "We'll need to look at the units tonight, check the installation. Bottom line — we got nothing from the boat. It happens, unfortunately."

"What about the sunglasses?"

"Partial, before they went swimming."

I squeeze shut my eyes, massage them. "You've got to be kidding."

"It'll be different next time," Joe assures me. "We'll set it up on land."

I can't help laughing. Sometimes it's the only thing left to do.

Joe fixes me with a look. "You still in, Porter?"

I think of Simon Cardinal, watching me sink while he fishes.

"Hell yeah."

I spend some quality time at the cabin along the lake with the cops of operation Kitten, going over in detail what Simon told me on the boat. It's clear that he was paid to create tension among the bands and disrupt the Cree election. It seems most likely this was aimed at undermining the plans of Sammy Cardinal to unite the bands in a common voice. It's less clear who paid Simon Cardinal to do this but it sounds ominously like it's connected to the huge oil sands interests up river, whose effluent inevitably arrives in the water supply of Fort Chipewyan.

"This is huge," says Waldren, cracking his knuckles.

"Colossal," says Markham. "Imagine this in the papers."

"No doubt," says Waldren. "The oil sands drive the economy of the province."

"Try the country," says Markham. "Then there's the States — our oil sands are the only large oil reserve in a nearby friendly country. Start monkey-wrenching with that and it becomes a matter of national security. Those boys are pretty heavy about that stuff. Next thing you know, we got the CIA up here."

"Just hold on," says MacFarlane. "You're working yourselves into a lather."

We're sitting on an ancient couch and odd assortment of chairs in the living room of the small cabin. The Mounties are all in rural camouflage — jeans and plaid shirts. It looks like a lumberjack union meeting.

"This is just a theory right now. We need some serious evidence."

"What's the next step?" I ask.

"Well," says MacFarlane, "like Joe told you, we need you to meet again with Simon. We won't rush it this time though. Give him some space to stew about it, maybe call his contact personally. If he does, we have his phone tapped and we have eyes on him steady. If he doesn't in the next few days, we'll have you make contact again."

"What do I do until then?"

"Just act natural, as though you're working for the Forest Service."

The meeting breaks up and I go to the ranger station, act natural, spend the next few hours doing paperwork. Luke wanders in, surprised to see me, tells me he's got the dog squared away with his dad. Scorch is penned behind the garage out back of the station, if I want to visit him.

I thank Luke, tell him I'll be sure to do that later.

"Did you hear about Bernice Whiteknife's uncle?" says Luke.

I stiffen. "No. What's going on?"

"There's two RCMP trucks at his place. I heard he had a heart attack."

Luke tags along as I head over to Cork's house. Two RCMP Suburbans and an ambulance are parked along the edge of the street out front. Two Natives sit in the ambulance, waiting, the need for their services clearly not urgent. The burgundy truck with the dented front panel is in the driveway. Several other vehicles are parked on both sides of the street and a small group of locals have collected in the front yard. Several I recognize from the sweat lodge. Helen Mercredi is hugging Sammy Cardinal. Tuber is sitting on the big stump, looking lost. I walk over, followed hesitantly by Luke. Sammy Cardinal whispers something to Helen Mercredi, who nods, releases him and turns to me.

"Porter," she says hoarsely. "So much sadness lately."

"What happened? Have you been inside?"

"I found him," she says, biting her lip. "Just come over to talk to him, you know, and he's dead. Sitting at the table. Flopped over, his face in a bowl of mashed potatoes. I tap him on the shoulder but he doesn't move."

"When was this?"

"About an hour ago."

I give her shoulder a squeeze, walk to the house, my mind working. I wonder what she went to talk to him about. I hesitate at the door, look around. Luke has remained with the crowd on the lawn. They're engaged in muted discussion. I knock on the door. Markham answers, now in uniform.

"Can I come in?"

"Just a minute."

He closes the door, returns quickly, ushers me inside. Rodney Whiteknife has been laid face up on the linoleum floor of the kitchen. He's pale, eyes vacant, bits of white mashed potato clinging to his face. Waldren and MacFarlane stand away from the body, talking with Dr. Cho, who glares, then continues a quiet discussion.

"You're sure it's a heart attack?" says MacFarlane.

"Signs all indicate infarction," he tells the cops.

"Can we package him up?" says Waldren.

Dr. Cho nods, signs something on a clipboard. While he's doing this I look around the small kitchen. The house smells of gasoline and cooking. The scatter of mechanical parts on the table have been pushed to one side to make way for a plate, a bowl of mashed potatoes, and a fry pan filled with greasy sausages. A cup of coffee has been knocked over on the table, a puddle of dark liquid drying on the floor. There are no signs of a confrontation. Markham waves in the ambulance people, who bring a gurney and body bag. When we make room for them to work, MacFarlane motions me over, down the hall.

"I can't believe he just had a heart attack," I say.

"It happens," says MacFarlane. "Doctor checked him over."

"Doesn't the Medical Examiner need to do that?"

"Up here, he is the ME. There'll be an autopsy later, down south."

I nod, thinking. "You had eyes on Whiteknife. What did he do today?"

MacFarlane shrugs. "Went to the doctor, who says he reported feeling poorly, then went shopping, came home, made supper, and keeled over."

"What about Collette Whiteknife?"

"We're still looking for her. No luck so far."

The EMTs are zipping the body into a black bag.

"What if he did something to her?" I say. "Stashed her somewhere?"

MacFarlane sighs. "Then we've got a real problem."

"Did you ever get that search warrant?"

"No, but we're here now. Show me that bag."

We go around a corner to the small broom closet. The bag is still there, stuffed behind the old vacuum cleaner. MacFarlane snaps on white latex gloves, reaches in, pulls out the bag. We kneel on the floor as he zips it open, looks at the contents.

"This is interesting, Cassel. Very interesting."

"What now?"

"We call ident. Process the house. See what else we can find."

# 13

.

I LEAVE RODNEY Whiteknife's house carrying with me a deep sense of unease. Collette Whiteknife has not been seen for several days and is officially listed as missing. Despite an organized search by the RCMP and community members, there is no trace of her. In the yard, I ask Sammy Cardinal if there's anything I can do to help with the search and he nods, tells me everyone is working together now. The bands are united. I can join one of the boats searching the river and local lakeshore. He doesn't specifically say he's looking for a body, but it's pretty obvious what is going through everyone's mind, after the drowning of Bernice Mercredi.

Both Luke and I join a group of locals in a boat.

We search downriver until dark, to the weir and back, find nothing.

Mark Middel invites me for supper, during which he grills me for details I can't discuss. I turn the conversation to how the Forest Service could assist in the search for Collette Whiteknife. Middel promises me the use of a helicopter the next morning. I drive back to the IA base, nervous and fidgety, don't sleep well. The next morning we fly the lakeshore and river, search extensively with no success. If she's in the water, given the currents, there's really not that many places she could be. It feels as though we're waiting for a body to bloat and rise to surface.

It's not a good feeling.

Late in the afternoon, I take a break, head to the IA base for a sandwich. I've been so busy with the search, and so worried about Collette

250      DAVE HUGELSCHAFFER

Whiteknife, I'd completely forgotten about Simon Cardinal and our impending meet but, when I return to my room for a few minutes of rest, I find him sitting in a chair, opposite my bed, thumbing through an old magazine.

"Fire Guy," he says, grinning as I walk in.

I stop, puzzled. His truck isn't outside. I have no idea where he came from.

"What do you want, Simon?"

"What do you think?"

"I don't have an answer for you yet."

"There are other things we need to talk about. Let's take a drive."

I want to tell him to get the hell out of my room, let me rest — he's the least of my problems right now — but it's clear I'll have to keep up my part. Perhaps Simon knows something about Collette, or what happened to Bernice Mercredi. Maybe even something about the Hallendry fire. MacFarlane assured me they would have Simon under continual surveillance, so now is as good a time as any, although I would have preferred a staged location, where they could have set up their microphones and cameras and whatever other high-tech spy gear they use. I don't have my James Bond sunglasses, or my emergency ball cap. We haven't rehearsed any scenarios, or exit plans. Our strategy is based on controlling the situation. I'll have to string him along for another meet, where the situation will be better controlled. For now, I'll need to get him to someplace where they can have him under direct observation.

"All right," I say reluctantly, follow him out.

He's wearing a ball cap, pulled low, his braids tucked underneath, and an oversized old green coat. He looks around the yard. There's no one here at the moment — the HAC boys have been sent back to Fort McMurray, and the local IA crew are based at a different location for the moment. Still, he seems nervous, his movements furtive.

"We'll take your truck," he says.

"How did you get here?"

"Caught a ride," he says, opening the door to my truck.

I hesitate, something bothering me but not sure what it is, then settle in behind the steering wheel. We roll out through the gates of the base. I'm expecting to take him to town, where it'll be easier for Special "O" to monitor, but Simon has other plans.

"Take a left," he says.

A right turn takes us to the highway, then town. A left turn takes us to a series of trails, little more than worn ruts between the trees, meandering through the rolling pine forest for miles. I'm not sure how Special "O" will monitor us out there.

"No, I think we'll go right," I say, and begin turning the wheel.

"I said left."

I hardly believe it when Simon pulls a gun from beneath his coat, points it at me.

"You must be joking," I say. Then I notice the pistol has a long barrel. It's not a long barrel — it's a barrel with a silencer.

A subtle shiver runs up the back of my neck, like a premonition that my life suddenly is about to change forever. Or end. It doesn't seem real but I force myself to focus. The silencer is professional equipment, illegal and hard to obtain. Given that Simon is a local, recruited more for his position than his criminal sophistication, I assume the gun is borrowed, meaning the situation has changed. Simon has contacted his employer. My cover is blown. I am in serious danger. The only thing in my favour is that I'm in control of the vehicle, and Special "O" is watching, although I doubt they can see the gun, held low inside the truck.

"Screw that," I tell him. "We're going where I say."

I turn the wheel farther right, press on the gas, feel a distinct waft of air across my face, synchronized with a loud popping sound. The window in the door of my truck explodes, flinging shards of glass against my cheek, and I slam on the brakes, lurch to a stop.

"Are you crazy?" I holler at Simon.

"Left," he says, gesturing with the barrel of the gun. He's got an excited wild look in his eyes and his hand is trembling. He's pumped on adrenalin and could easily lose control, start shooting. I need him to calm down.

"Okay," I say as evenly as possible. "Take a breath and calm down."

He points the gun at my head and I turn left, ease the truck onto the trail.

"Faster," he urges.

"Okay, okay. Calm down, Simon. I thought you wanted to talk."

"Drive," he says, gesturing again with the gun.

He directs me along the trail, telling me where to turn when it splits. After we've driven a few miles, he seems to relax a bit, the gun swaying in his hand as we bump along. I'm hoping Special "O" saw the window shatter and will find the glass on the road. I'm hoping they know exactly where we are. My hopes lift when I see a dark truck parked along the side of the trail ahead. Simon frowns.

"Stop here."

I brake to a halt about twenty yards behind the parked truck, tensed and ready. The doors on the truck open and two tall, dark-skinned men with short hair step out. They don't look Native. They're wearing leather jackets and one is carrying a black pump shotgun that I take to be a police model. The one with the shotgun takes up a position a few paces away from my door, gun hanging loosely at his side. The other approaches Simon's side of the truck. Simon rolls down his window.

"Any problems?" the man asks.

It takes a second for me to realize he's talking to Simon.

"No problem," says Simon.

"Why'd you shoot the window?" he says.

Simon gives me a half smile. "He needed a little convincing."

A jolt of fear passes into my chest like a knife. This isn't Special "O." Whoever these men are, they're working with Simon. The situation is quickly escalating. There are now three opponents and two visible guns. More firepower may be concealed. I tense my arms and grip the steering wheel, ready to make a run for it.

"I wouldn't do that," says the man with the shotgun, lifting it to point at me.

On the other side of the truck, the other man steps quickly aside. Simon flattens himself against the seat, presses the muzzle of the silencer against my ribs.

"Out of the truck," says the man with the shotgun.

It seems like a critical thing not to get out of the truck, but there's nothing stopping them from shooting me right here. I need to stall until Special "O" sends in the troops, so I carefully lift my hands from the steering wheel, open the door, and step out. Simon slides out after me and the stranger without a gun gets into my truck. I'm herded at gunpoint into the backseat of the other truck. Simon slides in beside me, jabs the muzzle of the gun into my ribs.

"Okay," I say, trying with little success to sound calm. "Now what?"

"Shut the fuck up," says the man in front. So much for talking.

My truck pulls ahead and we follow, continuing up the trail. We don't go far before encountering a long straight stretch of trail with a curve at the far end. The truck ahead accelerates suddenly, engine racing, thumping and rattling over the ruts, leaving us behind. I watch, perplexed, as the truck hurtles far too rapidly to make the curve in the trail. The driver side door opens and there's a black blur as the driver jumps out, tucking into a roll. My truck ploughs into a large pine, the impact shaking the tree. There's a tremendous thump, like a crack of thunder, followed by the tinkle of glass, then silence.

"Holy shit," says Simon, beside me.

I use the distraction to grab the barrel of the gun and try to yank it from Simon's hand. A shot goes off, punching a neat hole in the roof of the truck, but Simon refuses to let go. I have an intimate view of the side of his face, eyes bulged with effort. A split second view of an elbow, coming at me from the front seat, and a bright flash.

Darkness.

I regain consciousness with a throbbing headache. Someone is prodding me in the ribs with the tip of their boot. As my eyes flicker open, a dark face hovers above me, beyond which are treetops.

"Get the fuck up," says the man.

I stare at his face a few seconds longer, puzzled, until it comes back to me. This is the man who crashed my truck. Other than a long scratch on the side of his face, he seems no worse for wear. I prop myself on my elbows and look around. Simon Cardinal and the other man stand a few yards away. Past them, I see my truck, hood crumpled and front caved in against the trunk of a massive pine. The other truck has been turned on the trail, ready for a quick get away. I'm kicked in the ribs hard enough to cause a blossom of pain that leaves me nauseous.

"I said, get the fuck up."

I quickly scramble to my feet.

"Now we're going to have a little talk," says the man.

I look around. The man who kicked me has the pistol with the silencer held casually at his side. The other stranger has the shotgun. Simon, grinning with wicked anticipation, is unarmed. He has a full bottle of whiskey in hand. My truck is totalled. The other truck has two red plastic gas cans and a spare tire in the back. I raise my eyes, hoping to see a plane circling. Empty sky. Where the hell is Special "O"?

"No one is coming," says Simon.

"They're coming," I tell him. "They're watching you right now."

"They're watching my cousin."

I frown, puzzled, and Simon laughs.

"I paid my cousin fifty bucks to put on my jacket and drive my truck. People say we look a lot alike. He's at a friend's place right now, playing cards."

The dangerous tingle I had earlier returns, stronger.

"Start talking," says the man with the pistol, aiming it at my belly.

"What do you want to know?" I say, looking around again for something I can use. The realization that I really am on my own comes as a physical shock. My pulse quickens, pounding in my head, and my mouth dries. My vision is narrowing. These men mean to kill me and I am quickly nearing the threshold where logical thought is replaced by instinct. I can't let that happen and force myself to slow my breathing, focus on my surroundings. Both men are in their early thirties, tall and in good shape. They both have guns. I have no weapons. There's nothing around me of use, except sticks and stones. If I can't out-fight them, I'll have to out-think them, and try to piece together what their plan might be.

"I think he needs a drink to loosen up," says the man with the shotgun.

He grabs the bottle from Simon, thrusts it at me. When I don't take it from him, he swings a roundhouse kick at my ribs, which I barely manage to evade, ducking my midsection out of the path of his boot. He grins.

"That one was free," he says. "The next one won't miss."

I take the bottle, sip a bit of the whiskey. Warmth trickles down my throat.

"What do the cops know?" says the man with the pistol.

"How about you tell me what you know," I say. "I'll fill in the gaps."

I'm ordered to take another drink. I sip again.

"More," says the man with the pistol.

They keep forcing until I've taken a few ounces. Why do they want me to drink?

"I know you're full of shit," says Simon. "I had you checked out."

"The cops know you started the fires, Simon. They know who paid you."

"Really?" says Simon, sneering. "And who is that?"

There's a tense silence. It occurs to me that they want me to drink so it looks like I crashed the truck, which fits with my image in Fort Chipewyan lately. They've done their homework and it makes me realize I'm dealing with real professionals here. They look South American and I can imagine them working for some drug cartel. Their employers here have just as much money, and I have no doubt they've spared no expense, sending a clean-up crew. They'll need me dead in the crashed truck, and they'll need my injuries to be consistent with the crash. On the bright side, this means they won't shoot me.

On the other hand, they'll beat me to death.

"He's not going to talk," says the man with the shotgun. "We're wasting time."

He goes to the truck and returns with an aluminum baseball bat, which he hands to Simon. After a moment's consideration, he hands the shotgun to his companion and retrieves the two plastic gas cans, carries them over to my wrecked truck. I was wrong — they likely won't beat me to death. They just bludgeon me unconscious, to approximate the blunt trauma of the crash, then place me in the truck and light it up. I'll still be breathing for a brief moment in the fire — long enough to fill my lungs with smoke and char for when they do an autopsy. It'll look like a simple case of drunk driving.

"Take another drink," says the man with the guns.

I hesitate, looking at Simon. Something else has occurred to me.

"You know you're next," I tell Simon.

He grins, no doubt amused by what he sees as my last ditch effort.

"Think about it," I say quickly. "These guys are the clean-up crew."

"Take a goddamn drink," says the man with the guns.

I keep my eyes on Simon. "All we've got on you is simple arson, maybe auto theft."

"Don't listen to him," says the man with the guns. He tucks the pistol under his belt and raises the shotgun, pointing it at me, pumping a round into the chamber with a menacing metallic click. "Start chugging that booze."

"Think about it, Simon. Billions of dollars of oil sands investment on the line, all put in jeopardy because you can connect what's been happening in Fort Chip with who paid you. Newspapers. Public inquiries. Investigations. I'm the only person that's actually heard what you've said. When I'm gone, you're the only link that will be left."

Simon's grin falters. The man facing me tightens his grip on the shotgun.

"Shut up and drink," he says.

"Why do you think you're here right now Simon? Why do you think they're letting you see their faces? Because it doesn't matter — they're going to kill us both."

"Shut him up," the man by the wrecked truck yells to his companion.

There's a period of a few brief seconds when nothing happens. I see Simon's expression change as he thinks, caught in the grip of indecision. He's a few paces behind the man with the shotgun. The second man is twenty yards behind Simon. I tighten my grip on the bottle, aware that I have at least one thing to use as a weapon. Simon looks at the man by the wrecked truck, sees his hand slide toward something at his belt. Simon lunges at the man with the shotgun, stumbling and swinging wildly with the baseball bat.

The bat catches the man on the side of his knee and I drop as he jerks sideways, the shotgun firing, pellets buzzing past my ear, then we're both on the ground. He's on his side, shotgun pinned beneath him, and while he rolls to pull it free I kick my way over, club at him with the bottle, which glances off his shoulder and flies out of my hand. Face-to-face on the ground, I grab the shotgun before he can swing it over and we struggle for control. He kicks at me, hitting a hip, the impact twisting me sideways, but I manage to hang on to the shotgun. He yanks the gun along the ground, pumping a fresh shell into the chamber, heaves against my grip to swing the muzzle toward me. I push back and the muzzle swings away, pointing at the second man, still close to the wrecked truck, struggling to free something from his belt — a pistol. My opponent has his finger in the trigger guard, tries to wrench the muzzle towards Simon, who is struggling to his feet. Two bright red squares appear within range of the muzzle — the cans of gas — and I jab my elbow into the crook of the man's arm.

The gun barks, kicking in our hands.

There's a whump as a full can of gas explodes, followed by a rush of heat and a scream. I catch a glimpse of a figure rimmed in flame, flailing wildly. The man locked onto the shotgun with me snarls and heaves himself over, on top, straddling my chest. We're both still gripping the gun and he leans forward, forcing the length of the gun against my throat. I'm losing the battle — he has the advantage of weight and leverage. Simon Cardinal looms suddenly over him, baseball bat raised like a war club, face singed and fierce, long braids swinging. He catches the man on the side of the head. There's a sickening thud as the man is knocked off me by force of the blow; shotgun flipping out of reach. Simon staggers back, chest heaving, drops the bat. I scramble backwards on my elbows, twist and push myself up, see Simon reach for something on the ground as I stand.

When I turn to face him, Simon has the pistol pointed at me.

I lift my hands, palms forward. "It's over," I tell him. "It's done."

He looks crazed, lips pulled back, panting. The truck and pine tree blaze, sending up a column of dark smoke. I'm not sure what Simon will do. He looks around, at the sprawled form near my feet, the burning truck behind him, and the other man, inert on the ground, his jacket smouldering, then back at me, pistol still held rigidly in my direction.

"This is your chance to set it right, Simon."

A long moment of indecision. "Shit," he swears.

His shoulders slump and he lowers the pistol.

"How did this get so fucked up?" he says.

Behind him, the man with the smouldering jacket sits up, skin on his face red and split, like a man rising from the grave. He yanks a pistol from his belt.

"Behind you," I yell at Simon.

Simon turns as the man aims the pistol. Both guns are equipped with silencers and against the crackle of the fire I hear no shots, see only the jerk of the man on the ground, the twist of his body as he topples back to earth. Simon stumbles, falls to his knees. In a few steps I'm beside him, kneeling. He looks in wonder at the gun in his hand, drops it and falls onto his side. The front of his jacket is soaked with blood.

"Hang in there, Simon. I need you to set this right."

"I just wanted a big boat," he says quietly.

His head droops, eyelids flutter, and he dies among the pine needles.

A helicopter roars past overhead — the local IA crew, finally getting some action.

The helicopter circles and I see the dark faces of the Native firefighters peering down, eyes wide. Normally they would find an opening in the forest and land as quickly as possible to start fighting the fire, but with the crashed truck and bodies strewn about, this is anything but a normal fire call. So they continue to circle, assessing, no doubt discussing with Mark Middel on dispatch. I've already confirmed Simon and the two strangers are dead and, other than wave at the helicopter to let them know I'm okay, there isn't much I can do. The gas tank on the truck finally explodes with a percussive retort, sending up a ball of flame. Once the heat has dissipated, I scuff out with my boots the growing perimeter of surface fire creeping through the carpet of dead pine needles. It's not long before the responders begin to arrive. I hear sirens, see trucks winding their way along the narrow trail. Three RCMP Suburbans thump along single file, followed by an ambulance and two lumbering fire trucks. The entire emergency response capacity of Fort Chipewyan has arrived.

Waldren and MacFarlane park about fifty yards back.

"You all right, Cassel?" MacFarlane calls as they walk up.

I nod, feeling anything but alright.

"What the hell happened?" says Waldren, looking around.

Dugan and Verdon, the ident specialists, take charge of the scene. The EMTs confirm the dead are in fact dead and I explain how they got that way as Waldren and MacFarlane listen intently and take notes. Dugan flags a path for a fire truck and local firemen begin to hose down what's left of my pickup. After I've explained what happened, I do it again on camera, with Dugan recording. An EMT checks me over, digs a lead pellet out of my cheek, assures me I'll have a cool scar to impress the chicks. I smile, appreciate his attempt at humour among so much death. Then I'm removed from the scene, taken to town by MacFarlane where we continue our conversation in the interview room at the RCMP detachment. He brings me a cold can of Coke.

"Where were you guys?" I ask.

"He fooled us," MacFarlane says with a defeated shrug.

"What about the wiretap? He obviously contacted his handler."

"Cardinal must have had a contact arrangement we couldn't intercept," says MacFarlane, rubbing his hand over his receding apex of hair. "We're still looking, but all indications are that whoever was handling him was very good. These aren't guys you just hire off the street. These are professionals, probably ex-military or secret service types. They usually work for syndicates and can be very difficult to pin down."

"What does that mean for the investigation?"

MacFarlane thinks about this while I sip my Coke.

"As you can appreciate, this is a big deal politically," he says tapping a finger on the edge of the table. "Particularly with what just happened, so we'll have to proceed carefully, make sure the investigation is bullet proof. Right now, we don't have much to go on. All we have is a few broken pieces of audio from your meet on the boat. Our suspect is dead."

"And I'm your only witness."

MacFarlane nods. "We can offer you protective custody."

"Do you think that's necessary?"

MacFarlane considers. "Hard to say," he admits. "I think they were after Simon to reduce their exposure, and it was convenient to use you for the scenario they had constructed, without raising suspicion. At the same time, they could interrogate you but, from your description of the events, it seems this was a peripheral component of their plan. If they really wanted to question you, they'd have taken you somewhere private, and would have taken their time. These types of guys are very good at that."

"What about Collette Whiteknife? Did you find anything useful in the house?"

"Nothing that suggests a possible location or motive."

I think of Collette.

"I do think I owe you an apology though, Porter," MacFarlane says wistfully. "We found a Forest Service belt radio in his house, hidden in a bedroom closet. We checked the serial number with the Forest Service and found it was signed out to you. I have to admit we didn't put much credence in your story about the attack along the river."

"You believe me now?"

"Let's say, we find your story more compelling."

"Is Rodney Whiteknife's involvement more compelling as well?"

MacFarlane excuses himself from the room. I think he left to go to the washroom, but then it occurs to me that he might have gone to turn off the recording equipment — a suspicion that gains credence when he returns and fixes me with a hard look. "Normally Porter, I wouldn't discuss this with you, but after everything that's happened, I think you deserve a bit of latitude. I think you were onto something with the Hallendry fire, and that Whiteknife was concerned enough to go after you. The rape and revenge scenario fit the evidence, both yours and ours, followed by a destabilizing situation and an attempt at damage control."

"Do you still think he died of a heart attack?"

"It looks that way. We've got a rush autopsy scheduled to confirm."

MacFarlane excuses himself for a moment, no doubt to start recording again. We're joined by reinforcements from the Major Crimes unit, who've just flown in and want to hear my story first-hand, and we spend the next few hours going over it, again and again. It's past midnight when they kick me loose. MacFarlane hands me a small two-way radio, tells me they'll call me when they need to talk to me again. If I feel uncomfortable about my safety, I can use it to call them. And it's got a panic button, he tells me at the door, in case I need help and can't call. It's the budget witness protection program. They've reserved a room for me at the Lodge, just up the hill, and hand me a key. I stumble up the rocky path, barely conscious, fumble at the door with my key and crawl into bed, too tired to take off my boots.

I sleep late the next morning, wake up feeling as though my body is filled with sand. Everything is stiff and sore. The gouge on my cheek from the shotgun pellet blazes with pain when I grimace at my reflection in the mirror. The bruise around my eye from the fight in Fort McMurray has developed into an interesting shade of purple and yellow. There are new bruises on my torso, fresh and tender. I take a shower, head to the restaurant, wishing I still had the special tea from Dr. Cho. Although my table has a spectacular view of Lake Athabasca, rippling and gleaming in the sun, the effect is lost on me. I consider calling my fiancée, desperately wanting to hear her voice, but doubt I could keep my composure.

The conversation we need to have must be face-to-face.

After eating I wander outside, wonder what to do. The RCMP have yet to call me today and I don't want to go to the ranger station, face Middel and his endless questions. I don't really want to talk to anyone. I don't have a truck and decide to go for a walk, limber up my stiff muscles, take a route down the rocky hill, avoiding the RCMP detachment and ranger station. At first I fool myself into believing I'm headed nowhere in particular, but soon give up fighting the pull and walk faster until I arrive in the back alley behind Cork's house. I know the RCMP have already searched the house and it's virtually pointless for me to do the same, but I can't accept this feeling of powerlessness while Collette is missing. I knock to confirm no one is in the house.

The door is still unlocked.

I start in the kitchen. The dishes on the table have been cleared away. The spilled coffee has been cleaned up. There's no visible remnant of the death that occurred here so recently, or of the flurry of activity that followed. Still, I sense some residue. Perhaps an odour lingers and I picture Cork lying on the floor, bits of mashed potato sticking to his face. Pushing the image from mind, I work quickly and systematically, opening drawers, peering into cupboards. Nothing unusual and I move to the living room and bathroom. By the time I reach the bedrooms, I've become sloppy, fighting a sense of futility that saps what little energy I have. Who am I kidding? Trained professionals have already gone through the house with greater scrutiny than I could hope to replicate. I return to the kitchen, stare at the table where Rodney Whiteknife, aka Cork, died; remember when I first met him at the bar and asked him how he got his nickname.

*I pull out the cork, and it's all done.*

He seemed like a simple, likeable character. Then again, nothing in Fort Chipewyan has turned out anything like it first appeared. The fire at Hallendry's cabin. Cork. Collette Whiteknife. Simon Cardinal. Even the RCMP, running surveillance on me. My eyes track over the table and counters, come to rest on a plastic garbage can in a corner. It's one of those cheap rectangular things with a flip lid, which I take off, peer inside. Here's where the sausages and mashed potatoes went. I'm about to replace the lid but change my mind, dump the contents into the kitchen sink. It's a mess of food and wrappers and coffee grounds. The smell isn't great.

Using a spatula from a drawer, I move the contents around.

A brown piece of paper catches my attention. I pull it out, matted with potato.

It's immediately familiar.

I leave the garbage in the sink.

I walk quickly to the nursing station, pondering the implications. The brown wrapper is identical to the wrapper from the special tea given me by Dr. Cho. The day Rodney Whiteknife died he went to the doctor, complaining of feeling poorly. The doctor gave him something, like he gave me something, only now Whiteknife is dead. It's not a prescription, so it can't be traced, and the brown wrapper would be meaningless to the RCMP. It was the same doctor that served as the local medical examiner and pronounced the cause of death a suspected heart attack. It all seems oddly convenient and although I have no idea what role the doctor might be playing, or what his motive might be, I need to find out what he gave Whiteknife.

The young Native receptionist tells me to take a seat.

I sit on a hard plastic chair, fidget for a few minutes in the waiting room, surrounded by others waiting to see the doctor. This could take hours that Collette might not have. I return to the reception counter, the receptionist frowning as I approach.

"It's urgent that I see the doctor now."

"First come, first served," she says.

I lower my voice. "Police business."

She purses her lips, gives me a look that indicates she doesn't feel even this is sufficient cause to break the mandatory queue, but tells me she'll ask the doctor. She returns quickly, ushers me into a small exam room, from which she has to evict an old Native man, speaking quickly to him in Cree. He gives me a sharp look, nods, and shuffles out. Feeling like a heel, I thank them both, take a seat in the exam room. The doctor arrives a few minutes later.

"What is problem today?" he asks, looking harried.

"You remember the tea you gave me?"

"No more tea," he says stiffly. "We already discussed."

"Who else did you give tea to?"

His dark Asiatic face becomes subtly wary. It's not much, but it's there.

"Did you give something to Rodney Whiteknife?"

"Cannot discuss other patients," he says, waving a hand dismissively.

"I can come back with a court order," I say, bluffing just a bit.

"You come back when ready," he says brusquely. "Now, I have work to do."

He's gone as abruptly as he appeared and I'm left with the distinct impression he's hiding something. Unfortunately, there doesn't seem to be much I can actually do without a court order and I leave the exam room, stop at the front counter to thank the receptionist again and tell her I'm done. She barely notices me. Feeling put-off, I head toward the door.

"Mr. Cassel?"

I turn back. An older Native nurse stands with the receptionist at the counter.

"Yes?"

"I'm glad I caught you. I have message here from the hospital in Fort McMurray. They've been trying to contact you now for several days."

I thank her, puzzled, ask if I can use a phone. She shows me to a tiny office, closes the door, and I punch up the number on the slip of paper she gave me. A woman answers.

"Good afternoon. Addictions outreach."

"I think I have the wrong number."

"Your name, sir?"

"Porter Cassel. I have a message that someone called from this number."

"One minute," she says. "Yes — that was us."

"I don't understand —"

"Mr. Cassel, I understand your reluctance," she says, her voice assuming a practised patience, "but I assure you we are here to help and are completely confidential."

"Look, I really think there has been a mistake."

"No mistake, Mr. Cassel," she says, her tone becoming brisker. "We are a referral service provided by the hospital in Fort McMurray, where you had blood work done last week. Your tests indicate a high level of several very addictive compounds, Mr. Cassel, so we were notified. That is the purpose of our call, sir. We are here to offer you addictions counselling, if you are willing to make that commitment."

The phone in my hand feels suddenly sticky and there's a distant buzzing in my head.

"Are you still there, Mr. Cassel?"

"Yes," I say faintly. "What substances are we talking about?"

"I'm sure you already know, but we can discuss this in more detail at an initial consultation. We'll also discuss a plan. Are you currently in urgent need of a detox service?"

"No, I'm just in need of some answers," I say, and hang up.

After I leave the small office I stand for a moment in the waiting room, debating another confrontation with the doctor. Other than a few too many drinks in the past several weeks, I haven't knowingly taken any medication, legal or otherwise. The only way drugs could have entered my system would be through the special tea given to me by Dr. Cho. This explains the euphoric effect of the tea and why I craved it so intensely, to the point of needing to drink to replace the effect, falling back on a previous addiction. It also explains a lot of other things, such as my sudden outbursts and aggressive behaviour. The bar fight in Fort McMurray. Headaches, nausea and itching. And the trembling. What did Waldren say when I reported finding the jar with the testicles?

*He's got the DTS so bad he's practically vibrating.*

Delirium tremens — or DTS — are an effect of withdrawal from an addictive substance. At the time I thought nothing of his comment because I thought I had some underlying medical condition that was causing a suite of worsening symptoms, and the tea was helping me. Now it seems the tea was causing the symptoms. The doctor was systematically addicting me.

But why?

I decide I'm not quite ready to confront him. As appealing as the idea might be, it will only bring up his defences, making it more difficult to find answers. I need some time to think this through. I leave the clinic, stand in the small gravel parking lot in front of the building. Distracted and irritated I look for my truck, realize I no longer have one and, cursing, decide to walk to the monument overlooking the lake. Perhaps there, with the openness of water spread before me, I can figure out what to do next.

*Credibility*, I think as I walk around the corner of the nursing station.

The doctor must have been attacking my credibility — there's no other reason to hook me on drugs, other than to impair my ability to function. Same idea behind having Collette Whiteknife sleep with me. But why would he feel the need to do this?

Standing in the back alley, I look at the nursing station, wondering.

I shake my head, walk past the squat complex of trailers for housing transient medical staff. A small car, parked at the rear of the trailers, has a broken cover on its brake light assembly. I stop, rooted, instantly make the connection. This is the car from the night when I followed Cork. This is the car of the person who picked up that awful package.

It's parked behind Dr. Cho's unit.

Why would the doctor want Rufus Hallendry's testicles?

For a moment I stand in the alley, consider the possibility that I'm simply losing my mind. It seems the easiest explanation. There has to be a better explanation. I try the back door on the doctor's temporary accommodation. It's locked.

I kick it open.

There's a short hall with a mat for boots. Two doors face each other; one to a bedroom; one to a bathroom. Both rooms are neat and sparse, as though no one lives here. Small kitchen at the end of the hall, beyond which is a miniscule living room facing the street. Drapes are drawn over the window. No pictures on the walls. Spending only a few days here a month is obviously not worth the effort of making it homey. I return to the bedroom, open the closet. Two suits. The dresser holds a few pairs of socks, underwear and several shirts. You could put all the doctor's possessions into one suitcase — which, I suppose, is the point. The kitchen has the usual kitchen stuff — pots, pans, plates, cutlery — but not much of any of it. I do find a shrink wrapper in a cupboard, which seems odd, but you never know what the previous tenant might have left behind. Another cupboard holds several large boxes of chocolates — the type you might buy as a gift for a friend. The fridge has milk, two cucumbers, lettuce, radishes, and five boxes of baking chocolate. This guy has both ends of the food spectrum covered; perhaps he's hoping it'll average out. I do a quick pass through the living room, but there's really nothing to search here, spend a minute exploring the bathroom vanity cupboard. Shaving gear. Soap. I return to the kitchen, troubled by the inconsistency of the boxes of baking chocolate, examine one of the boxes, open it up. It's chocolate, all right — a heavy brick of the stuff. Dark and bitter, this isn't the type of chocolate you would eat recreationally.

Shrink wrapper. Chocolate. Boxes of chocolate.

I open the cupboard and pull out several of the big gift-type boxes of chocolates. Two of them look brand new, covered in plastic wrap. One has been opened — or has yet to be wrapped. Perhaps the doctor is smuggling drugs. I open the unwrapped box. It's half-filled with big oval-shaped chocolates, with a larger one in the centre of the box. Maybe the guy just really likes chocolate. I pick one out, find a large kitchen knife and cut the chocolate in half, expecting a creamy centre, caramel, maybe cocaine.

What's inside is hard and leathery. Blackish-green fluid seeps out.

I take another and peel off the chocolate coating. It looks like the pig galls I found in Rufus Hallendry's garage, but why would the doctor be coating pig galls with chocolate? I think of the dead bear I found near Hallendry's cabin and realize these aren't pig galls — these are bear galls, illegal and highly prized in Korea and China. The doctor is smuggling them in as chocolate treats. I pick out the chocolate in the centre of the box, larger and shaped differently, chip off the chocolate coating. There were wires for drying something in Cork's garage as well, which I assumed were for beaver castors, or fish, or something legitimate like that. Perhaps they were both selling bear galls to the doctor. The coating on this one flakes off easier, revealing pink mottled skin with short wiry black and grey hairs. There are stitches on one side, like a baseball, holding together two rough flaps of skin. When I realize what I'm holding the shock causes me to fumble and drop it.

A scrotum and testicles — probably once attached to Rufus Hallendry.

I take a step back, disgusted as I look down at the thing on the floor. Damn — I have to pick it up again, take this to the RCMP. I pull a sheet of paper towel from a spool under the counter, lean over. The floor creaks and in my peripheral vision something moves. I manage to turn my head in time to see a dark leather shoe coming at me. The kick hits me hard in the ribs, knocking the wind from me as I crash to the floor. I just have time to lift my head and see Dr. Cho turn, lips set in a hard line, before another kick connects with my head. A bright flash and I'm flat on my back. The ceiling seems to drift slowly, like a cloud on a summer day. Specks of light descend and wink out.

My thoughts drift too, trying to latch on to what happened.

Suddenly, Cho is above me and I see a needle heading for my neck. A jolt of adrenalin and I lunge to the side, feel the needle penetrate into my shoulder, scramble frantically back, crab walking, Cho after me, trying to pin me down with his foot. I grab at the foot, miss, get the side of his shoe hard against my cheek, push back and slide under the kitchen table. Under here, I have protection from above and can kick at anything within range.

Chest heaving, I watch Cho's legs, wait for the next attack.

It doesn't come. I realize the needle is sticking from my shoulder and yank it out. The syringe is nearly empty. He's waiting for whatever he gave me to work. Already, I feel faint. I trace my hand along my leg until I find the little radio the RCMP gave me in its pouch, feel through the thin leather for the buttons. Transmit or panic — any will do. Numbness in my shoulder is spreading into the muscle of my chest and back. I slide over enough I can see Cho. He stands a few yards back, tensed and waiting.

"Why did you kill Rodney Whiteknife? Was it over bear galls?"

"He was just a tool," says Cho. "A dull one."

"But why? Bear galls aren't hardly worth anything here."

"You westerners know nothing of face," he says vehemently.

My voice is beginning to slur and I'm starting to feel lightheaded. If I'm going to make it out of here, it's going to have to be on my own, and soon. I release my grip on the radio, slide my hands beneath me and crouch under the table, as though I might sprint out. Cho watches, wary. I'm drugged, the clock running out, and beat-up. Cho clearly is a martial artist and knows that as soon as I show myself from under the table, he has me. Or he can wait, and he has me. I'm not prepared to let him have me either way and I rise suddenly, taking the table with me. Tilting it forward, I grab the supports and charge at him, use the full expanse of the table top like the front of a bulldozer. He wasn't expecting this, tries a kick that deflects up and sideways over the face of the table, knocking him off his feet. I stagger, dark splotches in my vision, lose my balance and fall forward, pinning Cho beneath the over-turned table, with me on top. As he struggles to rise, the table begins to break, the seam between the two sides of the top separating over his back. If he manages to break free, I'm done for. On the counter, just above me and to the right, I see the handle of the knife I used to cut open the chocolate, grab for it and swing the knife around. As Cho gets his legs under him, I thrust the knife as hard as I can through the crack in the two halves of the tabletop, hear a scream.

The table collapses beneath me, falling into a dark silent pit.

In the blackness I hear only my breathing until that too is gone.

## 14

MY EYES BLINK open to a blazing overhead light, eclipsed suddenly by a white coat. Dr. Cho has escaped from beneath the table and is closing in to finish me off. I thrash blindly to push him away, find I'm tangled by cords.

"Whoa — easy there," calls a strange voice.

It takes a moment for me to realize that I'm not in danger. A nurse and an older man in a white coat — a different doctor — have retreated a few steps from my bed. Weak, shivering and confused, I push myself up on my elbows and look around.

"You're okay now," the doctor says. He has grey hair and kind eyes.

"What happened? Where am I?"

"Can you tell me your name?"

"Porter Cassel."

"Do you know what day it is?"

"I'm not sure. It's been a bit of a blur lately."

The doctor smiles, seems pleased with my response. "You're in the hospital in Fort McMurray. I don't have all the details, but I can tell you that someone injected you with a powerful anaesthetic. Your blood pressure was dangerously low when they brought you in. After we stabilized you we brought you back slowly. You're going to feel a bit strange for a few hours. You may experience some confusion, disorientation, or difficulty thinking clearly. This is normal. It will take some time before the effects of the anaesthesia are completely gone."

"Anaesthetic?" I say, puzzled,

"You were fortunate that it was given in the muscle."

The needle I pulled from my shoulder. "What happened to the guy that put it there?"

"I can't answer that one for you," says the doctor, checking my pulse. "I believe there's a member of the local constabulary waiting to speak with you, though. Perhaps he knows."

The doctor confers with the nurse, then turns back to me.

"You are going to be just fine, Mr. Cassel. You've got a lot of general trauma to the head and torso, including a cracked rib, so I advise plenty of rest. We'll give you a pain killer when we let you out of here."

"When will that be?"

"Tomorrow perhaps, but we'll see."

"No — I've got to get out of here right away."

The doctor chuckles. "I admire your spirit, but have concerns about your body."

"You don't understand," I say, thinking about Collette Whiteknife.

"Patience, Mr. Cassel," the doctor says, laying a veined hand on my arm. "You're not going to be back to your old self for at least twenty-four hours. Your body is recovering from a major drop. You can't operate a motor vehicle. Your muscle coordination and control are going to be impaired. And you shouldn't be making any decisions for the next day or so, so you might as well lay back and get some rest, enjoy the hospitality of our lovely nurses."

The nurse, an older lady, beams at me.

I settle back, troubled and restless. The nurse takes my blood pressure; still a bit low, then I'm on my own, listening to the bleep and sigh of the hospital ward. I'm woozy and close my eyes. I don't get to rest long.

"Cassel," says Waldren, coming into the room. "Good thing we gave you that radio."

"What are you doing down here?"

"I escorted you on the medivac. We've got a few questions."

"Me first," I say, struggling to sit up.

"Let me get that." He presses a button on the side of the bed. "Better?"

"Yeah. So what happened to the doctor?"

"He's down the hall, with a punctured lung. You got him good."

I glance at the door and Waldren chuckles. "Don't worry, he's under guard."

"He'd better be — he's got a mean snap kick. You found the bear galls?"

Waldren nods. "And something else."

I shudder, remembering the hideous lump in my hand. "What's your theory?"

Waldren sighs, puffing out his cheeks. "We're still working on it. Forensics are running DNA from the testicles, which they can compare to a sample they took from Hallendry's crispy critter. Hell of a thing," he says, shaking his head, "cutting off a man's balls."

"What do you think it means?"

"It's a pretty strong statement, emasculating a person like that."

"You still think it was about the rape?"

Waldren places a hand on the bed rail. "I don't know, Porter, but the bear galls do complicate things. We thought we had a pretty clear case up until now. Older man in the company of two younger females gets drunk, rapes one or both of them. Relatives find out and go medieval on him, then get stupid when the law starts to sniff around."

"But the doctor isn't a relative."

"Exactly," says Waldren. "What reason does he have to be involved?"

"Were some of those bear galls fake?"

Waldren frowns. "We haven't checked. What are you thinking?"

"Hallendry's brother Charles told me he was sending pig guts up for his brother to make lure for trapping. What if Rufus Hallendry was selling bear galls to the doctor and decided to slip in a few pig galls? How would the customers react if they noticed the slip?"

"They wouldn't be happy," says Waldren. "It'd be like buying cocaine and finding out someone sold you baby powder. The supplier would lose credibility."

"He would lose face."

"You may be onto something. Maintaining face is a big thing in business over there. Right up there with loyalty. But tell me something — what tipped you off?"

"Magic tea."

"What?"

I explain the tea the doctor gave me, the effect it had, and finding a similar wrapper in the trash at Rodney Whiteknife's house. My blood test and the call from the hospital.

Waldren's expression goes from excited to sombre.

"This explains the bag of beans we found in Cho's residence."

"Magic beans?"

"Yeah, we sold a cow for them. No, they were castor beans."

"Doesn't sound nearly as interesting."

"They're magic if you want to kill someone. Castor beans are used to create an extract called ricin. Six thousand times more toxic than cyanide. Depending how it's ingested it can be pretty quick and it's nearly impossible to detect in an autopsy unless you're looking for it."

"What if he gave it to Rodney Whiteknife?"

"Might look like a heart attack."

We're both silent for a moment.

"So let me get this straight," I say. "Dr. Cho was buying bear galls from Rufus Hallendry and Hallendry slipped in a few pig galls to top up an order. The doctor looks bad and has to save face, so he hires Rodney Whiteknife to kill and castrate Hallendry and burn down his cabin so it looks like an accident. Then he ships the poor bastard's nuts to his customer to show he's taken care of the problem. Finally, to limit exposure, he poisons Whiteknife."

"Holds together so far," says Waldren.

"But why hire Whiteknife? The doctor could have bumped off Hallendry himself."

"True," says Waldren, drumming his fingers on the bed rail. "Killing Hallendry would have been easy for the doctor, but the other thing would have been messy. There would have been a body to explain, that was missing a few parts. Might have seemed better to get a local to do the dirty work, incriminate himself, then quietly take him out."

"No mess. No connection to him."

"Exactly."

"And none of this is related to Simon Cardinal?"

"Not that we're aware of," says Waldren.

Something else occurs to me. "What about the rape?"

"If there was a rape. Makes a good cover story."

"There's only one person who knows the truth about that," I say.

"Yeah," says Waldren. "And she's still missing."

Waldren grills me for more detail for the next hour, then leaves to brief the rest of the team in Fort Chipewyan. I try to rest, but can't stop thinking about everything that's happened. I try to get in to see Dr. Cho, but the door is blocked by a rather large Mountie, who won't so much as let me peek in the narrow slotted window on the door. I wander to a common room, flop onto a sagging couch and brood about Collette Whiteknife, run through every possible place she could be, and what has been done to look for her.

I find no answers. Every place she might be alive has been searched.

A salesman on the television tries to sell me laundry detergent.

A frail old man totters into the room, towing an IV stand.

My eyes come to rest on a large faded wall map of the area from Fort McMurray north to the territorial border. Lake Athabasca is a long wide tract of blue. I peel myself off the couch, stand in front of the map, visually tracing the shoreline and river where we've searched. Currents would move a floating body inevitably downstream, to be caught on the weir. We've looked there. Repeatedly. My gaze wanders northeast along the lake into Saskatchewan. Uranium City. Fon du Lac. Then back in Alberta, where a small speck in the centre of the lake catches my attention. A tiny island surrounded by an ocean of water.

Egg Island Ecological Reserve.

I frown, stare at the little speck. The label dwarfs the island.

Something about that island bothers me.

Cork, at the grocery store, getting into my face when I asked about Collette.

*She's having fun without you.*

Then having the audacity to toss something into my cart.

*You should have some eggs. They're good for you.*

"Damn," I curse, startling the old fellow on the couch.

He peers at me, squinting. "You all right, son?"

"I need to charter a plane."

I know the nurse in charge will give me a hard time about leaving without clearance from the doctor, so I simply decide to call a cab, change out of my backless hospital gown and into my grubby clothes, and walk out. I can explain later. On second thought, I find a pen and write a quick note on a napkin, which I leave on my bed. Then I walk out. Or try.

"Mr. Cassel —"

I ignore the nurse calling out to me from the nursing station.

"Mr. Cassel —"

I hear her running to catch up and I stop.

"I'm sorry, Mr. Cassel, but where are you going?"

She's a young attractive redhead who needs a bit of sun. I shake her hand.

"Thank you so much for your generous hospitality, but I have to go."

She pulls away her hand. "Oh — no, you can't go without the doctor's release."

"Actually, I can," I say. "But I promise not to operate any equipment for the next twenty-four hours, or to make any major decisions. Well, any more major decisions."

She's not impressed. "Even if you do go, there's paperwork."

"No time," I say, and walk briskly away. I hear her take a few tentative steps after me before turning back to the nursing station. No one else tries to stop me and I climb into a waiting cab. A minute later, the hospital is behind me and I'm on my way to find Collette.

I have the cab take me into the river valley, past the old downtown core, to what is locally known as the Snye. It's an old oxbow of the Athabasca River which flows through Fort McMurray and serves as the runway for a float plane company. The cab drops me in front of a small faded white building. There's no one inside. I walk down to the floating dock, find a pair of legs sticking out the open door of a float plane.

"You open for business?"

The owner of the boots, a young stubble-cheeked pilot, backs out of the plane, steps down onto the float. "Hello there," he says, extending a hand, which I shake.

"I need to fly to Egg Island."

"You can't," he says. "It's an ecological reserve, closed to the public."

"That's why I need to go there."

"Well, we could fly over it, so long as we don't go too low."

I hire him on the spot, providing we can leave immediately. He checks his watch, guesses he has time for a quick flight. When the sticky point of payment comes up, I mention that I'm with the Forest Service.

"I don't know," he says, lifting his ball cap and scratching his head. "I usually get a call and an aircraft request, with the codes and all that."

"Do you take Visa?"

"Yeah, that'll do."

I'm anxious to get into the air, but we go to the office, where he takes my credit card, runs it through an old manual imprint machine, has me sign something. If I'm wrong, this will cost me everything I have left in the bank. If I'm right, I might just save Collette. It's a chance I'm willing to take and we return to the plane, belt ourselves in.

"You a biologist?" he says as we taxi to the end of the oxbow.

"No. A fire investigator."

"I didn't think there's anything on that island to burn. It's just rocks."

The plane roars and surges ahead, floats ploughing through the water, skipping across waves, then the water releases us and we're airborne, lifting over the highway lined with cars, the bridge and the Athabasca River. The north end of Fort McMurray sprawls below us. Soon the first of the massive oil sands excavations come into view. An area the size of a city has been stripped of trees and soil to reveal an expanse of black sticky ground. Manmade rectangular lakes shimmer with temper lines of floating hydrocarbon. I think of Simon, dying among the pine needles, seduced by his big boat. Below me is seduction on a far grander scale. I wonder if anyone will pay for what happened in Fort Chipewyan, or for what might be going downstream into their drinking water. More than likely, the big oil machine will continue to run unobstructed, lubricated by its own success. My concern lies ahead on a much smaller piece of ground. I ask the pilot why Egg Island is designated as an ecological reserve.

"Some sort of rare bird nests there," he says. "A tern, I think."

Below us passes an ocean of pine trees, draped over old sand dunes, interspersed with lakes like dropped puzzle pieces. The trees peter out closer to Lake Athabasca, surrendering to an area of active dunes. At the north end of the dunes, where sand meets the big lake, is Williams Point — where Collette was rumoured to have gone camping. We've scoured the area by helicopter and found no trace of her. As we fly over the broad expanse of Lake Athabasca it occurs to me what a perfect location Egg Island is to hide someone. It's surrounded by enough water that single engine aircraft cannot fly to it. As well as being incredibly remote, it's off limits. Even if a plane flew over, it would difficult to see anyone from much of a height.

There is one type of plane that can fly there though — a float plane, and as I peer down past the long metal floats my pulse quickens. A tiny dot of land is visible far below us, no larger than a fly speck on the windshield.

"Can you take us farther down?" I ask the pilot.

The plane tilts and we descend, level out.

"Lower, please. I doubt the birds are there already."

The pilot considers, drops us into a steeper descent. It's difficult to estimate size with nothing around but wave-crested water. Still, the island scarcely seems to increase in size as we draw closer. From a thousand feet of elevation it is clear the island is perhaps a hundred yards across, little more than a round heap of cobble, bare of all vegetation but a few shrubs. As the plane levels out, I squint to see anything against the glare of the surrounding sunlit water.

"Can you take us down closer?"

"Sorry buddy, but a thousand is as low as I'll go."

We pass the island, make a wide turn, head back.

"Holy shit," says the pilot, peering down. "There's someone down there."

We drop sharply and I see a tiny form, barely distinguishable against the light brown cobble, whipping something back and forth. Closer, I recognize Collette Whiteknife, waving a grey sweatshirt, her anxious face peering up at us. The pilot buzzes low across the island, to let her know we've spotted her, then banks the plane into a turn and lands into the wind. Soon we're puttering and bobbing toward the island. My whole body aches but I barely notice, focused on the mound of cobble sticking out of the water and the frightened girl waiting for us on shore. When we're close, the pilot cuts the engine and I open the door, step down onto a float. Collette sloshes into the water, staggering, arms stretched in front of her. She's shivering, gaunt and sunburned. I'm worried she'll fall into the icy lake in her hurry to meet us.

"Stay there," I call to her. "We're coming to you."

She's shaking when I grab her arm, pull her up beside me on the float. She hugs me fiercely and we nearly fall. I manage to grab hold of a wing strut.

"Thank God," she sobs.

I brush hair away from her face. "You're okay now."

She clings to me, wisps of hair tickling my face in the breeze. I look past her at the island, wonder what she must have gone through these past few days. She had plenty of fresh water, but nothing else. No way to make a fire. No way to signal a passing plane or boat. The island has nothing for shelter against the sun, cold or wind. There's nothing here but rocks with bits of downy feather stuck between them. She'd have been hypothermic at night. Without food to replenish her energy, it would only have been a matter of time before she died of hunger and exposure, or a big storm washed over the island and took her with it. I guide her along the float and into the back seat of the plane, where I check her over. She's suffered from exposure but otherwise seems unharmed. She keeps trying to hold onto me as I work.

"You're okay. Just let go for a minute."

Reluctantly, she releases her grip on my clothes.

"Porter?"

"Shh." I put a finger to her lips.

"She okay?" says the pilot.

"I think she's going to be fine. Do you have any food on board?"

"I might have some lunch left from yesterday."

He rummages in the rear cargo compartment, returns with a thermos and lunch pail.

"Might be a bit stale, but there's a sandwich and some coffee."

Collette attacks the sandwich, quickly drains the coffee. When she's done, I strap her in, close the doors of the plane, ask the pilot to take us to Fort Chipewyan. I take the seat next to Collette in the back, pull on a headset against the roar of the engine, watch the nose of the plane rise as we take off. Collette sits stiffly beside me, hands clenched together in her lap.

"What happened?" I ask her through the headset.

She remains silent. A few moments pass.

"I have to tell you something, Collette. Your uncle, Rodney, has passed away."

Her shoulders sag and her lip trembles.

"I'm sorry. Were you close to him?"

She shakes her head, stares out of the window.

"What really happened at that cabin?"

For what seems a long time, Collette Whiteknife stares out the window of the plane at the clear blue sky and I wonder if we'll ever know what happened that night in Rufus Hallendry's cabin. Then she takes a deep breath, looks straight ahead. Her voice is clear but halting, as though the only way she can let out her story is in small manageable pieces.

"It was supposed to be a practical joke. Get Smokestack drunk. Bernie and me. Then he was going to do something funny to him. Didn't tell us what it was, but said we'd like it. So we did some hot knives, drank quite a bit. We were all pretty zonked. When Smokestack started to stumble around, my uncle came in, told us to wait in the truck."

"Did you see him do anything to Hallendry?"

She shakes her head.

"Was he carrying anything when he came out?"

"An old tin can. I don't know what was inside."

"You don't want to know. What happened next?"

"When he ran out of the cabin, there were flames shooting out the window. He told us not to tell anyone about it. The next day he sent Bernie to work at the fire."

"And the rape?"

Collette lowers her head, shakes it subtly no.

"What about the cabin by the river?"

She stares at her feet. "He told me what to say."

"Did you tell me *anything* that was true?"

"One thing," she says quietly. "At the party — I told you I liked you."

"Wonderful. I feel much better."

She places a hand tentatively on my leg.

"We didn't do anything, Porter."

Her hand is surprisingly warm. I brush it away and she flinches.

"It was my uncle's idea. But you passed out. I just stayed in the room with you."

"Why are you telling me this?"

She turns away, looks out the window.

"You said you were engaged. I didn't want this hanging over you."

For a few minutes there's nothing but the roaring vibration of the float plane.

"Thanks for letting me know."

The pilot looks back and I catch the reflection of his half smile in the curve of the windshield. It's not everyday he has this much drama in the cockpit. Collette leans her head against my shoulder and nods off to sleep as I watch the shoreline pass below, pick out the dark smudge of the Whiskey Creek Fire, then the sprawl of Fort Chipewyan's buildings against pink and grey granite. It dawns on me that my hands have stopped shaking and the pressure in my chest is gone. I've survived the Whiskey Creek Fire, Simon Cardinal, Rodney Whiteknife, and Dr. Cho. I'm going home, to see Telson, healthy and with a clear conscience.

It's good to have my life back.

# Acknowledgements

I would like to thank the many members of the Royal Canadian Mounted Police who shared their expertise in the fields of crime scene investigation, forensics, autopsy, poisoning, case management, surveillance, and fire investigation. Without exception, they were cooperative, courteous and enthusiastic in response to my many inquires. In particular, I would like to thank Sgt. Gordon Petracek, Forensic Identification Specialist; Cpl. D.B. (Bruce) Hamblin, Forensic Identification Specialist: Sam Andrews, Medical Examiner; Cpl. Keith Sanford, Major Crimes; and Cpl. Lorne Doktor (aka Doc), of Special "O." Thanks due also to Craig Hockley, Head of Special Investigations and Forensic Services, Fish and Wildlife Division, Alberta Sustainable Resource Development (ASRD), and Morgan Kehr, HAC Coordinator, Forest Protection Division, ASRD. Dr. Robert Jarvenpa, of the Anthropology Department of the University at Albany, provided a historical context to intertribal conflict. Archie Waguan shared his experiences as Chief of the Mikisew Cree First Nation. Special thanks also to Doris MacDonald of the Aseniwuche Winewak Nation for the experience of a traditional Native sweat lodge.